Also by Paul Preuss

SECRET PASSAGES

Paul Preuss

TOR®

A TOM DOHERTY ASSOCIATES BOOK
NEW YORK

This is a work of fiction. All the characters and events portrayed in this book are either products of the author's imagination or are used fictitiously.

SECRET PASSAGES

Copyright © 1997 by Paul Preuss

Edited by David G. Hartwell

A Tor Book
Published by Tom Doherty Associates, Inc.
175 Fifth Avenue
New York, NY 10010

Tor Books on the World Wide Web:
http://www.tor.com

Tor® is a registered trademark of Tom Doherty Associates, Inc.

The publishers wish to thank W. D. Snodgrass for granting permission to reprint his translation of "An Archaic Torso of Apollo," by Rainer Maria Rilke.

Excerpt from "The House in Winter," from The October Palace by Jane Hirshfield. Copyright © 1994 by Jane Hirshfield. Reprinted by permission of HarperCollins Publishers, Inc.

ISBN: 0-812-57148-7
Library of Congress Card Catalog Number: 97-7600

First edition: August 1997
First mass market edition: August 1998

Printed in the United States of America

0 9 8 7 6 5 4 3 2 1

For Debra

SECRET
PASSAGES

1

At the edge of a high terrace, under a grape arbor supported on slender columns, two men sat watching the autumn twilight. Below them the lights of Athens rippled in the thickening haze; the shadow of the Acropolis rose like a stone ship on a phosphorescent sea.

"The fellow was competent enough, occasionally creative," said the taller man. Manolis Minakis poured brandy into balloon glasses and slid one across the marble tabletop. "It wasn't a complete waste of time."

"You said the same thing about Ostrovsky when you gave him the sack." Richard Wingate was small and neat, with manicured nails and graying hair trimmed close to the skull.

"Bloodless characters, with passion only for their next publications," Minakis replied.

"Ambitious youngsters, rather, not religious acolytes. And they agreed to help you, despite the absurdly remote location and your insistence on secrecy."

Minakis raised his glass—"*Yeia sas,* Richard"—and leaned back comfortably, his blue cotton sweater draped loosely over his shoulders. "It's good of you to defend them. And they did teach me an important lesson."

"Which is?"

"That I need something more than a bright young experimentalist."

Wingate's laugh was dry. "You need a disciple."

Minakis did not reply, but studied the purpling sky through the curve of his glass. Behind him, over the tile roof, a pale glow in the sky announced a fat moon rising.

"Who's the next candidate?" Wingate busied himself lighting a thin black cigar with a cylindrical brass lighter. "I'm sure you have someone in mind."

"I'm thinking of Peter Slater. Presently in Hawaii."

"Slater. Really." Wingate blew a thin stream of smoke. "How do you propose to lure him away from his comfortable position to follow you into the desert?"

Minakis grinned, baring white teeth under a broad gray mustache. "There are signs that, like Saul on the road to Damascus, Peter Slater has recently undergone a conversion. He is willing to admit that the world is real after all, even at the quantum level. I intend to discuss this with him at Delos II. Of course, I also intend to make him question the worth of his heretical new beliefs."

"And if he doesn't choose to attend Delos II?"

"I'm afraid the whole affair will have to be postponed."

Wingate shook his head. "Am I to understand the corporation is underwriting this conference just so you can play devil's advocate to Peter Slater?"

Minakis raised his brows, all innocence. "The invitations are strictly Papatzis's concern. I only suggested that it would be appropriate to invite those who were at the first Delos."

"I had no idea Slater was that old."

"He's an ancient—almost half as old as you or I. I'm told he's on the verge of acquiring an instant family, by marrying a woman who brings her young children with her."

"Then why not let me pull a few strings and have him invited to CERN for a year? Surely it will be easier to move your experiment to Switzerland—which I've been trying to convince you to do since you started—than persuade Slater to move his family to Greece."

"I trust you'll find a way to indulge me," Minakis said complacently. "That is, if you haven't grown weary of my stubborn quest."

"Really, given the chance, slight as it is, that you will someday get around to changing the world with these experiments of yours . . . Well, I'll find out what I can. But don't set your heart on acquiring Slater as a junior colleague."

Minakis's black eyes reflected the curve of the moon. "Don't concern yourself with my heart, Richard. Whatever will happen has happened."

Anne-Marie walked barefoot at the edge of the surf, hugging her daughter to her shoulder, and Jennifer crowed in ecstasy when the high waves crashed beside her, partly because her mother squeezed her extra tight each time. But on Anne-Marie's face tears mixed with the salt spray. The cool breeze, the warm sunshine, the thunder of the turquoise ocean, every sensation reminded her of yesterday's happiness; with every retreat of the seething water, the wet sand beneath her feet slipped away as if she were sliding back into the sea.

For half a year she'd been living an anticipatory dream, of building a home with a man she loved who would be a loving father to her children—a life filled with the simplest of pleasures, the things most people have, what seemed to her a normal existence—a life she had hardly dared dream of before she met Peter. At last she would belong in one place in the world, belong there by choice, instead of drifting or running or being held prisoner to someone else's whims. As soon as the divorce was final, as soon as Charlie had finally accepted the inevitable and done what was right, she and Peter would marry. The dream would come true.

But when she came home from her job at the ad agency that day, the baby-sitter told her about the thick envelope that had arrived in the morning mail. Before the door closed behind the woman, Anne-Marie had ripped open the envelope.

Re: Marriage of Phelps.

Dear Anne-Marie; I am pleased to inform you that the court has entered a judgment of dissolution, effective 1 November. . . . Because the dissolution was contested, the court has decided a number of issues. While we were not given everything we asked for, nevertheless . . .

Her fierce hope exploded in despair. She had lost; Charlie had won. He had won the right to carry Jennifer away for weeks at a time, and worse, much worse, Carlos would go on living with him. Charlie had taken her son. The daughter who was more Peter's than his, the son who was not his at all.

For an unknown time her mind was filled with no coherent thought but instead with a kind of howling light. Then she heard her ten-month-old daughter's tiny voice—"Ma, Ma"— and felt a tug on her skirt and forced herself to bend and take up the little girl, to flee the beach house, to trudge the sand where the blurred light resolved itself into waves making their thundering landfall.

The lawyer's letter lay open on the kitchen table, beside the stiffly folded judgment. She had not read the letter a second time, had not read the judgment at all. Why should she? Without her children, what did the rest matter? She was through with lawyers and judges and social workers and hearings, through with trips to California to beg for what was hers, through with postponements and empty days waiting in motel rooms, through with decisions made without her. What was left to her was what she had never used but should have begun with, the truth. Charlie's money and connections wouldn't save his pride when he heard what she had to tell him.

As for her own pride . . . that was only a part of the dream.

Jenny was tiring of the beach walk; she fretted and struggled in her mother's arms until Anne-Marie soothed her. "We'll go back, honey. We'll go home now." She walked toward cottages standing among palms and ironwoods at the edge of the sand, and when she was far enough from the surf, she set the girl down. After a few moments of staggering and falling down and bulldozing the sand, Jenny was glad to be carried again.

As they came near the house—all angles and raw wood and salt-streaked plate glass, a modernistic bachelor's pad too small for the three of them, but in the months since Anne-Marie had moved in, she and Peter had yet to find better quarters—Anne-Marie saw Peter's antique Triumph turn into the driveway and pull up behind her Honda in the carport. She felt a sudden rush of relief, an urge to run to him and hide in his arms.

Then she remembered the letter. She wished she hadn't left it out where he would find it. Inevitably he would feel sorry for her, and his pity would drain what strength remained to her, the strength of her anger. With each step from the beach to the deck, she willed herself to erase all expression from her face.

Inside, past the Baldwin baby grand that took up half the living room, Peter turned from the kitchen counter, where he was busy emptying ice trays into an ice bucket that held a fat bottle of champagne. "Great! I won't have to start the celebration without you."

Anne-Marie stared in confusion. Had Peter seen the judgment? Did he think it was good news? But it lay undisturbed on the dining table.

"Da!" Jenny twisted toward him and flung her arms wide. "Da!"

For a moment the dream flowed back, dissolving, but even in tatters comforting her; she broke into a smile, her pale eyes shining. Peter dropped the ice trays on the counter and crossed the living room in three long strides, flinging his arms wide to surround them both.

Anne-Marie met him with a soft kiss. Meanwhile Jenny hooked her sharp nails in his ear and tugged.

"Oww!"

"Welcome home, Da," Anne-Marie said as he freed himself from Jenny's grip. She set the baby girl on the floor. "What are we celebrating?"

"The Greek islands, Ma, all expenses paid—kids too, if we want to bring them—and all I have to do is give one short talk to a bunch of people I've been dying to trap in one place."

"Fantastic. This just came out of the blue?"

"I mentioned I was at a conference a few years ago, only time I was ever in Greece? The sponsors are putting on Delos II, and they want us old-timers back."

"Good for them. When do we go?"

"Not until spring. The time will fly."

"Mm," she murmured in agreement. "Tell you what, let me feed the cherub while we're waiting for that bottle to get cold."

"Food fight!" he called gleefully. "This demands suitable accompaniment."

He leaped to the piano, seated himself with a flourish, and—while Anne-Marie wrestled Jenny into a high chair and covered her with a bib—plunged into the urgent, falling and climbing runs of the final movement of Beethoven's "Moonlight Sonata," making it sound like the score to a Buster Keaton movie, no moonlight in evidence. Peter's hands raced over the keys, and Jenny squirmed frantically in time to the music, shrieking ecstatically every time she managed to divert an incoming spoonful of pureed squash into her hair or onto the floor or, best of all, back onto her mother.

Through the noise and mayhem, Anne-Marie smiled and laughed and imagined herself having as much fun as they were.

Two hours later Jenny was asleep in her corner of the little bedroom. Peter and Anne-Marie, having raided the refrigerator and made a quick supper of leftovers, sat close on the wooden love seat on the deck, sipping cold champagne as the sun sank into the sea off Kaena Point.

Anne-Marie snuggled herself closer into the curve of Peter's arm. "I got a letter today too." She was too close for him to see her face, but she felt his chin resting on top of her head.

"A letter. And?"

"I'm single again. Or will be, first of the month."

He put his glass down on the deck and pulled her closer. "That will never do," he said softly. "Will you marry me?"

"I don't know. When?"

"Second of the month?" She said nothing, and for a long

time he didn't realize she was crying. He waited until her sobbing subsided and she was breathing evenly again. "I didn't mean to rush you," he said. "The third will be fine."

She pulled away and looked up at him, her pale eyes rimmed in red. "The rest of the letter wasn't good news. I wasn't going to tell you."

"Carlos?"

She bobbed her head and swiped at her nose with the back of her hand. "And Jenny. I was a fool to think I could beat Charlie."

"What exactly was the decision?"

"Carlos has to live with him while he's in school. I can have him for a month in the summer and two weeks at Christmas. And weekends, if I'm in San Diego. And he can have Jenny in the summer—after she's two—and any weekend he's here."

"That doesn't make sense. We'll fight it. Together. We can hire people to see how he treats Carlos. We can reopen the case."

"No more courts," she said with heat. "Charlie stole him. He says I ran away. He lied, and he paid other people to lie. He did it to punish me, not because he cares about Carlos. He never spent any time with him before. But he claims *I* abandoned *him*."

"Then I think the first thing you ought to do is schedule a trip to San Diego to see your son. Surely the settlement gives you that much. It's been a long time."

"I will. But I'm not leaving it at that." She stared at the ruddy glow on the horizon where the sun had gone down.

"Anne-Marie . . ." Peter put his hand on her shoulder.

She twisted her head and looked back at him. Her smile came jerkily. "I . . . won't do anything stupid. Don't think I'm crazy."

"I know you're not crazy." He pulled her to him again, and she clung to him as if he were the only fixed thing in her life.

Later that night, when Peter lay sprawled under a sheet, one arm dangling to the floor, snoring steadily, Anne-Marie crept out of the bed. She peered into the crib, where Jenny's tiny snores were as steady as Peter's, then went into the living room and found the cordless phone and carried it onto the deck.

She punched a long number on the pad and listened to the click of the circuit connecting. She heard the phone's nasal buzz. High overhead the moon was small and bright, washing the stars from the sky, but in Switzerland, almost halfway around the world, it was the middle of the morning.

Two weeks later: in another part of Switzerland, the intercom chortled softly in Richard Wingate's office. He pressed the button. "Yes, Rudi . . . Good, bring it in."

The Andwin-Zurich Building was hardly distinguishable from any of the modernist glass-and-steel corporate headquarters overlooking the lake and the mountains, but Wingate's office was deep inside it, a windowless room paneled in carved oak from a twelfth-century abbey. One panel opened on oiled hinges, and Rudi Karl entered carrying a thick report. He was a young man with a blond ponytail and the wiry build and deep tan of a downhill skier.

He laid the report on Wingate's long desk, as big as a library table. "Wait here," Wingate said, and Rudi took a chair at the end of the desk, sitting motionless as Wingate opened the report and read, quickly and silently:

> . . . Upon the retirement of Bronislaw Lasky, head of the theory department, Slater agreed to assume the chair. During the next six months he produced numerous papers on theoretical particle physics, exploring new areas opened by a flood of data from the reconstructed proton-antiproton collider (see Appendix II).
>
> Last spring Slater's output of theoretical papers abruptly slowed. A number of review articles have since appeared under his name with titles such as "Things, Objects, and Quantum Field Theory" (see Appendix III), which his colleagues have characterized as "a useless rehashing of questions that have persisted since the formulation of quantum mechanics seventy years ago," and "physics for philosophers."
>
> According to several sources, TERAC's director has

asked Slater for more theory and less history and philosophy, but this request seems to have met with incomprehension. A colleague suggests that "Peter always did have a tendency to think that whatever interests him is supremely important. Until now he's been lucky. . . ."

" 'Until now he's been lucky,' " Wingate said aloud, and looked up from the document. "I told Minakis we ought to get Slater to CERN, but I doubt that any of the world's high-energy physics labs are in the market for philosophers these days."

Rudi nodded in solemn agreement, patting his silk tie. Wingate went back to reading. For five minutes they sat in silence, until Wingate flipped the cover closed and leaned back in his chair.

"Well, Rudi, based on this, I think I'd better tell Minakis to forget about Slater. Even if Slater doesn't care about his job, the other fact that stands out is that Mrs. Phelps—his fiancée, I mean . . ."

"Ms. Brand."

"If she has any influence over where he lives, her first choice is likely to be southern California, where she can be close to her son."

"Before you make your recommendation," Rudi murmured, "depending on how important . . ."

"It's important to Minakis."

"May I?" Rudi leaned forward, reaching for the report. "Here in Appendix VI, biographies of next of kin . . ."

"I don't see any help for us there."

"Ms. Brand's brother, Alain . . ."

"Mm, the fellow who sells old books. What about him?"

"I've heard his name mentioned in other circles."

Wingate raised an eyebrow. "What circles? Coins?" His assistant had a fondness for ancient coins; since many of the world's leading dealers were located in Switzerland, he was well placed to indulge his hobby.

"Not only coins. It occurred to me, given Ms. Brand's brush with the law in North Africa . . ."

Rudi let the suggestion dangle until Wingate impatiently

broke the silence. "That was years ago. Recreational drugs according to this, not antiquities. Anyway, apparently they haven't seen each other since they were children."

"But in Appendix IX, telephone logs . . ." Rudi found the page he wanted and slid the report back in front of Wingate, holding his muscular index finger against the long list of phone numbers. "Alain Brand's bookshop in Geneva . . ."

Wingate peered at the log. "Eleven minutes, sixteen minutes, twenty-three minutes, almost half an hour . . . four times in the last two weeks. What have they found to talk about after all these years?"

Rudi shrugged. "Without a phone tap . . . illegal, of course . . ."

"I can't imagine we'll learn anything useful." Wingate leaned away and steepled his fingers under his chin. "All right, see what you can find. But only at this end. You'd better go to Geneva and handle it yourself."

2

A brass bell jingled discreetly as Anne-Marie pushed open the door of the bookstore. When she stepped across the threshold, her pulse accelerated; bookshops were among her favorite haunts, but she'd long avoided this one.

Not that it was a scary place. The light through its many-paned windows was diffuse and warm, reflected from the high brownstone walls across the Grand Rue; it had a nice scent of wood polish and old paper; its mahogany shelves were filled with high-priced editions covered in gold-embossed leather—Lord Byron, Mary Shelley, Rousseau in English translation—the sort of souvenirs of Geneva that investment bankers from Illinois or South Africa or Australia would take home to display in their libraries along with other handsome books that they never read.

The clerk, a young woman with black hair pulled back in a knot, looked up and assessed Anne-Marie as a casual tourist who might spend a few Swiss francs on a paperback classic or a leather bookmark but was not here to do any serious buying. She hunched down on her stool behind the rostrum and went back to perusing the commodities columns in the *Tribune de Genève*.

Anne-Marie moved slowly among the shelves, letting her eye range along the titles, noting the occasional fine old volume among the reproductions. Here was a Descartes in a locked glass case, there a Voltaire. A sixteenth-century English translation of Caesar's *Commentaries* was displayed on a reading stand in the corner. She knew the content of these works intimately, most as ragged paperbacks from her school days at the Sorbonne, but a few from their earliest appearances in print, even in manuscript, from her researches in the Bibliothèque Nationale in Paris.

A door opened quietly in the back of the shop. Edgy despite her best attempts to stay cool, Anne-Marie swung in its direction. The handsome young man who faced her widened his eyes and pursed his lips in a tight O, mocking her expression. "Excuse me, dear, but *I'm* the one who should be surprised. You're twenty minutes early."

Alain was older than she was by two years, and his lank hair was the same glossy chestnut as hers, their mother's legacy, but his eyes were green, not blue, after their father's. He walked quickly to her side and, before she could lean away, wetly kissed the air beside her cheeks, one side then the other.

His lips stretched into a smile. "Were you ever early in your whole life?"

"I can't wait to hear why you asked me here, Alain," she said softly, willing herself to be friendly.

"I am warned, then. But we cannot talk in my shop." He batted his eyes at the clerk at the rostrum. "My sister and I are going to lunch, Edith. We'll be back in an hour."

"All right, sir."

"I'll tell you what," he said with saccharine cheer, bearing down on her, "if a customer should happen to stumble in, try something new, why don't you? Just for me."

"Yes sir? What would that be?" The woman's red lips barely moved when she spoke.

"Pull your nose out of the newspaper. Offer to help. Maybe we'll sell something."

"My apologies, sir," she murmured, shoving the paper farther under the rostrum.

Under the clerk's spiteful gaze, Anne-Marie allowed her brother to pull her out onto the street. They walked in hurried silence along narrow cobbled streets, Alain humming tunelessly to make it clear he did not wish to speak. She followed him with difficulty; her skirt tugged at her knees and her low heels found every crack in the paving, while he moved like a male model on a runway, his gleaming alligator slippers neatly skipping past dirt and puddles, his tan summer-weight suit and silk tie flowing insouciantly around him.

They came to a cramped hilltop square, from which rose the abrupt and inelegant towers of the Cathedral of Saint Pierre. To the right of its portico, modern steps went down under the pavement.

"Do you know of the excavations beneath Saint Pierre? One of our more famous attractions?"

"Certainly I know them."

"Well, pretend it's your first time." His bright grin was dangerous, a little mad.

"I thought we were going to lunch," she murmured, shrinking from him.

"And I thought *you* wanted to talk about private matters." His grip on her elbow was as tight as his grimace. "Not in a crowded café, thank you."

He pulled her down the steps to the subterranean gate. Upon reaching the ticket seller, a diffident old gentleman in a tweed suit, Alain hesitated and patted his pockets. He turned to her, all innocence. "I seem to have come out without any cash."

At that she laughed. Alain, true to form: had he ever paid for anything he could get someone else to pay for? She opened her purse and paid the ten francs for the tickets. They went through the turnstile into the cool darkness.

They walked along steel catwalks suspended over an eerie tangle of ruins beneath the floor of the cathedral, moving through shadows into pools of light thrown from hidden fixtures. In this place Julius Caesar had established an outpost of Rome; four centuries later Rome still ruled the West, and a Christian bishop had built his palace here. From the compost of ancient walls and paving stones and trash heaps and bone pits rose the massive piers which supported the medieval structure over their heads.

Alain stopped under an eroded gargoyle and turned to face her. "How are you and Peter getting along? Still newlyweds? Still the lovebirds, are we?"

"Do you feel safer in the dark?" she asked. "Do you think I won't dare start screaming in a museum?"

"I suppose that would be foolishly optimistic."

"Peter and I have a very good relationship."

"Why do I imagine that you sound like you are giving a deposition? But perhaps that's the point. A respectable marriage, a respectable husband—next time maybe you can use them to sway the court in your favor."

"Why are you being such a shit? What have I done to you, except to ask for your help?"

His smirk was gone. "I won't waste your time. I fervently wish you'd go away, but after months of your letters and phone calls I get the idea that you're not inclined to do that."

"I told you I'm prepared to pay you, Alain. All your expenses and more."

"How can you possibly compensate me? This is a conservative town, the soul of Protestantism, in which I scrape out a living selling expensive curios to the greedy and self-satisfied."

"You deal in more than curios."

"Precisely my point. And while the rare-book business is understood to be full of scoundrels, one cannot prosper in the business if one is *known* to be a scoundrel. Especially if one identifies one's *self* as a scoundrel." His voice had dropped to a creaking whisper.

To Anne-Marie it sounded like a stifled shout. "I'm not asking you to do me a favor. Charlie has my son because he has money. Now I have money too."

Alain sighed expressively. "I did a bit of research on your new husband"—he raised an open hand—"nothing sinister, just a routine credit check. Peter Slater may be better off than most, but he's not wealthy."

"He has enough. And he's worth more than money, Alain."

"Well, he's never going to make any money studying quarks, or superstrings, or whatever they're studying these days. If you had to marry a scientist, you really should have married someone with an interest in computers. DNA. Pharmaceuticals. Something like that."

With effort, she quelled her rising anger. "How much are you asking me to *compensate* you?"

"We'll get to that." He spoke plainly, his false cheer forgotten. "I've told you, I'm ashamed of what happened. . . ."

"It didn't just happen, Alain."

He recoiled from her fury. "What I did, then. I can't undo it. And really, I'm not the only one who . . . I mean, your boy is all right, after all."

The blood rose in her cheeks, darkening her face in the dim light. "Charlie is doing this to punish me," she said. "Not because he loves Carlos. Carlos is alone. He spends his days with hired nannies."

Alain looked distressed, but not on her account. "Oh dear, we're about to repeat ourselves."

"All I want from you is a drop of blood, Alain. A strand of *your* DNA."

Fine beads of perspiration decorated his nose. "You want rather more than that. You want a confession."

"A simple statement of the facts. No one will ever see it except you and me and Charlie." She felt calmer now. As despicable as he was, at least he was honest with himself. She leaned toward him, so close a casual observer might have thought they were lovers. "Tell me what you want. Just tell me."

"Let's walk a little," he said. "Pretend I'm showing you the sights."

They moved along the catwalks, through the thick walls of the cathedral's foundations and, still below ground, outside the massive building and under the street. Here the tunnels were more constricted and the roof was lower, made of reinforced concrete.

Alain stopped beside a Roman mosaic floor. All the stone and glass chips that made up its quiltlike pattern had been cleaned by the excavators and left almost as bright as new, but the floor lay buckled like a sheet of wet cardboard. "Your husband's in Mykonos now, isn't he? Attending a conference?"

"Yes he is. I'm supposed to be there with him." For the first time in their conversation, her brother had surprised her. What did he care about a physics conference?

"There's another man there, I'm told, also a theoretical physicist. His name is Minakis."

"Greek?"

"Evidently, although he spent most of his life in England and Switzerland. He's over seventy by now. He made good choices when he was still active"—unlike her new husband, Alain meant, as if scientific choices were obvious, or even wholly voluntary—"took out patents in superconductors, started a company you may have heard of, Andwin-Zurich. Today, even I would call Minakis wealthy."

"Is that the reason you're interested in him?"

"He's an amateur archaeologist. Amateur, but not really—now and then he writes for professional journals. The point is, within the past few months photographs of certain artifacts have been circulating. Unpublished stuff said to be in private collections. Reliable people tell me the collection is Minakis's."

"What kind of artifacts?"

Alain reached into the pocket of his double-breasted jacket and brought out a sheaf of Polaroid prints. "Three Middle Minoan painted cups"—he spread the prints like a hand of cards—"an alabaster vase carved with a harvest scene"—holding them up to the light—"a Late Minoan votive in the form of a gold *labrys,* a double ax."

She lifted her gaze from the spectacular ax. "I thought you were a book dealer."

"My interests are eclectic."

Again she waited; it got easier with practice. He had never discussed his business with her, but she knew that like herself he was unacquainted with hard work of the conventional sort. Who were these "people" of his who were so interested in Minakis? He must have sponsors, backers—buyers, perhaps.

"Minoan artifacts are extremely rare outside Crete, even in museums," he continued. "Sir Arthur Evans had a deal with the local authorities to take some of what he found at Knossos back to England—it's at Oxford now—but that was before Crete was part of Greece. These days the Cretans won't even let the National Museum in Athens borrow pieces, never mind letting them out of the country. I'm told that the last time the government tried, half the population of Iraklion surrounded the museum in town and the other half went out to the airport and stood on the runway to keep the riot police from landing."

"Yes, I heard about that." He wasn't exaggerating by much.

"The ancient Minoans did get around. There have been finds on the mainland, some Aegean islands, Asia Minor, the Levant, Egypt—but nothing much compared to even a minor site on Crete. The people I've talked to are very anxious to have a look at what Minakis has found."

"The Greek government must be anxious too"—she smiled thinly—"since it's illegal to conceal archaeological finds."

Alain shrugged irritably. "What I'm saying is, good-quality Minoan artifacts are among the rarest and most valuable objects one can hope to come across."

"And you think you've come across a trove of them."

"I haven't, but maybe *you* will." Alain went on, oblivious of Anne-Marie's shocked expression. "This Minakis is an awful man, they tell me, who'd rather insult a person than say hello. But you have an excellent reason to visit Mykonos, an excellent reason to introduce yourself; you've spent time on Crete, you speak Greek, he's a colleague of your husband's. And you certainly know how to handle a bad temper—I've seen you charm favors from a—"

She cut him off. "I'll be your spy, why not?" If it had been any less important to her, she would have made Alain persuade her, made him work for it, but that would be a waste of time. "And meanwhile you'll take a blood test and sign an affidavit."

"We'll talk about that later, depending on what you learn."

"I'll even steal his damned treasure for you, Alain. I want my son back."

"There's no need to steal anything."

"Do we have a deal?"

He drew a silk handkerchief from his breast pocket and daintily patted his sweating face. His skin was as damp and pale as the underground. "All right. If you'll do this for me, I'll do what you want."

She rummaged in her purse. "Put it in writing. Before I leave here." She handed him her address book, opened it to a blank page, and gave him a felt-tipped pen.

Alain stuffed his handkerchief back in his pocket and took the book and pen. He scribbled hastily. "Don't try to steal anything, Anne-Marie," he said as he gave them back to her. "Just tell me where he keeps it."

She read his scrawl, then slapped the booklet closed and turned away, no longer willing to share either anger or hope with the man who had dragged her into the pit. Impatiently she sought the stairway to the surface.

Eight hours later Anne-Marie was climbing again, pulling herself wearily up the last flight of apartment-building stairs. She'd been on trains all afternoon, Geneva to Paris on the TGV, transferring to the suburban for the trip to Saint-Germain-en-Laye. When she came out of the underground station in front of the château, it was already dark. She didn't bother to look for a taxi, just slung her overnight bag over her shoulder and set off through the village streets, grateful for the opportunity to stretch her legs.

But her mother, who *owned* this prime piece of real estate and lived on the highest floor, could not keep its lift running because she would not let repairmen do their work for more than a few hours without accusing them of malingering or theft, whereupon they invariably cursed her and walked off the job. Which gives her a perfect excuse not to fix anything, Anne-Marie thought, as she paused to catch her breath on the dim fifth-stage landing, under a fifteen-watt bulb on a timer that would extinguish itself any second now.

Her mother had buzzed her in at street level but hadn't yet opened the apartment door. Anne-Marie was reaching for the doorbell when she heard a key in the lock and the slide of a bolt. Then another bolt. The door opened an inch.

"I didn't think you could get up here so quickly," her mother said, peering through the slit. At that moment the light loudly clicked off, plunging the hall into darkness.

"Let me in, Mama. No one's holding a gun to my head."

"No?" Her mother squinted cautiously, then loosed the chain and pulled the door open a little wider, still holding it in front of her like a shield. "Then why mention it?"

Anne-Marie pushed into the apartment. "How's Jenny?"

"In her crib. You should not be surprised if she sleeps all night, after what she ate for lunch. Your child is voracious."

"Is she eating you out of house and home, Mama?" Anne-Marie walked down the dingy hall to the spare room, where she slept on a fold-out couch when visiting. "After only one day?"

"My apologies. I should have said she has a very healthy appetite." The older woman sniffed and fell silent.

Inside the spare room, Anne-Marie tossed her bag on the folding couch and turned to face her mother, a woman with eyes as fierce as her own, who had once been almost as tall and slim as she, now with wide hips and tired shoulders and a mass of dark hair dramatically streaked with gray. Anne-Marie drew a breath and tried to soften her hard words. "I'm sorry, I know you didn't mean it. It's been a long day."

They were interrupted by the appearance of Jennifer, who grinned shyly from behind the doorframe, winsome in polka-dot pajamas that left her feet bare and her toes curling. Seeing that she was seen, the dark-haired little girl swiftly hid herself behind the wall.

Anne-Marie eyed her mother, holding a finger to her lips. After a second, Jennifer poked her head out again. "*Peek*aboo!" Anne-Marie cried, which made her mother wince and caused Jennifer to crow ecstatically. Anne-Marie swooped forward, picking up her clown-suited little girl and squeezing her close, whirling her around in the narrow hallway while Jennifer giggled and screamed with pleasure.

An hour later, after her daughter had given up her excited play and lapsed back into sweet sleep, Anne-Marie and her mother sat across from each other at the dining-room table, a piece of wreckage Madame Brand had acquired at the antiques-andham market in Châtou. Under a yellowing bulb in a flyspecked ceiling fixture, they ate bean soup out of mismatched bowls.

"Alain looks fine," Anne-Marie said. "His business seems to be doing well." Her mother hadn't asked, but Anne-Marie thought she might like to know.

"Mmph." Madame Brand was intent upon a spoonful of soup.

Anne-Marie leaned away from the table. "We had a long talk about what's between us."

After a long silence the older woman said, "I'm glad you're willing to talk to him again."

"He admits the truth. To me, anyway. Maybe soon he'll be willing to admit it to others."

"I don't know why we can't put all that behind us. It was so long ago. God knows it was a hard time for us all."

"Are you defending him or yourself, Mama?"

"Why does he never come to see me? Is it because you've made him afraid to face me?" Under the ceiling fixture, Madame Brand's face was a tragic mask. "Why do you cling to the dead past? Are you determined to torture yourself forever?"

"No more than you." Anne-Marie looked around the apartment, at its stained and peeling wallpaper, its dirty windows, its flea-market furniture. "You're a wealthy woman. You own an apartment building in one of the best suburbs of Paris, and you live in it like a beggar. Why don't you show yourself some respect?"

"And *you* think money can be taken for granted, because you never had to work for it. All your life you got it from men . . ."

"You mistake me for yourself," Anne-Marie said angrily.

". . . even what you *inherited*. Well, your father has been dead a long time. He can't sell recordings forever." She seemed grimly satisfied at the thought, even though the money to be lost was mostly her own.

"I'm not so sure of that," Anne-Marie replied. "Eric Brand is more popular on CDs than he was on LP records; maybe he'll be an even bigger star when they invent the next . . . Oh, *merde.*" She slumped in frustration. Once more she'd let herself be tricked into her mother's game of contingencies. "Anyway, my point was, you own this building, thanks to Papa's royalties. If you don't let it fall to pieces, it will give you a living forever."

"No one lives forever, dear," her mother said primly.

"Some people never live at all," Anne-Marie answered. "You left Algeria a long time ago. Long before you had Alain and me to worry about. You're not a little girl anymore. You don't have to steal bread. You don't have to eat stewed rats."

Her mother said nothing, only dipped her spoon into the soup and brought it slowly to her mouth, sipping noisily at each spoonful as if it were the last she might ever taste.

Watching the performance with amusement, Anne-Marie conceded defeat. She dipped another spoonful of her soup and swallowed it. She said, "You'll be glad to hear that Alain and I have agreed to do as you suggest—put the past behind us. He's going to do what I've asked, and in return I'm going to help him with . . . a business matter. Unfortunately it means I have to be gone—a few days at most. Will you keep Jennifer a bit longer?"

Madame Brand looked up from her soup, her voice soft, her expression full of resentment and hurt. "What will that new husband of yours have to say about all this traveling?"

"I'll ask him tomorrow. I have to see him by myself, without Jennifer. For Alain's sake."

Her mother looked at her as if this were a tissue of lies not worth pulling apart. "I will be happy to keep the little girl as long as you want. I think she is happy to be with me."

"I know she is, Mama. She loves you. She knows you love her."

Madame Brand looked away, momentarily forgetting her soup. "Hmph," she said, her eyes bright with tears.

3

Under the springtime sun, Delos was an arid sliver of granite strewn with marble. Minakis waited patiently as hired caïques, modified to hold tourists instead of fish or lumber, puttered across the strait from Mykonos and deposited their cargo, sunburned European and American and Asian passengers who stepped ashore, peered at their maps, and started straight up the rocky slope to the east, enticed by the gathering shape of the amphitheater on the hillside and the guidebook's promises of mosaic floors in ruined Hellenistic villas.

Peter Slater was one of the caïque passengers, but he turned away from the others and meandered among the jumble of wrecked buildings at the water's edge. He moved with a tall man's angular grace. Impatiently raking his long-fingered hand through his sandy hair, he looked younger than his thirty-five years. His fair skin was flushed in the heat and bright with sweat.

Peter followed the Sacred Way of this once most-sacred island, which led him into a field of ruins only a classical scholar could have made sense of. He was not a classical scholar. He could not see what was once there, only what was

there now: the hard ground, the tough grass, the low courses of
stone relaid to sketch out the building plans of the ancient sanctuary, with a few column drums, a few white marble herms, set
upright to suggest the vanished third dimension. And underfoot, the paving stones and low stone steps of the Sacred Way,
a riverbed of stone deeply carved into smooth hollows by a
centuries-long stream of shoes and sandals and bare feet . . .

To the uninitiated, to Peter, it could only be glittering wreckage. More than the ruins were bright; every crystal in the granite of the low, barren hillside glistened with refocused sunlight.
He came upon a curious pair of white boulders looming in the
ruin field and stopped to peer at them.

Minakis, stalking him silently, wondered what he made of
the pitted and eroded gobbets of stone. He approached, making
no effort to be silent but moving up silently nevertheless.

" 'We will not ever know his legendary head,' " he said,
" 'Wherein the eyes, like apples, ripened.' "

Peter turned to find a man as tall as himself, as slim and
erect, but darker, more used to the sun—and upon inspection
much older, his eyes as black as lava and his teeth, under his
broad gray mustache, whiter than marble. Teeth and eyes and
height, that is what registered; Minakis was used to it.

"Professor Minakis. I didn't see you." He offered his hand.

Minakis shook it neatly, then turned his eye to the weathered
remains. "You know the poem?"

"Rilke, isn't it?"

"Yes, 'An Archaic Torso of Apollo.' I was inspired to learn it
because of this ruin. Not every kouros was Apollo, but this one
certainly was."

"This one?" Peter looked at the two trapezoidal boulders that
were once a statue. One would have been the upper torso, now
chopped off and set upon its waist; the other, two or three yards
away, must have been the pelvis.

"It was almost twenty feet tall, made on Naxos at the end of
the eighth century. The pedestal—it's still over there, by what's
left of the Naxian house—is inscribed, 'I am the same stone,
figure and base.' The Naxians had a habit of carving these
things in one piece, right out of the mountainside."

Peter looked across the grassy court to the rows of stone Minakis had indicated. "What happened to it?"

"Pirates tried to carry it off. It was so heavy they had to cut it up just to drag it this little distance. They must have decided it wasn't worth the trouble. Delos had been in ruins for more than half a millennium, but the unfortunate thieves were hundreds of years too early to capitalize on our modern appetite for stolen antiquities."

"Do you remember all of it?"

Minakis's eyebrow lifted. "All of it?"

"The poem."

He began again without preamble. His accent was educated British overlying native Greek.

" 'We will not ever know his legendary head
Wherein the eyes, like apples, ripened. Yet
His torso glows like a candelabra
In which his vision, merely turned down low,
Still holds and gleams. If this were not so, the curve
Of the breast could not so blind you, nor this smile
Pass lightly through the soft turn of the loins
Into that center where procreation flared.
If this were not so, this stone would stand defaced, maimed,
Under the transparent cascade of the shoulder,
Not glimmering that way, like a wild beast's pelt,
Nor breaking out of all its contours
Like a star; for there is no place here
That does not see you. You must change your life.' "

"Change your life?" The imperative caught Peter by surprise. His laugh was a dry sound in the dry surroundings. "Easy to say."

"Perhaps not so easy for the poet." Minakis stepped back. "Forgive me. I've thoughtlessly interrupted you."

"Nothing to interrupt."

Minakis persisted. "The others went that way. You came this way. I assume to be alone."

"They have guidebooks. I'm following my nose."

"Then your nose is good. But of course you've been here before."

"No. What makes you think so?"

"You were at the first Delos. Your paper on neutral kaons made a stir. You had interesting things to say about field theory."

"I never left Mykonos, actually; I hardly left the villa. In those days I didn't pay as much attention to . . ." Peter waved his long fingers and, after a momentary pause, passed them through his hair. And then, almost absentmindedly, he walked off. Minakis caught up and walked beside him in silence, moving with easy strides over the bare ground, listening as Peter spoke. "Delos I was ten years ago—quantum theory seemed as natural as water to me then; I could play in it without a care. If I'd had any sense of history, I would have recognized that I'd swallowed the Copenhagen interpretation whole."

"Back then, you insisted that the quantum world is not a world at all," Minakis prompted him. "No microworld, only mathematical descriptions."

"Yes, I was adamant. Those who protested were naive—one has to be willing to tolerate ambiguity, even to be crazy."

"Bohr's words?"

"The party line. Of course Bohr did say, 'It is wrong to think that the task of physics is to find out how nature *is*. Physics concerns what we can *say* about nature.' Meaning that when we start to talk what sounds like philosophy, our colleagues should rip us to pieces." Peter smiled. "They smell my blood already."

"Do not think I am not after your blood." Minakis bared his teeth in a happy grin.

"Thanks for the warning."

"But do consider that I am an old man, well past my theoretical prime. Not averse to philosophy."

They came to a row of stone lions, some shattered, some almost whole, crouched on stone pedestals—lean female creatures carved to show their ribs, their skins stretched over coiled haunches. The iron rods that propped up the marble fragments had seeped rust, staining the marble like dried blood. To the east, where the lions stared, a drained lake bed full of reeds lay motionless under the high sun. The stillness was disturbed by a bright green lizard, breaking cover to swim across the bending reed-tops.

Peter glanced at Minakis. "Let's say there are indications—I have personal indications—not convincing, perhaps, but suggestive, that the quantum world penetrates the classical world deeply." He was silent for a moment, then waved his hand at the ruins. "The world of classical physics, I mean. I suppose I've come to realize that the world is more than a laboratory."

"We are standing where Apollo was born," Minakis said. "Leto squatted just there, holding fast to a palm tree, and after nine days of labor gave birth to the god of light and music—who was a bloodthirsty savage. What did the world know of laboratories then?"

Peter said, "Even to me, my search seems foolish. Worse than philosophy. Metaphysics. Ideology." He pressed his lips together. "So if you are after my blood . . ."

Minakis held up a thin hand, his fingers as long as Peter's and, in the everywhere-reflected light, almost transparent. Peter, usually so fluent, stood as if transfixed.

Maintaining his hieratic gesture, Minakis turned to face the rocky hill that loomed to the east. On the far side of the vanished lake a woman was descending the path from the temple of Isis, her bright cotton skirts flowing about her knees, her dark hair stirring in the breeze of her passage.

Minakis dropped his hand. Peter's gaze slipped away, upslope. He squinted in puzzlement, then called out, "Anne-Marie!"

She walked toward them, raising a well-used 35mm Canon to her eye. She tweaked the focus and adjusted the exposure with practiced skill while she levered the film forward and clicked off half a dozen frames, never losing her stride. Watching her, Peter brushed his scalp absently, lost in admiration.

Suddenly she was standing in front of him. "Hello, handsome." Dropping the camera into her bag, she took his hands and gave him a wifely peck on the lips.

"You weren't coming until tonight. I would have met you."

"I caught an early plane. I just missed your boat. I've climbed over half this pile of rocks." She brushed at her dusty skirts, then looked up and smiled at Minakis.

"Professor Minakis," Peter said, "my wife, Anne-Marie."

"I'm very glad to meet you, Mrs. Slater."

"Actually it's Brand," Peter said, "Her own name."

"Call me Anne-Marie." She offered her hand and watched with approval as he shook it firmly, not trying to kiss her hand or bow or do anything smacking of fake charm. "You're from Crete?" she asked.

"What makes you think so?"

"Well, a name that ends in *akis*."

"Not much of a clue."

"Your broad shoulders, then, and your wasp waist, and your height—and, if you will forgive me, your very good looks. Vaivaios, eisai apo tin Kriti, apo ta oroi Kriton."

"You speak Greek?" Minakis's eyes were fixed upon hers.

"Pend'-exi lexeis, mono."

"More than five or six words, I think."

"Anne-Marie speaks eight modern languages fluently," Peter said proudly. "She studied literature at the Sorbonne."

"I was a poor scholar. But I lived on Crete a short while."

"Doing magazine photography," Peter said. "She's an excellent photographer."

"Mostly I was doing drugs. Then I got married." She darted Peter a warning look: *Let me speak for myself.* "Not to Peter. That was later."

Minakis watched the edgy exchange. "I can't resist asking you what any other Greek would have asked by now. . . ."

She smiled. "Two. Not Peter's, though."

After an instant Peter caught on. "Oh yes. Jennifer lives with us, she's one. . . . She's with her grandmother now?" He raised an eyebrow at Anne-Marie, who nodded. "And Carlos is six; he, uh, he's going to spend time with us this summer."

"When do you plan to have . . . ?"

"No plans," Anne-Marie said, cutting off the inquiry.

Minakis nodded. "I will now stop being a Greek. Have you been to Delos before, Anne-Marie?"

"Once. I spent my time running up and down rocks, glancing at things out of the corner of my eye, scared I'd miss the boat back. So far, this trip is no different."

"We can walk around a bit without worrying about the boat," Minakis suggested. "I know the curator. If necessary, she'll send us back in her launch."

"Shouldn't we check with the woman first?" Peter asked. "I can't be stuck here all night."

"It's true, my friend will probably insist we stay for dinner," Minakis said, nodding solemnly. "And if we get too jovial, we may have to be her guests overnight. Yes, Peter, I think you do risk missing tomorrow morning's talk . . . what's it called?"— the peremptory hand came up—"I remember now: 'Amplitudes versus probabilities in reduplicated space-time,' isn't that it?"

"I'll take your word for it."

"Warmed-over Hawking. You can afford to miss it, in my opinion." Minakis hesitated. "Oh my, please forgive me. I've just remembered that Hawking was your thesis adviser."

Anne-Marie's expression made her preference plain. Peter thrust his hands into his pockets. "Never mind. We'll be glad to have you show us around."

Minakis grinned a glittering grin that said, *Of course you would.* He turned and walked away, pausing at a discreet distance to admire the afternoon sun on the columns of the temple of Poseidon.

Meanwhile Peter leaned toward Anne-Marie and wrapped his fingers around her bare arms, on the verge of pulling her to him—"I'm just so happy to see you!"—but she evaded his hungry gaze. He leaned to kiss her, a light kiss on her mouth. Then, feeling her tension, he let her go. "Jennifer's okay? Your mother's all right?"

"Yes."

"Anne-Marie . . ."

"Let's talk later. When we're alone."

Together, not touching, they walked toward Minakis. He was an indistinct silhouette in the afternoon's shimmering light.

* * *

Hours later, after a tour of the island and its museum that would have exhausted even a scholar, they gratefully agreed to an early dinner with the ephor of antiquities and her husband in their square little house beside the square little museum above the sacred compound. Through clerestory windows, the westering light was honey colored on the walls of the airy dining room and on the fragments of statues that decorated it. The long table was set with dishes of gleaming black olives and slabs of white cheese, bowls of pink *taramosalata* and plates of green salad, loaves of bread and sweating jugs of wine; the aroma of roasting lamb came from the kitchen.

"My good friend Manolis here has often tried to enlighten me concerning reality," said the ephor, Popi Gorgopoulou, an energetic woman in her forties whose stiff yellow-blond hair was prematurely streaked with gray, "but I have never been able to make sense of his explanations." She directed her fierce attention upon Peter. "You are famous for your theoretical work, according to my friend. Also according to my friend, you are interested in the nature of reality." She lifted a glass of purple wine. "So I made him promise to bring you to meet me. I invite you to explain reality to me."

There was a moment's silence during which Popi's husband took the opportunity to make a trip to the kitchen; so far he had added little to the conversation besides his hearty smile, for he was not confident of his English, which the others were speaking in deference to Peter, who did not speak a word of Greek. Meanwhile Peter savored a morsel of marinated octopus and wondered just when Minakis had promised to produce him.

"Two years ago," Peter said, after pausing to swallow, "I would have had to decline your invitation. I was as much a logical positivist as Werner Heisenberg, who was suspicious of the word 'reality.' "

"Was he really?" Gorgopoulou asked, amused.

"Because, said Heisenberg, while such words lend themselves to sentences that produce pictures in our imagination— he used the example, 'Besides our world there exists another world, with which any connection is impossible'—such sentences have no consequences and therefore no content at all."

"But surely reality is what we can see and hear and feel," said the ephor. "Our experience. Our sense impressions."

"Most of us can agree on that," Peter said, "but if that were all we had to go on, we wouldn't know much about the world. We continually make assumptions, we fall into habits, we build little rational constructs on top of our sense impressions. I've seen the sun come up most days of my life, unless it is cloudy, so early on I concluded that the sun really does come up every day whether I see it or not. And I can think of good reasons why it should do so. And that becomes part of reality."

"A modest assumption," said the ephor.

"Not so modest. The realm of sense impressions *plus* the rational constructions we base upon them extends a long way, all the way from distant quasars down to the smallest virus. But try to look at anything much smaller . . ." Peter shrugged and speared another fragment of octopus tentacle with his fork.

"Please don't keep us in suspense," Anne-Marie said dryly, twisting her wineglass between her fingers.

"When we try to look inside atoms," Peter said, "not only can we not see what's going on, we cannot even construct a coherent *picture* of what's going on."

"If you will forgive me, Peter," Minakis said, turning to the others. "He means that we can construct several pictures—that light and matter are waves, for example, or that light and matter are particles—but that all these pictures are inadequate. What's left to us is the bare mathematics of quantum theory."

"As you've said before, Manolis"—Popi Gorgopoulou broke in enthusiastically—"and according to quantum theory, the microworld doesn't really exist?"

"More precisely," Minakis suggested, "according to the prevailing interpretation of quantum mechanics, the question of whether the microworld has an independent existence is meaningless."

"Yes, but do you *believe* that?" she asked. "You, Peter. Do you really believe there are two worlds, one that doesn't exist and one that does?"

Peter found Minakis looking at him across the table with an expression of wolfish amusement. "I used to," he said. "No more. Quantum theory works, but it doesn't tell the whole story."

"Then you believe in one world," said the ephor. "One really *real* world."

For a moment, no one said anything. Finally Peter nodded. "I'd like to."

Anne-Marie said, "Note the conviction."

Minakis said to Gorgopoulou, "Whatever the really real world is like, my friend, it is not what you might imagine."

"And you, Manolis?" she asked. "Can you imagine it?"

"I can imagine the real world." Minakis's smile was enigmatic. "Alas, in the time available to us tonight, I could not begin to describe it to you."

After dinner they took up their glasses of sweet *mavrodaphni* and moved away from the table. The ephor and her husband took Anne-Marie to see the Cycladic sculptures whose fragments were displayed in the hall of the adjacent museum; speaking Greek, *kyrios* Gorgopoulos was not at all reticent.

Meanwhile Peter followed Minakis onto the stone terrace that overlooked the ruin field of Apollo's sanctuary. The fat sun was wobbling toward the horizon across the narrow strait between Delos and its neighbor island Renia, backlighting the marble rubble with orange light.

"Professor Minakis, people speak highly of you, but I'm afraid I'm not familiar with your work." Talking physics, Peter tended to bluntness. "Tell me more about this real world you imagine but can't describe."

Minakis turned away from the view of the sunset. "Are you familiar with John Cramer's transactional interpretation of quantum mechanics?"

"No I'm not."

"Some years ago Cramer followed up Feynman's and Wheeler's proposal that the self-energy of the electron can be eliminated if one assumes the existence of advanced-wave solutions to Schrödinger's equation for electromagnetic waves."

"Which proved to be a red herring."

"I'd prefer to call it a useful mistake, given the subsequent course of cosmology and quantum electrodynamics."

Peter shrugged.

Minakis leaned closer, his back to the spectacle of the setting sun. "Also possibly useful, I think, for removing the absurdities of quantum mechanics generally. Cramer takes Feynman and Wheeler several steps further, you see; he develops the notion of an exchange, or transaction, between what he calls 'offer' waves—analogous to the wave function describing any quantum event—and 'confirmation' waves, which are emitted backward in time by the absorber of the consequences of the event."

Peter cocked his head quizzically. "That makes it sound as if every quantum event is a negotiation between the past and the future—between a cause and its effect." In full sunlight Peter's skepticism was plain.

"Although Cramer's scheme is only an interpretation," Minakis replied, his shadowed expression unreadable, "in my view it is much more sensible than the Copenhagen interpretation and at least as logical as the many-worlds interpretation. But Cramer assumes it can't be tested . . . that it makes no predictions which differ from those of standard quantum mechanics."

"You disagree?"

"Theory is indispensable, of course, but I was always one of those chaps who are happiest getting their hands dirty in the laboratory," Minakis said. "Read Cramer. I'll give you his papers. Then we can talk."

Popi Gorgopoulou came onto the terrace, leading Anne-Marie by the hand. "Time to go, you two, while there's light to see by."

Peter saw his wife radiant in the orange light, her pale eyes afire, her soft clothes wrapping her form in the evening breeze like a statue of Victory. He felt a rush of desire, having nothing whatever to do with the abstract matters he had been discussing a moment before.

But her pale gaze was fixed on the man behind him. On Minakis.

* * *

By the time the ephor's launch drew alongside the stone quay in Mykonos harbor, the stars were out overhead and the bars and discos were warming up, their big speakers throbbing. The quayside was filling with boisterous tourists; a few feet away a party of tanned young Scandinavians piled out of a taxi, laughing, and Minakis commandeered the cab.

Peter and Anne-Marie rode with him to the sprawling villa on the hill above the town that housed the Delos II conference. Minakis rode in front and paid the fare efficiently before Peter could muster even a feeble protest; the three of them parted at the gate with promises to find one another tomorrow.

Peter led Anne-Marie through the olive-planted courtyards along paths dimly lit with low fixtures. It would have been a perfectly quiet night except for the attenuated revelry that floated up from the town below. He showed her into the guest-house they'd been assigned by the conference organizers and flipped the switch that turned on the bedside lights.

It was not much bigger than a motel room, just a bedroom plus a WC with shower, but pleasantly furnished in varnished pine and rough cotton, with oil sketches of Byzantine churches and blue seas hanging on the whitewashed walls. The villa staff had already moved Anne-Marie's single bag into the closet.

"A nice place," she said, "to be alone with you."

"It looks a lot better tonight than it did last night."

She came lightly into his arms, loosening her knees and pressing the length of her body against his. They had never been alone through the long afternoon and evening; every look he'd had of her had fed his desire, even when she was mocking him. As she kissed him hungrily, making little sounds of want, she pulled his shirt free of his trousers and insinuated her hands, impatiently undoing the buttons from his throat to his belly. His long-fingered hands supported her bottom as she leaned back, opening his shirt, smiling at what she could see of his spare, muscular body in the warm lamplight, then pulling her own cotton T-shirt over her head—shaking out her dark fragrant hair—pressing her cool bare breasts against his smooth chest and kissing him again, probing his mouth with her tongue, working at his belt buckle while he caught the elastic bands of her skirt and panties in his thumbs and pushed them down over her flaring hips.

They stumbled over their clothes onto the bed, snorting with muffled laughter, their mouths still pressed together. She drew her knees up under his arms and clasped his sides with her thighs while her hands found his hard buttocks, and he found her center.

Time was confused; they lost the sense of what was supposed to come before what, and for a burning interval their laughter and need and exultation were scrambled. Then she groaned and arched, and he pulsed. Within a few falling seconds time reasserted itself—

—and they heard the ticking of Peter's travel clock on the table under the lamp.

"I missed you," he said, his nose and forehead against hers, peering into her eyes that, this close, were one pale eye.

"I could tell," she said. "Could you tell I missed you?"

He chuckled. "I got that feeling, yes." He gently disengaged and sat up beside her. "Tonight's a bonus. I thought I would never have you alone again."

Her fingernails meandered across his belly, but she said nothing.

"Tell me about Geneva. What was so urgent about what your brother had to tell you?"

"Not as exciting as he made it sound. Turns out he had an assignment for me—he'd pitched a story to the editor of a Swiss business magazine."

"Let me guess. Professor Minakis."

She pushed her face into his side, laughing, blowing hot bubbles against his skin.

He laughed too, but not so freely. "This was supposed to be a vacation. Kids and all. You're working, Jennifer's with your mom—not much left of that scheme."

Anne-Marie looked up. "You're working too. I should be done by the time you are."

"By tomorrow afternoon?"

"I'll interview him, make a few pictures . . . the two of you together, if you'll let me. He seems quite taken with you."

"You seem quite taken with him," Peter said quietly.

She turned away, rising naked from the bed. She sought something to cover herself in her garment bag hanging from the closet rail, while she tried hard to calm her temper.

The first time they'd met they were in a temper, challenging each other. She was married to Charlie but had left him alone with Carlos, just long enough for a photographic assignment to cover the dedication of the giant TERAC accelerator in Hawaii. She'd been drawn by the sound of Bach on the piano, a complex and unmelodic piece Peter was playing in the midst of a big party of physicists and their spouses and hangers-on—a piece her father had performed to critical raves. Peter wasn't as good as her father, of course, but for an amateur he was very good. She'd fallen in love with him that night, and he with her, but both were wary of their feelings, and after a few turbulent days they had separated. Months passed between the first heat of their romance and the re-emergence of what they could trust as love, months during which Anne-Marie left Charlie forever, and Jennifer was born; their emotions were still on shaky ground and could crumble beneath them without warning.

"I'm sorry, it was a stupid thing for me to say," Peter said from the bed, watching as she pulled a black silk kimono over her nakedness. "But sometimes I wonder if I know who you are."

She shook her head and turned away so that he could not see her tears. "I'm sorry to hear that. Don't expect me to spell it out for you." She sounded angry, even to herself. She hated sounding that way. The anger she felt wasn't against Peter; it was her defense against despair.

4

Early the next morning Minakis left the villa and walked down the rocky slope overlooking the harbor, toward Mykonos town below. Doves had softly announced the coming day, but already the light was hard, reflecting heat from the shimmering surface of the water. At this hour, with the shops closed and most tourists still in their beds—only an occasional German drinking his breakfast beer—the overcrowded town could have passed for the pleasant village it had been half a century ago.

He walked through the narrow streets to a little square by the sea, where a coffeehouse was open early for the convenience of fishermen, and sat at a table under a pungent eucalyptus. A sleepy waiter brought him boiled coffee and a slice of *galaktobureko*.

Minakis pulled a string of amber worry beads from his jacket pocket and began absently clicking them through the fingers of his left hand. The view from his table was a pretty cliché: the three whitewashed windmills on the promontory were for snapshots, not for grinding grain, and the houses along the seawall with their wooden, Turkish-style second-floor balconies overhanging the waves housed boutiques, not families. But small boats with saints' names painted on their bows—*Ayios Nikolaos, Ayia Varvara*—still hauled out on the strip of yellow sand, and fishermen still went out lantern-fishing on calm nights. Last night, coming across the strait from Delos when the sky was tinged with the smoky afterglow of sunset and the water was as smooth as oil, the fishing lanterns were a floating galaxy, which their launch cleaved like a slow rocket.

At dawn the fishermen carried their catches to market, then spread their purple nets to dry on the quays and squatted beside them, sewing up the tears. On the beach a few feet in front of Minakis a gang of dark-skinned fishermen who could have been medieval pirates were bent over their nets, wielding spike-like needles and purple polyester thread.

As he sat clicking his worry beads, Minakis contemplated the progress of his own fishing expedition. Yesterday, on Delos, his hopes had been confirmed: Peter hadn't once spoken of observations or measurements, only of *reality;* he was on the verge of abandoning quantum conservatism for a much older conservatism. It remained to convince Peter that his search was noble but that he was hopelessly lost, that only Minakis could lead him out of the dark wood of quantum field theory.

Peter was not the only challenge, however. Until the moment of his first sight of Anne-Marie, while she was still a distant figure descending the sacred hill of Delos, he'd begun to think that his scheme to lure her and her husband to Crete was working after all.

Richard had assured him that Anne-Marie's brother had practically salivated at the photographs of the Minoan artifacts "rumored" to be in Minakis's possession—that Alain had leaped at the hint that his sister was just the person to do his dirty work for him. Minakis had not fretted about the cool cynicism of entangling Anne-Marie in his affairs just to bind her husband more closely. But until yesterday, when the first distant sight of her had raised the hairs on his neck . . .

His banter with her had been a precarious performance. Something about her—he could not imagine what—made him feel as if he were in the presence of the uncanny.

He sipped his bitter coffee, and when he looked up, he saw Anne-Marie walking toward him across the little square from the direction of the sea, her dark hair stirring about her face, her battered camera hanging by its strap from her shoulder. For a moment he went cold, as if she had caught him in some sacrilegious act. "Anne-Marie," he called. He stood up and slipped his worry beads into his pocket. "Good morning."

She stopped and shaded her eyes against the direct sunlight. "Is this place open? Can I get something to eat?"

"Of course." He waved at the waiter, who was already hurrying toward them, less sleepy now. "Tell me what you'd like."

Anne-Marie turned to the waiter impatiently. "Ena galaktobureko, parakalo, kai ena kafes Ellenikon, metrio, kai ena potiri nero, poli krio."

"Malista, kyria." The waiter bobbed his head and hurried away, and Anne-Marie sat down, smoothing her blue denim skirt over her brown legs.

"Pardon my presumption," Minakis said. "I forgot that you don't need an interpreter."

She smiled crookedly. "I make allowances for Greek males."

He studied her with circumspect pleasure. Her sandaled feet were powdered with beach sand, and her white cotton blouse was unbuttoned to the curve of her tanned breasts. A beautiful and decisive woman, he thought, who does not doubt the reality of the world she sees through those pale, fierce eyes. How deeply does she see into it?

She returned his impertinent gaze and said nothing.

"If I may ask," he said. "The breakfast at the villa is very good, very eclectic."

"Is that meant as a recommendation?"

"I mean you could have gotten anything you wanted there."

"You're here, not there. Assume my reasons are like yours."

Clearly he didn't think they were, and presently she admitted as much.

"No, not like yours. I followed you." She brought her camera up to the level of her chest and levered it to the next frame.

"Followed me? Oh, because Peter's already at the morning talk, I suppose . . . ?"

She aimed at him and snapped the shutter, all in one quick motion, then thumbed the lever to the next frame.

Minakis hid his surprise in rambling talk. "I confess I have little use for Hawking's 'imaginary time.' A mathematical stunt to get rid of the Big Bang, apparently because he finds singularities distasteful."

"Thanks so much." She snapped the shutter and thumbed the lever again, pressing her mobile lips together to suppress a grin.

"For . . . ?" He raised an inquisitive eyebrow.

"For explaining what doesn't interest me in terms I don't understand." She said it with more humor than heat, keeping her eye to the viewfinder. She snapped one more frame, then let the camera dangle from its strap. "I followed you to take pictures of you. And to ask you about yourself. I decided that while Peter was working, I would work too. I suspect you would make an intriguing subject for a magazine piece."

"I'm flattered." And impressed. He knew the truth more completely than she could imagine, and he knew how carefully she had to step around it. Yet nothing she said was untrue.

The waiter brought custard and coffee and cold water. Minakis watched as she ate hungrily, following each forkful of sugar-dusted pastry with a sip of coffee, then a sip of water. Finished at last, she sat back in her chair. "That was good."

"Mm. The only better I know is in Iraklion, at a place on Fountain Square. Two places, these days. Two brothers shared a restaurant, but they got into an argument and split it down the middle. They haven't said a word to each other in years. The tables are shoved up to the line, so if you want to start a fight, just put your plate down on the table beside you. It will vanish into the enemy kitchen. Then come the gruesome threats and the arm waving."

She laughed happily, letting down her guard. "You showed us a wonderful time last night. I meant to thank you. Peter too."

"Alas, my repertoire is exhausted."

"You mean you're not a tour guide at heart?"

"Nude beaches aside, Mykonos is a very ordinary place."

"I think you showed us Delos because you want to know Peter. And right now you're dying to hear everything I have to tell you about him."

"And do you have anything to tell me?"

"I heard him claim an interest in reality last night. But I think for him reality means a kind of aesthetics, something he can deal with rationally, at arm's length."

Minakis took a sip of his bitter coffee. "I would like to know how you came to that conclusion. When did he first . . . ?"

She smiled again, faintly. "I'll let him tell you what he wants you to know. The truth is, I'm really not interested in talking about him this morning. Peter, Peter, Peter. Say it three times and be done."

Minakis straightened in his chair. "Forgive me, I've behaved extremely rudely."

Her gaze was hard upon him. "Now tell me about what I'm interested in. Tell me about Manolis Minakis."

"What is there to tell?"

"Oh, the usual things. Are you married? If not, why not? How many children do you have? If none, what's wrong with you?" She bared her teeth. "Nothing personal."

Her teasing delighted him. "I was married once, for a short time, a very long time ago. My wife died. As for children . . . none that I know of."

"No bride stealing, no sheep stealing, no blood feuds?" She pouted. "A dull story, for a man of Crete."

"Although I was born on Crete, Minakis is not the name I was born with."

She brightened. "That sounds like the beginning of a tale."

"A long tale, much too long for a demitasse of coffee."

"I'm in no hurry."

He paused, entranced by the teasing impatience that animated the beautiful face before him. He, who had perfected the art of intimidation, who had meant to draw her into his web, had been disarmed by her, invited to spin his web for her amusement.

"I was born in a village below Mount Dikti, above the Lasithi Plain," he said at last. "A village too small to appear on most maps. But as a man named Pendlebury once said—and it is still true—'maps of Crete are in any case woefully inaccurate.' My mother's name was Sophia. I never knew her."

5

"Yip! Yip!" The girl raced up the thorny mountainside, hardly breaking stride as she hurled sharp stones from her apron pocket at the sheep and goats that fled from her and her mongrel dog. She was imitating the dog—"Yip! Yip! Yip!"—a matted black-and-white cur who bounded ecstatically after the sheep, nipping at their hocks with his eyes rolled back in his head, although without the girl to set an example he would never have dared cause such commotion. The bedraggled sheep ran this way and that, clattering over the rocks, spilling miniature avalanches down the steepening slope, their efforts to escape frustrated by the frantic dog and the girl's missiles, which forced them to climb higher still, while the handful of goats in the flock went along with what must have seemed an exciting game of tag. Above them, Dikti's limestone cliffs were golden in the evening light.

"Sophia! Curse you, stop that!" a male voice roared, echoing from the cliffs. "Come here! Come here!"

"Yip! Yip!" she cried, urging the panicked sheep upward. But the dog stopped and nervously cocked an ear to the man down the mountain. Nikos Androulakis, Sophia's father, had once been as adept at chasing sheep and goats over the crags as she was, and he was not kind to dogs.

When her father started up the slope, Sophia turned to watch, planting her shoes wide in the dirt and squatting on a boulder. She rested her jaw on the heels of her hands and set her elbows wide upon her knees; her bare elbows poked through holes in her blouse and sweater; her skirts hung in scallops. The flock, no longer harassed, milled around bleating.

Androulakis picked his way unsteadily among the rocks and thorns. Soon enough he was pawing the earth just to keep himself upright. Sophia guessed that he'd been sitting in front of Louloudakis's place all afternoon, drinking the raki he distilled himself, while the other village men sipped boiled coffee. At last he staggered and glared up at her, still a hundred yards down the slope but close enough for her to see the sweat shining on his forehead, and his heaving chest.

"You won't obey?" he cried. "To the devil with you, you whore of Babylon!"

At thirteen, Sophia was vague about his meaning, but whenever Papa Kriaris, the village priest, sang those verses of Revelations about the Whore of Babylon in church, he wore an expression of disgust on his bearded face, so it was probably worse than an ordinary insult.

Scowling, she stood up. She jammed two fingers of her right hand into her mouth and whistled at the flock; instantly the animals launched themselves down the mountain, tumbling past her. She followed in their dust, gangling down the slope, while the dog trailed at a safe distance.

As she passed close by her red-faced father, he drew his arm back and swung at her, open-handed. The tips of his fingers stung her ear. She tossed her head and straightened her back and kept on down the slope. He lunged after her, this time aiming his fist at the back of her head, but she ducked away, and he stumbled and fell hard to one knee. A second later, feeling the hurt, he bellowed in frustration.

She didn't laugh; she pointedly ignored him. Like the goats, her downslope progress was a dance among the rocks.

*   *   *

The dozen raw stone houses of Ayia Kyriaki—the name means "Holy Sunday"—sheltered three extended families, fewer than a hundred people when everyone was at home. The village clung to the slopes of Dikti above a wide arroyo that wound through the almond groves of the Limnakaros Plain, a watercourse that was dry most of the year but became a rushing torrent when the snows melted. At the foot of the little plain the seasonal waters fell through a cleft into a gorge that opened into the Lasithi Plain below—verdant Lasithi, six miles across and three thousand feet above sea level, ringed with mountains and sporting a necklace of twenty villages. Poor Ayia Kyriaki was alone in Limnakaros, a thousand feet higher and hidden from its neighbors behind a stony ridge.

By the time her father had descended to their house at the top of the village's single street, Sophia had already driven the flock into their rock-walled pen against a limestone outcrop. When Androulakis pushed through the gate into the courtyard he found her seated demurely beside her mother on a bench beside the door, her apron full of bean pods, helping to hull broad beans into an iron pot. The dog lay on its belly beside the beehive oven that was still warm from the afternoon's baking, eyeing him nervously.

Androulakis said nothing but limped past the women, through the open door into the house. They heard him rattling around inside, making more noise than he needed to.

"You have been tormenting him again," Sophia's mother said in a harsh whisper.

Sophia snapped a pod and said nothing.

"You must respect your father, child." At thirty-five, Katerina's face was browner than her daughter's and netted with deep wrinkles. Long ago she might have been pretty, perhaps even cheerful, but Sophia could not remember any expression on her mother's face less bleak than the one she wore now.

"He does not respect himself."

"Hush." It was a whispered plea. "Why do you cause trouble for nothing? No matter what people think of him, they will think worse of you."

"They do already," Sophia muttered.

Androulakis came out of the dark doorway, his walking stick in his hand. A net *sariki* was wrapped tightly around his head, dangling its knotted black tears across his brow, and a gray wool *sakouli* bulged at his side; the neck of a raki bottle protruded where the drawstrings puckered the mouth of the bag. The knees of his black pantaloons were red with dirt, and the backs of his hands were striated with thorn scratches. He'd shoved a big curved knife into the sash around his waist.

"You are going somewhere, Niko?"

"What does that matter to you? You are the witch who foisted this accursed child on me." Saying it, he did not look at Katerina, but stared at his pale-eyed daughter with hatred. "May you be happy together."

"But you will be home for dinner? The bread is fresh. There is still some lamb. And onions for the stew."

"I will never enter this abode of demons again." He hauled himself across the courtyard and through the gate, slamming it behind him so hard that a loose board fell to the ground.

"Ha!" Sophia jumped to her feet, spilling beans from her apron onto the ground. "His friends will drag him back here—after he drinks himself to sleep," she said, loudly enough to be heard in the street.

Any other mother in the village would have screamed at this obstinate child, beaten her, sent her to bed hungry, but Katerina knew that nothing she could say to her daughter would bend her from her self-destructive course. In truth, she feared the girl was mad.

"Here is what I imagine happened next," Minakis said to Anne-Marie, pausing to sip his bitter coffee, "although I was not there to see it, for it was almost a year yet until I was born."

"Tell me how you can imagine any of this?"

"Later an old woman told me things."

"Oh, things . . . ," she said skeptically.

"And when I pressed her, the truth slipped out."

"Well, that explains it." Pale-eyed, Anne-Marie returned his black stare without flinching.

Minakis supposed that he could read her thoughts easily:

here is an old man indulging himself, taking advantage of her curiosity—yet she finds it an amusing story, and by necessity she has as much time as he wants to take.

His amber beads came out of his pocket; he twirled them through his fingers. He would take a little more of her time.

"I picture the disreputable Androulakis outside his gate, hearing his daughter's insults but telling himself that he chooses not to dignify them. He limps down the cobbled lane a few dozen paces to the village square, a level space with the chapel on one side and Haralambos Louloudakis's coffeehouse and one-room general store on the other. He notes the mules tethered to the stone trough in front of the cistern, one saddled, the other packed with odd bundles wrapped in canvas.

"A stranger sits at one of Louloudakis's tables, surrounded by village men competing to keep his glass full of raki; Louloudakis and his two boys hustle back and forth, bringing plates of olives and cubes of cheese and fragments of grilled sheep's liver. In the mountains, nothing is of more urgent interest than a *xenos,* a stranger and therefore a guest—who quite apart from whatever news he might bring is sure to be odd and interesting in his own right.

"This one certainly is—a thin young man with glossy hair and a neatly trimmed mustache, who instead of a mountaineer's baggy breeches and high black boots wears a blue serge suit and scuffed brogans. He's holding forth, making a speech: 'Thrace is ours, and the Aegean Islands. And soon Smyrna, best of all.'

"Androulakis stares at him, avid with curiosity, and stares even more hungrily at the feast. But when he tries to push his way into the circle, his neighbors act as if he isn't there. He has to peer through a wall of shoulders.

" 'Smyrna is to be ours, you say?' Stavroudakis is the oldest man in the village and half deaf; he doesn't know he's shouting and wouldn't care if he did.

"The men are passing something from hand to hand, a flat piece of cardboard. As it is about to change hands in front of Androulakis, he reaches between the two men in front of him and plucks it away. It's a photograph showing a city's waterfront, with masts in the foreground and palm trees and pines and white European-style buildings reflected in the waters of a wide bay.

" 'After five years, if the people of Smyrna vote to unite with Greece, then it will be done,' says the stranger.

"Now Michalis speaks up, a man who owns more almond trees than anyone else in the village. 'How could they not vote to unite with Greece? Smyrna *is* Greece.'

"Androulakis's brother-in-law, the priest, snatches the photograph out of his hand, but he has seen enough.

" 'Venizelos has worked a miracle,' yells old man Stavroudakis, louder still, and the others join in. 'To Venizelos!' 'To his health and ours!' 'Many more years to him!' The men drain their glasses and slam them down, but as soon as the stranger's glass hits the table someone pours it full again, and Androulakis, hovering outside the circle, is increasingly annoyed. He was the last to join the group; they should have offered him hospitality.

" 'So much for Smyrna,' he insists. 'What of Constantinople?'

"Now the circle opens to him, for he has asked the obvious question. 'The Allies maintain their garrison there,' says the stranger, looking at him for the first time. 'They will make sure the sultan keeps his word.'

" 'Well . . . next year, maybe,' says Androulakis with a kind of grim satisfaction. It's a catch phrase: *Next year in Constantinople.* Grinning at his own cleverness, he yanks the bottle from his *sakouli* and proposes a toast. 'I'll drink to next year.'

"They cannot but join him, pushing his bottle away and standing him to a glass of Louloudakis's best. 'Next year in Constantinople!'

"Stars burn over Dikti, hardly dimmed by a lopsided moon rising over the almond groves. The men progress from shouted toasts to shouted verses, celebrating their fathers' victory over the Turks—most of whom were not Turks, of course, but their own Greek neighbors, converts to Islam.

Take up your blade and stab the earth and stones,
Warriors' blood stains your blade; it breaks on their bones.

"Aside from a spill of yellow lantern light from Louloudakis's doorway, the night sky provides the only illumination in the square. At the edge of the shadows, women and girls advance and retreat, staring with wide eyes at the stranger and repeating in whispers what they can hear about him: 'He comes from Athens.' 'He is here to make pictures of the mountains.' 'He brought his machines on his mule.' Katerina is there among the watching women, and Sophia too.

"Finally the priest's wife pulls the priest out of the circle, and the rich man and his sons drag the stranger and his mules off to their house. Left without entertainment, the others wander away to their homes, and Androulakis is alone with his bottle. He sits watching Louloudakis's boys rinse glasses at the trough. Soon the oil lamp goes out, and their father emerges into the moonlight, pulling the door shut behind him. '*Kalinichta,*' says Androulakis, but they ignore him.

"Now he's alone, his bottle almost empty; his *sariki* has come untied and fallen to his chest. He's sworn never to go back to Katerina's house, but of course he's sworn that many times; only once, long ago, had he found the energy to walk all the way down through the almond groves, down through Lasithi and on down out of the mountains. That time he'd spent a few days in the *ouzeries* beside Kastro's harbor, watching caïques and fishing boats sail in and out, and when his cash was gone he'd made the long walk back.

"So he sits in the dark, disgruntled. Beside him on the table-top is the photograph in its cardboard frame; Androulakis picks it up and peers at it by moonlight—there are fewer minarets in this city of Asia Minor than there are in Christian Kastro. Surely it is a kind of paradise on earth.

" 'I'm glad you found it.' The stranger has come out of the shadows and stands watching. 'I was afraid someone had carried it off.'

" 'Smyrna is a grand place, is it?' Androulakis asks, his speech slurred.

" 'As you can see. It is more beautiful than Nafplion, more beautiful than Thessaloniki.'

" 'More beautiful than Kastro, even?'

"The stranger shrugs, not wishing to give offense. 'All the nations of Europe do business in Smyrna. Everyone speaks Greek, but they speak Italian and German and English as well. Turkish and Arabic too, naturally.'

" 'I curse the Turks.'

" 'Of course you do.'

" 'A man could do well there?'

" 'That land has been Greek since the war against Troy.' The stranger smiles. 'Certainly a Greek patriot could do well for himself in Smyrna.'

" 'I could do well for myself?'

"The stranger studies him as if weighing the question. 'You are more than a farmer, I suppose. More than a herdsman?'

" 'You saw the iron windmills in Lasithi when you were coming here? When I lived there I made them by the score. In my hands, iron is like leather in the hands of a saddlemaker.'

" 'Well, then. A gifted, decisive man. Who could do better in Smyrna? There will be need of artists in iron, in the Greater Greece.' The stranger leans forward and lifts the photograph from Androulakis's hand, then bows and turns away.

" 'Malista,' whispers Androulakis. 'This time I will not give up; I will not come back.' In Kastro he will find a ship to Athens—or to Asia. 'I will do well for myself. And for Greece.' He raises himself from the table, dragging his wool bag with him. He walks unsteadily across the square and takes the lower road, toward the almond groves and the beckoning moon."

Minakis stilled his restless worry beads and paused to watch Anne-Marie, trying to judge the effect of his tale spinning.

"I'd be inclined to say that you have an impressive imagination, Professor," she said, her eyes wide with challenge, "if imagination weren't so simple—lazy, even—in the absence of facts."

"You are a photographer, an artist. Rightly concerned with authenticity."

Her face grew hot. "Meaning we fake it for a living?"

"I meant the opposite. Your medium—any artistic medium—
is so easily manipulated that you must struggle against it to tell
the truth. Reality *is* the physicist's medium. Reality and mathematics. We must struggle to tell truths that are not the accepted
truth. Imagination is what we value most."

"What possible ground of reality do you have for the tall tale
you just told?" Anne-Marie replied testily.

"The reports of eyewitnesses—although they came to me at
second hand."

"By all means tell me more."

He felt himself absurdly threatened by this woman whom he
had imagined he could control. He spun his worry beads, and
spun them again.

"It was Sophia," he said at last. "She watched Androulakis
and followed him out of the square. She had hidden in the shadows with the other women; when the stranger left, when they
had given up watching and gone home, she had lingered. Now
she crept silently after her father, as far as the edge of the village.

"There she stayed, watching Androulakis haltingly descend
the path beside the watercourse, until his shadow-figure dissolved into the moonlit fretwork under the almond branches.
When at last she lost sight of him, she smiled.

"Yes, I think she must have smiled. Certainly she was satisfied."

6

My grandfather never came back to Ayia Kyriaki. He had spoken of Smyrna with patriotic fervor—this from the priest's wife, Katerina's sister, who had it from the priest, who had it from the photographer—so Katerina chose to believe that her husband had joined the army. The Catastrophe made heroes of countless missing persons. In that Royalist adventure, Smyrna was burned to the ground, thirty thousand Greeks were slaughtered, and a quarter of a million swam for their lives. Six months later, the Great Exchange: a third of a million Greek Muslims were sent to Turkey; a million Turkish Christians arrived in Greece."

Minakis rattled the spoon in his empty coffee cup and pushed back his chair, his eyes burning with the apparent memory of events he had not been alive to remember, but which were topics of Greek conversation to the present day.

"Katerina and Sophia didn't have to wait that long for their troubles to begin. . . ."

"Hey, you clumsy thieves! You think I don't see you?" Sophia watched from the ridge as the Louloudakis boys, Theo and

Dimitris, climbed the hillside toward her and the flock. They came within a few yards of the stragglers, studiously ignoring her, before they began shouting and whistling and driving off the nearest animals.

She ran toward them, shouting as she ran. "You think your father will not hear about this? Your mother will not know? The whole neighborhood will hear that you are stupid thieves, and cowards without honor!"

The little one, Dimitris, proved too sensitive to ignore Sophia's insults. He stopped chasing sheep and turned to face her. "*You* are without honor!" he called back in his clear, high voice. "Your father left you. You are a whore. And your mother is . . . your mother is the *mother* of a whore."

Stones from her apron were already in Sophia's hand. She flung the first and hit Dimitris in the side of the head. He shrieked and clapped his hand to his ear; bright blood seeped through his fingers, and he wailed louder at the sight of it.

Eight-year-old Theo paused in his frantic herding. "You go to the devil," he yelled at Sophia, shaking his open hand in the five-fingered curse, just before her next stone caught him in the neck. He screeched wordlessly and, seizing his throat, burst into tears.

Down the mountain she came, the stones flying from her hand as if from a sling. The boys fled in panic.

No one said anything in the village that night or in the days that followed. For Louloudakis to accuse Sophia of hurting his boys would have been to admit their bungled crime—after all, only primitives from western Crete were sheep thieves. But on the next night, someone threw garbage over the wall of Katerina Androulakis's courtyard. And each night after that, until the night when Sophia, perched on the wall waiting, heard approaching footsteps on the cobblestones and said loudly into the darkness, "Those who want to use this place as a dump must pay a tax." She hurled a stone, bouncing it high off the wall of the house downslope, where it fell clattering to the street. "Did you understand me? You will pay a tax"—she threw another and heard a solid thunk and a surprised cry of pain—"to the doctor."

Amid complaining curses, the footsteps retreated, and from that night on no one would come near Sophia or even speak her name aloud. She was a creature of a kind they had never encountered, and though they imagined much, they knew nothing of her. Sophia, the daughter of Androulakis the ironsmith, a manually gifted lout, and Katerina the would-be village scholar, who had read the dozen books in her possession so often they were crumbling—and taught her daughter to read as well, which was a useless and dangerous art in a woman.

Who knew of Sophia's dances among the thorns and rocks of the highest peaks? Who knew whom she might have met on the wild heights, whom she might have enticed to those heights with her gray-eyed smile and flashing brown limbs? Who was she really, in the eyes of the man who first desired her? Only a laughing child-woman? Or the Lady of the Animals, or a *neraïda* who enticed men, under the noonday sun, to momentary bliss and everlasting disaster . . .

Who knew of the young girl's passion and humor? Who knew why she despised hypocrisy and seized everything vivid that life had to offer? Did anyone really know—or did they merely assume the worst—that it was Sophia who had perpetrated the worst scandal in village memory, who had crept into the chapel of Ayia Kyriaki after midnight, Christmas night of 1921, and scraped the eyes out of the fresco of the Virgin and saved the scrapings in her kerchief and then walked barefoot in the thin snow that covered the cobbled street of the village and blew the scrapings of paint out of her hand through a crack in the shutters of a certain room in a certain house? And that when she did these things—if it was she—that she was not only barefoot but completely naked.

That was a potent spell, but unlike the usual lovelorn village girl who needed a presiding witch to go with her on such a blasphemous errand, Sophia would have needed no one.

The man upon whose sleeping face the powdered saint's eyes had fallen sought her out within the week, high up in the snow-covered mountains where he had peculiar business but she had none at all, except to meet him there, laughing, and to draw him into her secret grotto and to lie with him there, her heat warming him against the winter cold, his ardor causing her quick pain and fleeting ecstasy.

"All-Holy Mother, how can this be true?" Katerina whispered the words, then fell silent, her jaw slack, her palms pressed to her cheeks. Silently she beseeched the icons of Nicholas and George and the Virgin, paper prints framed in dark wood that were set on the shelf beside the dying fire. Sophia huddled in the corner below them, almost invisible in the feeble glow of the embers. Her body shook with sobs and shivered with the cold.

The girl had been running away into the winter mountains; Katerina had badgered her for it. But it was only when she had seen her daughter's uncharacteristic morning nausea and tears, noticed her shielding her tender breasts, which upon inspection were swollen larger than a normal fourteen-year-old's, that she guessed the truth.

Roused from her bitter meditation, Katerina stood up and went to the hearth and reluctantly put another billet of olive wood on the coals. There was only a little firewood left in the house. It was late March, and the nights were bitter cold. Yesterday the sky above Limnakaros had spit multiple lightning bolts, as if dead Zeus were returning to the mountains of his birth; snow and freezing rain blanketed the valley, and Dikti's crest was invisible. She turned to stare at her daughter. "Who did this?"

Sophia only shook her head, hiding her face in her hands.

"You were raped," Katerina said.

Sophia shook her head again.

"It does not help us, it makes no difference, but tell me you were raped."

"No, Mother."

"Who *did* this with you? Your no-good cousin? One of the Michalis gang? Who robbed our honor?"

"None of them." Sophia smeared the back of her hand across her face. "It's my fault, nobody else's."

"I don't think so. You are not the Virgin Mary."

Sophia sat up and moved closer to the fire. She stared into the flames. "I'll kill myself."

"Don't speak blasphemy, child."

"What can I do but kill myself?" Sophia started crying again, silently this time, letting the tears flow down her cheeks, where they wetly reflected the firelight. "I won't go down and be a whore in the towns."

"No," Katerina whispered. "Before that, I would kill you myself." In the silence the olive wood caught and sputtered with brighter flame. "We must keep this a secret. You must bear the child secretly."

"What good will that do," Sophia wailed, "after my child is born?"

Katerina did not answer; she did not know what to answer. "We must keep the secret," she repeated. "When spring comes you will stay with the flock in the high pasture. Stay there, don't come back. Stay until your time. I'll bring you what you need."

Sophia fell silent. If her mother wanted to delay the inevitable, who could blame her? To Sophia, whether she killed herself now or later would not make much difference.

Winter fitfully softened into spring. In the first week of April Katerina and Sophia moved the flock out of Limnakaros, up steep slopes to pastures lying beyond the ridge of Dikti, already fragrant with thyme. Here Katerina's father had built a round shepherd's hut of flat stones and perched it on a spur of rock, with a view across the pine forests that fell away down to the south coast and the blue Libyan Sea.

The ewes and nannies were already round and heavy; the morning after the women arrived at the hut, the first lamb tumbled out. Alerted by the excited barking of the dog, Sophia was there to watch the birth. She'd seen it happen often, but she watched with new curiosity. The wet, staggering lamb found its legs within minutes, and was soon making drunken attempts to run and jump.

Sophia put her hands under her sash and felt her hard abdomen. If only a human baby had the self-reliance of a lamb. The thought unexpectedly saddened her. What were lambs for, but to slaughter?

She went into the stone hut, where Katerina was vigorously sweeping out the winter's trash. "We have to make this a fit place to live," Katerina said, as if to explain her obsessive sweeping.

"I'll be fine here," Sophia said.

"Not just for *you*," said her mother.

In the hut there was a low stone bench for a bed, and a table made from rough planks laid on stones, and two low stools in front of the fireplace. On the walls hung black iron tubs for boiling milk into cheese.

Sophia and Katerina arranged the bedding they had carried up from the village on the back of the ancient donkey. They hung a tight-woven red rug to cover the worst of the fissures in the curved walls and another ruined and patched rug over the open door. There wasn't much more they could do, given the dirt floor and the smoke-blackened walls; men were meant to inhabit these ugly heaps of stone, not women. Men were supposed to herd the sheep and cut the firewood and boil the milk into cheese. When there was no man around, a girl could do the job.

For breakfast, they ate cheese a year old and hard shepherd's bread soaked in oil. Soon Sophia would be busy with the cheese making, milking the animals and cutting wood and boiling the milk and squeezing out the whey. Then she would have fresh, soft *mizithra* for breakfast, and—with a little honey mixed into the white cheese—for a moment or two life would be smooth and sweet. She laughed aloud, delighted by the thought, then covered her mouth when she saw her mother's troubled stare.

Sophia watched a long time when Katerina, on foot, led the ancient donkey back over the ridge—to ride the animal would be to shorten its life, and where would they get another when it died? Then Sophia skipped back to the hut. She loved this place better than anywhere. Her mother's father, of whom Katerina still spoke reverently, had chosen it for its good water; he had laid a channel of carved stones from a natural basin, into which copious amounts of water seeped from a fissure in the ridge, down to the trough where the animals now drank. The trough and the hut and the low-walled milking pen were on the edge of an airy precipice. Sophia stood there, looking down on drifting clouds that were still pink with morning light, listening to the water that overflowed the trough and fell two hundred feet into the pine forest below. The smell of pines, the morning light, the sound of falling water—her heart lifted above the clouds.

"My mother lived in that place all spring and summer. I think of her singing to the sky, rehearsing lullabies, making little toys for her baby out of wood and cloth and string, skipping and dancing and dreaming of the hard times and good times that awaited her and her child."

Anne-Marie watched Minakis quietly, betraying no emotion.

"But that's all imagination; I have no evidence for it, not even secondhand reports."

"I'll trust your imagination," she said.

His gaze faltered and he looked down, as if surprised to find a coffee spoon in his hand and no coffee in his cup. He waved at the waiter and indicated their empty cups, then turned back to Anne-Marie. "My grandmother told me that once or twice a week she climbed over the ridge and brought my mother what she needed—bread and oil, a honeycomb, wild greens, a mended sweater, a shawl she had sat up nights weaving. Meanwhile my mother grew heavier with me. Everyone in the village knew where Sophia was, but they left her alone because—now I'm guessing, for my grandmother never would have told me this—they were afraid of her."

Anne-Marie smiled. "From what you've told me, they had good reason."

Minakis nodded. "She was formidable. I think they believed, quite literally, that she was a demon. You've heard of *neraïdes?*"

"Water nymphs? That's ancient mythology."

"In the villages, we still believe in them. Beautiful women who love to dance in the wildest places. Sometimes they can be tricked into marrying ordinary men. But you mustn't betray them, or they will steal your voice and drive you insane."

Anne-Marie's sophisticated smirk faded when she realized Minakis wasn't smiling.

"I think that someone was telling spells against her," he said, looking at her as if daring her to contradict him.

"Who was telling spells?" she asked.

"They say priests don't tell spells, but I think it was Kriaris, the priest."

Anne-Marie hesitated. *We still believe in them.* How much was included in Minakis's version of reality? A door had opened, just a crack, and beyond was darkness.

For a long time he was quiet. When he spoke his voice was a dry monotone. "The time came for her to be delivered. August, the hottest, driest month, but subject to sudden storms in the mountains . . ."

Lightning hit the triple peaks of Dikti in multiple bolts that flickered and flared white. Thunder followed instantly, crashing through the rain. The night was a livid landscape of wet rocks alternating with nothing visible, only streaming blackness.

Sophia and the dog worked the bleating sheep into the stone pens near the cliff-edge. When the last of them was in the pen she staggered into the hut; there was no door to close against the night, only the tattered rug. The dog followed her inside, shaking himself vigorously before flopping down by the fire. Sophia was drenched and shivering, and as she collapsed on the hard bed she was seized with sudden apprehension. She gasped and clutched her belly.

She did not want to do this now. Not without her mother beside her. Not at all. But her belly contracted and she knew she had no choice.

She hauled herself to her feet, forcing herself to move while she could. She went outside again and hauled a tub of fresh water from the trough. Already the storm was passing, moving west, and stars were coming out overhead.

Inside the hut, Sophia struggled out of her rain-soaked clothes, standing as naked as on that winter night when she had magicked the father of her child, the child who now insisted upon being born. The dog watched with a kind of sympathetic curiosity as Sophia piled wood into the fire pit. She pulled a rough blanket around herself and sat down again, waiting.

She did not have to wait long before the next contraction squeezed her, forcing her to cry out. She fell back on the stony bed; her eyes sought out the polychrome of Saint Nicholas that her mother had brought from the village and pegged high on the curving wall, where Sophia could see it whenever she lay down. Wordlessly she beseeched him. Nicholas was the patron saint of children—of maidens, not mothers—but Sophia was still a child. Her eyes bored in upon the saint's dark eyes under his high, curly-fringed bald dome, her vision narrowing as wave after wave of pain engulfed her below.

She screamed until her throat was raw, until she felt rather than heard herself. The heavens echoed her cries with distant thunder, as if the sky had been hollowed out. She thought she would die and tried not to wish for death.

Hours passed; the fire blazed and then collapsed into embers which slowly cooled to ashes—

—and at last everything was silent and dark.

Then Sophia heard a tiny cry. She was so spent that she wasn't sure she hadn't died. She tried to move. Reaching down between her legs she found the bloody child and brought it to her breast, dragging the umbilical across her empty abdomen. A male child. He rested there, wrinkled and twitching, crusted with white wax and splattered with red blood, crying a long time before his cries faltered into whimpers.

The dog came and licked at her shoulder, shy and suspicious, then sniffed with great interest at the bloody afterbirth that had slid onto the floor, until she hissed at him and made him retreat. She sat up then, swaying with fatigue and loss of blood, and when the dizziness passed she stood carefully and laid the baby on clean raw wool on the floor beside the bench. She bent to bite through the cord, then knotted it, expecting him to cry again, but he made no sound. Her head swam as she made an effort to gather the bloody blankets from the bed and wash the gore off the stones. She tenderly rinsed her baby in the iron tub she had filled with spring water. His miniature fingers and toes enchanted her; they twitched against her breast and ribs.

Naked, holding her son, she pushed aside the rug over the door and went into the cool morning air. The western sky was black and full of stars, but in the east, toward the peak of Lazaros, the horizon was already glassy red. As she looked up, a bright meteor scored the sky, and a few seconds later another followed, even brighter. It was August, and the dawn sky was alive with falling stars.

Sophia walked a few steps farther, to the edge of the cliff. The water from the stone trough bubbled as it fell; a breeze was stirring the pines below, invisible in the darkness. The sheep bleated in their pen. After the night's rain, the earth smelled fresh; it smelled of pine sap and thyme, of astringent limestone, of wet sheep and new babies. She felt the coolness of the air and hugged her baby closer. She turned back to the hut.

Moments after she entered it, the ground heaved once, then settled. Outside, vested ravens cawed at the brightening sky, their ill-tempered screams echoing from the peaks.

Katerina had risen long before dawn and started the climb from Ayia Kyriaki, leaving the donkey behind, bringing with her only a little marmalade in a pottery jar and a loaf of fresh bread. The last part of the climb in the dark exhausted her, as it did every time; the slope was loose dirt and rocks lying at the angle of repose, falling away with every step. After an hour's hard work she reached the crest of the ridge and stopped to catch her breath.

Sophia's child was due, and still Katerina did not know what to do about it; she had no one to ask for advice. Kriaris the priest was her brother-in-law, his wife her own sister, but she didn't trust them or anyone else in the village. She couldn't take the time or risk the gossip of making a trip to Kastro, where perhaps she could talk to someone in the metropolitan's office—to ask about charities, or possibly to find honorable employment for Sophia. If one thing was clear, it was that neither Sophia nor her child could live in Ayia Kyriaki.

Katerina saw the first hint of dawn in the east and set off grimly along the path. She was almost in sight of her father's stone hut when the earth heaved and made her stagger. When for a moment it steadied, Katerina trudged on. No one on Crete was a stranger to earth tremors.

But when the whole mountain jerked sideways with a screech, pulling the ground out from under her, she cried out, "All-Holy Mother!" and fell down hard. She lay on her side, clutching her bag close with one hand and crossing herself repeatedly with the other, while loose rocks clattered and skipped past her head. The ground shook for almost half a minute. When she could get up, she ran.

The hut lay all in a heap, its dome collapsed inward. Seeing the ruin, Katerina cried out again, wordlessly, and threw herself upon the rubble. She pushed the square-cornered stones aside as fast as she could; they were heavy, and she had no strength, perhaps because in her heart there was no hope.

She found the dog first, its black-and-white fur matted with blood. It whined and snapped at her, and she left it half buried where it lay. She worked to pull the rocks away from the fire pit, supposing, without thinking it through, that anyone inside the hut would have been beside the fire. But when she had made a hole all the way to the bare earth, she found no one.

The bench next. She pulled away a rock to which the paper icon of Saint Nicholas was attached. She pulled away another, and found her daughter's foot and ankle beneath it, bruised blue. Crying aloud, half choking on her sobs, she pulled the rest of the stones away from Sophia's body. Sophia lay there naked, coated with blood and dust, unmoving, making no sound.

Beneath Sophia's arm, between her dead body and the stone bed, a baby wriggled and choked and sneezed on the dust.

7

believe my grandmother must have considered doing away with me right then, with the handiest chunk of rock."

Anne-Marie was sure Minakis was joking, but she waited with what she hoped was an unreadable expression. He grinned at her confusion.

"Fortunately for me, there was the matter of the property."

"What property?" She begrudged him the question. Beneath the surface of their exchange a struggle of uncertain dimensions was going on, of which they were both aware.

"Katerina had brought to her marriage a few parcels of land near the village, some almond trees, which her husband had neglected, being too inebriated or perhaps too proud. He was from Lasithi, not from our village, and he must have suffered the common slander that he was living off his wife's dowry." Minakis twirled his worry beads carelessly, as if to suggest that all this was unimportant. "Nevertheless, with him vanished and their daughter dead, when Katerina died her relatives would inherit."

"Her relatives? You mean the priest's wife?"

Minakis nodded. "My aunt Eleni, yes. And through her

Kriaris and eventually their son. But even if I was a bastard, that land was legally mine when my *yia-yia* passed away. Kriaris was almost as poor as Katerina, and a much more desperate and greedy character. It was only a matter of time until he tried to rob us—through some legal fiction or by simple violence."

"You really think your grandmother would have killed you because of that?"

"At the moment, seeing the daughter she loved lying dead and a raw newborn helpless in the rubble . . . ?" Minakis paused. "Of course, she would have had to hide my body."

"What a gruesome thought."

"Katerina was capable of gruesome acts, like all desperately poor people. But—like all village women—she was also fervently religious. I owe my life to her faith."

Having made the decision to sacrifice honor on earth for the sake of honor in heaven, Katerina confronted practical choices. The first she made automatically; she killed the tortured dog, smashing its head with the largest stone she could lift. Then she took up the baby boy and washed him in the cold water of the trough. She laid him aside while she carefully covered over her daughter's body with the stones that had crushed her, to protect her from the ravens.

Most of the flock had panicked and scattered, but a few sheep loitered in the broken pen. She got a little milk from a ewe; the others she let go.

The morning air was sharp and clear, cool but growing hotter under a cloudless sky. Katerina, the baby bundled in her arms, went the long way down the mountain, picking her way slowly over hard rock, avoiding the steep saddle where the clay, always ready to slide, had been turned into a kind of red grease by the night's rain. She reached Ayia Kyriaki in the heat of the afternoon, when everyone else was inside or napping in the almond groves under what shade they could find.

She laid the baby on her bed and unwrapped him, studying him at length for the first time. He lay there, alert, making no sound except quiet grunts and sighs, his milky eyes unfocused but searching. His sex was swollen and red, and the severed cord that hung from his belly was as purple as a bad bruise, but he was at peace with the world, and intensely curious.

As she peered into those new eyes, it seemed to Katerina that there was something supernatural about his calm. She'd fed him from a twisted rag she'd soaked in ewe's milk, and it had satisfied him all morning long. Now she fed him again—he accepted the rag as if it were a natural teat—and after crossing herself three times, she left him there alone in the shadowed house.

She walked through blinding sunshine and midday heat to her sister's house, the priest's house beside the chapel. The two buildings formed a little courtyard in front of the one-room school where a teacher from Lasithi taught the village children twice a week. Katerina banged on the door. After a long time, Eleni opened it.

"What do you want?" Eleni's eyes were heavy with sleep; her stiff black locks had escaped their ribbons.

"I must have a *tama* from the chapel. I must offer to the All-Holy Mother. It's an emergency."

"You're being silly. Come back later."

"This minute. I have to see Kriaris. *Ade.*"

Eleni looked at her sister's face with resentment, but whatever she saw there persuaded her. "All right, come in. I'll get him up."

Kriaris came out of the back room, his clothes askew, his shirttails hanging out of his trousers. He pulled at his beard, the symbol of his spiritual authority. "What do you want, Sister?"

"I want a *tama*. Show me what you have."

"Can't this wait until a decent hour?"

"Are you so busy?" Katerina pushed her face at his. "Have you been slaving in the almond groves all day? Making yourself thin chasing sheep?"

"You are making yourself hateful," Kriaris complained. "What do you want of me?"

"I told you, a *tama.*"

"Come on then." Furious, Kriaris pushed past her, out of his house and into the chapel a few steps away.

Katerina followed him into the cool, frescoed barrel vault. He had already disappeared behind the iconostasis, a carved cedar panel made splendid by icons of Nicholas and George and the All-Holy Mother. Defying the custom that women were barred from the mysteries, Katerina pushed through the curtain; it was, after all, just a wooden partition, and Kriaris was back there rooting through his collection of *tamata.*

"Which one do you want?" he demanded. "They're all here, all that I have. Look for yourself."

She looked into the tray and saw the pressed tin cartoons lying in heaps like discarded playing cards. Eyes, hearts, stomachs, limbs, figures of men and women and children—they had been used before, some often; they were blotted with candle wax and had scraps of faded ribbon stuck through their perforations. That did not annul their efficacy. Katerina poked among them with a forefinger until she found the image of a fat, smiling baby. "This one," she said, holding the tin rectangle up to the light from the slit window.

"Difrango," said Kriaris without looking at it, his hand out.

An extortionate amount, but after some fumbling she produced a worn two-drachma coin from her apron pocket and pushed it into his palm. "For the *tama* and a candle."

She went back through the screen and set the offering on the rail beneath the icon of the All-Holy Mother. She looked at the baby lying there, smiling under Maria's protection, and tears started from her eyes. From a nearby table she took a wax taper and lit it from the oil lamp burning in front of the Virgin. She crossed herself and, bowing her head, murmured a prayer.

Kriaris squinted at her through the curtain. "One of your relatives has been blessed with a child?"

"I have been blessed," said Katerina. "Do not remove this"—she touched the *tama*—"I don't want you selling it again. Tell me when you require another contribution."

In the half light his goatish eyes swelled with curiosity. "I don't understand you, Sister. You say you have been blessed?"

"My beloved daughter, Sophia, has been taken by Christ and Maria this day into heaven." Katerina fixed her brother-in-law with a penetrating stare, trying to search out the representative of Christ that lurked within the covetous village priest. "If by now you have had enough time to wake up from your nap, you can help me bring her body here for burial."

"Sophia is dead?" His tongue darted out to slicken his lips.

Katerina said nothing, only left him standing there, astonished, as she walked to the chapel door and, to his weak sight, dissolved into the dazzling midday sunlight.

"The priest did his sanctimonious best to help my mother to a decent burial. The whole village turned out to burn candles over her corpse, piously reassuring themselves that she was dead. They put her in the churchyard under a slab of limestone, the best my grandmother could afford."

"You were safe, then?" Anne-Marie asked.

"Safe?" Minakis grinned, showing his teeth under his mustache. "I'm told that I never cried; it was almost as if I understood my precarious position. Days went by before Kriaris learned that Katerina's interest in the tin image of a baby had nothing to do with sad memories of her daughter, but with the reality of me."

"How did he find out?"

"She brought me to him and demanded that he baptize me."

"*Impossible!* You cannot ask it of me. Go down to Kastro, make your confession there."

"I have nothing to confess, Brother."

"I will not condone your daughter's sin." Kriaris looked at the calm baby in her arms as if it were something loathsome, a thing of filth.

"Whatever his mother's sin, this child was born into the world with no more sin than you or I."

"Are you teaching *me* the doctrine of the church?"

"The doctrine of the church is God's love, not your ignorance."

At which he cursed himself for ever lending her his seminary texts, where such theological questions were argued. "I won't do what you ask. Find somebody else."

"Brother, you haven't heard me. I want you to baptize him."

"I heard you. I refuse."

"And I want you to be his *nonos*."

"Get out! Get out!" He took Katerina by the arm and tried to shove her toward the door, but she was stronger than he was and stood her ground, pulling the baby away from him. He stumbled and had to let go to keep from falling. He turned on her, screeching in fury. "You mock me! Sponsor a bastard? You do not even know his father's name!"

"It would be a generous thing for you to do. It would be honorable. I understand all that, and so—"

"You understand *nothing*."

"So for nothing I will sell you half my land."

"What? What are you saying?" He hesitated, his face wet with perspiration. "Your land for nothing—what does that mean?"

"Be the boy's godfather. Take half of my land—his land—now. We'll make up a bill of sale."

. Through his open mouth, spit dribbled onto Kriaris's beard.

"If he survives, you'll get the rest too," Katerina continued. "I'll make a will and give it all to my sister."

"You can't do that," said Kriaris, who understood these matters; neither custom nor law would permit Katerina to disinherit her descendants.

Because Katerina was a reader, she too understood these matters. "Perhaps the boy will not be good to me in my old age. Perhaps I'll be forced to repudiate him."

The priest wiped his mouth with the blood-spattered towel he wore around his waist—he'd been dressing a lamb in the schoolyard when Katerina had barged in on him. She was right: if the boy survived, he could make his own living; he wouldn't need any land. It *would* be generous, an honorable thing for Kriaris to do. "You must say nothing about this," he said.

Katerina held the baby closer to her breast. "My left hand will not know what my right hand is doing."

"And so I was baptized. The little church was full of the curious. It was a bit unusual for the priest to be the godfather too, but Kriaris managed it without making obvious mistakes. He sprinkled the oil on the water and said the priestly words and then the godfather's words—'I surrender this child, baptized and anointed and given over to God'—and handed me back to my grandmother, who had succeeded in making Kriaris the guarantor of my safety on every possible level, spiritual, physical, and social."

"So *now* you were safe."

Minakis laughed. "I'll tell you how much Katerina trusted her neighbors. The day she brought me down from the mountain she went out and cleared the ground around the house of weeds and trash, anything flammable. She repaired the gate, and she scattered broken pots along the walls and around the edges of the roof, to make noise if anyone disturbed them. She sat up late every night with her father's shotgun across her lap, a weapon with a fearsome reputation, with which the old man claimed to have killed a Turkish soldier in the rebellion of 1889. She made sure her neighbors knew she had it. No one had ever thought of Katerina as being as terrifying as her daughter, but for my sake she was determined to make herself terrifying."

"She must have succeeded," said Anne-Marie.

"She had the help of fate. The day of my baptism, everyone came to stare at us. Knowing her, I suspect she looked straight back at them, though it must have pained her. The day *after* I was baptised, Louloudakis's older boy, Theo, the would-be sheep stealer who had made the sign of the devil at my mother, complained of soreness under his eyelids. He had trachoma, pinkeye, a common disease then, and it half blinded him. He was not the only victim of the disease; within the month three other people who'd been in the chapel that day, and of whom it was remembered that they had openly criticized my dead mother, came down with trachoma." Minakis's smile was rueful. "The villagers knew with folk certainty that they were victims of Katerina's evil eye, and after my baptism they were afraid to look at her; they blamed every accident or misfortune on her. The *tama* of the baby vanished from the Virgin's icon. Someone wrote *panoukla* on my mother's tomb, in blood."

"That means plague."

"It also means a female demon—my mother's reputation before I was born, the reputation my *yia-yia* inherited. The next summer Katerina hid her valuables and took me into the mountains. Without help she rebuilt the collapsed hut, and there we lived from early spring until late autumn. She did what business she had to with villages on the south slope and came back to Ayia Kyriaki only in winter. No one disturbed her property. They were afraid to touch it."

Anne-Marie was momentarily dizzy, appalled by what she was hearing. "How hard that must have been. How hard for you."

He shrugged. "It was life, how was I to make comparisons? I spent my boyhood quite happily, with an indomitable old woman for a parent and a flock of sheep and goats for playmates."

"She wasn't old," she said, surprised. "You said she was less than forty."

"In Crete, in the 1920s, she was an old woman."

8

For seven years, much of that time spent in the high mountains, Katerina tried to hide her worry from the growing boy. Sometimes when Manolis was alone with the flocks, chasing sheep and goats on two skinny legs almost as nimble as their four, he caught his *yia-yia* spying on him from a distance and laughed, taking it as a game. It was no game to her, and she knew it was no help to him to see his grandmother always hovering like a guardian angel, an angel carrying a shotgun. A real guardian angel, yes. That would have been helpful. That she prayed for.

But she could not follow him everywhere. As he grew tough and self-reliant she despaired of trying, and at last grudgingly allowed him to roam on his own. He was a tireless explorer; before he was eight years old he had circled the mountains.

To the west the landscape was grim and fantastic, layers of limestone lifted out of some ancient seabed and cooked and bent like stiff dough into loaves of earth-bread—only cliffs and caves there, few bushes and fewer trees. The south was precipitously wild, blue-shadowed with oaks and pines, with springs spewing from every crevice in the rocks to water miniature paradises that glimmered with flowers and birds. On the eastern slopes there were labyrinths of eroded limestone spires and top- iary forests of holly oaks, their bizarre shapes sculpted by tree- climbing goats. Selena to the north was an expanse of naked rock, so high and pale and gray as to have taken its name from the moon.

This wild landscape was thickly populated, not only by the shepherds and farmers who lived in the villages that nestled in the canyons and clung to the heights, but by vampires and water sprites as well, of whom Katerina warned Manolis. He believed her warnings and managed to avoid them. In every village he made a friend or two—schoolmasters especially, because they could sometimes be cajoled into lending him books—except his own.

One day, as he was bounding along the ridge above Ayia Kyriaki, pursuing a fractious lamb—at two thousand feet below the cliff-edge, the village was practically beneath his feet— something smacked hard into a boulder a yard away, sending up a spray of rock dust, and an instant later he heard the *crack* and simultaneous echo of the gunshot from the cliffs. There was nowhere to run on the barren ridge. He dived, rolled into a heap behind the melon-sized rock the shot had struck, and lay still, arranging himself so that he looked right at his assailant, a stick figure far down the slope on an opposing rise. Possessed of a mountaineer's natural *teleskopia*, Manolis could see exactly who it was, a boy who would have had no trouble com- ing up the mountain after him.

Evidently he didn't have the courage; instead he stood watching, waiting for Manolis to get up. Finally, perhaps hop- ing that he'd hit his mark but not willing to find out for sure, the would-be assassin turned and scurried away down the hill.

Manolis felt something in him melt like wax in a flame; the terror that he had not let himself feel now reduced him to tears. Why did they hate him so? Sobs shook him, until finally he wiped tears and snot away on the back of his dirty hand. His self-pity soured into fantasies of revenge. One of these nights, with some clever arrangement of ropes and stones and pig manure . . . Meanwhile he lay still on the hillside, giving the incompetent shooter plenty of time to get away.

After that day, Katerina gave Manolis his great-grandfather's shotgun to carry when he went alone in the mountains. The gun had a single hexagonal barrel of rippled blue Damascus steel; it was almost as tall as he was.

He and his grandmother had no choice but to spend the winters in the village. Kriaris the priest fulfilled his duties as *nonos* to Manolis by setting his lumpish son as guardian over his bastard nephew, but the younger Kriaris was lazy and indifferent, and most of the time Katerina insisted that Manolis stay out of his sight, out of sight of everyone in the village.

At first he hated the cold months when he was confined to his grandmother's dark house and its courtyard, but soon he came to love winter's compensations, when Katerina helped him learn his alpha, beta, gammas and read to him from the Bible and her father's tattered history books. She recited the tales her father had told her of Crete's heroic struggles against the Turks and Venetians and Saracens, along with her own tales of the saints and angels and demons that had always lived unseen among the living.

When they were together in the mountains, she taught him the *Erotokritos,* making him repeat it after her, month after month, until he had memorized all ten thousand lines of Crete's epic poem. In this feat, however, he was no different from the illiterate shepherds who also knew it by heart and would recite it for hours on end, like Homeric bards, around a long night's campfire.

Shortly after his eighth birthday, Manolis and Katerina brought the flock down from the mountain earlier in the year than usual. The village school had acquired a new, full-time teacher. Manolis was full of anticipation; Katerina was full of fear, but she would not let her precocious grandson grow up an ignorant shepherd.

"Good morning, everyone," the schoolmaster said firmly.

"Good morning, sir," the class replied, in ragged unison.

"Who wants to say the prayer this morning? You?" The

schoolmaster consulted his notebook. "Your name is Sta-vroula?"

The little girl bobbed her head and blushed.

"Go on, child."

She stood up beside her chair and recited the prayer in a high, clear voice, never stumbling until the conclusion: "And forgive us our debts, as we forget—mm, *forgive*—our debtors, and deliver us . . . And *lead* us not into temptation, but *deliver* us from evil." She sat down abruptly and gazed up at the new teacher in stunned bliss.

Yannis Siganos contemplated the ten young faces in the room that peered at him in awe or resentment. Six-year-old Stavroula was the youngest. The room's oldest and most sullen face belonged to fifteen-year-old Dimitris Louloudakis, who Siganos imagined must consider himself a prisoner in a room-ful of babies. Siganos could sympathize. Despite his tailored wool suit, despite the longish nail on the little finger of his right hand that none too subtly boasted of his education and pro-claimed him above peasant labor, the young teacher was just another boy from the neighborhood, from Tzermiado in the Lasithi Plain, lucky enough to have a merchant father who could afford his university education. Having secured a teach-ing credential, he'd found himself right back where he came from, assigned to the smallest village in the Lasithi nome.

"Those in the higher class—I mean Nikolaos, Christophoros, Sotiris, and you, Dimitri—take the book to the back of the room and turn to the chapter on the Age of Perikles. Share it," he said, forestalling the objection on Dimitris's sour face. "I'll question you after the younger children have practiced the alphabet." Chairs scraped in the narrow, whitewashed room. Besides the chairs and the teacher's table and an iron stove in the corner, a slate board on the wall was the room's only furni-ture. Siganos took up a piece of chalk. "The rest of you say after me: *alpha, vita, ghama.*"

The younger children were enthusiasts. *"ALPHA! VITA! GHAMA!"*

"Very good." Siganos energetically chalked the letters on the board, firmly pronouncing them aloud. He'd gotten as far as *omikron, pi, ro* when he realized he was no longer being echoed. He straightened and turned, scowling, and found the children whispering and staring at the schoolroom's open door.

A boy's thin figure was silhouetted against the bright light of the courtyard, a boy wearing scuffed high-topped shoes and ragged canvas shorts and a threadbare wool tunic. He was long legged and curly headed, of indeterminate age because he was hard to see in the glare.

Siganos said, "You are here for school?"

The boy nodded.

"Come, child, come inside. And close the door behind you."

The boy stepped inside and carefully pulled the door closed.

"What is your name?"

"I am called Manolis Androulakis, sir."

Stavroula's eyes widened and she leaned out of her chair and whispered to Christoula Michali, who giggled.

"Be quiet!" Siganos said angrily, and the girls froze.

For a moment the silence was deep enough to hear the buzzing of grasshoppers in the courtyard. Then Dimitris Louloudakis snuffed and hawked and spit on the floor.

Blood rose in the young schoolteacher's face. He took four long strides to the back of the room and struck the boy hard across the cheek with his open hand. "Have you no respect?"

"I did not mean any disrespect to *you*, sir"—the formal words of apology were undercut by Dimitris's dark look, which filled Siganos with unease; the boy seemed already a grown man with a grudge, old beyond his years—"but you don't know what that one is."

"That one? Is that any way to speak?"

"That one is the devil himself." Dimitris glared at the newcomer, his voice rising. "His grandmother is the witch who made my brother blind."

"That is ignorant, un-Christian superstition. You may not say such things in this room"—Siganos, sensing a pending crisis of authority, worked himself up—"and you may never spit on the floor. Apologize or leave here this moment."

Dimitris turned his implacable gaze back upon the teacher,

whose handprint still glowed on his cheek. Then he stood up and walked to the door, flinging wide the door Manolis had just closed, letting it crash against the wall as if trying to hit the newcomer with it.

Siganos followed him as far as the doorway. "You can come back to school when I have talked with your father," he called, too loudly, but Dimitris did not even look back.

The schoolmaster closed the door and returned to the blackboard, eyeing the newcomer with irritation. "Sit down, sit down, over there. We are learning the alphabet. You are to say the letters out loud."

In a high, clear voice, Manolis said, *"Alpha, vita, ghama, dhelta, epsilon, zita, ita, thita, yiota, kapa, lamdha, mi, ni, kzi, omikron, pi, ro, sighma, taph, ipsilon, phi, shi, psi, omegha."*

Like the other students, like Siganos himself before he'd gone to Athens and had the Cretan accent ridiculed out of him, Manolis's pronunciation was atrocious. Yet he obviously had no need to learn the alphabet. Siganos polished his schoolmaster's fingernail against his vest and, sighing quietly, turned to the other children. *"Alpha, vita, ghama . . ."*

When the midmorning break came, the older boys got up a game of kickball in the little courtyard between the school and the chapel, using a sheepskin tied into a ball. The two girls sat on the porch and put their heads together, whispering secrets. Manolis stood beside the schoolhouse door, watching. The September sun reflected heat from the limestone flags, and grasshoppers droned in the still air, thrumming a bass line to the ballplayers' high-pitched shouts. Dikti rose above the rooftops, serene and softly gray, near and distant at the same time, as if its crags were part of a different landscape in a different time.

The gate in the wall across the courtyard was open; Dimitris Louloudakis was leaning against the jamb. He beckoned Manolis silently. *Come here, come here.*

Manolis considered the invitation. He knew Dimitris well, though they'd never been introduced; he'd heard what Dimitris had just said about him in the classroom, his odd words and phrases resonating with other things Manolis had picked up by eavesdropping on street conversations from behind his grand-mother's wall.

He crossed the courtyard. His eyes were not on Dimitris but upon the ground, searching the swept pavement for stones. Stones were what he used to ward off angry dogs he encountered in his wanderings across the slopes of Dikti. Stones comforted him.

There were no loose stones here. Manolis reached the gate and stopped, and raised his eyes to Dimitris. "What do you want?"

"I want to see you close, child. To see what devil's spawn looks like."

Manolis leaned forward and peered up, open-eyed. "Can you see me now?"

Dimitris flinched away. "Don't try to give *me* the eye."

"I wouldn't," the little boy said reasonably. "You don't have anything I want." It was envious people who cast the evil eye, his grandmother had told him.

Dimitris flared. "May your balls swell up anyway."

"Why do you say those things to me?"

"Because your eyebrows grow together, stupid." But the boy showed no fear, so Dimitris tried to mount a more persuasive show of menace. "Because of your mother! She was a demon and a whore."

The schoolmaster came into the yard. "I sent you home, Dimitri. When I talk to your father, I'll ask him where you were today."

Dimitris turned away quickly, glad for the excuse to leave, but he paused on the other side of the wall, out of Siganos's sight, long enough to whisper to Manolis. "Look out when you go home tonight, devil's child."

Manolis, raising his hand as if to wave good-bye, pinned the older boy with his intense, unemotional gaze. For a moment time faltered; Dimitris Louloudakis stood still in his tracks.

You, looking so fierce, your name means "little flower," and your nickname means "parsley." Do you believe in the evil eye? Ponder this.

Manolis lowered his hand and let his gaze flick away. "I

always look out where I go . . . to make sure I don't step on any tiny little parsley plants, *Maindanaki*."

Dimitris spit and crossed himself and fled down the narrow lane. Manolis was delighted, so taken by surprise that he laughed out loud.

"You shouldn't have insulted him, child."

Manolis turned to find the schoolmaster peering down at him. "He shouldn't have insulted my mother, sir. She's dead."

"Has your son told you why I sent him home today?"

Siganos had refused Haralambos Louloudakis's offer of a raki at a table on the square, preferring to talk with the man inside his store, out of sight of curious loungers. To Siganos, a merchant's son, there was something comforting and familiar, something almost luxurious about the cool interior, with its barrels of wine and cured olives, its crates of oranges and coils of stiff new rope, its sacks of flour and bins of dried beans that stood open on the stone floor, its shelves stacked with loaves of sugar, cans of tobacco, bars of fragrant soap from Rethymnon—whatever the citizens of Ayia Kyriaki could not conveniently grow or make for themselves.

"He told me." The storekeeper's lips barely moved under his stiff mustache. "Now listen, young Mr. Schoolmaster, you're new here, but you have to know that that Androulakis bastard is an evil influence and a provocation to the other students."

"He is a very quiet and inoffensive little boy, Mr. Louloudakis. He can read, and he can add and subtract and multiply and divide. Apparently his grandmother taught him."

"The devil knows what they get up to with each other, living up there on the wild mountain."

"Who was the boy's father?"

"Nobody from around here." Louloudakis found that the sacks of dried beans on the floor needed rearranging; he bent over them busily, his back to the teacher.

Siganos's eye took in the rest of the place, the counter with its enameled basin beside the iron stove where Louloudakis boiled coffee in a long-handled copper *briki,* the nearby shelves with rows of glasses and bottles of cloudy spirits. His glance fell upon the trophies mounted high on the back wall, the pine marten and the wild goat's head—and the shotgun that rested there on wooden pegs. Unlike the typical villager's ancient fowling piece, this was a fine weapon with a barrel of blued steel and an ebony stock inlaid with silver. For a moment Siganos forgot about Manolis. "May I ask you about . . . ?"

"You already did. His mother was a filthy girl, a wild girl, the witch who scratched out the Virgin's eyes in the chapel; she wandered everywhere. What happened to her was God's will."

Siganos was reminded of his purpose. "Surely people must have talked about her—who did it to her. Made some guesses."

"Nobody *knows* who got the bastard on her"—Louloudakis stood up and turned angrily on Siganos—"but I'll tell you this much: he'll be the only one in your school if you let him stay. How will you explain an empty schoolhouse to the politicians who think we need a full-time teacher, Mr. Schoolmaster?"

Siganos paused to consider the question, trying to conceal his surprise at the depth of the man's rancor. "I thank you for the advice," he said as coolly as he could. "I'll start thinking about it now—about how I'm going to explain why an entire village does not wish to obey the law."

Louloudakis's mustache twitched involuntarily. "You mean to let him stay?"

"The law requires it, sir."

"Politicians in Athens," the storekeeper said contemptuously.

Siganos said, "We have been a modern state for over a century, and only this year—at last!—we have a constitution. Thanks to those politicians in Athens, Ellas is a nation, not a collection of primitive tribes. For your own sake and the sake of your sons, you should learn to respect the law." Having delivered himself of this admonition, and finding his cheeks radiating in the gloom, Siganos turned and left the store.

Over the next three days the population of the schoolroom dwindled, until Manolis was the only student in the room. On the fourth day even Manolis was absent.

Siganos waited in the empty schoolroom, his face getting

warm. He wiped the sweat from his mustache. *Benighted peasants, refusing their children an education because of some incomprehensible feud . . . perhaps they will have to be taught a stern lesson.*

The door opened without a knock. Haralambos Louloudakis came in, followed by half the men of the village. Standing at his blackboard, Siganos watched them drag themselves in and shuffle about, arranging themselves with their backs flat against the walls, many of them hoping to be inconspicuous.

"Good morning, gentlemen," Siganos said. "Have you brought your children with you?"

"We don't want Manolis Androulakis in this school," Louloudakis said without preamble. "You can take his part or you can take ours. Either way, Mr. Schoolmaster, you'll take what comes next."

Siganos didn't try to stare Louloudakis down—a waste of honor—but instead shifted his gaze to Stavroula's father and asked him, "Is that what you think, *kyrie* Stavroudakis? You think little Androulakis is a threat to your daughter?"

He got no answer, only a defiant and embarrassed stare. He asked each of the men the same question and got the same lack of response. A few such crude exchanges conveyed the message: law or no law, Manolis Androulakis was a pariah.

Yannis Siganos was a well-intentioned man, but he was also a realist. "All right. I'll see what I can do about your fears."

He was aware of the eyes that followed him as he walked up the steep street in the midday sun. He said good-days to the black-clad women perched in their gateways, but only a few murmured replies, and none smiled back at him.

He came to Katerina's gate and rapped on it with the back of his hand. There was no answer. He knocked again. "*Kyria* Katerina? Are you at home?"

"*Kyrie* Siganos?" The voice was barely a whisper from the other side of the gate.

"May I talk with you?"

The bar scraped back and the wooden gate opened enough to

admit him, but Katerina did not show herself to the street. Once he was inside she quickly barred the gate again.

"Come inside the house, sir. I can make coffee."

"Please don't trouble yourself."

"No trouble. I am honored. Inside, please. Come."

Siganos could not refuse the woman's hospitality, so he let her lead him inside; it was almost noon, but here the shadows were thick. He saw household implements and a few cooking utensils beside the fireplace. Icons on the wall. In one corner, a shelf with a dozen tattered books; except for the Bible and the *Erotokritos* he did not recognize their titles, only their age.

"The coffee will take just a moment."

It occurred to him that she would be saving fuel for the winter. "No coffee, please. If you have a little cold water, that would be very satisfying."

"Yes, of course, right away."

"Is Manolis at home?"

Katerina nodded and bobbed her head toward the inner room, past the wide arch that divided the house in half. Siganos could see little but the outline of a chair and a chest and a bed inside; his eyes needed time to adjust to the gloom. He stood waiting quietly, listening to the woman as she moved behind him, collecting cups and tipping water from a jug.

As the pupils of his eyes slowly widened, Siganos realized that the amorphous form on the bed was not a pile of bolsters; it was the boy, who seemed to be asleep. Siganos stood and approached him cautiously. "Are you all right, child?"

Manolis rolled over and sat up. Even in the shadows his puffed-up bruises, some of them still bleeding, were enough to make Siganos wince.

"How did this happen?"

"I met some boys when I was going to school."

"Some boys? How many?"

"Three. They didn't bother me too much." Manolis's face twisted in a sudden grimace, meant to be a grin. "Their faces aren't so good either."

No good to ask the names of the attackers; no doubt their parents, following Louloudakis's example, would defend their children's right to assault whomever they pleased. Siganos considered what comfort he could offer. "It wouldn't be good if this happened every day," he said feebly.

"I can go there and back by different ways."

The teacher perched himself cautiously on the side of the bed. He laid his fingers on the arch of the boy's tough bare foot. "Manoli, I think that you are more . . ."—he didn't want to say more intelligent, although that's what he meant—"more ready to learn than the other students. What if I taught you alone? One person to another."

"After school?"

The truth: *"Instead* of school. You don't have to go there at all. I'll be your tutor."

"Say yes, child." Katerina's raw voice was passionate behind them. "Papa Kriaris also advises it. There is no community for us here. You can learn your lessons despite that." She bobbed her head toward Siganos. "I bless you, sir, I bless you."

Siganos turned to her. "Mother, you mustn't hope for much."

"Why do I have to stay away from the others?" Manolis demanded, leaning forward from the bedclothes. "They will like me soon. I can *make* them."

"Never," said Katerina.

"They are only children, Manoli," Siganos said. "Sometimes they can be made to behave. But they can't be made to feel what they don't want to feel."

"Why don't they want to?" Manolis asked.

"Because they haven't been taught well," Siganos said.

Manolis looked back at the teacher, his dark eyes wide in his bruised face. "I want to be taught well. I want to learn what you know."

Siganos, looking into those wide eyes, suspected that the boy already knew more than he realized, that he had yet to discover what he knew. "We'll make plans, then. We'll make arrangements," he said, patting the boy's bare foot, its sole as stiff as shoe leather. "I'll teach you what I can."

9

"In the first three months he read every book in the school-house, even the most advanced," Siganos said. "*After* school, while I sat there watching, because I had to carry them back again next day."

It was an autumn evening and already dark outside; Yannis Siganos and his cousin Georgios were perched beside the stone fireplace in Georgios's house in Tzermiado, a small house in the biggest village on the Lasithi Plain.

"You helped him through them," his cousin suggested.

"Very little. I was supposed to be teaching him, but it was all I could do to keep up. He was voracious."

"Is his grandmother so gifted a pedagogue, then?" Georgios asked skeptically. "Surely he's a bright child, as you say, and very curious—but he must have seen those books before." Georgios's wife and her mother had pulled their chairs close on the other side of the hearth and were steadily shelling a heap of black walnuts while they listened to the men talk. Mutton chops sizzled on an iron grill over olive-wood coals; the smell was enough to make Siganos's jaws sting with saliva.

"Maybe, but he'd never seen a book in English. It was a year later that I happened to be carrying a copy of *Treasure Island,* by Robert Louis Stevenson. You've read Stevenson?"

Georgios thrust out his chin, a silent no. The women gazed at Siganos as if he himself were speaking some incomprehensible foreign tongue.

"Anyway, the boy found the book and asked me questions about the Roman alphabet, and in a few minutes he was sounding out words on the page. Pronouncing them oddly, but still . . . it was as if I could see ideas forming in his mind."

"He took this book from your *sakouli?* He is not only curious but bold."

"It's a story of pirates and hidden treasure, what boy wouldn't love it? But to read it, he had to learn a foreign language and a foreign system of writing. After a month of instruction, no more—and the loan of my English lexicon—he read it straight through. Later I brought him other books. *Voyage au Centre de la Terre,* by Jules Verne. *Kinder- und Hausmärchen,* by the Grimms. Using them he learned to read French and German too. I helped, but he has a gift."

"What good can it do him? No father, no mother, no prospects. He will spend his short life in these mountains." Sparks popped and flew up the chimney, sending shadows dancing through the chilly room. Georgios leaned toward his cousin. "Listen, my child, I want to hear no regrets from you. Go back to Athens with a good conscience. You've given two years of your life to that filthy one-street village and the filthy peasants who inhabit it. You were wise not to challenge them. They're the sort that wouldn't hesitate to toss you over a cliff."

"In Iraklion, that's what they say about Lasithi," Siganos replied irritably, "that up here in the mountains, we'd as soon slit a throat as say *kalimera.* In Athens, that's what they say about Crete. In the rest of Europe, I expect, that's what they say about Greece."

"How wrong are they?"

"Well, we ought not be proud of it." Siganos stared into the fire. Then he glanced almost apologetically at his cousin. "I didn't tell you about the arithmetic—I mean the mathematics. You know I was never good at numbers. Between you and me,

I didn't completely understand what I was supposed to be teaching the older boys. There's a book of algebra, but most of it was just a puzzle to me. This past year, when I had difficulty, I asked Manolis."

"Really."

"He explained it to me."

"What makes you think he knew what he was talking about?"

"He made it seem rational, simple—I could understand it myself, I could teach it to others. To you, if you dare me."

His cousin thrust out his chin again. The sizzle of chops and the creaking of hot coals filled the silence.

"He'll waste his life up there, you're right about that," Siganos went on sadly. "What's to be done about him?"

Although the women said nothing, he felt their disapproving gaze. He glanced at them, then back at his cousin. Their answer was plain enough. *Nothing.*

That fall, Manolis stayed on the mountain. The schoolmaster had gone to Athens, and at Louloudakis's instigation there would be no one to replace him—no one to teach school in Ayia Kyriaki and no one to tutor Manolis. . . .

On a late November morning he and Katerina started the flock down the mountain, retreating before oncoming winter. The sky was veiled with cirrus. Far below, sickled yellow almond leaves were falling away in the breeze, drifting beneath the smooth gray branches, making the narrow plain of Limnakaros into a bowl of silver and gold. They descended at a businesslike pace, not wishing to diminish the reserves of fat on their robust animals. But Manolis, full of energy, often darted ahead, far down the slopes. As they approached the slide he scrambled back and took Katerina's hand to help her down. All innocence, he looked at her with bright eyes. "Tell me again, Grandmother. What is a whore?"

"Be quiet," she gasped, her knees and toes already suffering from the descent. "Don't you think I know what you've been hearing? Those who say these things to you will burn in hell."

They half slid down the talus while he considered her words. "So my mother *was* a whore. And I *am* a bastard."

Katerina set her thin lips and trudged on, but she did not let go of the youngster's hand; instead she gripped it tighter. If she had been a few years younger, if he had been any less long-legged and agile, he would not have been helping her; she would have been dragging him down the slide. When at last she spoke it was with determination. "Once and for all, your mother was not what you said and you are not what you said. Your father was"—her brows knotted in an anguish of improvisation—"an Englishman."

"An *Englishman?*" Manolis was astonished. He had read a great deal about the English—pirates and explorers and clever children who lived in a rainy land full of toads and rabbits and hedgehogs—but the only Englishman he had ever seen depicted was in a photograph in one of Katerina's old books.

"A fine young man, a very fine young warrior," Katerina said, "and *his* father was a very great lord, and very rich . . ."

"Oh, Grandmother." Manolis laughed happily. "You are making a joke."

"He was an officer in the English army and a true friend of the Hellenes," Katerina insisted, raising her voice. "He married your mother secretly."

This news silenced the child's laughter. How was it possible to be crowned in marriage *secretly?* Manolis had witnessed two marriages in the village, when Stavroudakis's youngest son had married Michalis's oldest daughter, and when Louloudakis's cousin had married Michalis's youngest daughter, and those were grand coronations, involving everyone in the neighborhood; indeed, he and his grandmother were the only ones who had not been invited.

"But then the Catastrophe! The greatest of misfortunes, the ruin of our family!" Katerina descended with more vigor, gasping for breath and hoping her grandson was still too young to ask the most awkward questions, too young to realize the absurdity of the yarn she was spinning. "Before he could announce that he was Sophia's husband, your father was killed—like your grandfather—fighting the Turks in Anatolia."

"Fighting the Turks with Grandfather?"

"Yes, exactly."

Manolis considered this. The stories about *Pappou* Niko, his mother's father, were no kinder than the stories about his mother. Surely his own father was a better man than that. But an Englishman? "Why did you never tell me?"

"What good could it have done for you to know?"

"I always wanted to know about my father. You only said he might come back one day, that I should wait for him to tell me."

"You would have repeated what I said. The others would have laughed at us, worse than they do now. Anyway, it makes no difference."

"*You* care about it," he said, daring to defy her.

"It was your parents' secret, my child. They took it with them to their graves. Now it is our secret."

"Why do you tell me now, if you want it to be a secret?" Manolis persisted. "I want to know more about him."

In his distress Katerina felt her own. She paused to rest, her chest heaving. In truth, she had never met an Englishman, and all she knew about the English were the stories her father had told her of the reign of Prince George, of the Great Powers, of fiery young Eleftherios Venizelos. But her vivid imagination had always been at its best combining elements of the familiar. She conjured up a creature of mythic proportions even as she described him to Manolis: a man with a saber at his side and a white pith helmet on his head—a helmet crowned with a spike!—resplendent in a high-collared tunic with gold buttons down his front and gold stripes on his sleeves, wearing black patent-leather shoes on his feet and white gloves on his hands. She gave him a noble family and great deeds and manly virtues. Let the dead Englishman be capable of every refinement of honor and paternal feeling. Let him stand for everything that Manolis—and Sophia, and Katerina herself—had lacked in childhood.

Never mind that she had described the very photograph Manolis remembered from the old book. The splendid male icon found a niche in his mind and gleamed there as he and Katerina made their way downslope, herding the animals in

front of them until at last they came to the rock pen beside the
last house on the edge of Ayia Kyriaki.

Manolis gnawed at a chunk of shepherd's bread soaked in sour
wine. Dead thorn branches burned on the hearth. "How do I
know he even cared about me?"

"He cared about you," Katerina said with passion. "He loved
you, even if he never saw you; he wanted the best for you."
Having embarked recklessly upon this mythic journey, there
was no reason to hold back now. Her eyes widened, catching
bright reflections from the fire. "He left you a treasure."

"A treasure?" For all her fantastic notions, Manolis had never
had reason to doubt that his grandmother believed what she told
him. "What kind of treasure?"

"He didn't tell anyone. Or if he did, only your mother."

Manolis chewed off another chunk of bread. "Where?"

"He didn't tell anyone *where,* child. Only that . . ."—she hesitated; Manolis waited—"it is under the ground."

"Somewhere on the mountain?"

Katerina shrugged.

"Then I will look for it."

"Next year. In the spring."

"I'll look for it now. Until the first snowfall."

"That is foolish. Why do you want to hurry?" Tears started in
Katerina's eyes. But if she despaired at what she had begun, she
said no more about it that night.

Early the next morning Manolis packed his *sakouli* with
shepherd's bread and hard cheese; he hardened himself
against Katerina's pleas and left, almost running up the
mountainside.

He might have searched for signs of buried treasure in his
favorite grottoes and glades, or on the promontories where he had
lazed and dreamed of a legendary past or a future as hazy-bright
as the sun seen through the mountain mist—places where he had
sometimes contemplated an infinite regress of other worlds,
which might include so improbable a manifestation of reality as a
father who was an English officer. He might have spent his days

visiting every site that had caught his fancy during his years of far-ranging travels.

But he already knew where to look.

He reached the shepherd's hut through a cold mist, in a flurry of snowflakes that gave him pause. He had promised his grandmother to come down the mountain at the first snowfall—but these feeble flakes would never reach the valley floor; it wasn't snowing down *there*. He squatted inside the soot-blackened hut beside a fire of sticks, huddled in his wool cape, carving hard slivers from a block of cheese with his great-grandfather's knife.

Vampires and *neraïdes,* demons and witches, saints and angels had inhabited the overlapping worlds of his childhood, but in the books he had borrowed from Siganos and other schoolmasters, other worlds had acquired substance, populated by heroes ancient and modern—Perikles and Alexander and Venizelos—and gods, pagan and Christian—Apollo and Hermes and Christ. Among them was the tale of Theseus of Athens, who had come to Crete to slay a bull-man at Knossos. In the villages of Dikti it was said that the English, who had been digging in the ruins of Knossos long before Manolis was born, had uncovered the Minotaur's lair.

When Theseus was a little boy he lived in the Peloponnese, and there his father had secretly married his mother and left a treasure for him under a great stone. Only his mother knew where the stone was, and she had lived long enough to see Theseus lift it. If Manolis's mother had lived, she would have told him where to find his father's treasure; it would have been in a place she knew well.

Impatient, Manolis put down the hard rind of cheese, left the fire, and pushed aside the dirty rug that hung over the entrance to the hut. Snow swirled erratically; he felt its sting on his face more than he saw it in the bright mist.

He walked a few steps to the stone trough at the edge of the cliff. There was only a damp stain in its bottom. Katerina had told him that this trough was once always full of water that overflowed and spilled into the forest below. But since the earthquake that killed his mother there had been only a trickle in it; now they had to water their animals half a mile away. Where had the water gone?

Manolis walked uphill along the stone channel that fed the trough, back to the fissure that had been a spring, a black crevice in the crust of frozen snow that lay over the rocks. Already shivering with cold, he peered inside.

He went back into the hut and gobbled the last of the cheese and put on every piece of clothing he had with him—wool trousers over his wool drawers, a goat's-wool sweater over his tattered cotton shirt, his wool cape over all. Then he gathered up the sticks he hadn't burned and knotted them into bundles with scraps of wool cord. He found a handful of matches and stuffed everything into his *sakouli*.

Moments later he squeezed his way into the crevice. Except where his own shadow blocked it, diffuse daylight illuminated the rock face ahead of him. There water trickled over a spongy mat of algae and dripped into the catch basin of his great-grandfather's stone channel.

When he held his breath and kept very still, he could hear a rush of water deeper in the earth below.

He sat back on his heels and studied the rock face. It was a chunk of limestone that had fallen from the ceiling of the narrow passage where once the spring had issued, blocking it off. The water he could see was oozing down the front of the fallen block; the water he could hear was flowing beneath it.

There was a black space between the fallen block and the wall, and other black spaces among the jumbled rocks on the floor of the passage. If he could move one of those rocks, he could look further inside. He put his back and shoulders into lifting what appeared to be the smallest block; it was slick with mud and algae, but he got his hands around one sharp corner and heaved, pushing back and forth—

—until suddenly it came loose and tumbled away, out of his hands, bouncing and echoing into an invisible crevasse. With it the earth gave way beneath him, and he plummeted after.

He hit on his bottom and struggled to get his feet under him while sliding down a muddy slope in the darkness amidst a tumble of stones—slowly at first, though he couldn't quite stop himself because the mud was as slippery as grease. Then faster, plowing through the mud. Then his feet were out from under him—panic suddenly rising—and he was falling free, and he screamed.

He crashed into an invisible floor, which knocked the scream out of him. He screeched, struggling to get his breath back, until finally he got some air into his lungs. In the blackness he groped in his bag for a bundle of sticks and a match. Everything was wet and slimy, but he found his matches and struck one. When the fire bloomed in his hand, when his eyes adjusted to the glare, he looked around.

His ragged breath caught fast in his windpipe. He was sitting in a boneyard. Skeletons lay everywhere on the muddy rocks, big skulls and little skulls, leg bones and arm bones, high-arching rib cages and deep pelvises gleaming bright in the flicker of the torch. But all were streaked and grotesquely shadowed with black fungus.

Manolis didn't hear himself whimpering as he held the flaring torch over his head and peered into the gloom. Overhead, water dripped from veils of stone to fall upon stalagmites as big as tree trunks growing from the greenish mud. He could make out the slope he'd slid down. A stream of water poured swiftly down it. He was not in hell, then; he was *not* in hell. He could get out of this place.

The torchlight revealed artifacts scattered among the bones, lying where they had fallen from the necks and waists and hands that once supported them. Belt buckles glittered in the mud beside vertebrae; mingled with the skulls and arm bones were necklaces and earrings of carnelian and blackened silver, and green copper bracelets and loops of amber worry beads on corroded chains, and finger rings and bits of rotted cloth, and ancient weapons—sabers and pistols and long guns from the last century.

Manolis stood up and stepped cautiously among the skeletons, whispering to himself. Not prayers. Logarithms. The most comforting thing that came to his mind.

All these people must have died at once. The skeletons of infants lay in the bony arms of what had been their mothers or grandmothers or aunts or sisters; rusted guns lay in the grip of fleshless fingers, cocked but not fired. Mildewed scraps of rugs, piles of black sticks that were collapsed chairs, rotten wooden chests which had burst to expose crockery and kitchen utensils—these testified that the cave had been used as a hiding place more than once. On a closer look, some of the bones were not human at all; they were the familiar bones of sheep and goats, brought into the cave as food or to hide them from the enemy. Up in the apses and crannies of the cave roof lay more bones, the remains of those who had tried to escape sudden doom.

Had Manolis's great-grandfather, when he built the channel from the spring, known of this slaughter? He would have been a boy in '66, a young man in '78, a grown man in '89 and '96; each time the Cretans had risen against the Turks, the fighting in the mountains around Lasithi had been fierce. He *must* have known this place. Where else could he have acquired the leather-bound books that were now his daughter's, if not by looting the dead?

And Katerina, had she known of this place too? But she would not have kept such a momentous secret: if she had known of this place, they would not have been so poor.

He went quickly from one skeleton to another, taking a bracelet, a silver belt buckle, a wedding necklace of coins, a loop of amber worry beads on a chain, things that could be discreetly sold for a bit of food or clothing, things that would please his grandmother, things he wanted for himself, stuffing his *sakouli* until his torch crumbled into sparks.

He lit another torch from the last of his kindling and searched for a way out. If he stayed close to the falling stream, he could find his way back up in the dark, though he would be soaking wet when he reached the surface—which meant he might freeze before he got down the mountain. There was a rougher, drier path up the wall to the right. Hard going in the dark, but staying dry was worth it.

The torch burned fast as he started up the slope, and it was guttering by the time he reached a massive cross section of fallen stalactite that blocked the path. The only passage was a narrow ledge beside a yawning gap in the floor. The torch sucked itself out. Panic battered him; in daylight he no longer believed in vampires, but here . . . in the darkness he felt the presence of the unburied, their bones cleansing and reknitting, red flesh growing on slick white skeletons.

As he groped in the darkness, inching upward on all fours and feeling for purchase in the clay, his hand came upon sharp flakes of what felt like broken pottery. Hardly thinking, he scooped them up and stuffed them into his *sakouli*.

A quarter of an hour later he came out of the mountainside into sunlight. The mist had retreated to the forest below, leaving cold blue sky to arch over the world. His heart lifted.

His hands were dirty and he was covered with mud outside, but inside his layers of wool he was still dry. He laid out his treasures on a flat rock, rings and earrings and bracelets and necklaces, lapis and amber and carnelian stones afire in the sunshine, tarnished silver settings testifying to their purity by their blackness. And beside the jewelry, a few shards of pottery.

He picked them up. They were almost weightless, delicately made and intricately painted, black and red on pale gray. On one piece were zigzag red and black branches that Manolis recognized as thorny spurge, on another, broken in the middle, half a lively fish. Manolis had kicked his way through countless broken pots in his treks across the mountains; in some places sherds were as common as acorns in an oak wood, but those were mostly rough pink scraps that could have come as easily from a flowerpot broken yesterday as from an ancient vessel.

Not these. He stared at the painted fragments in his fingers; he'd never seen anything that called to him so immediately from the distant past of his daydreams. . . .

"They were scraps of typical Middle Minoan pottery, styles common in Central and East Crete," Minakis said calmly, as if trying to soothe Anne-Marie's visible agitation. "Of course I didn't know that then; I'd barely heard of Minoans."

The unexpected revelation made her dizzy. Minoan pottery? Was this cave the source of the artifacts she had come to find?

It was a question she couldn't ask. "What about all those *people?*"

Minakis's gaze shifted to the sea beyond her. "It must have been 1866, the worst of the uprisings. When Turkish soldiers threatened the villages, caves were good places to hide and easy to defend if necessary: anybody coming in was blind and a plain target against the sky. But eventually the Turks figured out how to attack without risk. They built brushfires outside the entrances that sucked out all the air. They did that at Melidoni, at Milatos. On Dikti too."

"A whole village just . . . snuffed out?"

"Who was left to look for them? My great-grandfather was probably the first to find them, when he built the trough."

"What did they say in Ayia Kyriaki? When you told them what you'd found?"

"Told them?" He peered at her with an expression of friendly curiosity. "I told no one. As for all those rotten skeletons . . . once I had persuaded myself there were no vampires in the cave, it seemed a fit enough burial place. I wasn't a religious boy."

She started to speak but reconsidered. Perhaps he was baiting her, laying some intricate snare. The way he claimed to have found the Minoan sherds . . . that part of his story was hardly convincing. Lightly she asked, "Did you ever go back?"

"Not for a long time. Until two years ago, I thought I had taken everything worth taking." His expression was cool, relentless. The worn amber beads clicked through his fingers. "Would you like to go there with me?"

With her surprise came fear, shaking her heart like a low-voltage current; she laughed to cover her confusion. "Oh yes I would. But I owe my husband a vacation."

"Take your vacation on Crete. Both of you."

She smiled as slowly as she could manage, struggling to calm her erratic heartbeat. "We will, I promise. But first I have to sell your life story for a pot of money. You promised to tell me how you got your unusual name."

"You ask with such depth of feeling." He let his beads wrap themselves around his finger and closed his fist, silencing them. "But as you wish."

10

On a winter night when Manolis was fourteen years old he came home to find Katerina sitting on the ground in front of the *phourno* in the courtyard. The bread inside the oven was baked harder than shepherd's bread, and the ashes were still warm, but she was cold.

He could give no voice to his anguish. He only sat on the ground beside her a while, rocking her body in his arms. Then he picked her up and took her into the house and arranged her on her bed, crossing her bony hands over her breast.

Manolis was a tall boy and very thin, all hard muscle and fine bone, with a face much like his grandmother's, too stark for good looks. Katerina had dominated his world. Besides the schoolmaster who had left for Athens so many years ago, she was the only one he had ever cared to please. How would it be to live here now, in a place populated exclusively by his enemies, where there was no one to love, to care about, to talk to and tease? He sat for a long time, hardly moving more than she did. At last he went for the priest.

* * *

They buried Katerina the next day. Besides Manolis, the only people at the funeral were Kriaris and his wife and son, who were there to insure against any appearance of irregularity. The priest hurried through the service, singing in a thin, unpersuasive voice, to which his lumpish son sang the responses in a disconcertingly sweet tenor. When her body had been interred under the same slab that covered Sophia, Papa Kriaris beckoned Manolis into his house next to the chapel. It was not a comforting gesture.

Kriaris went to a table in the corner of the good room and took a folded sheet of paper from the drawer. "You read well, child, and your grandmother could write well. Read this. It's her will and testament."

Manolis took the paper. He recognized Katerina's hand, the inked letters angular on the page. At first he read eagerly, grateful to learn anything of his grandmother's thoughts. But within a few lines he learned that Katerina had found him to be an *impious* and *cruel* boy—words he had never heard her use—and that she had determined that he cared only for himself and nothing for her, and that in her fear of not having a living in her old age she had determined to repudiate him, turning for protection to her priestly brother-in-law, to whom she had already ceded a portion of her inheritance and to whom she herewith ceded all her other possessions, namely her house and all its furnishings, her flocks of animals, and her remaining parcels of land.

Manolis looked up to see Kriaris eyeing him damply, a dribble of spit creeping into his beard.

"Did you make her write this?"

"That is an evil suggestion."

"When was I cruel to her? When was I impious?"

"Are you going to argue? You have no hope. In her own hand she has written out the grounds for disinheritance."

"Why did she write these lies?"

"Call them what you want."

Manolis saw his aunt Eleni standing in the shadows behind the arch, signaling to him, a finger to her lips, pointing at the door with her other hand.

Manolis coldly ignored her silent request. "Have you read

this, Aunt Eleni?" he demanded, holding up the paper. "I loved my grandmother more than anyone. You know it. And she loved me."

Eleni frowned. She stepped into the room and looked hard at her husband, and some signal crossed between them.

"Don't take it too hard, boy," Kriaris said gruffly. "You have time. There's time to work things out between us." He turned to his wife, but she had left the room. Kriaris looked back at Manolis, his expression venomous. "Forty days, until the memorial service. After that you must be gone from the house."

Eleni accosted Manolis as he crossed the courtyard. "Katerina did not betray you, child, she saved your life. My husband has been your protector since you were born."

"That's crazy," Manolis said, walking fast.

Eleni ran to keep up with him. "*She* promised him the land. You were a newborn, hardly a day old. She made him promise to keep you alive."

"If I'm alive, it's no thanks to a priest."

"Do you think Louloudakis would not have slaughtered you like a lamb, if not for my husband? Because of him, the schoolteacher was allowed to teach you after school. Because my son protected you, Louloudakis's sons left you in peace."

"I would have gone to school with the others, if your husband had been a *real* priest. Old man Louloudakis would not have chased off the schoolteacher and closed down the school, if your husband had been a *real* priest." Manolis choked; tears streamed down his thin cheeks. "And as for Little Parsley, he is lucky I chose not to kill him as he once tried to kill me. I would not have missed."

All along the street the old men and the women in black watched with undisguised satisfaction as they passed. When they reached Katerina's gate Manolis pushed it open, but Eleni stayed behind in the street. "You are still a child. You must listen to what I'm telling you," she cried.

Manolis turned, his hand on the gate. He saw the anguish in Eleni's face, the same deep lines as in his grandmother's face, drawn there by the days of her life. "What *are* you trying to tell me?"

"Leave Ayia Kyriaki while you can," she whispered. "My husband can no longer protect you."

His tears dried on his face as took in her words. "Let me thank you, Aunt Eleni. You have done all you could for me. Go back to your husband and reassure him that I know how inno-cent and kind and noble all your family have been to me."

She gasped at the force of his bitter sarcasm, at the hatred in his red-rimmed eyes. She crossed herself and rushed away.

Forty days had not quite passed before Easter came. On Great Friday night, Manolis climbed up and straddled his grand-mother's courtyard wall in a place he'd cleared of broken pot-tery. He could see a sliver of the town square, and people moving in the shadows. All evening long the church bells had been clanging at intervals, and the sound of Kriaris's thin singing, answered by the sweet chanting of his son, had wob-bled out of the chapel into the night air. Now a ragged cheer went up as the church door opened and Christ's coffin appeared—a lightweight coffin of pasteboard, covered with garlands of lilies and wild orchids—held aloft by two men pre-ceded by Kriaris, who was swinging a smoking censer, and fol-lowed by an acolyte carrying the empty cross. The coffin bearers paused every few seconds to allow men and women and boys and girls to duck under the coffin for good luck, laughing and shouting happily.

The coffin came up the street toward Manolis, passing beneath the wall where he perched, but the bearers didn't pause outside his gate or spare him an upward glance, only circled around behind the houses to the bottom of the village. Manolis could hear more people ducking under the coffin with joyful shrieks, all along the way. Before the procession had returned to the square and disappeared inside the church, Manolis had climbed down from the wall.

The next night he was perched on the wall again, listening to the clanging of the church bells and the incessant percussion of gunfire. His eyes stung with woodsmoke and gunpowder, his jaws with saliva, as the aroma of roasting lamb and kid wafted along the dark street. Come midnight his own Easter morning feast, bean soup and boiled wild greens, would be as meatless as if Lent had not ended. Kriaris had already grabbed his grandmother's animals and joined them with his own flock.

Manolis was not a weak boy, not without talent, not without vigor, but he was paralyzed by inaction, not knowing what to do when the time came to act. He had no resources. He had no hope. He looked up at the stars wheeling overhead, emerging slowly from behind the sharp line of Dikti's cliffs, moving toward the year's true beginning.

Suddenly there were shouts of *"Christos anesti! Alithos anesti!"*—"Christ is risen! He is risen indeed!"—and people came out of the church with lit candles, passing flames to those waiting outside, one candle to the next. Boys in the square pulled on the bell ropes, and soon the bronze bell atop the squat tower was swinging, swinging, ringing loud enough for God to hear. Beneath the shouts and clangor, Manolis heard the shrill notes of old Ariakis's panpipes—hesitant at first, then bold—and the shriek of a *lyra;* somewhere out of sight, Louloudakis was sawing wildly at the miniature violin poised upright on his knee, pouring out manic, skirling, half-Asian music. Even a villain could sound like an angel, if he could play the *lyra.*

A ruddy glow sprang up the stone walls of the houses, and a whirlwind of sparks climbed to join the stars. Judas was burning. A scarecrow of old clothes was Judas, scapegoat for all disappointments, blazing atop a brushwood pyre in the village square. On this night Judas was burning in a score of towns in Lasithi and in hundreds of towns throughout Crete—all over Lasithi and Crete and Greece, a galaxy of bonfires. There was not a soul in Ayia Kyriaki who was not gathered in the square to watch the traitor burn.

None of them had the slightest thought for Manolis. He left his barricaded courtyard and crept along the fire-reflecting cobblestones to watch like a woman from the shadows at the edge of the square.

At once he saw the *xenos,* a tall man with curling, straw-colored hair, a sharp face the color of bronze, a gaze that in the flickering firelight seemed supernaturally intense.

It was Easter at last, the first moments of Holy Sunday morning, the day for which the village was named, and the men were dancing to the pipes and the *lyra,* leaping and stamping their boot heels on the flags, swirling about with their arms raised high. *Christ is risen! He is risen indeed!*

The *xenos* danced with them. What grace and energy that man had! What prodigious leaps he made, as if he could fly straight up into the air! And what an appetite! Manolis watched in fascination as the stranger paused to devour lengths of boiled sheep gut stuffed with wild greens and the savory slices of lamb and kid that young Louloudakis pressed upon him. As the tavern keeper sawed away on his *lyra* the *xenos* raised a glass of raki to him and his son, tossed it back neat, and again charged into the dance.

The dancing stranger's bright gaze was like a lighthouse beam, flashing each time it swept over Manolis—who forgot himself, watching, and stepped forward out of the shadows. The stranger stopped short, and Manolis was startled to find the man's glittering eye fixed upon him across the width of the square.

"You, child. What are you doing there? Hiding?"

The music faltered. Every other eye among the villagers gathered in the square turned upon Manolis. He comforted himself that without the power of the evil eye, their hatred was nothing.

"Come here, child," the Englishman said. By his speech, which was almost but not quite perfect Greek, Manolis took him for an Englishman. Not an Italian or a Frenchman or a Russian, none of those other sorts of exotic *xenoi* his grandmother had told him about and his long-gone tutor had delighted in mimicking, but an Englishman. Manolis could run—what would that gain him?—or he could step forward. He walked into the square, conscious of his shabby clothes among the men in their polished boots and their black and scarlet

Easter finery. He went up to the stranger and boldly stared him in the face, hoping that his terror did not show.

There was something teasing and mischievous about the man, something aggressive about the thrust of his jaw and the twist of his thick lips. Close up, the mystery of his glittering gaze was solved, for Manolis saw that his left eye was made of glass.

"You're the one I've heard of, surely," the stranger said. "From my friend Georgios Siganos in Tzermiado."

"I don't know a *kyrio* Sigano in Tzermiado," Manolis said.

"But you know a few things, don't you?" The Englishman switched to English. "You know how to speak English."

"A bit," Manolis replied in English. "Not as well as you know Greek, sir."

The Englishman laughed, throwing back his head. "I was speaking *Cretan,* not Greek." He fixed his bright smile on Manolis. "I could go to the mainland with all these *oshis* and *Azhee Cheery-a-chees,* and they wouldn't understand me any better than an Albanian."

Manolis bobbed his head. "As you say, sir." But he wondered how else one would possibly pronounce the name of Ayia Kyriaki.

"My friend Georgios tells me you know the mountains. So you must know the footpaths to the south coast, over Dikti."

"I know these mountains."

"I could use a guide. Will you go with me tomorrow?"

"I will be pleased to go with you."

"Good, good. Sit down, eat some lamb with us."

Every face in the firelit square was a featureless mask, staring hollow-eyed at Manolis.

"I must leave now," he said firmly.

The Englishman raised an eyebrow and took account of the onlookers. "Meet me here tomorrow—later today, I mean. Not before noon! I plan to be drunk until then." He turned to Louloudakis. "Tavern keeper, fill the glasses of these good men."

At which the men began to shout, "Impossible, you are our

guest," and while the Englishman pretended to protest and finally bobbed and grinned in defeat, Manolis hurried back up the street.

Once again he perched on the wall of his grandmother's courtyard and studied the visible sliver of the village square, framed by houses in shadow. The music took up again; he caught a glimpse of the tall Englishman dancing the *sirtaki* with the other men while the pipes and the *lyra* whirled dizzily.

How had he picked Manolis from the shadows? Asking people in Lasithi about him—why? Manolis could hardly trust himself with the answer that pressed itself upon him. *He was English. His father was English. . . .*

At midday, Manolis dressed in his walking clothes and packed as many extra socks into his *sakouli* as it would hold. He found a last rind of kaseri cheese in the house and tossed it in; from the wall niche beside the fireplace he took the amber beads and the scraps of pottery he had secreted there years ago and pushed them deep into a corner of the bulging bag.

He took up his great-grandfather's shotgun, as familiar to him as a walking stick. Then he left his grandmother's house, walked out of its arched rooms with their heavy wood beams, leaving the frayed red rugs that hung on the whitewashed walls, the curled and faded paper icons in the corner by the fireplace, the spavined chairs and the warped table, the blackened kitchen utensils. . . . He went outside, past the dead grapevine, the tall jars standing empty, the iron scythes and wooden rakes and frayed panniers for winnowing grain that were stacked against the courtyard wall. He did not even glance at the *phourno* that had stood empty but for ashes since he had found his grandmother sitting dead in front of it. He went through the gate and left it open behind him. He would never come back. His only program and plan were to guide the Englishman over the mountain.

Ayia Kyriaki was asleep, everyone exhausted by the night's festivities and taking a long nap before rousing themselves to more celebration. The sunlit square was empty, except for the Englishman.

"There you are, boffin," he said cheerily. He was sitting by himself in front of Louloudakis's place, wearing a white wool sweater with a V-collar and baggy shorts and low-cut heavy shoes. An olive-wood walking stick carved with a hook leaned against the chair beside him. On the chair rested a *sakouli* in red and gray wool, more intricately woven than Manolis's own. "You're rather late. I did say noon."

"*Nai, mesimeri.*" Manolis's reply was edgy.

"Oh yes, *mesimeri*. It slipped my mind." He meant that noon and midday are the same word in Greek. Not knowing what he meant, Manolis had no reply. "Name's Pendlebury," said the Englishman, thrusting out his hand. "And you are Androulakis."

Looking at the outstretched hand, Manolis assumed the man wanted to hold his. They shook, and Manolis held fast. "*Nai, kyrie* Pendabri.*"

Pendlebury hesitated a moment before using his left to detach himself from Manolis's grip. "Right. What's all this you've brought with you? That bloody great gun! We're only taking a walk over the mountain."

Manolis glanced at the shotgun and his stuffed *sakouli* and again found himself speechless.

"Fine with me, naturally, if you want to carry it all. Shall we be going?" Pendlebury didn't wait for an answer. He expertly hooked the strings of his own *sakouli* over his shoulders, settling it like a backpack, and went off up the street toward the top of the village. Manolis hurried to catch up. They went past the house that had been Manolis's home until a few minutes ago—

—and kept on going almost at a run for the next quarter hour, straight up the gorge toward the rock slide that was the shortest route over Dikti. Despite his slender legs, the Englishman's vigor was astonishing; he was as strong as any mountain man Manolis knew. Were all Englishmen like this?

They climbed side by side, attacking the mountain. Pendlebury seemed much younger than any of the men in the village, but maybe all foreigners were like this. Maybe none of them looked their age. Of course Manolis, who was young, was swifter and stronger yet. But as he kept up with Pendlebury, both of them slashing their way up the slope, he sensed that the Englishman was irritated not to have outrun him.

"What happened to your eye?" Manolis shouted over his breath.

"What do you mean by that?" Pendlebury shouted back.

"Your glass eye."

"You are not supposed to notice it," Pendlebury said. He put on a burst of speed, but Manolis kept up with him.

Climbing beside him at a pace now furious, Manolis demanded, "Why did you want a guide, *kyrie* Pendabri? You know the mountain very well."

"Well, I do not *know* it. I've only been here once before."

"If you should have any questions, don't forget that I'm with you," said the boy.

Pendlebury glanced at Manolis with his skewed, bright glance, and kept on climbing.

They reached the ridge. In front of them, clouds swept up from the Libyan Sea like steam from a kettle, curling over the ridge and dissolving in blue midair, alternately obscuring and unveiling the wide view of the length of the island spread out to the east and west. Dikti's highest peak lay up the snow-covered spine to their left, eastward, and farther east, a little lower, was the peak of Lazaros. To the west, Aphendis Christos rose almost as high as Dikti, across a stony chasm.

"The three peaks of Dikti," Pendlebury said. "Do you think a man could do them in one day?"

"Why would he want to do that?"

"The challenge, *paidi mou.*"

"If he had no other reason"—no good reason, Manolis meant, such as chasing sheep—"I suppose he could."

"Well, it is a challenge." Pendlebury seemed restless. "Are you hungry?"

"I'm not hungry. It's windy on this ridge."

"Let's get on down then. To Vianos. You lead the way."

"Oshi, kyrie, you don't need me to lead you."

"You're my guide."

"If you go wrong, I'll tell you."

Pendlebury regarded the tall boy, whose hair was ruffled by the wind and whose dark eyes looked back at him expectantly. Then he shrugged and stepped off briskly across the rocky slope.

Manolis followed closely but hung back a little, not quite keeping pace, because he wanted to see where the man would go without prompting. They followed the worn path at first, as would anyone crossing the ridge. But when the main track veered to the right and started descending switchbacks, Pendlebury went left along the fainter trace. It was not the way to Vianos, but Manolis said nothing. He only smiled to himself.

Before long they arrived at the shepherd's hut where Manolis had been born and where he had lived more than half his life. Pendlebury squatted in front of it and gestured for Manolis to sit beside him. "We have to eat, else you won't be much good to me. Is this *mandra* enough out of the wind for you?"

Manolis dropped to the ground beside him. "Yes, this is a good place. Let's eat." He fished in his *sakouli* and brought out the chunk of kaseri.

Meanwhile Pendlebury brought soft bread and oranges and a bottle of yellow Lasithi wine from his own *sakouli*. For a few minutes they busied themselves cutting up the bread and cheese and peeling the oranges with their knives. Like Manolis's knife, Pendlebury's was a Cretan knife with a *mantinada* engraved on its blade, but Manolis suspected that the verse on Pendlebury's blade was the more bloodthirsty, for the Englishman seemed the sort who had to excel in everything—the sort of man who would command the instant admiration of any villager on Crete.

Pendlebury passed Manolis the bottle of wine. He took a swig and passed it back. They munched and chewed in silence, watching the clouds mob the pine forest below the cliff where they perched.

"So you know this place." Manolis jerked his head toward the tumbled hut.

Pendlebury looked around. "Why do you think so? I've never been here."

"Let me show you something." Manolis reached into the corner of his *sakouli* and pulled out his potsherds.

Pendlebury took them and peered at them with interest. "Middle Minoan One, I'd say. This pattern's rather like some spouted jugs I've seen from Palaikastro."

"They are Minoan? Like what *o kyrios* Evans found at Knossos?"

"Alike in that they are Minoan." Pendlebury seemed unsurprised that Manolis would know of Evans and the Minoans. "Styles differ. Depending on age, of course, and where they are found. These are characteristic of East Crete, but I've recently seen similar pieces in Lasithi."

"How do you know all this?"

"Because I am an archaeologist. Should I have mentioned that earlier?" Pendlebury smiled. "Until recently I worked at Knossos, for the British School—more accurately, for Professor Evans himself—and some of what I did there was sorting through broken pots, thousands of them dug up over the years. Whole mounds of them. So this sort of thing"—he jostled the sherds in the palm of his hand—"is my business. Where did you get them?"

"Here."

"Near this *mandra?* On the surface?"

"No, inside the cave," Manolis said.

"There is a cave nearby?"

"Why did you come this way, *kyrie* Pendabri? You know this is not the path to Vianos."

Pendlebury studied the boy, intrigued. "I didn't know that. I took this path because it seemed interesting to me. Why didn't you warn me, as you said you would?"

"Because I thought you were bringing me here on purpose. I thought you knew this hut. I was born here. My mother died here."

"I've never been here, child."

"And I thought you also knew the cave where I found those *gastria,* those pieces of pot."

Pendlebury thought a moment but declined to ask why Manolis assumed all these things. "Were you also hoping these scraps of pottery are valuable? Are you hoping to sell them?"

"I would never sell them," Manolis said passionately.

"Good, because that would be illegal," Pendlebury said. "We are crossing these mountains on this fine Easter Sunday, my child, so that I can look for just such things as these *gastria,* as you call them. A nice word, peculiar to this region." He held out the sherds, and Manolis reached out to let them drop into his hand. "Frankly I did not expect to find anything this interesting until we were much lower down. It may be that you have led me to a Minoan sanctuary."

After lunch Manolis led Pendlebury to the crevice where the spring had once run copiously into his great-grandfather's stone trough. The archaeologist stuck his head inside but was unwilling to squeeze past the fallen roof block that made further exploration difficult and messy. "Certainly worth a closer look," he said as he crawled back out, rubbing his hands vigorously on the seat of his shorts, "given a bit of leisure."

Manolis said nothing; his eyes betrayed his disappointment.

"I'm planning to be back, you know. I'm making arrangements to excavate a cave in Lasithi, near Tzermiado. The home of Zeus's parents, they say—Rhea and ghastly old Kronos, Father Time, who ate his children. You know of it?"

Manolis shook his head.

"It's just a small cave, but more interesting than its myth. What I've seen on the surface there is older than what you've shown me here. I'm bringing my wife, she's an excellent excavator, and we're going to do a proper job. So you see . . ." He broke off. "As for this place—until I can give it a proper inspection, can it be our secret?"

"Everyone who knew about it is dead," Manolis said.

Pendlebury took the remark as agreement. "Right then. It's getting late. How do we get down from here?"

"From here we go down to Christos," Manolis said without evident emotion. "Unless you want to stay on the mountain tonight."

"If I had a full bottle of wine, camping on the mountain would suit me better. Alas, you must lead us to civilization."

11

In the fog, among the pines, after an hour of precipitous descent that crammed their toes into their shoes, Pendlebury called out, "Look here, Androulakis . . . this mist . . . can't see past one's nose . . . well, I'm becoming *bored*. What are we going to do about it?"

From a Greek this would have been a challenge to a contest—a shooting match or a game of dice, given the time, or perhaps a poetry match to see who could make up the bloodiest or most sentimental *mantinada*. From an Englishman, Manolis didn't know what to expect besides the obvious, that they were already in a footrace.

"Come, come," Pendlebury insisted. "You were recommended to me as quite an extraordinary specimen. I *anticipated* meeting you. Aside from some potsherds any goatherd could have stumbled upon, you haven't shown me a thing."

Manolis took the insult as part of the game and tried to sound cheerful. "What were you expecting to be shown, *kyrie?*"

"Something adept, something original. Some *spark*," said Pendlebury in a demanding tone. "What are you good at?"

Manolis was fairly certain that cheesemaking was not the

answer Pendlebury wanted. "Only a little English," he ventured, *"peu français, klein Deutsch, ligo Ellenika . . ."* He winced. *"Sygnomi,* excuse me, not Greek, only Cretan."

"A little sarcasm while we're at it?"

"I'm said to be good at mathematics, *kyrie."* If Manolis played this right, perhaps he could trick the man into a riddling game. "Perhaps you would like to test me."

For long seconds they trudged through the pine forest over rocks that crumbled and fell away downhill faster than they could walk. Neither the loose rocks nor their footfalls echoed in the insulating mist. "Well, how am I going to test you?" Pendlebury said at last. "Numbers don't interest me much, never have."

"Mathematics isn't only numbers. There is geometry; there is logic." Meaning, even an Englishman should be capable of logic. "I read this puzzle in a book: a bear walks one mile south, then one mile west, then one mile north, and ends up where she started."

"Am I supposed to tell you where she started?" Pendlebury demanded grumpily.

"No, *kyrie,* tell me what *color* is the bear."

Pendlebury charged down the narrow path with vigor, pushed through thick pine branches, and leaped over a stream just above where it became a waterfall. He turned a fierce grin on Manolis. "The bear is white!" he cried.

"Truly, she is white." Manolis suppressed his glee.

"Yes, of course. If one goes south from the North Pole, goes west, then goes north again, one returns to the North Pole. Thus a polar bear!"

"Congratulations, *kyrie.* I suppose I will have to try again."

They plummeted down the forested slope, their heavy shoes scuffing up pine needles and mud, the long-legged Pendlebury still determined to outdistance the boy, and the boy determined not to be outdistanced.

"Now tell me this, *kyrie:* a man, not a bear, walks one mile south, then one mile west, then one mile north"—his words rushed out like the stream that tumbled past them—"and ends up where he started, and he didn't start from the North Pole."

"Impossible!" Pendlebury shouted back.

"No, geometry."

As they descended the wooded slopes, slant daylight came intermittently through the blowing fog. Except for their own hard breathing and heavy footfalls they walked in silence, reaching gentler ground at last, where the grass was thick and the forest thin, the pines having been burned to make pasture.

"If you can persuade me of this man's odd walk, lad, I'll confess that you are a geometer. So far as I can imagine, there is no place between the poles and the equator that one can walk *this* way for a mile and turn at right angles and walk *that* way the same distance"—Pendlebury swung his walking stick wildly as he indicated these turns—"and then turn right again and walk *that* way the same distance, and not end up someplace different from where he started."

"I'll explain it," Manolis said fiercely. "The man isn't anywhere near the North Pole. He's close to the *South* Pole, and he walks toward it until he is *sixteen-hundredths* of a mile from the pole. Then he turns right and walks a mile, always going due west, and then"—he laughed—"and then, you see, he has made a perfect circle around the South Pole!"

Pendlebury glared, speechless.

"So, when he turns right again, he goes north, back to where he started," Manolis concluded triumphantly.

"You'll have to draw me a diagram," Pendlebury said. They went on in silence through the dissipating mist. "Anyway, you said geometry, and you brought in numbers. Sixteen-hundredths of a mile," he said with disgust. "How many feet is that?"

"A little less than eight hundred and forty-five feet—actually the man would have to turn right at eight hundred and forty feet and four inches," Manolis said, after a brief pause. "The point is, *kyrie,* that a circle of that radius has a circumference of one mile. Approximately."

"Approximately? *Hah!*"

"One mile less approximately half an inch."

Twisted masses of limestone emerged from the thinning mist; the sun shone brighter in a sky that was bluer every moment. They walked briskly across the lush meadows, green springtime fields that would turn to tinder in the dry days of summer.

"Do you know what a polar bear looks like, Androulakis?" Pendlebury demanded grumpily.

"There are no bears on Crete, *kyrie*."

"You've been to the North Pole? The South Pole?"

"Nowhere but these mountains."

"What about your family? Any polar explorers among them?"

"My grandmother is dead. She owned some almond trees in Limnakaros, but she gave them away. My grandfather died fighting the Turks. My mother died when I was born, in that hut on the ridge—there was an earthquake and the hut fell on us. My father was an Englishman."

Hearing this flat recitation, Pendlebury, no longer bored and no longer playing games, dropped his challenging tone. "Your name isn't English, lad. There aren't many English boys with your looks."

"Their marriage was a secret."

Pendlebury didn't question this improbable explanation. "What became of your father?"

"I don't know. I was hoping that you . . . that you could help me find out."

Pendlebury must have caught something in the boy's tone, for he slowed his pace so that they didn't have to shout at each other. "Not likely I would know, unless he was an archaeologist."

"He was a soldier."

"Good for him, then." He glanced at Manolis. "I'm sure I seem ancient to you, lad, if not to myself. I'm thirty-one, and I imagine your father must be rather older. You would have been six or seven years old before I ever set foot on Crete. It's not likely I met him."

Manolis said nothing, but walked along the path without seeing it, lost in thought. So Pendlebury, according to himself, could not be his father; theirs was only a chance meeting after all, to be enjoyed while it lasted, for whatever knowledge or pleasure one could extract from it.

Pendlebury too was quiet, concentrating on the path, which suddenly pitched down again and narrowed to a single cobbled lane that dropped into a sheer crevice in the mountain. The path clung precariously to the cliff; a waterfall was audible long before they could see its silvery plume across the mist-filled gorge.

The watery music was interrupted by an insect *buzz* and *splat* against the cliff wall a foot from Manolis's head. He tackled Pendlebury from behind and threw him facedown on the cobbled path as the rock dust fell and the echoing blast reached them; in the same motion he rolled sideways, unslinging his shotgun, breaking the breech, shoving in a shell, snapping it closed.

Pendlebury started to sit up. "What the devil . . . ?"

This time the *splat* came closer to Pendlebury's head than Manolis's; he ducked. "You're not going to fire that thing?" Pendlebury whispered breathlessly, incredulous. "Those paper shells are old enough to be your grandfather's."

"They were my great-grandfather's," said Manolis, taking aim.

"But you don't want to *hit* anything."

"Why not?"

"Acts have consequences, Androulakis. You can't just shoot somebody on a whim. Somebody you can't even see."

"I see him. I know him. It wouldn't bother me much if I killed him."

"Listen to me, you're a boy. This . . . incident . . . it isn't your whole life."

"All right. I'll just drop that pine branch on his head." Manolis squeezed the trigger, and the great gun roared.

"What happened?" Pendlebury said, having prudently rolled away from the explosion.

"Listen now."

A thin, scared voice echoed in the canyon, calling, "You can't even shoot."

Manolis, plucking out the spent shell and shoving in another, called back in his loud, clear mountain voice, "I'll drop some more greens on your head, if you are brave enough to stay where you are, Little Parsley." Taking aim, he fired again.

When the echoes died away, the voice that came back was thinner and more distant and more frightened yet. "You can't hit anything. Don't ever come back, you devil's spawn."

A final *splat* of shot hit the cliff wall high behind them, nowhere close, followed by a distant echoing blast. After a long pause, Pendlebury asked in a nonchalant drawl, "What do you call this sort of path?" His face was still close to the pavement.

"Kaderimi," Manolis replied.

"A Turkish word, I think, but these paved paths were here a long time before the Turks." Apparently the Englishman liked to give lectures, even under fire with an audience of one. Perhaps it was a comfort to him. "Roman citizens may have walked where we're walking now."

"I wish I had lived when they did," Manolis said. He sat up.

Pendlebury sat up after him. "Do you imagine that life was better then?"

"Yes. No priests to grab everything."

Pendlebury laughed. "No *Christian* priests. Christians, Romans, ancient Egyptians, any variety one can name, priests will grab what they can. Occasionally to good purpose, one must admit." He nodded across the gorge. "Think he's gone now?"

"Long gone, *kyrie*. He's a coward."

"So, Androulakis, you mentioned your grandmother and her father, both dead, and your mother, also dead, and your father, who seems to have vanished. Do you have any living relatives?"

"I don't know."

"Where do you live?"

"Since this morning, nowhere."

"I'm serious, lad."

"I lived in my grandmother's house, but the priest took it. This is what I own." He patted his gun and his *sakouli*.

"I see." Pendlebury stirred uneasily. "We'd better get on. We don't want to be walking in the dark." He got to his feet. "You understand you're in my employ until we reach Vianos."

Manolis, who thought this a strange thing for the man to say, stood up and plucked the smoking shell from his gun. "I'll take you to Vianos. Not for money."

Pendlebury didn't answer; he turned away and launched himself recklessly down the narrow paved path overhanging the gorge. Within a few steps he was almost running, eager to assert his immortality.

They emerged from the gorge long after the sun had passed the pine-crested cliffs. The sky to the southwest was clear and soft, hung with a handful of planets and bright stars, and everywhere there was the sound of falling water, and the night air was full of the perfume of apple and cherry blossoms. Beneath them the village of Christos clung steeply to the precipice; warm light spilled from open doors and windows, and bursts of laughter and the sawing of a *lyra* floated on the evening air.

"I know the schoolmaster here," Manolis said. "I think he will give us a place to sleep tonight."

Anne-Marie caught herself sitting braced in her chair and forced herself to relax. Young Manolis had, after all, escaped alive; the man he had become sat across from her, his dark eyes watching her in veiled amusement.

"What would have happened to you if this Pendlebury hadn't appeared when he did?" she asked. "As if on schedule."

"I suppose if space-time were configured differently, Little Parsley would have killed me. Or I would have killed one of the Louloudakises and become a fugitive. Or anything else you care to imagine. But there is only one world, the one we live in. Perhaps you've heard the saying 'Even God cannot change the past.' "

"But why would an English archaeologist take an interest in a homeless Greek villager?"

"Pendlebury's interest in me was because he was a curiosity seeker and I was a curiosity, an unschooled shepherd boy with a reputation for speaking foreign languages, rather like a talking dog—it wasn't that I did it well, it was that I did it at all. When we got to the schoolmaster's house in Christos that night, Pendlebury was of course the center of attention, but he kept prodding the poor man and his wife to talk about me, about how many books I'd read, how many languages I spoke—and then he said that while I might be famous for my erudition there in Christos, in Lasithi I was famous for my riddles. 'Have you heard the one about the bear who walked one mile south . . .' "

"Was he mocking them? Or you?"

Minakis lifted his chin twice: no and no again. "Pendlebury loved us Greeks, the people of Crete most of all. He knew just how far to go with his bragging and boasting and teasing—just as far as we would go—and we loved him for it in return. He wasn't a sentimental man, though. He was a romantic in the true sense, and something about his meeting me on Easter morning struck him as an act of fate. As apparently it strikes you."

"What would you call it, if not an act of fate?"

"I regard everything that happens in the immensity of space-time as a species of fate." He settled his thoughtful gaze upon her. "Perhaps you will come to agree with me. But in Pendlebury's case, I think he kept me around to see what would happen next."

She smiled and opened her hands, surrendering, asking without speaking, What happened next?

Minakis laughed. "The schoolmaster and his wife offered us their bed, but we insisted upon sleeping under the house with the goats. I remember being awakened to a sound I took for a windmill, but it was only Pendlebury doing his jumping jacks.

" 'Kalimera, Androulakis,' he called cheerily. He was wearing only underclothes, and I was surprised to see how smooth and brown his legs were, more like a swimmer's than a hiker's. 'Join me, why don't you? Warms the blood, limbers the muscles, tones the appetite marvelously.'

"Well, I didn't join him, but neither could I go back to sleep. Five minutes later I lifted my face from my pillow of fragrant burlap to find Pendlebury seated on a wine keg, studying me with his bright stare and lacing up his walking shoes.

" 'I've been thinking,' he said, 'about those potsherds of yours. How long have they been in your possession?'

" 'A few years.'

" 'Years! Good heavens, lad! Don't you know the law says you must immediately report any antiquities you find to the authorities?'

"He was talking about potsherds. It was such an absurdity that I sat up, wide awake at last. 'You're joking.'

" 'Deadly serious. Look here, I'm afraid you'll have to come with me to the museum in Candia. I am determined to stay on good terms with the ephor of Crete—a very excitable fellow, name's Marinatos. I'll do what I can for you. Nevertheless you'd better be prepared to throw yourself on his mercy.'

"Pendlebury seemed mightily pleased with himself, making a citizen's arrest in a country of which he was not a citizen. But I had no objection. For one thing, I'd never been to Kastro, which foreigners called Candia. For another, I'd never seen a museum.

" 'You'll give yourself up without a struggle, then? Right . . . *Oh.*' Pendlebury winced as if a complication had just occurred to him. 'One wrinkle. I'd planned to spend a day or two investigating the coast south of Vianos. I'm afraid I'll have to keep you with me. Since you're under duress there's no question of my not paying for your time.'

"I managed to produce a frown at the prospect of earning money for nothing, and told Pendlebury to do what his conscience required of him.

"We pried ourselves away from the schoolmaster and his wife, who loaded our *sakoulis* with boiled red eggs and sugary bread and withered oranges, and soon we were racing each other across the wooded slopes toward Vianos, first one of us in front, then the other, leaping the occasional boulder or fallen tree with hardly a break in stride. I felt a swelling ecstasy unlike anything I had known since I was a little boy, unlike anything since those wild and childish days when my ignorance gave me the illusion of freedom. . . ."

12

Everywhere we went on the coast south of Dikti, Pendlebury made friends with the villagers, inspecting the antiquities they showed him and prospecting for himself—his one good eye could spot a bit of painted pottery sticking out of the soil ten feet away." Minakis began clicking his worry beads in quick-march time. "For days we raced up and down the dry red cliffs until he satisfied himself that he'd seen as much as could be seen on the run. When we retreated to Vianos, I thought my time in his company was coming to an end.

"He installed us under an enormous plane tree in the village square and allowed the locals to ply us with food and wine while he scribbled in his notebook—odd to watch a big man write such a tiny hand, but paper was worth something in those days. Along with his notes he scratched out maps indicating routes and walking times, drawing shorelines and craggy mountains so quickly it was clear that he'd been doing this for years, that maps of Crete were second nature to him.

"He had the gift of concentration. The villagers pelted him with questions, but he left me to do the talking and refused to linger when he was done with his work, telling them that there

was an urgent need to take his companion—me, that is—to
Candia, where I had an appointment with the ephor.

" '*Asteievasai!* You're joking, that's impossible, nobody
could walk to Kastro in less than a day!' they shouted after us,
as we raced away at our usual ankle-breaking pace.

"An hour later we were in country I'd never seen, and when
night fell we were still walking, up hills and down into
streambeds and up hills again, enough to make me lose my
sense of direction. Villages came into view, with lamps flickering in the windows of the houses; I lost myself in reveries of the
warmth and laughter and caring and tenderness of the families
who lived in them. I'd never known such families, but it seemed
a pleasant thing to imagine.

"Meanwhile I was trudging along behind this unyielding
Pendlebury, a sort of Bronze Man like the legendary Talos who
could circle the island of Crete three times in a day. It was long
after dark when he called back to me, 'Looks like we're not
going to make it to Candia after all,' his voice full of amusement. 'I know some people who live nearby. Maybe they will
give us a place to sleep tonight.'

"I had no idea what was so funny.

"We crossed a stream on a low stone bridge. A mass of dark
buildings without a single light showing covered the hilltop to
the right. I assumed it was an abandoned Muslim village, a
place of ghosts. Across the road, at the end of a long wall covered with vines, was an iron gate; Pendlebury pushed it open as
casually as if he owned the place.

"A house stood inside the wall. Pendlebury ran up the steps
to a veranda in back, waving at me to follow. He threw open the
door and shouted, 'Hilda! I'm home.'

"I was stuck behind him when he stopped in the doorway."
Minakis laughed at the memory. "It wasn't until he got out of
my way that I saw the ancient woman inside, swathed in layers
of starched cotton, enthroned on a chair with embroidered
cushions—and beside her, struggling to get up from a sofa with
little napkins on its arms, a man about as old as Pendlebury but
whose skin was as smooth as I had ever seen on an adult; on
this warm spring night he was wearing a necktie and a dark

blazer with a university crest embroidered on his breast pocket. Intending to surprise me, Pendlebury had surprised himself. These were the Hutchinsons, mother and son, and apparently it had slipped his mind that they were living in his house—that in fact it was now *their* house.

"Hutchinson and his mother were both as tall as Pendlebury, and I was convinced the English were a race of giants. When Pendlebury presented me to Mrs. Hutchinson I transferred my shotgun to my left hand, lunged into the room, and grabbed the woman's hand in mine and began pumping it up and down; my first attempt to pronounce 'Hutchinson' came out something like 'Shuckingzon.' She yanked her fingers to her bosom and said rather edgily, 'Charmed, I'm sure.'

"Then Pendlebury introduced her son, 'the Squire,' and told me he was the curator of Knossos, a term which meant nothing to me. Meanwhile he kept a grip on my elbow and tugged my hand away from the Squire's when I latched on to it, at the same time gently relieving me of my shotgun. I didn't try to pronounce Hutchinson again, but I did tell the Squire, 'Charmed, I'm sure.'

"Another woman came into the room, and catching sight of her, I forgot my English entirely.

" 'This is my wife, Hilda, the very fine archaeologist of whom I spoke.' Pendlebury's chest swelled up like a rock dove's with pride. Indeed, she was quite the most entrancing human being I had ever set eyes upon, small and dark, with pale skin but a bright smile. Compared to the Hutchinsons, I found her merely human scale a comfort. Having mastered the business of hand shaking, I took hers firmly but did not cling to it.

"She wished me a good evening. 'You could hardly have given my husband a better gift than to show him a new route over Dikti,' she said, and before I knew it she was sending us off to bathe, having relieved us of our weapons. . . .

"Despite my protests—and a moment of real fear— Pendlebury made me go first into that tin tub, which a servant woman had filled with hot water. I was accustomed to washing myself a handful of water at a time. I'd never taken my clothes

off to bathe, and no one but my grandmother had ever seen me
naked, and then only when I was an infant.

"Warm water, I quickly discovered, is narcotic. I lay there
outrageously exposed, trying to make sense of a day that had
begun on the familiar slopes of Dikti and ended in this strange
house. There was no sense to be made; it was surely a dream.
If life was sweet this moment, it had been sweet before, every
moment of sweetness preceded and followed by bitterness; it
was the bitterness that defined the sweetness, and the other way
around. Still, here was *this* moment. Best not to spoil it. The
water was warm, the soap was scented with flowers. . . .

" 'Out of there, Androulakis. It's my turn. Quick, quick, or
we'll miss a hot supper.'

"He towered over me as I stood up streaming out of the tub,
shocked awake and panicked by my own nakedness and by his.

" 'Clothes in the next room,' he said. 'Put them on.'

"I had never seen anything so fine as the dining table around
which the adults were gathered, the wine red cloth set with
painted plates and cups and bowls of steaming food, lit by tall
candles and with a centerpiece of purple irises. Mrs.
Hutchinson looked hungry enough to eat a donkey; they'd been
waiting for Pendlebury the whole long day.

"When he finally appeared, fresh from his bath and dressed
in crisp khaki trousers and a white shirt, they almost cheered.
He paused a moment, preening. His sun-bleached hair, wet
from the tub, was slicked back along his scalp, its natural wave
lending him the aspect of a *kouros*—an impression not at all
discouraged by his enigmatic smirk and the crystalline gleam
of his glass eye. He knew he was the focus of attention, and he
loved it. . . .

"The moment is vivid in my memory, yet I am ashamed to
tell you that I don't remember a word of what was discussed
around the table that night—although the history of archaeology would no doubt be richer if I could. I was enthralled, overwhelmed; I did not even take my hands out of my lap until I
saw all the others take up their soup spoons, and then I did as
they did, following their every maneuver, while the talk contin-

ued with no sign that any of them noticed me or my silence. All I can say for myself is that I didn't fall asleep before the main course. . . ."

Manolis awoke early the next morning and found himself on the sitting-room sofa, covered by a thin wool blanket. After a disoriented moment he remembered where he was and why he was wearing odd trousers. They were British trousers. The people who lived here had lent them to him.

They were kind people, but their solicitousness was excessive and alien; he felt constricted by the too-plentiful furniture in the room, by its fulsome decoration, the painted lampshades, the pictures of strange ruins in desert lands hanging on the walls, the folds of printed cloth that covered the windows. He kicked off the clinging blanket, found the door, and opened it to the morning air.

The terrace was surrounded by a garden, planted with fragrant jasmine and red hibiscus and pink oleander, overshadowed by palm trees and pines, with dewdrops trembling on every petal and leaf. Doves mused among the branches and waddled in couples along the path. Farther along, Manolis could see a bigger house of an unfamiliar style of architecture—fieldstone blocks set in mortar, overgrown with wisteria vines.

Down the path, the iron gate that he and Pendlebury had entered last night stood ajar. He went through it, pausing to seek his bearings before crossing the dusty road into the shadow of the pines whose masses of perfumed needles sifted the morning air. He was puzzled to find the ruined village he'd seen the night before cut off from the road by a high wire fence. He walked fifty meters along it until he found a locked gate. After a moment's consideration and a glance up and down the road, he climbed the fence and dropped into the enclosure.

What he came to first under the pines was a shrouded columnar shape as high as a roadside shrine, wrapped in a canvas sheet. He'd never seen anything like it, and he might have lingered to investigate but for the more enticing mystery that lay just beyond: walls and pillars, some fallen, some built recently but left unfinished, not like any abandoned village.

He walked past ancient walls made of enormous stones scarred by fire . . . paving flags and free-standing blocks of gypsum that looked to have melted in the rain like sugar lumps . . . pillars of modern concrete painted red and white and black, tapering downward, with narrow bases and swelling capitals that supported fragments of roof and passageway. . . .

He followed a passage to the right and found himself on a porch high above a brook, the one he and Pendlebury had crossed in the night. Ruined buildings with inverted columns littered the slopes of the gully below, thrown into stark relief by the morning light. The hillside opposite the stream was covered with rows of grapevines, their spring leaves translucent in the sun; farther away, a solitary peak rose from the jumbled hills and caught the same light. As if to frame that distant peak, a sculpture of ancient stone and modern concrete, an enormous rack of bull's horns, was set at the edge of the terrace.

On a restored wall nearby were big framed pictures, life-sized men with broad shoulders and narrow waists, carrying jars and vases; they were wearing only short aprons or straps around their loins, and their long black hair was decorated with plumes and flowers. And there were women with the same almond eyes and curling black hair, whose dresses covered their arms and shoulders with flounces but left their breasts bare. The wall pictures were patchy, as if parts of them were older, or were meant to seem older, but ancient or modern they were nothing like religious icons, the only pictures Manolis knew besides muddy photographs and illustrations in borrowed books.

What Manolis had thought was a village covered many times the area of Ayia Kyriaki; unlike any village he knew, the wrecked buildings on the hilltop were all perfect rectangles, all connected to one another as if the whole complex was a single structure. In the center was the biggest of the rectangles, an open courtyard with the remains of walls and colonnades on three sides.

The wall paintings confirmed what he had suspected when

he saw that first downward-tapering pillar. This was Knossos, the very Knossós that Sir Arthur Evans had dug out of the ground a third of a century ago, rebuilding it as he uncovered it. This was the palace of Minos, the heart of the Minoan empire; this was the labyrinth. Theseus of Athens had come here in chains, had made love to the princess Ariadne, had escaped with her and later abandoned her, but not before she had helped him slaughter the Minotaur.

All this Manolis had read in the books he had borrowed from every schoolteacher within a day's walk of Limnakaros.

Last night he had stayed in the home of the curator of Knossos. Whatever the title meant, perhaps it meant someone who could explain these wonders.

First he would have his fill of them. . . .

For an hour he climbed over the walls of the palace; descended a pillared staircase, winding down three stories of a light well to frescoed rooms below; studied pipes and channels that brought water inside the rooms and carried it out again—plumbing which did not exist in the villages of Dikti—and stood amazed before giant jars, their shape as familiar to him as the jars that stood in his grandmother's courtyard, as ordinary as the broken jar that was the chimney on the roof of her house, but half again as tall as he was and more than three thousand years old. He poked into airy living rooms and shadowy throne rooms, into dark chambers with massive square pillars engraved with the sign of the double ax, into basement store-rooms now open to the sky and lined with rows of even bigger jars.

Beneath the palace's reconstructed upper stories, locked behind wire-mesh screens, he found wooden trays full of broken pottery. Hundreds of boxes were stacked atop one another, all bearing neat labels, many in a spidery hand Manolis recognized as Pendlebury's. Manolis tried to picture the man who loved to run up and down mountains sitting quietly for hours poking through innumerable bits of broken jar and cup.

As he was trying to decipher the labels through the wire mesh, a shadow fell in the passageway. A man stood at the end of the narrow corridor; in a voice rough with age he demanded,

"What are you doing here, young man? Thinking of abscond-
ing with those potsherds?"

"*Sygnomi*, I am . . ."

"You are the famous potsherd thief John warned me of." The
man approached, wielding a thick cane. He was shorter than
Hilda Pendlebury, older than Mrs. Hutchinson, the shortest,
oldest Englishman Manolis had seen yet, with bright eyes, a
grizzled mustache, and a felt hat smashed down on his head,
dressed in a wool suit as rough as sacking. "You're trespassing
here. You're up to no good."

"My name is Manolis, I am—"

"*Another* Manolis. What am I going to do with all you
Manolises?" the irate little Englishman demanded.

"*O kyrios* Pendabri brought me here. . . ."

"You mean to say John *Pendlebury*."

"*Nai*, Pendabri."

"Pendle-*bury*. Oh, never mind. He intends to take you into
Candia, he told me. Couldn't find you; thought you'd made a
dash for it."

"Sir?"

"Well, what *are* you doing here?"

"Looking," Manolis replied. "This is Knossos."

The man squinted, his woolly brows fretting. "So it is."

"I have read about it. About King Minos and about Sir Arthur
Evans. When I saw that I was here, I wanted to explore."

"You have let yourself into the labyrinth, child."

"I knew it when I saw it."

"Did you?" The old man's mustache twitched. "Time and
again, earthquake and fire have brought these buildings low.
What you see here is only a fragment of a fragment of what
once stood here, and even the fragments are artificially linked.
How can you understand what you are looking at? How can any
of us?"

"I don't understand anything, sir. I'm only looking."

"You need a clew, child, such as Theseus had—Ariadne's
thread, that he took into the labyrinth to lead him out again.
Didn't John tell you he had written a guidebook to the place,
when he was curator?"

Pendabri had been a curator here? "*O kyrios* Pendabri didn't talk much about himself."

"Only talked about your potsherds, eh? Well, go on back now, he's waiting for you. Worried you haven't had your breakfast."

Manolis was eager to obey, but the unmoving little Englishman was blocking the way out. Manolis got up the courage to squeeze past him; once past, he turned back. "I wasn't stealing potsherds, sir. I'm not a thief."

"Aren't you?" The man raised a bristling eyebrow. "We're all thieves in this pursuit. Even if all we steal is time."

Manolis hesitated, not sure he understood the meaning of the English words. "How are you called, sir?"

"I'm called Arthur Evans, when they speak plainly of me." The man waved his cane imperiously. "Go on, child; go on back."

"So little Arthur caught you in the palace?" Pendlebury grinned knowingly at Manolis, meanwhile bouncing his happy three-year-old son upon his knee. Freshly shaved and wearing a cotton shirt with every wrinkle ironed out of it, surrounded by his family in the sunny garden of the house he called the Taverna, he was no longer an archaic *kouros* but quite the new man, a strictly modern European. "Were you really trying to get at the sherds?"

"I was only looking at them through the wire," said Manolis.

"Don't tease him, John," Hilda said. "A joke can go too far." She held her fretting baby girl to her shoulder, shading the girl's head with her palm.

"Androulakis is not a child, my dear. He stands up for himself quite well." If Hilda expected to hear more, Pendlebury disappointed her. He set their son on the ground and reached for an orange slice, leaning forward to let the juice spill on the flagstones. Meanwhile the boy spotted a fat green lizard and set off chasing it into the garden.

"Will you have some more fruit, Manolis?" Hilda asked. "Some more yogurt, perhaps?"

To show his gratitude to Hilda he would have eaten anything

she offered, but his overfull stomach threatened to cramp. "Thank you, Mrs. Pendabri, I have had a sufficiency."

Pendlebury suddenly stood up, grabbed a napkin from the table, dabbed it at his chin, and quickly tossed it aside. "Sir Arthur," he called, as the vigorous old man strode up the drive past the garden. "Will you join us for coffee?"

"Kind of you to ask, John. Good morning, Hilda," Evans said, doffing his hat.

"Good morning, Sir Arthur."

"No coffee, thank you, but I'll sit a moment." Evans climbed the garden steps. "No, you stay," he said firmly to Manolis, who had gotten out of his chair and was sidling away. "You're a growing boy. Eat your breakfast." Evans perched himself in the chair Pendlebury pulled out for him and cast a regal eye over the family scene, waiting for someone to address him.

Hilda was the first. "Have you seen the bust yet?" she cheerfully inquired.

Evans shook his head. "Wouldn't dare to peek under those sheets, shiver to think of looking at my own brazen image. I was in the metropolitan's office half the afternoon yesterday, but they won't be dissuaded from a public unveiling. He says we can expect over a thousand people! What am I going to feed them?"

"I believe you can rest easy, Sir Arthur," Hilda said. "Kostis and the others have been bringing in food for days."

"Ah, well." Under his brows, Evans's eyes were gleaming with amusement. He turned his attention to Manolis. "Then there's our young linguist and geometer and pottery fancier. He's already let himself into the palace."

"So he has confessed," Pendlebury said.

"Since that's the case, he certainly ought to have a look at what we've taken *out* of the palace."

"Yes, it's high time Androulakis and I were off to beard the ephor in his museum," said Pendlebury, jumping up again and straightening his shirtsleeves. "Don't forget those sherds of yours," he said to Manolis, "they're material evidence."

"Surely you're not planning to walk!" Evans feigned surprise, and Hilda smothered a giggle.

"It's less than three miles," Pendlebury said defensively.

"You'll ride with me," Evans declared. "I have business in town this morning. Walk back, if you feel the need to stretch your legs."

A long black shining automobile with running boards and a canvas roof rolled down the path, its fat tires popping the gravel. "Climb in here, John," Evans called from the back seat, leaning to open the door. "You sit up front, Androulakis. View's better from there."

Once through the gate, the car rapidly picked up speed. Between Knossos and Kastro the dry hills were green with leafy vineyards and flowering orchards. Manolis sat upright beside the driver, fascinated by the scenery tearing past at a fantastic rate, perhaps as much as twenty-five miles per hour. In the leather-upholstered back seat Sir Arthur, tiny to begin with and further shrunken by his eighty-four years, sank deep into the cushions, while Pendlebury hunched over to keep from hitting the canvas roof with his head.

"Athens was all aflutter," Evans was saying. "There's no doubt many quite moderate people have been shut away, on the excuse that they had something to do with the revolt. I was treated grandly at first—then almost prevented from getting on the boat in Piraeus."

"You must take action, sir," said the driver, breaking in, eyeing Evans in the rearview mirror. "The fleet is in mutiny. In the east they are shooting the *palikaria!*"

"I'd be much less apprehensive if you would watch where you are going, Kostis," Evans said crossly. "We can discuss the political scene later, if we must."

The honey-colored fortress walls of the city soon came into view. The road crossed a dry moat on a stone ramp and entered under a massive gate. The car was instantly surrounded by a crush of people and pushcarts and laden donkeys and overladen lorries; when Kostis tried to turn he was furiously waved off by a policeman standing in front of a barricade where workmen were digging up the pavement.

The black limousine moved on slowly, past Turkish houses

with overhanging wooden balconies, past the teeming market, its stalls piled high with fresh goods—glowing oranges, piles of fish the color of new-minted coins, skinned rabbits whose purple flesh was gaily decorated with tufts of fur on ears and tail. . . .

They inched past a square graced by a Venetian fountain, then turned through narrow back streets to another square overlooking the sea. Here a new concrete building was set hard against the old stone ramparts among plantings of palms and figs intended to mask its impertinent modernity. Kostis pulled the limousine to the curb.

"We dismount here," Pendlebury said to Manolis, as he opened the car door and unfolded himself from the back seat. "Thank you, Sir Arthur."

Evans smiled impishly. "Please convey my respects to the ephor."

As Evans drove off in his black chariot, Pendlebury led Manolis across the raw garden and through the tall doors of the museum. Inside, he gave the guard a friendly greeting; to Manolis he said, "Go wherever you want in here, but stay where I can find you. Oh, and let me have those sherds."

Manolis handed them over, and Pendlebury left him alone to wander the sunlit halls.

Disoriented, Manolis entered the first room. Low glass cases, wood framed and brassbound, stood in the middle of the wide floor, and taller cases stood against the cream-colored walls. The paper labels on the artifacts were handwritten in Greek, some in English and German and French and Italian as well, informing the visitor that these were Neolithic and Early Minoan finds, none of them younger than four thousand years old and many of them twice that age. Manolis was entranced by the clay models displayed in the tall cases, rough little pinched-out figures, full of life, which he took for children's toys. One showed three men wrestling with a bull, hanging haphazardly from its horns.

In the next room there were carved stone and molded clay figures, painted cups and vases, and tiny gemstones incised with strange scenes and mysterious picture writing. . . . These were a little less ancient, only thirty-seven hundred years old.

In each room, the dates decreased by a century or two and the wonders multiplied: two figurines of crowned women in full skirts, their breasts bare, their arms writhing with snakes. A clay disk stamped with spiraling hieroglyphs. Vessels in the shape of bulls' heads and lions' heads and giant seashells carved from hard black-and-white stone. Bronze cauldrons, bronze swords, bronze saw blades big enough to cut down cypress trees; heavy bronze axes sharp enough to hew house beams and ship keels; thin gold double axes for worship and ceremony; a multitude of clay leaves, burned reddish black, incised with an unreadable script. Burial tubs—in the Greek of the labels, these were called *larnakes*—made from intricately painted clay but shaped exactly like the zinc tub in which Manolis had had his first bath last night.

In every room, exuberantly sculpted and painted pottery, from giant storage jars to rotund pitchers wriggling with painted octopuses to delicate cups decorated with abstract designs in black and white and red . . .

Upstairs, the walls were devoted to murals: the Priest King (as the label called him) with his plumed headdress, the bare-breasted ladies of the palace, an astonishing depiction of acrobats playing with a bull—a girl grasping the enormous forward-thrusting curve of the horns, a boy doing a handstand on the animal's back, another girl standing behind the beast, ready to catch her flying comrade.

The reproductions in Knossos were flat copies; these had dimension and texture, their molded plaster bulging like flesh, but even these looked artificially new.

Not all of them were heavily restored. Manolis was taken by a small fragment of a fresco, repaired but wholly original, showing a big-eyed, red-lipped, impish young woman wearing a curious knot in her curly black hair.

While he studied it, Pendlebury came into the empty gallery. "I'm afraid it's bad news, Androulakis," he said, radiating mischief.

Manolis took in Pendlebury's expression and sighed, straight-faced. "So it's prison for me."

Pendlebury laughed, beaten to his punch line. "Not just yet. But the ephor says he has all the Middle Minoan *gastria* he needs right now, and there's no room for these in the museum." Pendlebury held out his hand, offering Manolis the sherds. "You'll have to keep them."

"Mm." Manolis pocketed the fragments. "I understand. The museum does seem very full."

"Always room for the unexpected. I aspire to add a few items to the collection myself."

"What I've seen, the Minoans were great . . . a great . . ." Manolis hesitated; he had never before been confronted by such an abyss of time, such evidence of vanished exuberance and vitality as he had found in this building, where the dead seemed more alive than the living in his own village.

When it was evident that he could not finish his sentence, Pendlebury came to his aid. "Any thinking person must stand in awe of that energetic and inventive race. But did you know, Androulakis, that most of what you see here was collected only since the beginning of this century? For hundreds of years before that, no one bothered to look even an inch under the ground—because of sloth and ignorance and superstition. All those Crusaders. All those Turks. Then in just five years, Sir Arthur uncovered Knossos. And meanwhile Halbherr was digging at Phaestos, and Miss Boyd was digging at Gournia, and the French and the Greeks were active too; the excavations at Malia, where they found the marvelous golden pendant with the bees—did you see it?—those were begun even during the Great War. We've hardly skimmed the surface. It costs more to dig now, of course, and there is rather less money to go around. But there is so much yet to find."

"Your life must be exciting, *kyrie,* to be able to find such treasures," Manolis said quietly. *Of course he had seen the bee pendant. Who could have missed it?*

"It's not the treasures, it's the knowledge. Look at this amazing girl," Pendlebury said, turning to the small fresco. "Sir Arthur named her *la Parisienne,* I suppose because Parisian girls were wearing their hair that way at the turn of the century, or because Parisian girls have always seemed a bit saucy to us English. She's alive. She's almost four thousand years old, but she's alive today, because of the spirit and skill that guided the hand that painted her." Pendlebury's bright gaze turned upon Manolis again. "And her blood is in your veins."

Manolis was astonished. "Those people were not like us," he said, thinking of the bare-breasted women and the men with their bare torsos and long hair and feathers.

"They were your ancestors."

"That can't be."

"Oh, you had other ancestors, Mycenaeans and Dorian Greeks and Romans and Byzantines and Saracens and Franks and so on. You're a mathematician, Androulakis, you tell me how many generations separate you from this woman. But I've studied you living Minoans, with your wide shoulders and your narrow waists and your dark grace and your laughter; I've seen you in every part of this island, which has always been your home."

"Approximately two hundred generations." Manolis's attention had drifted while he calculated; there was something comforting about labeling that gulf of years with a number. "Fifty-seven lifetimes."

Pendlebury smiled. "Yes. Thank you."

"You said it was four thousand years since this woman was alive. Assuming twenty years for a generation, seventy years for a lifetime . . ."

"Yes, Androulakis, I believe you."

Manolis refocused his attention on the little fresco. "*Was* she my ancestor?"

"Our business here is done," Pendlebury said; "it's time we got back to Knossos. Feel like a short stroll?"

Manolis grinned. "I'll race you."

13

On Mykonos the sun was high and the light was fierce, even in the flickering shade of the eucalyptus that overhung the little square. Minakis leaned away from his demitasse, which had only a smear of oily grounds left in it, and looked at his watch. "It's after eleven. You'll be getting hungry soon," he said to Anne-Marie.

"Perhaps *you* are getting hungry."

He smiled. "Perhaps. Before lunch, I intend to hear your husband's talk"—he searched the square for the waiter—"*Garzon! To logariazmo*—and afterward, we can attack the buffet at the villa. It really is far superior to anything we can get in town."

The waiter trotted to their table, adding up the bill. While Minakis reached into his jacket for his billfold, Anne-Marie drew a large, colorful banknote from her purse and put it on the table. He pushed it back. "I won't accept your money."

"Then the waiter will get a very big tip."

Minakis saw that she was serious. "I suppose things are done differently these days"—he took her bill and replaced it with a sheaf of smaller bills of different colors, pushing her change across the table—"and of course it would be a profound ontological error, not to mention a social error, to become mired in the past."

She brushed the hair from her eyes. "You're not mired in the past, Professor Minakis, you're reviewing it at my request."

"And flattered to be asked. But do call me Manoli."

They made their way through loud and crowded narrow streets, hemmed in by whitewashed walls and jostled by tourists, passing shop fronts that displayed bronze utensils and bright woven fabrics, gauzy shifts and blue-striped shirts and flimsy sandals, and postcards by the thousands—most of them scenic, many of them prurient, ancient Dionysian orgies painted on vases alongside modern Nordic nudes photographed live.

Minakis cut a path through the crowds as easily as if he were walking through a flock of sheep in a mountain pasture, with Anne-Marie following closely in his wake. It was a relief to reach the harbor, where the crowd dispersed over the broad quays.

They walked along the quay, past the crowded fishing boats and tourist craft. A white motor yacht lay moored by its stern in the Mediterranean fashion, its gangplank obscuring its name. Minakis took no notice of the boats; he resumed his story without slowing his pace. "Sir Arthur's big affair came the day after my visit to the museum. At midmorning the metropolitan arrived in golden robes and led him to the West Court of Knossos with lesser priests going before, swinging their censers and chanting. I tagged along in the train.

"Thousands of people were waiting, enough to repopulate the ruins—clustered on the ancient walls, hanging from the branches of the pine trees—some who'd started celebrating early were already falling into the ancient trash pits. The bronze was unveiled to wild applause. You've seen it: Sir Arthur guarding his labyrinth, an old man with a stern gaze and big ears and an aggressive necktie—not so much a portrait as a sketch in metal, much too modern for its subject, who was a thoroughgoing Victorian though he lived forty years into this century.

"I made no aesthetic judgments at the time, however. What a *glendi,* what a party it was! More people than I had seen in my life, all in one place on one day! They put a laurel wreath on Sir Arthur's head. 'So far indeed, as the explorer may have attained success,' he intoned, 'it has been as the humble instrument, inspired and guided by a greater Power.' Purest poppycock, but perfectly suited to the occasion.

"Afterward he entertained dozens of dignitaries in his villa, spending more money on food and drink in an afternoon than had been exchanged in Ayia Kyriaki since I was born. I was in the presence of the gods, and they were English. Pendlebury was my Apollo. Evans was my Zeus."

Minakis and Anne-Marie had reached the end of the quay. High above them, across a two-lane road busy with traffic, sprawled the gleaming white villa that housed the Delos II conference, crowning the dry slopes that overlooked the harbor. They dashed across the road between cars. Minakis began the steep climb without hesitation, his strides lengthening as the angle of the slope increased, and Anne-Marie struggled to keep up.

"That was to be Sir Arthur's final visit to Crete, the place that had made his reputation, the place he had put on the world-historical map. The next time I spoke to him we were in a different country. We might as well have been in a different century. . . ."

A few days after the festivities at Knossos, the Pendleburys and the Hutchinsons joined Sir Arthur for luncheon on the terrace of the Villa Ariadne, at a long table under the wisteria trellis.

Manolis had grown increasingly uncertain about his role in the affairs of the Knossos establishment. He hadn't been invited to Sir Arthur's luncheon—which would have terrified him—but his offers to help were ignored by the household staff. He hovered in the shadows inside the passageway to the kitchen, trying to stay out of the way of Kostis and old Maria as they trundled in and out, serving bowls of olives and garlicky yogurt and cheese-filled pastries and baked tomatoes stuffed with spicy rice and ground lamb.

Sir Arthur's store of cold champagne fueled the talk around

the table. He was an imperious host, with a store of scandalous anecdotes about the local authorities which he dared his guests to deny, or better yet to corroborate. "Of course you know the Greeks are ever more insistent that we drop the name Candia and call the place Iraklion, Mrs. Pendlebury," Sir Arthur demanded of Hilda, baiting her, "after Herakles, who I believe once paid a brief visit."

She declined to rise. "Iraklion has been the official name of Candia for a dozen years now," Hilda said mildly, "and no one I know pays the slightest attention."

Her husband, never one to avoid an argument, took up the gauntlet. "I don't blame the Greeks for preferring Herakles to the Arabic *khandak,* which means 'ditch,' after all. Would you name a castle for its moat?"

"Let them call it what they have always called it, John, Megalo Kastro," Evans returned. "Surely 'Big Castle' is sufficiently grand for anyone."

"That is a corruption of the Italian," Mrs. Hutchinson put in, "and from everything *I* have heard, the Venetians were a greater scourge upon Crete than the Turks."

"Perhaps they were, Mrs. Hutchinson," Evans replied, "but it is to the Venetians that the Cretans owe what notice they have deserved for most of the last two thousand years. I except El Greco, who at any rate preferred to live among Spaniards, but genius sprouts randomly and is always wild. I mean that the Venetians' principal business on Crete was the export of fruits preserved in sugar, known as products of Candia and therefore as 'candy.' Thus a new word entered the English language."

"So when we eat candy, we are eating something named after an Arab ditch," said Mrs. Hutchinson haughtily. "Frankly, Sir Arthur, I would have preferred not to have known."

Evans was flustered for an instant; then he laughed, delighted. "Quite right, Mrs. Hutchinson. I should not have raised the subject during luncheon."

Manolis, listening in the shadows, heard them talking about Crete the way they might have talked about their children, at once condescending and proud—as if they had invented the place for themselves. It had never occurred to him that he had a right to be proud of his homeland; he only knew, from his grandmother's tales, never questioning what she told him, that the people of Crete had struggled for centuries to be free of foreign control.

Old Maria came past, on her way from the terrace to the kitchen, and thrust a depleted bowl of stuffed aubergines at him. "Eat this, boy. You don't have to starve while you listen."

He took the bowl with a whispered *"Efharisto"* and began to eat, slickening his fingers with oil as he devoured the cold vegetables and bent his ear to the conversation of the English.

Sometime later, when Sir Arthur grew tired and excused himself to take a nap, Maria and the kitchen boy hurried to clear away the dishes. On an impulse, Manolis went out to help them.

"Androulakis! Wait here a moment. We've something to say to you," Pendlebury commanded.

The Pendleburys' and Hutchinsons' eyes were all upon him. The Squire was the first to speak, waiting until Maria and the boy had gone inside. "I'm told you're an orphan, lad."

Manolis fidgeted. What could he add to that plain truth?

"Not our business, of course. Can't adopt every homeless boy on Crete," Pendlebury put in gruffly. "But you seem to have a bit of promise. . . ."

"My husband means to say that he admires your exceptional intelligence, Manolis, which is widely reported, and which led him to you in the mountains," Hilda Pendlebury said gently, "and moreover that he admires your spirit."

"Well, of course that, yes," Pendlebury harrumphed. "You're a damned good shot with that old blunderbuss. And you're rather good with numbers."

"He means to say that he rather *likes* you," Hilda continued, "as do I. And he and I would like to do something to help you, in view of your present difficulties. If you will accept our help."

Manolis, having no idea what to say, said nothing.

"We're not here all year, you know," said Pendlebury. "Only a few months in the spring." He studied his glass, half full of warm champagne, and thoughtfully tossed it down.

The Squire said, "My mother and I are here rather longer during the year. We too would be glad to help."

For a moment they were all silent. Then Mrs. Hutchinson spoke up, her voice creaking. "Well, young man, if I were you, I would say, 'Thank you very much.' You don't want us all changing our minds, do you?"

"No, Mrs. Hutchinson," Manolis said. "I mean yes, I do thank you all very much indeed. But I don't understand."

"We have to work out the details, you see," said the Squire. "But in general, we thought we might employ you when we can, during the season . . ."

"The time when we excavate, the spring and early summer," Hilda explained.

". . . and put you in school when we can't employ you," the Squire concluded. "There's a rather good school in Candia."

"In Iraklion," Mrs. Hutchinson said firmly.

"In the city, yes. Provided you lived with one of the families here in Knossos, that is."

"Here? They would have me?" Manolis glanced toward the kitchen door.

"They work for the British School." Pendlebury grinned his fierce, condescending grin. "What's another Manolis to them?"

"And so, before the Pendleburys left Crete that summer, a place was found for me with one of the Manolises. With Manolis Akoumianakis, to be precise, known to everyone as Manolakis—who was the foreman of Knossos."

Minakis and Anne-Marie had reached the top of their steep climb. He breathed as easily as if he'd been for a stroll on the beach; Anne-Marie, coming up beside him, gasped for air. He admired the roadside asphodels while he waited for her to catch her breath.

"How did he feel about that?" Anne-Marie asked, between lungfuls. "Your foster father, I mean." Sweat beaded her hairline, and her pale eyes were mirrors in the heat.

"Manolakis and his wife had three sons and a daughter—also a niece who was living with them—who accepted me quite matter-of-factly. There is no such thing as a Greek who is not ruled by curiosity, but we knew better than to inquire too deeply into our mutual good fortune: I didn't ask where they got the money for my keep, and they never referred to it."

"What did you say, when they asked why you were there?"

Minakis grinned. "Something about a liking for potsherds."

Seeing that Anne-Marie had gotten her wind back, he started walking toward the villa. The driveway was a strip of fresh asphalt bordered by fieldstone walls and oleander bushes, leading through dry fields to the mansion's iron gates.

"Potsherds! They all had a good laugh at that. Old man Manolakis—I called him Uncle—told me about his first job at Knossos: when he was a boy he'd walked over Ida carrying bags of cherries to sell in Candia. That was in 1900, when Evans had just started to dig. Manolakis wasn't much interested in going back to his village, and he wangled a job washing potsherds. It didn't take long for Evans to see that he was good at recognizing what bits went with other bits. First he was promoted to chief potsherd washer. Then he became foreman of the whole dig. Here was I, boasting of my liking for potsherds to a man who was a potsherd virtuoso."

"Did that embarrass you?"

"In those days I assumed *everybody* knew more about *everything* than I did." Minakis smiled at the memory. "I had only two responsibilities. One was to vindicate the Pendleburys' faith in me by excelling in schoolwork—me, who'd attended school less than a week in my life. The other was to earn my keep. To do that I had to learn some archaeology."

They had come to the iron gate, which stood ajar. The watchman had vanished, having succumbed to hunger or the drowsy heat. Minakis looked at his watch. "With luck your husband is saving the best of his talk for last."

"I've heard it before," Anne-Marie said. "So, I suspect, have you. I'll join you later."

"Be sure not to miss the buffet. Here on Olympus the menu is nectar and ambrosia—almost as good as what Sir Arthur used to serve." He was smiling, but there was an edge to his voice.

Anne-Marie hesitated, puzzled, before she nodded. She turned and left him watching after her as she hurried down the path among the silvery young olive trees.

14

You all know Peter Slater," said the profusely sweating man in the dark suit and tie, "whose distinguished career includes the prediction of the mass of the Z-zero from first principles, and who predicted the mass of the inside quark and the existence of the I particle, and who was one of the participants at our original Delos conference. . . ."

Professor Papatzis went on reciting Peter's achievements longer than he needed to, as if to prove that Peter had not been invited to Delos II by mistake, for how could the organizers have anticipated what was being whispered on the terraces during the coffee breaks and cocktail parties, that Peter Slater had lost his edge, outlived his genius, befuddled himself with philosophy? Papatzis blotted his neck with a wadded handkerchief one last time, then handed Peter the lavalier microphone and wearily returned to his chair.

Peter nodded thanks and looped the microphone cord around his neck, taking in the audience of two dozen mostly middle-aged males dressed as if for a golf tournament, along with a scattering of hairy youngsters in sandals and two women in sensible skirts. Peter and the unfortunate Professor Papatzis were the only ones in the room wearing jackets, but Peter's was of silk, not wool, and he looked cool enough.

"I've borrowed my theme from John Bell, a title he never used but wanted to: 'Quantum field theory without observers, or observable, or measurements, or systems, or apparatus, or wave-function collapse, or anything like that.' "

Someone in the back of the room laughed mirthlessly, drawing out his snorts and chuckles like a barroom drunk. Most of the people in the room were distinguished heads of university departments, happy to let their younger colleagues attend conferences in Illinois or Birmingham or Frankfurt but keeping plums like the Aegean Islands for themselves. Which meant that most of them were quantum conservatives, the kind of people Peter was here to convert.

"An impossible goal, I agree," Peter said to the heckler, "but worth honoring even in the breach. You see, I'm hoping to undo a myth. The kind of myth that says it was Columbus who discovered that the Earth is not flat. That it was Copernicus who discovered that the Earth is not the center of the universe. That it was Freud who discovered, as he claimed to have done, that we are not rational beings. With apologies, Dr. Freud, we physicists knew it before you did. Long before you, we demonstrated that humans are driven by mental structures—space and time among them—which are not fully formed and are often unconscious.

"Freud, who had little science and less mathematics, was nevertheless right to claim a lion's share of credit for that most persistent of twentieth-century myths, that nothing is what it seems; that everything is a matter of interpretation; that nothing, ultimately, is real. In our own field, Freud's role was played by Professor Bohr and his Copenhagen cronies."

As a speaker, Peter usually had a knack for bringing his listeners in, but this afternoon most of them were as silent as a field of stones. Among them were some of the world's most self-satisfied theorists, Copenhagen-interpretationists all, who despised philosophy and were easily rankled by criticism— even implied criticism—and Peter was giving them both.

"For most of my life I believed in that myth, shared by theoretical physicists and psychoanalysts alike," he continued. "I believed what Heisenberg said, as most of you do, that trying to extract common sense from a quantum-mechanical calculation is like trying to understand a grammatical but meaningless sentence. I believed Bohr, as most of you do, when he suggested that comprehensibility and incomprehensibility are somehow mutually affirming. I was taught to laugh at stubborn old Albert Einstein—as most of you were taught—because he objected when quantum theorists claimed that the questions quantum theory could not answer were a priori unanswerable."

Peter fiddled with the switches on the tabletop overhead projector, glancing at the screen that hung on the stand behind him. "Can we have it dark, please?"

The heckler in the back called out, "Shouldn't we have a little light instead?"—which got a laugh.

Peter turned on him, smiling. "If you believe in Bohr's complementarity, sir, as I suspect you do, darkness *is* light"—which got as big a laugh, for no matter which side of a debate they were on, these people cherished a retort.

Meanwhile the staff of the villa closed the thick blue drapes that separated the lounge from the terrace, cutting off the hot light along with the fitful draft from the sea. Peter took a transparency from a folder and arranged it on the projector; a list of numbered propositions in his bold and graceful hand appeared on the screen behind him.

"Here's where the myth has got us. We know how atoms behave, and the constituents of atoms, to an astonishing degree of accuracy. We can describe with some confidence the first three minutes of the universe. But how do we resolve the mismatch between a single quantum system, such as our theory describes, and the statistical data we get from actual experiments? How do we explain the spooky action-at-a-distance of the instant correlations in the experiments inspired by John Bell? How do we cope with the measurement problem. . . ?"

The door at the rear of the room opened, admitting a shaft of natural light bright enough to overwhelm the projected image on the screen. Peter squinted into the glare as Manolis Minakis slipped inside to stand against the back wall, letting the door close itself behind him.

Peter went on. "How can we bridge the chasm between the realm of quantum characteristics and the classical world? Trying to solve this dilemma, some of our best and brightest have proposed that the world—including the most distant and ancient galaxies—actually comes into existence when we choose to *observe* it. I come before you penitent, an apostate Copenhagian, to tell you that observers are the most mythical part of the myth. The world is whole; it's here; it has always been here, since before there was anything in it more observant than quark soup."

Peter knew well that most of his audience, if pressed, would vigorously defend the role of the observer in quantum measurements. So with as much verve and charm as he could muster—though the black chamber radiated their offended disapproval—Peter prepared to launch himself upon the central dilemma of quantum theory, which was that it violated every thinking person's experience of the world.

Anne-Marie let herself into their guest cottage and snatched up the phone from the pine bedside table. "*Kalimera sas, kyria* Thanatopolou. I need to place a call to Saint-Germain-en-Laye, near Paris. Will you help me?"

Mrs. Thanatopolou was a switchboard miracle-worker; within minutes she had succeeded in connecting Anne-Marie with her mother. Anne-Marie was delighted that Jenny recognized her voice; she was reassured by Mama Brand's grumbling admission that she and her granddaughter were enjoying each other's company; she made herself sweetly patient with her mother's lengthier grumblings when she told her she would have to be gone two more days. Just two more days.

Finally the one-sided conversation was over. Anne-Marie hung up the phone and went to the cottage door and bolted it, just in case. . . .

"*Kyria* Thanatopolou, one more, please. To Geneva." She recited the too-familiar number and paced in tense tight circles, waiting for the call to go through.

Hardly an hour went by that Alain Brand didn't spread the photographs of the Minoan hoard on his desktop and pore over them with a magnifying glass. Painted pottery, carved stone, worked gold, extraordinary objects arranged on rough cloth on an uneven surface, taken with a flash camera. Who had taken them? How had they come into the possession of the ponytailed tough who called himself Karl? Alain had asked himself these question from the beginning. He hadn't asked them of Karl.

The office line buzzed. "Your sister is calling, sir."

He pushed the button. "Anne-Marie!" His voice was full of warmth. "Thinking about you this very moment."

She didn't ask what he'd been thinking. "I've found them—or at least I know where they came from."

Alain was startled. "Already?" Less than forty-eight hours had passed since they'd reached their agreement.

"He talked about the place, described it, but I'll have to go there to make sure. And tell you how to find it."

"Where?"

"Where do you think?"

"Anne-Marie, I . . . I was going to tell you . . ."

"Tell me what?" she demanded.

"I've been . . . I've had . . . Well, I don't think this whole thing is such a good idea after all." Alain gathered the Polaroids into a pack and slipped them into the locking drawer of his desk, as if to hide them from himself.

"I'm friends with him, Alain. There's nothing to worry about."

Oh but there was; since he'd sent her on her way, Alain had worried more with each passing hour, as he should have worried from the beginning. "I'm worried for *you,* Anne-Marie. . . ."

"Lies bore me." Her voice was cold. "We have an agreement. I'm doing my part, and when I've done it you'll do yours. I'll call you again in two days."

"Anne-Marie . . ."

But she'd hung up on him.

Alain wiped his brow. If she knew how much she frightened him . . . His sister was capable of terrifying rages; what had he set loose when he'd sent her to Greece? She was as high on his promises as she used to get on booze.

Because Alain Brand was a cautious man he had so far enjoyed an uneventful career. No warrants had been issued for his arrest, no countries had named him persona non grata, and nobody had threatened him with bodily harm. Dealers in ancient artifacts could rarely choose their suppliers, but they could be picky about their clients, and Alain picked his carefully. Like an alcoholic who knows that the only way to keep on drinking is to limit his intake hour by hour, day by day, until control becomes his obsession, Alain understood his own greed.

Yet when blond Karl had muscled his way into the back room of the bookshop and thrown the Polaroids onto Alain's desk, when he'd told him what he was willing to pay if Alain would only find out where these things were—not get hold of them, not even lay eyes on them, just find out where they were (Karl would take care of the rest)—Alain failed to laugh in the fellow's pretty face or show him the door. He knew that if he found out where the objects were, he'd want to see them for himself. Even so he just couldn't keep himself from listening.

He'd let Karl tell him about this Minakis, this rich Greek who had the pieces hidden somewhere. Tell him how his sister could get to know the man. Suggest that she'd do whatever Alain asked her to do—that they could make a trade—because there was something Anne-Marie wanted, something Alain would rather keep between himself and her.

How did Karl know so much about Alain and Anne-Marie? Why had Karl chosen to approach Minakis through him and his sister? How had the photographs come into Karl's possession?

All the multiplying questions . . .

The phone buzzed again. "Herr Karl to speak to you, sir."

"You said I was *in?*" The question was a furious squeak. "Sir?"

"Never mind." He punched the lit button. "Herr Karl! Good of you to call, but it is a bit soon to—"

"Your sister left Minakis less than half an hour ago—after she spent the whole morning with him. She called you yet?"

Something warned Alain not to lie. "As a matter of fact, yes. She's making good progress, but she needs time. A few days."

"A few days." By his tone, Karl didn't believe it. "Don't make me call you again."

Alain hung up, trembling. Wearily he sank his head into his hands and massaged his scalp.

He looked up with a sniff. So they'd tapped his phone. What next, if he didn't give them what they wanted? There was one way he could get off this train, and that was to give Anne-Marie what *she* wanted right now, no strings attached. That would put a cork in her bottle, and as for them, he could tell them no thanks, no deal, count him out—and what could they do?

But he couldn't get the Minoan treasures out of his mind.

Two days, she'd said. . . .

Anne-Marie let herself into the dark auditorium and stood against the back wall, straining her eyes to find Minakis in the gloom. On the dais Peter was gesturing at equations on the screen. She could see nothing but silhouettes and the edges of unfamiliar faces rimmed in reflected light. An unreasoning fear seized her, that Minakis had slipped away.

But he was there, only inches away, standing against the wall. Silently she nodded, pretending calm. He nodded back, his eyes reflecting the shining screen.

After a few seconds, Anne-Marie had no trouble finding her place in Peter's script. Moving in and out of the projector's bright glow, he performed with his usual grace, preaching what his colleagues didn't want to hear, pretending to be unfazed by their antagonism—although she suspected he was hurt more than he let himself show; all his life he'd been used to applause—and she found herself admiring his persistence.

There'd been a time when she'd been as enthusiastic about ontological questions as he was, a time when she would sit with her friends in a café or a dingy Left Bank loft for hours, sipping sour red wine out of a jug and sucking on a shared reefer, talking about meaning and being and signs and significations as if truth could be extracted from the flow of words like gold nuggets from gravel in a streambed. Their motive had been the opposite of Peter's; they wanted reassurance that the world was whatever they chose to make of it. But no matter how much they talked, reality remained. It was the stuff you had to deal with.

When Peter had started muttering about reality in his off moments a year or so ago, her excitement was briefly rekindled; she thought a theoretical physicist might have something more substantial to say on the subject than a bunch of under-graduates mangling literary theory. *The world we live in is a world of big things,* Peter began bluntly enough, when she pressed him to share his thoughts. *Our experience suggests that to change the position of something we have to move it from here to there, that to change the energy of a system we have to burn some fossil fuel, say, or roll a rock down a hill. These are continuous processes; they take time.*

We live in a world of big things, all right, Anne-Marie thought, a world in which the unfair, the random, and the foully obscene are as likely to make our lives hell as to give us fifteen seconds of fame, much less serenity—a world in which the greedy and evil are as likely to die in peace as the good and generous.

By contrast, quantum theory describes a tiny world that is grainy and discontinuous. A change in the position or energy of an electron near an atomic nucleus occurs not smoothly over time but abruptly, in no time at all. The state of a quantum system is uncertain before it is measured, Peter said, and any act of measurement—in which a big-world instrument forces a link to the quantum world—irrevocably changes things. Uncertainty is not mere ignorance: until the position of the electron is measured, it has no definite position; until the energy of the electron is measured, it has no definite energy. Heisenberg, uncertainty's creator, asserted that the quantum world does not *exist* except as a tangled set of likelihoods.

Anne-Marie asked him how scientists dealt with the split between a big, smooth, predictable world and a microscopic, grainy, uncertain world. Most of us just ignore it, Peter answered; after all, the mathematics gives the right answers. But the question had posed a dilemma to quantum theory's creators, among them Albert Einstein and Erwin Schrödinger. At first glance Schrödinger's wave equation of 1926, the workhorse of quantum mechanics to this day, appeared to restore classical meaning to quantum processes. Schrödinger thought there was a reality and it consisted of waves, continuous and propagating smoothly through space, taking time to do so. What look to us like particles are only little bunches of waves, he ventured.

Schrödinger's equation held up, but not his interpretation. It turned out that Schrödinger's waves could not have a real existence in space-time; instead, it was argued, they were graphs of probability. Einstein hated these probabilities, and he hated what they led to: his friend Niels Bohr's complacent Copenhagen interpretation. Bohr proposed that cause and effect were irrelevant in the quantum microworld; he insisted upon the distinction between the ordinary world and the quantum microworld. The former can be understood, Bohr said, but the latter can only be described.

Where does the quantum world end and the classical world begin? At five atoms? Fifty atoms? A trillion atoms? Bohr had no answer, which emboldened others to take the Copenhagen interpretation even further—the illusory classical world has no real, independent existence either, they proclaimed; it is somehow brought into existence by the very act of measurement. Anne-Marie knew the feeling. As a poet had put it:

> Or perhaps it is
> that the house only constructs itself
> while we look—
> opens, room from room, *because* we look.
> The wood, the glass, the linen, flinging themselves
> into form at the clap of our footsteps.

Einstein, incredulous, demanded of a friend, "Do you really believe the moon exists only when you look at it?" His friend pondered for many years and wrote, after Einstein was long dead: "The twentieth century physicist does not, of course, claim to have the definitive answer to this question."

To Einstein, causality, limited by the speed of light, was the essence of experience. Einstein said that separate events which influence one another must somehow be in touch with one another, and the fastest possible way was at the speed of light.

To prove his point, in 1935 he and two young associates proposed the Einstein-Podolsky-Rosen experiment. In this imaginary experiment, two identical particles interact and then go their separate ways. A measurement is done upon one of them, establishing its position, say, or its energy. What does that measurement tell us about the *other* particle?

Quantum theory says we cannot know anything about the state of a particle until we measure it—that whatever quality we set out to measure does not exist with any definiteness until it has been measured. But these identical-twin particles set out *together.* If we know the position of one, we can infer the position of the other. If we know the energy of one, we can infer the energy of the other. Each measurement establishes an aspect of *reality*—so Einstein and Podolsky and Rosen asserted—not only of the particle measured but also of its distant twin.

Common sense finds no problem here. Why does quantum theory have a problem here?

Because, Peter explained, according to quantum mechanics neither particle has a definite position or energy until it has been measured. A measurement of one particle *forces* the state of both, even if the unmeasured twin is well on its way to Jupiter by now. And by the way, the "information" the distant particle receives about its own state reaches it infinitely faster than the speed of light—it gets there in no time at all.

Why must the distant particle be uncertain about its state? Why does a remote measurement *force* that state rather than merely reveal it? Why can't quantum theory admit the preexisting *reality* of the states of both particles?

Because whatever you find is an aspect of your whole experimental setup, Bohr replied. Different processes, different realities.

Because quantum theory is not an adequate description of nature, said Einstein and Podolsky and Rosen. There must be a way around uncertainty. There must be more to nature, perhaps "hidden variables" that, if we knew them, could explain what quantum theory cannot.

Heisenberg argued that hidden variables are worse than

unnecessary, they're impossible. Then a young American theorist named David Bohm showed that hidden variables *are* possible in nonrelativistic quantum mechanics, but for thirty years no one paid him any attention until an Irishman, John Stewart Bell, demonstrated that you can have quantum mechanics or you can have hidden variables, but you can't have both. Bell suggested that it was now possible to settle the question by actually performing the Einstein-Podolsky-Rosen *Gedankenexperiment.*

Bell showed how to make the *Gedanke wirklich,* Peter said, the thought real. Measure one particle, then the other. Measure the spin of an electron pair, say, or the polarization of a pair of photons. If your measuring devices are aligned just so, you should find perfect correspondence. Which tells you nothing—that's what you'd expect. But if your measuring devices are *not* perfectly aligned, there will be a discrepancy.

Here's the gist, here's the crux, Peter had exclaimed, and listening to him, Anne-Marie had been certain that some great revelation was imminent. If the microworld is smooth and continuous after all, and there are hidden variables which can explain why it looks otherwise, the discrepancy between measurements will be so big, *this* big—but if quantum mechanics is right, and the microworld is grainy and discontinuous and the uncertainty relations are the best we can hope for, the discrepancy will be different. That difference is known as Bell's inequality. To save Einstein's classical, smooth, causal world you cannot violate Bell's inequality.

Experimenters soon began trying to violate Bell's inequality. Their experiments fit on bench-tops and used pairs of photons. Quantum mechanics predicted that polarizers would show a certain correspondence between the states of the photon pairs, while hidden variables would show a different correspondence, and Einstein would win.

Quantum mechanics won.

The experiments kept getting more refined. Quantum mechanics kept winning. Telling her this, Peter got more frustrated, and Anne-Marie knew the great revelation would not be forthcoming. *The perfect experiment hasn't been done yet, but as Bell said, it's hard to believe quantum mechanics works so nicely for inefficient setups but is going to fail badly when enough refinements are made. We have to look at what the experiments tell us, and they tell us that causal information can move faster than light. Which makes me wonder why the causes we see always come before their effects, and why we never get messages from the future. . . .*

Effects before causes. Messages from the future. Anne-Marie had read a science fiction novel once about people who could foretell the future: they did it to demonstrate that not knowing what happens next is what makes life possible. Their grail was "unknowing." If she had the choice, she would welcome a message from the future, even if it persuaded her that life was not worth living at all. Best to get the bad news over with.

In the hot auditorium, in her sweat-drenched reverie, she sensed Minakis moving nearby, standing up straighter, and she tried to focus on what Peter was saying, to find her place in the script again.

". . . for example, are virtual particles real? They're useful devices, certainly, but it's a mistake to argue whether or not they're real just as it's a mistake to argue about whether the electron really goes through one of the slits in the two-slit experiment. . . ."

Peter had moved beyond Bell's inequality, beyond nonrelativistic quantum mechanics into quantum field theory, into symmetries and local coordinate systems, into a tangle of fiber bundles, mathematical entities beyond her comprehension. But she knew where he was headed, and it was far short of where he claimed he wanted to go; in the end he retreated into word games like any undergraduate.

"Once again we're fooled by our language," he said. "We have to make an effort to remember we're not talking about particles at all here, even if the imagery is useful; we're talking about the processes in which fields couple. . . ."

A voice boomed in the darkened hall. "Professor Slater, if you will permit me."

"Professor Minakis, is that you? Sorry, I'm blind up here."

"I am bold enough to say what our colleagues are too polite to say."

"Please do."

"That your equations are very pretty, but we don't know what you're trying to prove. Which makes us wonder why you're telling us all this."

Peter's smile turned to a grimace. "If you'll indulge—"

"You start by saying the world is real," Minakis interrupted, "then you draw a distinction between commonsense reality and objective reality. Is that a distinction with a difference? You banish the word 'observer' from our vocabulary, then you tell us the objects in the world that seem most real to us are already conceptualized in our minds—replacing one form of mentalism with another. Immanuel Kant couldn't have put it better, but is there any advantage to today's working physicist in what a Prussian noodler wrote two hundred years ago?"

"I hope to persuade you that the philosophical advantage is worth a great deal, namely the recovery of a meaningful concept of reality," said Peter.

"Then you will have to show us a scheme that solves real problems better," Minakis replied. "How else are we to choose between Bohm and Bohr, or Bell and Born, or Schrödinger and Heisenberg, or whomever?"

"I'm prepared to discuss an approach that—"

"In the fifteen minutes that remain to you? You should have started by showing us how your predictions differ—quantum mechanics versus whatever. Demonstrated that your scheme is more accurate."

"Both schemes yield equivalent results, as I hope to show."

"If that's all you hope to show, I wish you well," said Minakis's voice in the darkness, "but you must forgive me for wondering why you are taking the trouble."

A moment later the door opened, admitting a column of sunlight. Minakis's shadowy silhouette momentarily blocked it, filling the doorway, and then he was gone.

Others quickly followed by ones and twos. Peter found himself facing an emptying room. Anne-Marie watched him standing there helplessly. As much as she felt his pain, there was nothing she could do for him. She pushed herself in front of two guffawing men and fled into the sunshine.

15

The olive-shaded courtyard bustled with the villa's white-uniformed staff, busy carrying serving dishes to the buffet and setting places at tables scattered among the trees. Dazzled by the midday glare, Anne-Marie took a moment before she spotted Minakis on the lower terrace, talking to a tanned staffer in white.

Minakis, his back to the low terrace wall, saw Anne-Marie and waited for her as the young man nodded and turned away; behind him the blue-and-white harbor embraced its tourist fleet.

"That was horrible," she said. "You deliberately humiliated Peter."

"No, I challenged him," Minakis replied serenely. "Your husband has undergone a profound crisis of faith. He has rejected everything upon which his former success was based—the worldview of Bohr, of Heisenberg—and he seeks an alternative. I came to this conference hoping to hear him propose a new path. Instead, as indeed you warned me he would, he rehearses old ideas because they seem new to him. It won't do; he needs to transcend this pack of stale paradoxes. He needs a fresh approach, which can only come from himself."

"Or from you?" she said, anger coloring her cheeks.

"I would be honored to exchange ideas with Peter Slater, whenever he is ready to listen."

"Do join us for lunch, then—this buffet you were so excited about. You two can exchange away."

Though her invitation was issued through clenched teeth, he pretended it was genuine. "I don't think Peter wants to hear what I have to say just now. He has a lot of baggage to sort through." He smiled sadly. "As I do, in fact. I've made arrangements to leave the island this afternoon."

"Because you didn't like his speech?" Anne-Marie felt sudden panic. "It meant that much to you?"

"I thought I made that plain. It was the reason I came."

"It's not fair. You promised to tell me how you got your name." Her smile was a lopsided pout, as if to convey that her temper had been an act.

He stared at her from his imposing height, as if passing judgment on her sincerity. "I enjoyed our conversation this morning, perhaps because you made me do all the talking. If you want to talk more, come to Crete. For now, good-bye." When he put out his hand she thrust hers out awkwardly, surprised and offended, but he took it warmly. "My invitation still stands. Be my guests on Crete, you and Peter."

"Where in Crete?"

"You know where to find me. Do me the favor of giving this to your husband." He handed her a sealed business envelope, thick with folded pages. "Oh, and be sure to try the *garithes me feta* while they're still hot. And the Minos Kava, very cold. It goes well with shrimp."

She glanced at the envelope, and when she looked up, he was walking away. This time she didn't run after him, for with sudden conviction she knew that his invitation was bait.

He was right, of course; she knew exactly where to find him on Crete. She had done her best to seduce him into giving away his secrets, but he had told her only what he wanted her to hear.

A plump young man wearing a T-shirt with a picture of Einstein sticking his tongue out approached Peter and Anne-

Marie at their table. Not noticing or not caring that he had interrupted their meal, he went on like a movie fan about his admiration for Peter's work on the I particle. Peter was gracious, flattered even, until the fellow came around to the present moment.

"Reality? Don't know about that. Won't get anywhere until you tackle string theory, quantum gravity. Solve that, what you call reality falls out of it. Rest is a waste of time. My opinion. Not alone, either."

Peter made demurring noises until the self-satisfied youngster grew bored and went away. Peter waved cheerily after him. "Be sure and don't kick any stones," he called. He turned back to Anne-Marie with a bleak smile. "I'd say the early reviews are in: 'Slater goes too far but not far enough. Tilts at windmills, falls off hobbyhorse.'"

In the dappled shade they were enjoying sizzling shrimp baked with cheese and herbs in copper pans, along with a cool bottle of the Cretan wine Minakis had recommended. No one else had interrupted them since they'd sat down, much less asked to join them, and Peter was quickly sinking into melancholy. "Then there's Minakis," he said. "I saw you with him afterward. Did he add anything to his oh-so-useful remarks in the hall?"

"He says you're stuck on old ideas because they're new to you. He says you should come up with something original."

"He's being most helpful today."

"You asked."

"But no content; he really has nothing to say. Which may be why he didn't stick around to elaborate."

"He said you weren't ready to hear what he had to say."

Peter twisted in his chair, watching the table across the courtyard where the string theorists were holding court, four of them squeezed around a table the size of the one he was sharing with Anne-Marie, plus another half a dozen kibitzers—a couple of the gray eminences included—all crowded as close as they could get, clutching their plates to their chests, everybody yakking at once.

"I should have known better, about Minakis," Peter said.

"You've got to watch out for these New Age geezers. One good idea in their life; then they can't get a decent job for forty years, and they turn into little maharishis."

Her skin grew hot. "You don't know what you're saying."

"It's exactly what happened to David Bohm," he said, heedlessly cutting her off. "The Zen of the Tao, or whatever. Woolly Dancing Masters. All that metaphysical New Age crap."

"New Age is the last term I would choose to describe Manolis Minakis," she said.

"Old Age would suit you better?" Peter asked.

"Don't be a shit."

"All right, let's just drop the physics gossip." She leaned away from him, furious. He leaned away too, as if they were repelling magnets. "Sorry I said anything. Forget it. How much more time do you have to spend on this Minakis story?"

"Not much longer."

"What about Jenny?"

"Jenny's fine for a couple of days," she said defensively. "Mama may have ratty wallpaper, but she loves her granddaughter."

"That's a fine evasion. We were supposed to be on vacation. Does the vacation move to Paris now?"

"I don't know. Why not?" She stared around, distracted. "You've got to meet Mama sometime."

"I look forward to it." With an effort, he relaxed his shoulders and softened his voice. "If she's as fierce as you claim, she's a natural phenomenon."

Anne-Marie smiled tightly. "A little more time, please."

They ate the rest of the meal in silence, and afterward Anne-Marie said she was feeling dizzy and needed to take a nap. In other words, leave me alone. . . .

He let her go. He didn't want to hang around the villa where his wife and everybody else seemed to be signaling how much they wished he'd go away, so he decided to oblige the crowd and take a walk in the hills.

Not a good time for a walk, the hottest hour of the day, everything shimmering in the rising air: the dusty roads, the stone walls, the dry fields, the blue sea discolored by coppery reflections. He passed whitewashed towers with crisscross openings under their roofs and stones projecting like spear points from their ridgelines, exotic structures that wobbled in the radiant heat like visions from the *Arabian Nights*. But they were only dovecotes.

His mind wavered and swerved, one by one to the people he thought he knew but couldn't make sense of, from his new wife, so passionate and prickly—and lately so vague and evasive—to old Minakis, as smug and imposing and out-of-date in his own way as the rest of the seniors in the crowd, to his junior colleagues who lived in the immediate futures of their careers, constantly fretting that the fashionable questions were becoming passé. And thence to his tiny stepdaughter, Jenny, who lived only in the moment . . . and finally to his first wife, Kathleen, someone he hadn't talked to in almost two years.

Kathleen had been a colleague, a mathematician, who'd left him because he'd become obsessed with questions of physics that he couldn't bring himself to discuss with her. By the time he was willing to share them it was already too late for their marriage. It was a long time after that, when he thought he was a different person, freer, less obsessed, someone who had learned to care about other people, a *better* person, that he'd asked Anne-Marie to marry him.

What he hadn't realized and should have was that he was still in thrall to physics—to its motives rather, to a quest for the nature of nature, of the world itself—and that wherever his current obsession led him, no matter what he came up with this time, there would be no acclaim from his peers, no reward in this lifetime. Nor could Anne-Marie, however much she wished him well, share his passion.

Equally what he hadn't realized and should have was that Anne-Marie was herself obsessed and unwilling to share her obsession with him, except that it had something to do with her determination to gain full custody of her son. Peter had never met her ex-husband, Charlie Phelps. He'd spent a lot of time with Jennifer, a happy child whom he adored, if in a distracted way. He'd spent a bit of time with little Carlos too—well, a long weekend at Disneyland, anyway—and they'd gotten along, as far as any boy with sorrows to bear and a well-developed sense of self-preservation would allow a strange stepfather to get along with him, but Peter knew he would never share the fierceness of Anne-Marie's determination to have Carlos around the house.

Unable to communicate to each other what gripped them separately, the first months of their marriage had been filled with more tension than all the months that had gone before. And somehow Minakis had come along at just the wrong moment, pushing himself between them.

Minakis. The thought of him made Peter switch mental channels; he found himself rehearsing what he *should* have said when Minakis challenged him in the lecture hall at noon.

Because Minakis was right: most of Peter's musings on reality could be reduced to Kantian cant. The Bell-inspired experiments stopped woefully short; having all but proved that reality was nonlocal—that at the quantum level, the past and the future were intimately tangled, because the effects of quantum measurement were not "timelike" but "spacelike," meaning simultaneous—they hadn't so much as hinted at why this was so.

Reality was deeper than quantum mechanics, deeper than space and time. At the ultimate substrate, everything was connected. Peter even thought there might be a way to prove it, and last night Minakis himself had hinted at a similar view of things. Too bad neither of them had had the guts to spell it out in front of the lunchtime crowd.

Causality was the rub: if information could be transmitted instantaneously, effects could happen before their causes. If that were so, the world should have dissolved into chaos. Not structured mathematical chaos. Real yawning chaos, the black throat that swallows everything.

Peter balked at that. If all events are connected before and after they happen, part of a seamless multidimensional field, cause and effect are simply labels for sets of coordinates. Einstein wouldn't have objected to such a worldview, though

Heisenberg certainly would have. On this view, if causality is an illusion, then uncertainty is too. What if we cling to the uncertainty relations because they give the comforting illusion that causes *don't* have necessary effects, that the ordering of events is *not,* after all, determined . . . ?

Peter was walking faster and faster, along a dirt track that crested the island under the sky's pale dome. A stone in the road stopped him; he paused to nudge it with his loafer—beneath his trouser cuff the white skin of his bare ankle caught the light—and seeing that, he laughed, and suddenly he found himself back in the world of ordinary and quite extraordinary things, switching mental channels again.

Thinking of Anne-Marie.

He was high on the dry ridge above Mykonos, looking down on the white town and the blue harbor. A big private yacht was moving out into the strait, a steel vector on the water.

The guest cottage at the villa was empty. He'd thought Anne-Marie was here to chase Minakis around the island, to record her interview and take her pictures. But she'd never completely unpacked her suitcase, and now her luggage was gone; she hadn't so much as sat down on the freshly made bedspread.

A business envelope lay in the middle of the bed, with Peter's name printed on it in neat block letters. He ripped it open and stared, uncomprehending, at the photocopied pages of notes and equations handwritten in a minute hand, at the ink sketches drawn freehand with an artist's precision.

He picked up the telephone. "Peter Slater, Mrs. Thanatopolou. Would you connect me with Professor Minakis's room . . . ? He did? I see." He almost hung up, then said, "My wife and I discussed travel arrangements last night, but I'm afraid I was a bit distracted and . . . yes, that would be helpful."

He waited. "Was that to the harbor or the airport?" It was as much as he dared ask without making it obvious that his wife had run away.

Mrs. Thanatopolou did not know where the driver had taken Anne-Marie, and the driver, busily ferrying scientists away from the villa on the last day of the conference, would not be back for at least half an hour. Peter thanked her and hung up.

He turned his attention to the inked notes and sketches. There were references to a 1931 paper of Erwin Schrödinger's; there were references to a 1986 paper of John Cramer's; there were references to more recent papers of Gunther Nimtz. There were diagrams of an optical device with beam splitters and a test-pattern reference, some kind of interferometer that included a unit labeled "black box." Maybe that was supposed to be funny.

But when he looked more closely at the details of the so-called black box, Peter lapsed into the kind of creative narcolepsy that had occasionally led his parents, when he was still a child, to be concerned for his mental well-being. He saw the possibilities. . . .

The black box was a magazine of crystalline channels, each of so fine a dimension that it was narrower than the amplitude of a photon of the laser light Minakis's device was designed to shine through it—in essence forming a barrier to that light. But quantum theory allows particles to occasionally tunnel through barriers; the transit time is constant for a given setup, and if the barrier is sufficiently wide, a particle tunneling through it can apparently get from one side to the other faster than the speed of light. No one knows why; some argue the effect is an illusion. It's a tiny effect in any case, but Minakis's black box was designed to amplify it many times.

Unlike Bell-type experiments, there need be no randomness in a signal communicated via the black box. If Minakis's setup worked, even on a minor scale, it could topple the traditional notion of causality.

Peter had often speculated on what it might take to prove that there was an implicate order to the world—David Bohm's term for a connectedness deeper than classical cause and effect—but he had never gotten this far. In these handwritten pages were some of his own half-baked experimental ideas, ideas he had never shared with anyone, because he had supposed he would need an accelerator as big as CERN or TERAC to test them,

here laid out and referenced and refined, the necessary apparatus boldly specified—and it would fit on a bench-top.

He stood up abruptly and began to pace. Minakis's name
appeared nowhere on these pages, no signature, no self-
reference, but Peter had no doubt that this was Minakis's work.
He opened the door of the stifling bungalow to the blaze of the
afternoon. In the full heat of the sun he knew plainly that to find
Anne-Marie he needed to find Minakis. He badly wanted to
find them both.

16

When Delos and Mykonos were smudges on the northern horizon, framed by the yacht's spreading wake, Minakis came up to the bridge. *La Parisienne* was 160 feet long, built in Holland as a whaler tender but refitted for luxury; its deep draft, meant to take on the monstrous swells of polar seas, made for a smooth ride in the Aegean, which was often choppy if rarely monstrous. Today the sun was hot and the air was serene; only the yacht itself disturbed the surface of the water, and glittering dolphins played in its bow wave.

"What time do you expect to put in, Captain?" Minakis asked.

"Shortly after seven, sir." The captain was a youngster from Hydra, late of the Greek coast guard, who had come along with the boat when Minakis purchased it from its previous owner.

"Everything went well in Athens?"

"Customs made noises, but I showed them the documents from FORTH. That was good enough."

"Good. I'd hate to think about putting the pieces back together after their meddling." Minakis watched the horizon, unsquinting, his dark eyes proof against the glare of sea and sky. "I'll stay aboard tonight and go up to Limnakaros tomorrow. Meanwhile, no interruptions."

"Very good, sir."

In his cabin on the main deck, Minakis pulled linen curtains over the portholes to cut the glare and settled himself in the mahogany armchair at the built-in secretary. From his briefcase he took the originals of the notes and drawings he had left for Peter Slater. Critical parts of the apparatus were stored in the captain's safe at this moment, handcrafted optical units benefiting from two years of trial and error with his former assistants.

But would Peter be on hand for the next stage? Minakis leaned back in his chair and closed his eyes, feeling the long waves of the boat's movement through the sea. Since Delos, since his carefully plotted ambush of Peter had been interrupted by the early arrival of Peter's wife, nothing had gone quite as he'd planned.

For one thing, he hadn't planned to spend the whole morning telling his life story to Anne-Marie. For another, he'd surprised even himself by lashing out at Peter's naive assault on the limits of the Copenhagen interpretation. Among theorists under thirty, that battle was won; Copenhagen was assumed to be seriously deficient. What to do about it was the question, and a sophisticated redefinition of reality was not the answer.

Minakis had intended to tantalize Peter, to persuade him that Minakis was on the verge of a breakthrough and that Peter could help him find it. He had never intended to bolt and run, leaving raw notes and drawings, mere unsupported documents; instead he'd envisioned philosophical arguments under the olive branches and the stars—arguments he would win, of course. Now he worried whether the papers alone were enough to entice Peter to seek him out. . . .

Why had he fled to Crete? Because of Anne-Marie. But that was no answer; it was an enigma. Before yesterday she had been a case history, a piece on his chessboard. If he could give her an urgent need to visit him on Crete, she would overcome any reluctance Peter had to come along. That was his plan.

Then he'd seen her, descending the stony hill of Delos.

This morning she had flattered and coaxed him with innocent lies, without a hint of guile. Charming, but no mystery; he knew what she wanted, so why did she affect him so? In her pale eyes, he sensed depths he could not fathom.

For half a century he had shunned love. His only liaisons had been short affairs, never devoid of calculation. Only two women had ever deeply engaged his desire and his imagination—both when he was so young as to have been a different person. With the first of these he had never even held an intimate conversation.

His fantasies had been too long suppressed, and suddenly they bubbled up. Anne-Marie—the partner he might have imagined for himself, if he were Peter, if time were more flexible, if events were not so firmly tied to their space-time coordinates, if anything could happen . . .

If one could live one's life again.

In the spring of 1936 John and Hilda Pendlebury began excavating a cave in the cliffs on the eastern edge of the Lasithi Plain. On Manolis's first holidays from school he went to join them, starting from Kastro before dawn, walking across low ridges and through broken ravines as the sun rose higher, then up the sheer north scarp of the mountains on a switchback *kaderimi,* one of those roads whose foundations, Pendlebury claimed, had been laid by the Romans. "On Crete, knowing the distance is useless," Pendlebury was fond of saying, grandly. "Times alone matter." Manolis didn't need to be told that; he did the twenty-six miles to Lasithi in six hours without ever breaking into a run.

In the spring sunshine Lasithi's circumscribed plain was a quilt of blue and yellow wildflowers, of fields of scarlet poppies and new green wheat, every field with its windmill, thousands of white canvas sails turning atop squat strap-iron towers, facing into the northerly breeze and creaking merrily as they turned. Walking through the plain with the smell of new growth drenching the air, with the windmills singing in the wind and snow-crested Dikti serene against the sky, Manolis felt a rush of unfocused joy.

He came to Tzermiado, which a year ago would have seemed a metropolis to him but after Kastro was only another village. He asked directions to the cave of Trapeza and walked a few hundred yards farther, to a tabletopped bluff that rose above the village. A narrow path climbed steeply between low walls shaded by carob and olive and oak; a scramble at the top took him to a ledge in front of the cave's narrow entrance.

The ledge was surely busier than it had been for several thousand years, with village men squeezing past each other in the entrance, those going in carrying empty baskets, those coming out carrying baskets full of mud, which they dumped in front of two women seated on camp stools, who sorted through it, pulling bits of bone and pottery and carved stone from the filth.

Hilda Pendlebury was one of the women; beneath her kerchief a few wet strands of hair were plastered across her brow. "Manoli! We didn't expect you so soon." She stood, wiping her muddy hands on her long apron. "Do you know Miss Money-Coutts?"

The younger woman, equally drenched in sweat, nodded acknowledgment but remained seated and did not break her concentration.

"Oh yes, from last summer," Manolis said. "She helped *ton kyrio* Pendabri catalogue the sherds."

"For which history will remember me," said Money-Coutts, sparing him a wry glance as she pawed through a handful of mud, "if for nothing else."

"You've come to see how we're doing," said Hilda.

"I've come to see *what* you're doing, *kyria*," Manolis said. "Everybody talks about archaeology, but I've never seen it done."

"You've seen more than you think," Hilda said. "Thousands of potsherds and the tedious accounting of them. There's not much more to see except the digging up of them. If you want to see that, go right in." She pointed to the cave entrance.

Manolis brightened. "Thank you, I will."

The entrance to the Trapeza cave was a gap between two leaning slabs of rock, into which had been set a door of iron bars in a heavy wooden frame. Manolis stood aside as a man carrying a basket of mud emerged. Then he ducked into the twilight interior.

He was in a room as big as a village house, roofed with stone and floored with mud, decorated by stumpy stalactites and stalagmites and lit by daylight from the entrance. Nothing about this cave struck him as unusual or interesting; he'd poked his nose into lots of places like this. A yellow light showed at the far end of the chamber, and in that light he glimpsed moving shadows. He went toward it.

There, in a lower chamber lit by paraffin lamps, the excavators were at work. The whole mud floor of the place had been peeled back like the skin of a corpse, and underneath were bones, the fragmentary remains of small bodies, their knees pulled up to their chins, buried under only a few inches of soil and not nearly so well preserved as the bones Manolis had found in his own cave. John Pendlebury was down on his knees beside one of the shallow graves, scraping at a crumbled skeleton with a narrow trowel, bringing the scene into existence as if with an artist's brushstrokes. So intent upon the moment was he that Manolis did not dare announce his presence; he crouched beside a stalagmite and peered down upon Pendlebury as he worked.

"Oh there it comes," Pendlebury murmured. "Oh there it comes." He reached into the grave and grasped something and gently moved it. "Oh bravo!" He held the thing aloft in the yellow lamplight. Manolis couldn't see what it was, a bronze spearpoint perhaps, or a dagger. Pendlebury laid the corroded spike of dark metal carefully aside and jotted in his little notebook, then went back to his scraping.

Manolis dodged another workman carrying a basket of dirt, then let himself down over the slippery stones into the lower chamber. *"Kyrie* Pendabri."

"Androulakis!" Pendlebury got up from his knees, ducking to avoid the low ceiling. *"Kalimera!* Damned good to see you."

He thrust out his muddy hand, and Manolis shook it firmly. "Heard you've been giving the schoolteachers what for."

"Oh . . . well. They say I ask too many questions."

"Impossible," Pendlebury said firmly. "The way you ask them, perhaps."

Manolis said nothing, trying to hide his distress with an innocent and inquisitive gaze.

"We must have a talk about it." Pendlebury looked around. "Gentlemen, an intermission. Tea and sunshine." He scrambled up the short slope to the upper level of the cave and, bending low, turned to give Manolis a hand. "Here to help us out?"

Manolis jumped up the slope he had just slid down. "Today and tomorrow—if I'm to go back to school." Not that he would have minded skipping the rest of the year.

"Splendid, splendid." They dodged the rock overhangs and emerged into the blinding afternoon light, Pendlebury pushing Manolis ahead of him onto the ledge. "If you've come to learn a bit of practical archaeology, I can't think of a better teacher than Money-Coutts here, when it comes to sorting things out." Miss Money-Coutts and Hilda looked up from their muddy work. "Would you mind taking on a pupil for the next day or two, Miss Money-Coutts?"

"If he doesn't mind getting his hands dirty," the young woman replied, concentrating on her work.

"Right, and let's all wash up. Androulakis, do the honors, will you? At the moment you're the *only* one with clean hands."

Manolis made tea on the camp stove (that day and the next and on many afternoons thereafter) with all the ceremonies of pot warming and cozying that he had learned from the Squire and Mrs. Hutchinson. Later he sat beside Miss Money-Coutts, sifting sherds from the mud, trying to follow her example and listening for her sparse hints on how to clean artifacts without destroying them, adding what he gleaned to what he had already learned from Uncle Manolakis, his foster father at Knossos.

That night and the next he slept in the house of Siganos, the local schoolmaster, the cousin of his old tutor (who was now a journalist in Athens and in constant trouble with the government). Well before dawn on the second morning after his arrival, he walked the twenty-six miles back to Kastro and his classes.

He made the round-trip every weekend until school let out for the summer, when at last he was free to spend every day of the dwindling season at the dig. As the season drew to a close, Hilda Pendlebury joined her husband in scouting other promising sites in the neighborhood, leaving Manolis to spend mornings and afternoons alone with Money-Coutts on the ledge outside the cave, rooting through ever-fresh baskets of mud—occasionally resting his eyes by gazing into the distance, over the tops of the oaks on the hillside to the windmill-studded plain below, trying *not* to peer at Money-Coutts.

But always there was Money-Coutts, her sun-browned face lambent with perspiration, her mouth bent in a small moue of concentration, her green eyes sometimes just glancing away from his. She never acknowledged his fervent glances except by the lifting of an eyebrow, for she was many years his senior, though she looked as young as any Greek girl Manolis's age.

All that season the British School excavated the cliffs above Tzermiado. By June the picture was almost complete. The cave of Trapeza had been occupied in Neolithic times by people who were among the earliest to reach the island. Centuries later their descendants, the Minoans, were using it as a burial place and a shrine, and so it remained until the Minoans transferred their worship to a more spectacular cave at the opposite end of the Lasithi Plain. In that place, Psychro, during the last decade of the nineteenth century, Hogarth had brought up golden treasures; Psychro was one of those caves that claimed to be the birthplace of Zeus.

Pendlebury told the tale grandly, of Kronos eating his children, of Rhea substituting a stone for the infant Zeus and hiding him to be raised on milk and honey by Melissa the bee-nymph and Amalthea the goat-nymph. "But if Zeus was born in Psychro, and if Psychro succeeded our Trapeza as a site of worship in the Bronze Age, ipso facto Trapeza was the home of Zeus's parents. It was a rather modest little cottage, but never mind; we have excavated the home of Kronos and Rhea, the home of Father Time and Mother Earth's daughter, the Great Goddess of Crete herself. Which is what the inhabitants of Tzermiado will tell you to this day." He helped himself to a tumbler of the strong green wine from the pitcher on the table, tossed it back in a single throw, and drew his thumb across his wet lips.

Seeing the enraptured look on the faces of the students at the table, Hilda spoke up. "But whether that story has been passed down from the Bronze Age or Professor Hogarth put it in their heads forty years ago, who but John would venture to say?"

"No need to make a choice," Pendlebury replied. "Who's to say Hogarth didn't simply prod their race memory?"

The students—Money-Coutts too—laughed at this, but Manolis didn't join in; he thought Hilda had touched upon something deep. On his first visit to the Iraklion Museum, Pendlebury had suggested to him that he was a descendant of a pretty Minoan girl pictured in a four-thousand-year-old fresco. How much of our history has been put into our heads? he wondered.

It was a question he took with him when the digging season ended. It never went away; instead it grew in him, taking different forms as he grew older. *How much of the past is merely the present projected backward? How much of the present is conditioned by what we have not yet experienced . . . ?*

When John Pendlebury came back to Lasithi the following year, he was alone and in a sour mood. Hilda was ill, and he'd suffered professional setbacks. Hiking and climbing, always his boast, was now his solace; while his students dug and sifted through rock-shelter burials and a settlement on the limestone bluffs above Trapeza cave, he scoured the ramparts surrounding the Lasithi Plain, desperate to find a new and more spectacular site.

"I visited your cave," Pendlebury said one night when he'd returned late to Tzermiado after a long trek. "Found sherds, left them where they were. If it ever was a shrine, it wasn't an important one. More likely a den of thieves."

They were sitting alone at the table in front of the *apothiki,* the abandoned house the British School had rented in which to study and store their finds. The villagers were in their homes, and the students had staggered to their rented beds, exhausted.

"Not worth excavating?" Manolis said.

"Too remote for an organized expedition. What I got for my pains was a wallow in cold mud. And missed another chance to do the three peaks of Dikti."

In the light from the paraffin lamp, Pendlebury looked haggard. His shirt and shorts hung loosely about him. In former years there had been a provocative smoothness to his long-muscled frame, a glowing finish to his bronze limbs that would have been natural on a swimming champion but looked too polished on a hiker. The smoothness was gone now; the bronze was ropy iron, and both his eyes, the flesh and the crystal, glowed eerily in shadowed recesses.

Pendlebury poured wine from the jug on the table and drank deeply from his glass. "You didn't tell me about the bodies."

Manolis said nothing.

"Your affair. Can't say I blame you for keeping the secret from your old village gang. Still secret, rest assured. Anything in that cave, you're welcome to it."

The end of the 1937 season was approaching when Pendlebury summoned Money-Coutts and Manolis to accompany him on a closer inspection of a site a mere half-hour's scramble from Tzermiado. It was called Karphi, the Nail.

Manolis had known the place as long as he could remember; it was a landmark on the northern scarp of Lasithi. He followed close behind Pendlebury and Money-Coutts, hoping to see it this time not with a shepherd's eye but an archaeologist's.

They climbed over thorny pastures and shattered gray rock to come upon the Nail from above. As they walked over the edge of the massif, the world dropped away beneath their feet. Looking down, they saw sheer cliffs interrupted by verdant olive groves and vineyards, plateaus of cultivation where white villages nestled among vertical gorges; 3,600 feet below them, the Cretan Sea glittered like cold metal under an approaching layer of cloud.

They kept walking, onto the thin ridge that connected the Nail to the fortress cliffs of Lasithi. The rock here was pale gray and hard, its strata standing on edge, sculpted by wind and water into points and blades and sinister knobs. The ridge formed a little saddle that was filled with rubble and overgrown with thorns.

"These are walls," Pendlebury said, pointing to fractured stones lying atop one another in heaps, "and they weren't built by shepherds—not last year and not last century." He dropped to one knee and scratched in the red clay that filled the interstices of the stony ground. He brought up a sherd and handed it to Miss Money-Coutts, who pushed the hair out of her eyes to study it. "Don't say what you think," Pendlebury told her. "Let him have a chance."

Money-Coutts handed the sherd to Manolis. He spit on his thumb to rub away the mud. The clay was pale pink, with a whitish slip on which he could make out part of a black triangle filled with close-set parallel lines. "Late Minoan III?"

Pendlebury cocked an eyebrow. "A fair guess. Money-Coutts?"

"Sub-Minoan," she said. "Almost Protogeometric."

"This was their last refuge." Pendlebury swung his walking stick across the panorama of precipices on three sides. "This is where they came when the palaces burned, when the barbarous Dorians overran the lowlands, when Minoan Crete fell. Here and at Vrokastro and at Kavousi. Here the Dark Ages began."

The cries of vested ravens, rising with the flowing mist, announced wet gray clouds that suddenly welled up around them, closing in as they roamed the stony heights. Pendlebury leaped ahead, shouting to be heard in the damp wind. "We could be back in the Neolithic, back with those first poor seafarers who were so terrified of the sea that they hid in mountain caves. Here men built robber castles where their ancestors built shrines. There's a whole fortified town on this peak, and work enough for years."

Manolis hung back with Money-Coutts, who was making no attempt to keep up with Pendlebury, although she threaded the paths among the stones and thorns nimbly enough in her jodhpurs and high-laced boots. Without looking up, Money-Coutts muttered, "This business of the robber castles will go into his book. John never throws a good line away."

In his cabin aboard *La Parisienne,* Minakis took a copy of Pendlebury's book from the shelf above his bunk, the original 1939 edition, sheathed in a clear plastic library cover: *The Archaeology of Crete,* subtitled *An Introduction.*

He smiled at the subtitle's false modesty. Pendlebury's book wasn't an introduction, it was a condensed encyclopedia that noted every site where a telling sherd or artifact or bit of wall had been found, period by period, from the Neolithic to the Roman, along with estimates of how long it should take an athlete like himself to walk from one place to the next. For although Pendlebury described his pace as "half-way between a running messenger and a party of merchants," it was more like that of the running messenger.

The book was sent to press a year after Pendlebury began work on the Nail, and it included some of what he found there. In 1938 Hilda came back to Crete with her children in tow; she and John made wonderful discoveries, including a clifftop shrine that had been sacred to the Minoans long before the site was a fortified town. That season Manolis really learned to dig and draw and photograph; he learned to reconstruct the wreckage of the past. But what the archaeologists found was what they expected to find, for they lived under the shadow of war, and to them the ruins of Karphi were the remains of a beleaguered people. Pendlebury imagined himself with those Dark Age survivors, bracing for the last battle; perhaps he even looked forward to it.

Minakis stretched himself upon his bunk and opened the book, looking for the thousandth time at Money-Coutts's bold ink drawings of potsherds. He smiled now at the memory of his desperate passion. He had not thought about Mercy for years; he had done little to preserve his own past, the human emotions of his past. Any researcher could learn facts about him, but not what had mattered at the time. After the archaeologists have stripped away the material evidence, what is left? Data. Space-time coordinates.

Peter was right to echo Kant. In the end, meaning arises only from experience.

Minakis sighed. Six hours to go until Ayios Nikolaos, and a whole night ahead. He would take the time to set down a few reminiscences. Peter might like to read them someday.

Anne-Marie might like to read them too. Unless her interest was sheer pretense.

17

Peter knew nothing about Minakis except that he was said to have done early work on semiconductors, half theoretical, half practical, back in the 1950s before Peter was born. Peter knew little about the solid state and had never read anything Minakis had written.

Now there were these drawings and notes spread out on the bed beside the suitcase that Peter was packing as quickly as he could. What slowed him down was that he kept stopping to ponder some facet of Minakis's scheme. Though solid-state physics had little in common with particle physics, no branch of physics was unaffected by quantum theory, and it was evident that Minakis had thought about its paradoxes long and deeply. It was equally evident that he had a flair for experiment that Peter lacked.

Earlier, when Peter had tried to track Minakis down, he'd learned about the yacht, which had left Mykonos shortly after one o'clock. But Mrs. Thanatopolou didn't know its destination and she had no luck trying to raise *La Parisienne* on the villa's satellite phone. Mrs. Thanatopolou put Peter through to the University of Athens, where Minakis occasionally lectured, and she did most of the talking for him until the secretary yielded up an Athens street address and a phone number. But there was no answer at the number, not even a machine.

Peter thanked Mrs. Thanatopolou for her efforts and hung up, then stacked a couple of cord adapters and plugged his laptop into the phone jack. He hunched over its tiny keyboard, searching for traces of Minakis on the net. The net was wide in space but shallow in time: he found references to a few of Minakis's recent articles and letters in *The Oxford Journal of Archaeology, Revue archeologique,* and *Praktika tis en Athinais Archaiologikis Etaireias,* but Minakis didn't seem to have published any physics papers lately. When Peter finally snapped the laptop shut and stuffed it back in its bag, all he had was a list of articles about archaeology.

Well, he would have to go to Athens anyway; it was impossible to get anywhere in a hurry without going through Athens.

There was one more call he ought to make. He hadn't spoken to Jenny in three days; he'd expected to see her when her mother arrived on Mykonos. Not that she was likely to hold it against him . . . and what would he say when Madame Brand answered the phone? "I called to say hello to my stepdaughter, Mama, and by the way, it seems I've lost track of your daughter, my wife. . . ."

Maybe he'd call Paris from Athens. Right now he had a plane to catch.

It was almost 5:00 P.M. when Anne-Marie got through to her mother from a phone booth in the Olympic Airlines terminal in Athens, after waiting twenty minutes for the call to go through, but finally, "Hello, Mama . . . I'm good. . . . Yes, Peter's good too. Everything's fine, marvelous." She stared at the wood panel of the telephone cabinet, enduring her mother's worried interrogation and listening for sounds of Jennifer in the background. "Would you give her the phone, please? Just so she can hear my voice. . . ."

Bumps and breathing.

"It's me, darling. Can you hear me?"

More breathing, then a joyful "Ma!" Then a clink as the receiver hit the floor.

"What, Mama, a duet? Certainly I'd like to hear it." She heard her mother's voice almost whispering the words of the nursery song:

> " 'Ainsi font, font, font
> les petites marionettes.
> Ainsi font, font, font
> trois p'tits tours et puis s'en vont . . .' "

And in the foreground, Jenny's cheerful, arrhythmic huffing: "Fon, fon, fon, fon."

Anne-Marie laughed. "Bravo! I'm sure she's having a grand time, it's really good of you. . . . I'm on my way to Crete, but I don't know where I'll be exactly. . . . A day or two. Peter sends his love, can't wait to meet you at last. . . . Truly, he said so. . . . He *would* tell you himself, except he's not here right now. We'll call you later. . . . Good-bye now."

At last Anne-Marie hung up, weary with the effort of polite conversation.

Ever since she'd arrived in Athens the loudspeakers had been announcing that all departing flights were delayed due to "technical difficulties." People were elbowing their way to the ticket counters and shouting at the clerks—Greeks, especially when they're unhappy, don't stand in line—and knots of dejected travelers were camped out on hard plastic chairs in the waiting rooms. Evidently one translation of "technical difficulties" was "labor dispute." To get to Crete she would have to go by sea, and she barely had time to make the overnight ferry from Piraeus.

The taxi stand outside the terminal was built like a cattle ramp, with iron railings to contain the crowd. Anne-Marie dived in, suitcase and camera bag swinging, but suddenly froze when she saw a familiar tall figure ahead of her and almost had to bite her tongue to keep from calling his name: Peter.

She pretended to have trouble with her suitcase, allowing frantic men and women to push past her. Peter was standing at the curb now; she watched surreptitiously as he let two men push past him to grab taxis that hadn't reached the front of the line. Finally he got wise. He blocked the next man who tried to get by him with an elbow; then, as a cab came swerving in off the coast road, heading for the taxi rank, he loped to the back of the line of cabs and cut off another queue-jumper; Peter had swung his bags into the back seat and dived in with them before the cab had come to a full stop. The driver gunned around the loading cabs in front of him and headed back to the coast road on squalling tires.

Anne-Marie had to laugh, even as she hoped Peter's luck didn't last. She needed a day alone with Minakis without him.

Bumper cars at fifty miles an hour—rush hour on a boulevard with three painted lanes of traffic that somehow accommodated four, plus motor scooters that buzzed through the gaps like angry wasps—and twenty-five minutes later Peter reached the Intercontinental Hotel, still fuming.

An hour later, as dusk was settling over the city, he was ready to try again. It was a short cab ride to Minakis's address on a low hill in Pangrati.

The three-story building was a fortress with no windows on the ground floor and only a single massive wooden door, although it looked to be opulent, with balconies and arbored terraces and glazed tile roofs and a fine view of the Acropolis. City lights glistened for miles around in the purple twilight, but the rock on which the ancient High City stood was a dark silhouette. Peter rang the bell repeatedly; no answer. He climbed back into the waiting taxi.

He had hardly closed his hotel-room door behind him when outside his window, across the streaming traffic on Syngrou, the Parthenon came suddenly alight, blazing with garish yellow and red and blue—*son et lumière,* the instant history of Athens.

He'd had no luck in Athens. Crete, then. But it was a big island. . . .

He swallowed his pride and picked up the phone. Maybe, after all, his mother-in-law could suggest where to find his wife—

"Yes, Mr. Slater?" responded the hotel operator.

—when it occurred to him that he knew someone, a former colleague now working in Crete, who would surely know Manolis Minakis if he was in the neighborhood.

"Operator, I want to reach . . . I think it's called the Foundation for Research and Development, in Iraklion."

"I have a Foundation for Research and Technology, Hellas," said the operator.

"That's it." FORTH, that's what it was called. . . .

"No one answers, sir." It was late, even for Greeks. "If you would like to try again another time, here's the number. . . ."

Anne-Marie arrived in Iraklion harbor at dawn, sitting upright in the ship's second-class lounge after a fitful night.

The bus ride to Lasithi revived her. It was a good and soulful bus, whose young driver had decorated his windshield with garlands of lace and pictures of saints and nightclub singers. He sang along at full volume with the tapes he played on his cassette machine—he favored Maria Pharantouri and the music of Theodorakis—while the conductor went up and down the aisle punching tickets and rolling his eyes at the driver's high notes. After a few miles the bus left the tourist clutter of the coast; the air grew sweeter as it climbed higher. Poplars shimmered and grape leaves glistened in the sunshine; villages went by quickly, and the road pitched ever more steeply as the mountainside grew wild.

"Thymos! O thymos!" cried a woman in black, lowering the window beside her seat. Soon half the passengers in the bus had lowered their windows; some were sticking their heads out, sniffing the air as enthusiastically as puppies. *"Thymos!"* they exclaimed. Even over the diesel fumes, Anne-Marie could smell the wild thyme on the slopes. In her fatigue she shed happy tears, as if the scent of thyme made her nostalgic for better days.

Memory is a charlatan. The months she had spent on Crete had been among the most desperate of her life. After seven years she had returned to undo what had been done to her here—not even to undo it; perhaps the best she could hope for was to finish what had been started here.

* * *

The bus let her off in Ayios Georgios, and she got a lift from a farm boy who claimed business in Ayia Kyriaki. His name was also Georgios, like the dragon-slaying saint in the miniature polychrome that dangled from the mirror of his Toyota pickup. He asked the obligatory questions and quickly learned that yes, she was married, and yes, she had children, and yes, when her own business in Ayia Kyriaki was done she would be rejoining her husband. She was here only to make a few photographs of someone who lived in the village, she told him.

"That must be the rich man who bought a house there three years ago," he said, "but he hardly ever stays in it."

"I'm only here on a job."

Having gotten what news he could from her, Georgios spent the rest of the trip lecturing her on the inevitable triumph of the KKE in the coming elections—never mind low ratings in the polls, the demise of the Soviet Union—due to the moral superiority of the Communist Party over the Socialists of PASOK, who were a bunch of fascists no better than the right-wing New Democracy Party. She listened politely, allowing herself a tiny smile at the icon of Saint George dangling from his mirror.

The road was new, a lane of raw dirt that a bulldozer had scraped out of the cliffside, climbing steeply up the gorge until it entered the plain and reverted to a rutted track through the almond groves. Georgios's pickup plowed through almond petals drifted like snow.

He squeezed the truck into Ayia Kyriaki's single narrow street and stopped beside the cistern in the village square. Anne-Marie climbed down and looked around avidly, seeking what she had imagined.

Sure enough, she knew the place. Here was the chapel and here was Louloudakis's place, with men sitting in front of it who could have come straight from Minakis's narrative—a bearded priest in dusty robes, a gray-haired ancient in baggy pants with a *sariki* drooping on his brow—except these weren't quite the vigorous fellows she had pictured from Minakis's description; these were old men and frail. There were other people on the terrace she hadn't pictured at all, two big boys and a big girl, all with white-blond hair and pale Nordic eyes, stretching their long tan legs out of their canvas shorts as if they owned the place, eyeing her with the annoyance of tourists who think they have found the end of the world only to be interrupted by *you*—their presence partly explained by the sign beside the door that read, "Zimmer. Rent Rooms. Chambres a louer."

Anne-Marie reached into the truck bed for her suitcase, but Georgios was quicker. "You must allow me, *kyria,*" he said, as he yanked it over the tailgate and set it on the ground.

They stood there a moment, nothing left to say; it would be an insult to offer him money. "Let me take your picture," she said.

He brightened at the prospect. She pulled the beat-up Canon from her camera bag and fitted it with a 50mm lens. She waved at him to pose in front of his truck—this way, no, a little more that way. Behind him, the late-morning sun lit the squat church tower across the square and the gray-gold cliffs of Dikti beyond.

"Is it a Polaroid?" he asked through his clenched grin.

"Sorry, no, I'll have to send you a print." She snapped four frames while she talked, then four more. Letting the camera fall from its sling, she pulled a pen and a pad of standard releases from her bag. "Put your address here. And sign your name, if you don't mind me using your picture in a magazine."

He wrote carefully and handed the pad back to her. "Do you need help, finding this man you are supposed to photograph?"

"How many doors are there to knock on?" she said tartly. Then, more gently, "Forgive me, Georgio, I'm tired. I can find the house myself."

"Andio, kyria." He got back into his truck and drove away up the narrow street. His only business in Ayia Kyriaki had been to give her a ride.

"Anne-Marie! What a pleasant surprise." Standing at the open gate, wearing a black silk shirt and tan corduroy trousers, Minakis looked more at ease than he had on Mykonos.

By contrast she felt bedraggled. And miffed. "Why surprised? You invited me."

"Only that you got here so soon." He took her suitcase in one hand and her elbow in the other, drawing her into the courtyard, away from the curious eyes of the villagers who had followed her to his gate.

Again she had the sensation that she knew the place. A recent coat of whitewash had rendered the house and walls almost antiseptically clean, but the beehive *phournos,* the walls of the courtyard crested with scraps of broken pots . . .

"And Peter? Is he with you?"

"I came alone."

"Ah." A complicated expression—regret trying to hide itself—rippled across his face. "I wonder, did you . . . ?"

"I gave him your envelope. We didn't have time to talk. I expect he'll join us soon."

His charm grew wary. "Did you have a pleasant flight?"

"I couldn't get a flight out of Athens, some kind of work slowdown. I slept sitting up in the second-class lounge of the ferry from Piraeus."

"You must be exhausted," he said sympathetically.

"I'm wide awake. And like Squire Hutchinson's mother, I'm hungry enough to eat a donkey."

He smiled. "That won't be necessary. I made an early-morning visit to the market in Ayios Nikolaos."

"How did *you* get here so fast?"

"My yacht reached Ayios Nikolaos last night."

"Oh." She swept the hair from her forehead, the involuntary gesture he found so endearing. "I didn't know you had a yacht."

Lunch was an appetizer of urchin roe followed by red mullet rubbed with herbs and grilled over coals in the fireplace, accompanied by sliced potatoes deep-fried in olive oil and a salad of lettuce and shrimp and hothouse tomatoes with oil and vinegar and herbs. Anne-Marie ate with dedication.

They were sitting at a table that looked a hundred years old, upon which he had set gay pottery and fresh flowers so picturesquely that it might have been one of those slick magazine spreads Anne-Marie occasionally photographed. He poured the

last of a bottle of cold sauvignon blanc and apologized for not
having had time to build a cellar of good local wines.

At last she looked up from her empty plate, smiling bliss-
fully. "You are a marvelous cook."

"Hunger is the best sauce. Cervantes, I think?"

"You must learn to accept a compliment, Manoli." She
sipped her wine. "Now I'm brimming with questions."

"Of course. You're here to interview me."

"The boy who brought me here said you're hardly ever in
residence. Where do you live?"

"I have a house in Athens. And I spend time on my yacht."

"I can't picture this place as a weekend retreat."

He feigned surprise. "Even with all the rugs and pictures?
My restaurant range? My inside plumbing?"

"Oh, you've made it lovely. But why are you *here,* in your
grandmother's house? I took you for someone who wants to
understand his life. . . ."

He cocked his head, inquiring, inviting her to go on.

"Not the sort who wants to relive it," she finished.

Minakis watched her, bright-eyed and quiet as a cat. "You're
right," he said at last. "We live our lives once. And until yesterday it had never occurred to me to look back at my own in such
detail." He propped his elbow on the table and put his chin in
his palm and studied her. "I'm afraid it's not going to be as easy
as you hoped."

Her pale eyes widened; she tried not to betray her sudden
apprehension. She no longer had any doubt that he knew why
she was here—but was he willing to bargain? Did he know how
much she was willing to give?

"You've inspired me to try my hand at autobiography, you
see," Minakis said. "I spent yesterday afternoon and most of the
night at it." He got up and went into the room beyond the arch,
returning with a manila folder. He put it beside her plate.
"Completely raw, no doubt filled with error and self-delusion."

"Sounds like an autobiography, all right." Was this his bargain? She covered her confusion, opening the folder to a thick
pile of yellow lined pages torn from a legal pad, filled with line
after line written with a felt-tipped pen in a tiny hand.

"Tell me what you think of it. Honesty counts." He wasn't smiling. "Then I may answer more of your questions."

She gave him a wry look and, leaning back in her chair, began reading his spare, demotic Greek:

In the spring of 1936 John and Hilda began excavating the Trapeza cave above Tzermiado. On my first weekend free of school I went to join them, starting before dawn, walking the twenty-six miles to Lasithi in six hours. There I encountered Miss Money-Coutts on the ledge in front of the cave, where she and Hilda were washing sherds. When I saw her in front of the cave it was as if I were seeing her for the first time. . . .

18

Never having confided his passion to Money-Coutts or anyone else in two seasons of digging on the Nail, Manolis had no one to confide in now. Back at Knossos in the stifling summer heat, he escaped into the cool depths of the labyrinth, where the Squire had put him to work cataloguing boxes of sherds. Manolis had learned the Knossian pottery styles from Uncle Manolakis, his foster father, and though none of the Brits said it out loud, they considered him an expert.

One morning he was sitting on the cool floor of a basement storage magazine with his back to a wall four thousand years old, a crate of dusty sherds beside him and a sketch pad in his lap, with a pool of diffuse light descending through a grate in the concrete floor over his head—he could hear the shuffle of tourists' feet and the murmur of foreign languages above him—when a shoe scraped in the corridor.

"Who's that?"

Elpida Pateraki came into the light. "Good day, Manoli."

"Good day to you, Elpida. What are you doing here?"

"I thought, if you didn't mind, that I would keep you company for a little while."

He shrugged. "Not much here to interest you." She was his foster cousin (however one labeled these relationships); he saw her every day in the crowded Akoumianakis household.

"I'm interested in what you're doing. But I don't want to bother you."

"What I'm doing is listing these broken pieces of pot."

Her look encouraged him to elaborate. Indeed she had a most encouraging look; her green eyes glowed and her black curls tumbled over her ears, and in the shadows her white teeth shone in a shy smile.

"Where and when they were found," he went on, feeling a sudden sense of importance. "What period they came from. What sort of vessel they were part of—if I can tell. Sketching the pieces that are the most characteristic or unusual. Not many people would find it interesting."

"But you do," she said, her voice knowing and sympathetic. "Don't you want to be an archaeologist?"

"That's not possible," he said automatically. "Maybe I can be like Uncle Manolakis and help a man like John or Sir Arthur."

"Why not a woman like Hilda or Mercy?" she asked, teasing.

"A woman?" The idea hadn't occurred to him. Not that English women couldn't be archaeologists—almost all the English women he knew were archaeologists—but to direct an excavation?

"Like Miss Boyd," Elpida said, "who dug at Gournia and Kavousi. Mercy told me about her. I asked Mercy if she thought I could be an archaeologist."

"*You?*" A Greek girl an archaeologist? This was a fantasy. "Miss Boyd was a rich American."

"Mercy said I should let nothing stand in my way," Elpida said calmly. "She said there are better things for women to do than cook and sew."

"She did?" It sounded like something Money-Coutts would say, although Manolis had never discussed these things with her. But if Money-Coutts had said it . . . . "If you want to become an archaeologist, do your best."

"If I do, that doesn't mean I'm not good at cooking and sewing," Elpida added.

"I didn't say you weren't," Manolis replied crossly.

She showed him the basket she had been holding behind her. "I brought bread and cheese and marinated bulbs. And a little wine. Because you didn't come home for the midday meal yesterday."

"I was thinking about other things."

"I have often watched you thinking. May I sit beside you?"

"Well . . ."

"Thank you." She settled herself with the lunch basket between them. "Now tell me about these broken pots."

So, taking a deep breath, having already developed a fondness for lecturing—and with Elpida's green eyes encouraging him to suppose that she was fastening upon his every word— he did.

Elpida looked nothing like Money-Coutts. Money-Coutts was of average height, and she dressed in slacks or sensible skirts and military-style blouses, while Elpida was as tall as Manolis and full-figured, and she wore long black skirts that dusted the ground. Money-Coutts had brown hair cut short and fair skin that burned pink in the Mediterranean sun. Elpida was brown all year round, and her curling hair was raven black, and her eyes were as green as beryl, her eyebrows thick and dark, her nose bold, her lips wide and mobile. Money-Coutts had straight brows and a thin nose and a rather blunt mouth; she was an English beauty. Elpida was a Greek.

A beauty, oh yes. Manolis wondered how he had missed it before. But her full metamorphosis in his imagination—from childish cousin to desirable female—happened slowly.

She came to visit for an hour or two every day for the rest of the summer, bringing their midday meal, which always included some delicacy. She made him talk about potsherds and tell her about the Minoans—whatever he had learned from Evans and the Pendleburys—and he wondered if she was really as interested as she seemed.

They gossiped about the English. When it came to Money-Coutts, Manolis spoke cautiously, but Elpida spoke with innocent delight of how happy Mercy was with her Greek fiancé, how sad Mercy was to be parted from him. Everything she said seared Manolis's heart. Before long his heart was so thoroughly seared that it no longer bled, and he looked back at his infatuation from a distance.

Meanwhile little accidents occurred in the basement storerooms of Knossos: Elpida paused to adjust a shoe just as Manolis entered a corridor, so narrow he could not help but bump into her; Elpida dropped a serving spoon as they sat eating on the basement floor, and her breast lightly brushed his arm as she bent to retrieve it; he stopped in that same narrow corridor, and she collided with him, and he shocked himself by turning and kissing her clumsily—and was shocked again when she responded urgently for an eternity, several seconds at least, the two of them pressing as much of themselves against each other as they could manage, aided by the constrictions of the ancient walls, before she broke away and stepped back, staring at him, saying nothing, her eyes and mouth hungry, nevertheless shaking her black curls decisively and backing away.

That time he turned and left the palace; they left separately and secretly, as they always did, and she did not come back before the summer ended and the school year began.

After school on a cool October evening, as they walked past the palace toward Knossos village from the stop where the bus had left them, he shared a secret with her. "I have been studying the Minoan writing. The clay leaves."

"Oh Manoli!" Her face was bright with excitement. "How did you get permission?"

"I have the Squire's keys."

Her expression cooled. "That's forbidden."

"Perhaps the English own the land where the palace stands, but do they own the past?"

"What have you done?"

He told her. He had been going into the labyrinth on mornings when he was supposed to be at school, or evenings when he could claim to have been delayed. Slipping silently through the pines, into the ruin, he had opened the padlocks and swung

back the wire-screen doors and helped himself to the stacks of
clay tablets upon which the Minoan scripts were inscribed.

Strange writing carved on sealstones had first drawn Arthur
Evans to Crete in the 1890s. On the island the sealstones were
called milkstones, because village women valued them as
amulets to ensure the flow of mother's milk; often Evans could
not persuade the women to part with them, no matter how much
money he offered. Later, digging in Knossos, he found a trove
of similar writing, including thousands of inscribed clay tablets
not much bigger than willow leaves, baked hard and burned
purple in the conflagration that had destroyed the last palace.

But as the years and then the decades went by, Sir Arthur published only part of what he found. In 1909, in *Scripta Minoa*, he
described tablets with so-called hieroglyphs, and others bearing
the script he called Linear A, but he never published more than
a few samples of the script he called Linear B. The unpublished
tablets stayed locked in the basements of Knossos.

There Manolis crouched in the darkness, copying the signs
in his notebooks, working late by the light of a shuttered lamp.

"What have you learned with all this spying?" Elpida's eyes
were bright with concern, but equally with curiosity.

He stopped in the road and turned to face her. "I would not
have told you if I couldn't trust you."

"You can trust me"—she reached out to touch his arm, but
there was a green glint in her eye—"as long as you let me go
there with you."

A few days later he whispered to her to slip away after the dinner chores and join him in the palace. Elpida's cousin Phylia
saw them with their heads together and smiled wickedly, but
Elpida said, "Don't worry about her; she won't tell."

They crouched together in the cold basement; above them,
snow fell silently through the pines. It was early November, the
winter's first snowfall. He held up a leaf of burnt purple clay he
had been sketching by lantern light.

"I've copied dozens of these. I mean to copy out all the most
characteristic tablets, sign for sign." There was a way of relat-
ing the signs, he told her, a translation that might produce

meaning—a thin meaning, devoid of sounds and devoid of reference to *things*—but at the very least a meaning of relations among signs. "It's why the roots of words are units, but the beginnings and endings of words change by rules. It's why the order of words in different languages is different, but always according to rules. . . ."

"Do you know the rules?" She looked at him with an intensity that insisted he go on.

"Only a few." He could not find words for his conviction that underlying everything in language was mathematical regularity. "There must be almost three thousand of these tablets stacked in the palace magazines. Only a few hundred are Linear A. So I started with Linear B."

"Uncle Manolakis says Sir Arthur said you shouldn't try to interpret them."

"Don't worry, I'm not saying the writing is Hittite or Babylonian or something."

"Uncle Manolakis says Sir Arthur said the tablets aren't poems or letters, just lists of animals and things."

"Elpida, never mind what Sir Arthur said"—he was bold enough to take her hand and squeeze it—"let me show you what he meant. Some of these have a picture of the thing they're about, a chariot or a tripod or a storage jar." He tapped the fingers of his free hand at a hieroglyph on the clay tablet. "The signs for numbers are plain enough: a tripod—that's three-footed—or a two-eared or a three-eared or a four-eared jar. Numbers up to ten. John claims they used ratios and percentages."

"Do you think so?"

"I don't know yet."

He showed her more tablets. The Minoan scribes had often separated words with slashes in the clay, which made it possible to compare signs even if the words were meaningless.

"A lot of words are repeated with three different endings. I'm trying to copy every example I can find."

Elpida leaned closer and, in comradely fashion, laid her hand on the back of his neck. "If you want to be finished before Easter, let me help you."

For a moment he said nothing, because he was not thinking about copying signs. He leaned toward her, but she pulled away and turned her face aside, with a groan that was a promise.

He said, "Yes. I could use some help."

On winter nights, after the evening meal was finished and cleared away, they pored over their schoolbooks by the light of an oil lantern on the table in the Akoumianakis kitchen. Not everything in their notebooks was schoolwork.

Sister Phylia pressed them hard, wanting to know *just* what they were doing, and only when she left them in peace could they take stock of their progress.

By March they had determined that the endings of some of the words on the tablets changed in specific ways—five kinds of words, each with three endings: five sets of signs that consistently changed to three other sets of signs.

"Nouns," Elpida said. "Tripod, jar, chariot . . ."

"And the changes are declensions," Manolis agreed. "Which means we can pull them apart." He sketched a grid in his notebook and wrote *alpha, epsilon, iota* across its top and *1, 2, 3* down its left side.

The signs of Minoan script were syllables, not letters of an alphabet. By laying out a grid—vowels along the top, consonants down the side—and by putting each sign onto that grid according to the way it behaved in the supposed declensions of the supposed nouns, Manolis and Elpida began to prize apart the relations among the sounds of Linear B. They could do that even though they could not know how those sounds sounded, much less what they meant.

Late one night Elpida asked, "How many languages *do* you know?"

They were sitting in the kitchen in the dark, having blown out the lamp, and he could hardly see her, just the sheen of her black hair limned in the moonlight through the window, but he could smell the Rethymniot soap she washed with and the wild herbs she cooked with and the too-clean, too-scrubbed odor of the hand-me-down clothes she wore.

"From schoolmasters and their books I learned what the conquerors spoke—Indo-European languages, mostly, and Turkic and Arabic."

Rapt in the cold darkness, she wanted him to tell her more, to tell her everything. He thought she meant everything he knew about languages.

"I can hardly wait until John comes back," he said, "to tell *him* what we've found. . . ."

On a sunny April morning in 1939, John Pendlebury took a stroll with Uncle Manolakis and his grown sons on the heights above the Kairatos stream, which skirts the palace of Knossos to the east. Manolis, the youngest, the foster child, brought up the rear. The wheat was green and the grapevines were putting out translucent new leaves; the chalky yellow earth was spangled with wildflowers, anemones and crocuses and asphodels and irises in a dozen shades of red and white and purple, bending and trembling in the warm breeze from the south which blew at the men's backs, surrounding them with perfume as they talked of the war.

A month ago, Germany had occupied Czechoslovakia. A week ago, Italy had invaded Albania, and it was clear that Mussolini lusted for Greece. A few days ago Micky Akoumianakis had enlisted in the army, and his younger brother Minos had applied for the navy.

"The first strike will be from Albania," Pendlebury said, as if he relished the event, "but Crete controls the entrance to the Aegean, and the Italians hold the islands to the east and north. So we'll be next."

Old Manolakis pulled his wide straw hat farther down on his forehead to shade his eyes from the glare. "Will you be on Crete when the Italians come, John? This year you left your wife and children in England. That was wise of you. Next year, I think, you'll be in England with them."

Pendlebury struck the dirt with his walking stick. "England can't stay out of this fight. I know this island better than any Englishman alive."

"Better than any Cretan alive."

Pendlebury put on a humble face. "Modesty requires . . ."

"The map of Crete, I meant to say," Manolakis added, which brought a laugh from his sons. "Cretans don't have much use for maps. We know of your affection for us, John, but after all, you are an Englishman."

"Let's talk cartography then," Pendlebury said, hiding his hurt. "If I were an Italian general trying to take Crete . . ."

"You would be wise to have written your will," said Micky fervently. He was of late a law student at Athens.

"Bravely spoken, my child," said Manolakis. "Strive to contain your ardor while our English friend tells us what's on his mind."

Pendlebury slashed through the wildflowers with his stick. "I want you to see this place as I see it, Old Wolf. Mountains to the east and west. Iraklion to the north, with the best airfield on the island. To the south the wide beaches of the Messara—the only place where landing craft can come ashore in numbers. And right here, the road that connects them." With his stick Pendlebury gestured across the stream, where the ruins of Knossos were exposed; from the palace narrow traces of the ancient paved road extended north and south, and beside it the modern road. "This ridge commands the center of Crete as it did four thousand years ago. Any enemy of Crete must take these heights. Any defender of Crete must hold them."

"We have long understood this," Manolakis replied. "Perhaps as long as the English. Perhaps longer."

"You are with me, Manolaki?"

"Why would you think otherwise, my child?"

"We'll slaughter them before they reach Yannina," said Micky.

Nobody could find a suitable reply to Micky's martial boast. But Mussolini's troops were one thing. If (more realistically, when) Hitler and the Wehrmacht got into it . . .

Young Minos said, "Surely the women have made us a meal by now."

The women had. The men ate on the jasmine-scented terrace of the Villa Ariadne, and when at last they had fallen silent, exhausted by their warlike passions and lulled into slóth by the lavish midday meal, Pendlebury, whose skin had the high bronze color that made him seem to glow in the afternoon sunlight, turned his skewed gaze upon Manolis, who had not said a word during their tour of the heights.

"Ready for a few months of honest toil, boffin? Ready to trade the books for a bit of hod carrying and sherd washing?"

"I'm eager to go back up to Lasithi."

"Not eager for the dirt and the pots, I venture." Pendlebury poured cloudy green wine into his tumbler and offered him the jug, which he refused. "Not, I fear, on account of Money-Coutts."

This brought drowsy chuckles from the Akoumianakises, who had kept an ear open while contemplating their digestions.

"For the mountains," Manolis said, his face hot.

"To the mountains, then." Pendlebury sipped his wine. From Pendlebury, who never apologized, his live eye upon Manolis signaled a concession.

Manolis was not appeased. "Have you done the three peaks of Dikti yet, *kyrie?*"

"This year, I hope."

"I have, twice. Let me know when you decide to try again."

Pendlebury straightened in his chair. "You mean to race me?"

Manolis shrugged. "We'll compare times, if you like."

"I have never yet met a boffin I couldn't outrun."

"Have you met a boffin you could not outthink?" During the pause that followed Manolis ignored the grins and whispers of the others and concentrated on Pendlebury, who studied the tumbler in his hands a long while before he looked up and smiled dangerously.

"Try me, my child."

When the Akoumianakis men had gone off to Knossos village, Manolis withdrew the notebook from his *sakouli* and spread it open on the table in front of Pendlebury. "I put the signs on the grid according to the declensions. Vowels across the top, consonants down the side. Five vowels, alpha, epsilon, iota, omikron, probably upsilon. The consonants, I'm not sure of. There are at least fourteen."

"Which Indo-European language?" Pendlebury asked, peering at the inked matrixes.

"Kyrie?" Surely it was a trick question. "Any of them. Persian. Anatolian. Greek."

Pendlebury looked up. "You speak classical Greek, do you, Androulakis?"

"Oshi," Manolis said, emphasizing the Cretan pronunciation. "But I have a lexicon."

Pendlebury harrumphed, turning his attention back to the grid ruled on the page, its interstices filled with carefully copied Minoan signs. Some were simple and universal—a flail, an ax, a circle with a cross inside, which was the primitive mandala—but many were as intricate as Chinese ideograms. "Ingenious, truly ingenious. We ought to call you Minos, if that weren't your foster brother's name. Little Minos, then. *Minosakis."* Pendlebury let the book fall closed. "You're not the first, of course."

"Kyrie?"

"Not the first to propose that the scripts represent an Indo-European tongue. You've been preceded by a long line of distinguished scholars. All as mistaken as you, I'm sorry to tell you. Minoan is Minoan, Little Minos. Distinct. Unique."

"You're right about Linear A, sir. There don't seem to be any of the—"

"Look here, child, there's no important difference between A and B. A couple of dozen signs fell into disuse, a dozen new ones were added; fundamentally it's the same script, refined a bit for use by a new class of clerks. Today we would call that sort of person—what's the fashionable word?—a *bureaucrat."*

Manolis said, "I don't think they are the same language."

Pendlebury laughed. "Let me tell you the news. On my way here through Athens I met with an American who's been digging in the far west of the Peloponnese. He's found a Mycenaean palace that he claims is Nestor's Sandy Pylos. You know who Nestor was?"

"Homer's famous windbag."

"Quite. At any rate, Professor Blegen uncovered an enormous cache of tablets and brought a couple of hundred with him to Athens. He was good enough to let me have a look. They are inscribed with the Minoan script"—Pendlebury tapped his fingers on Manolis's notebook—"but the signs aren't combined in the same way. Maybe our Minoans taught Nestor's savages how to write. Perhaps *their* language was Indo-European. Perhaps it might even have been a barbaric form of Greek. It wasn't Minoan, though. It wasn't the language on our Knossos tablets."

"Kyrie, would you tell me how carefully . . . I mean, how long you were able to study Professor Blegen's tablets?"

Pendlebury's face lost its cheerful expression. "You're a bright lad, Little Minos, but do keep in mind that everything you know about ancient Crete you learned from me."

Manolis hesitated before he nodded.

"I suppose this is some sort of adolescent rebellion," Pendlebury said grumpily. "Now I don't sympathize with that. Sir Arthur would be very unhappy to know that you've been poking about in the tablets. He would consider it a breach of trust. Why, he practically tore Sundwall's head off, that poor old Finn, for copying tablets out of the *museum* without his permission."

"Nobody else knows what I've done." Manolis's heart sank as he lied. Elpida knew, and understood.

"Well, then." Pendlebury's hands twitched where they rested on the notebook. "You're not a philologist, child, you're a gifted and utterly untutored mathematician. This was a damned clever attempt at deciphering a sort of code, I'll give you that, even if it is all wrong."

"As you say." Manolis reached for the notebook. He had to pry it from under Pendlebury's fingers, while Pendlebury fixed his glassy stare on the boy.

"You and I have a greater problem than deciphering the Minoan script, Androulakis."

Manolis didn't answer. He was mulling the year's hard work his mentor had just dismissed.

"Despite your best efforts to the contrary, they're going to graduate you from that high school," Pendlebury continued, undeterred. "A few weeks from now—and don't think your teachers haven't considered this—you'll be cannon fodder. As for me, granted that I'm impossibly softhearted, but I don't like to imagine you in the passes of Epirus, chasing Italians through the snow."

Manolis looked up, sensing an affront. "Micky's going into the army. Why shouldn't I?"

"I admire Micky," Pendlebury said, "but Greece can spare a lawyer for the front lines. You're a different sort. Sir Arthur would prefer to have you at Oxford, but I think he'll go along with me when I put you up for Cambridge."

Manolis could only stare in confusion. Oxford? Cambridge? In his lap the notebook in which he had painstakingly begun the decipherment of Minoan Linear B lay forgotten. "Cambridge?"

Pendlebury took another swig of green wine. "Assuming they'll have you," he said, sounding genuinely cheerful.

19

Anne-Marie kept a thumb in the sheaf of pages and went into the kitchen, a room Minakis had added to the back of his grandmother's house. She found him drying the lunch dishes and arranging them on the shelves of a varnished pine cabinet.

"I'm curious," she said.

He turned and smiled, encouraging her.

"You said you don't believe anything in the past could have happened differently. If you had deciphered Linear B, that certainly would have rewritten history."

"I didn't decipher Linear B. Like many others, Elpida and I made a start."

He closed the dish cabinet and turned, leaning against the counter. "Of course Pendlebury was wrong, spectacularly wrong. Blegen's Pylos tablets were the same script as the Knossos tablets, the same as the tablets Wace found at Mycenae, which Ventris and Chadwick later used to prove that Linear B was Greek. John's authoritative bullheadedness forever put me off the track."

"I see your point." Anne-Marie suppressed the other questions that teemed in her mind and quietly left him to the dishes, while she went back to the reading of his scribbled manuscript.

On the last day of August 1939 I left the harbor of Elounda in a flying boat. . . .

I said good-bye to Elpida on the pier where Micky had driven us. I hardly dared to look her in the eye; neither of us expected to see the other again.

With a horrible roar of engines the airplane lifted from the bay. I looked down in naive wonder at the sea and the islands and the cloud tops passing below. My head should have been full of mythological images, of Daedalos and Ikaros fleeing Crete, but I was thinking of Elpida.

When I had told her of Pendlebury's response to our work with Linear B, she was angry on my behalf—chiding me for giving up too easily, for fearing to offend Sir Arthur. I protested that that wasn't the reason, that Blegen's cache from Pylos had persuaded John that the Minoan script was unique, just as Sir Arthur maintained. I believed him, I said.

"You have to believe him," she replied. "He is your *sadalos.*" She meant that without a powerful sponsor, a patron for whom one must be prepared to sacrifice even one's convictions, no Greek can hope to prosper. It was then that I told her that Pendlebury and Evans had offered to send me to university. This time she was angry for her own sake, and left without saying another word.

When I went up to the Nail—everyone knew it was the last season—Elpida stayed at Knossos. I was surprised that she insisted on riding to Elounda with me in Micky's automobile. She was silent the whole trip. My last image of her was of brooding silence.

Three days later I was in Cambridge, a labyrinth of stone and brick passageways, darker than usual, because while I was en route Britain had entered the war—windows were blacked out, and no lights were displayed at night. But I was a connoisseur of labyrinths; I was intrigued by those damp and echoing passageways.

Having known members of the British School in Crete, I

thought I knew the English. Not so. I found myself surrounded by pink-cheeked schoolboys, so earnest at their sports, so quick to trade insults, so susceptible to drink. We were required to wear black gowns that made us resemble beardless monks, and like monks we were locked inside fortresslike colleges after curfew. Yet—and this was strangest of all—we had the freedom to consort with respectable women without a chaperone, a freedom I found almost too terrifying to contemplate. In Crete, dishonor was death. The most dangerous thing that Elpida and I had done in the basements of Knossos was not to rifle Sir Arthur's crates of Minoan tablets but to be there alone together. In England it was not punishment that terrified me. It was English girls.

In some ways I benefited by my foreignness. I was impervious to English class distinctions, which were based upon one's pedigree and accent. I was a barbarian; anyone who dealt with me had to form his opinion de novo. Most simply consigned me to the category of wog. Among the others I made a friend or two.

This was the *Sitzkrieg* after the collapse of Poland, the so-called phony war, but tension was high as everyone waited for the next blow to fall. Greece was no democracy, but it was democracy's ancient home, and the fact that it was menaced by the Italians was in my favor. The English were more sentimental about my homeland than I was, possessively so. Lord Byron was often quoted. I was amazed to learn how many Greek treasures the English had benevolently removed during past upheavals—mainly, I gathered, to protect them from us Greeks.

During the month of September I took tea with the Pendleburys every week at their home, although John was often away, busy recruiting officer candidates among the undergraduates. Through some complicated system of favors I never understood, I found myself not at John's old college but at King's, better known for its theater than for its mathematics. Alan Turing was a grand exception; had Britain not entered the war a day before I arrived I might have had him as a tutor. But the code breakers had already whisked him away.

I had two whole rooms of my own in a narrow tower, with

a view through stone casements of neatly mowed grass three stories below. How alien that tame growth seemed to me! Inside my cramped but private rooms I learned to boil water on a gas ring, trying, without success, to acquire a taste for tea.

I was the only one of my class to propose an exhibition in maths. My don was a harmless young "moral philosopher," the Cambridge term for a scientist, whose head was in the clouds of Boolean algebra. The university lectures saved me. G. H. Hardy made a profound impression—he was the mathematical purist who sponsored Ramanujan, the Indian genius.

Opposite was Wittgenstein of the famous leather jacket, enamored of using ordinary language to destroy mathematical proof. In his seminar I heard for the first time the famous Liar's Paradox: " 'All Cretans are liars,' said Epimenides the Cretan." I didn't take it personally. This Epimenides was no doubt from Sphakia, a notorious nest of thieves.

As for my free time, a train ride would take me to country the English thought wild—lakes, moors, granite tors, chalk cliffs overlooking the green sea—and I walked through my loneliness in a wet landscape as exotic as the moon.

Along with the bread and cheese in my tidy British knapsack, I brought books. What one reads gets entangled with where one reads it. Just as I will always associate *Treasure Island* with a shepherd's hut on Dikti, I will always associate *Principia Mathematica* with the highest peaks of the Pennines—half as high as Dikti but wild enough in their own damp way. I could afford such books because Pendlebury had arranged a grant, in which I overindulged, buying too many expensive volumes. In my rooms I read constantly and "sported my oak"—undergraduate slang for keeping one's door closed so as not to be disturbed.

Among the few people to whom I opened my door was Richard Wingate, three years my senior and also a maths exhibitionist. Our don had introduced us, and after one of Hardy's lectures we exchanged a few words; next time we went to a shop in town for a pastry. In Richard I had found a rare thing, a friend—one I hoped who could translate the unspoken languages of an alien universe. He was a diminutive but graceful young man, his hair always trim, his suits always spotless and crisp, and he had a lurking sense of humor.

He was an Etonian with many old-school connections, and he soon offered to introduce me to his undergraduate society, the Epistolarians. The dozen or so members met in one another's college rooms or occasionally in hired rooms in restaurants, dandied up in evening clothes—where, after a supper of raw beef and burnt pudding, someone would be tapped to give a speech on a topic such as "free will versus determinism" or "moral conscience versus social custom."

Having attended three or four of these meetings as a guest—wearing borrowed togs—one night without warning I was called upon to speak. I managed to suppress stage fright long enough to give an impromptu talk on "the utility of absurd propositions," consisting of a few scattered musings on Maxwell's demon and Zeno's paradoxes suggested by my recent discovery of Russell and Whitehead. My wholly unoriginal conclusion was that thought experiments, even when they appear to violate common sense, give rise to fresh ways of thinking. Afterward Richard seemed much stimulated, perhaps more by sherry than by anything I had said—I had no idea whether he or anyone else had grasped what I was talking about. No matter. It was made known to me, in the crab-scuttling manner then in fashion among English undergraduates, that I was welcomed into the club.

I spent Christmas of 1939 with Richard and his family at what he called their city digs, a town house in London that was the grandest private dwelling I'd yet seen. Richard was the presumptive heir of a textile fortune; his father, who had been granted some kind of nonhereditary title, was an admirer of Oswald Mosley, the British fascist, and over supper the old man thundered that we Greeks would do well to admit the moral superiority of the fascist philosophy and the natural and historical hegemony of the Italians over the Greeks. I mumbled something about sovereignty. What more could I say? Metaxas's government was a dictatorship as oppressive as Mussolini's.

Whereupon Richard launched himself upon a defense of the

Greece yet to come (a vision of which I had heard nothing) so vigorous that his father ended by accusing him of Communist sympathies. When Richard replied, "What if I am a Communist?" his father threw down his napkin and left the table.

After a few moments of silence, Richard and his mother and I finished our supper by discussing the season's theater.

Richard's mother fondly thought of her grown boy as a toddler; in that big house we were put in twin beds in the same upstairs room. Nothing remarkable to me—I was used to sleeping anywhere, with whatever donkeys, dogs, cats, sheep, goats, or strangers happened to be on the premises.

I had already fallen asleep when a movement awoke me. I found Richard beside me in my bed, sliding under the sheets. "Manoli," he whispered, "do you have any idea of my feelings for you?"

"We do get on awfully well," I said in my best British, trying to understand exactly what he meant.

Evidently this was not an adequate response, for Richard pushed closer and began snapping the elastic of his underpants in what I suppose he thought was a provocative fashion. "Have you ever made love to another man?" he asked, with tremulous urgency.

"Actually, I have never made love to anyone."

"But you must have wanted to."

"A man? I don't see how it's possible."

"Oh, it's possible," he replied. His breathing was now quite ragged. "Let me show you."

I sat up and almost fell out the far side of the narrow bed. "No. No thank you, I mean. I'm not really interested. I mean my interest is strictly academic. I mean . . ."—by now I was practically stuttering—"I mean I'm really *not* interested."

He was quiet a moment. Then he asked, in a wounded tone, "Have I done anything to offend you?"

"I have the greatest affection for you, Richard. You are a good friend to me"—I came close to admitting that he was my only friend—"but I simply don't . . . well, you see, this business . . . that is, I like *women*."

"You can't really *know* that. You just said you've never had any experience."

"Nevertheless . . . I suppose I was born that way." To myself, I sounded as if I were apologizing.

He tried a different tack then, pretending cool amusement. "If you find my proposition so absurd, you owe it to yourself to expand your thinking. You were the one who argued for the utility of absurd propositions."

Which so agitated me that I recoiled and *did* fall out of the bed. "That argument is specious," I said, leaping up again. "I was referring to *thought* experiments. This is hardly the time or place for a moral-scientific dispute."

"Not much of a Greek, are you?" he said in a snide tone, and when I asked him what he meant by that, he gave me a thumbnail lecture about the sexual and philosophical propensities of the classical Greeks, much of which was news to me. I could only reply that, since I was from Crete and the furthest thing imaginable from a classical Greek, I was sorry if I had disappointed him; now I hoped he would allow me to get some sleep. Whereupon he heaved himself out of my bed and back to his own, and I heard no more from him that night except an occasional expressive sigh.

The next morning it was as if nothing had been said. Richard was as blithe as ever. We toured the city; at the London Zoo I saw my first polar bear—my first bear of any kind. I told him the story of the riddling game with Pendlebury ("Any polar explorers in your family, Androulakis?"), and Richard laughed, and I realized that I liked him very much and hoped the awkwardness of the night would not mar our friendship. When he saw me off on the train to Oxford the next day, he was all smiles.

Sir Arthur Evans had invited me to visit him at Youlbury, his country home near Oxford, a snug, warm place on a hill, filled with treasures from his explorations and travels. He was eighty-seven years old and full of vigor. After we traded gossip—he wanted to know all about the Hutchinsons, what the Pendleburys were up to in Lasithi, the fortunes of the Akoumianakis clan, and so on—he engaged me in archaeological debate as if I had something sensible to say.

I was tempted to open my heart and tell the old man what was on my mind concerning Linear B. I didn't, and I lost my chance, and a good thing I did, for he was fierce on the subject and never changed his opinion. I left Youlbury with an attack of homesickness, the worst since I'd come to England.

A few nights later Richard came to my room in the company of two football-playing Epistolarians whom he knew I disliked—whether he'd brought them or they'd brought him I don't know, but shortly they began trading crude remarks about the filthiness of Greeks generally and my own shortcomings in the way of appearance, intellect, and manners. Richard just stood by with a peculiar, sad expression on his face. I told him I wanted to speak to him privately.

"Oh, I don't think so," he said.

After that I saw him occasionally across a lecture hall or on the far side of the refectory, but we never said another word to each other at Cambridge, and I never went to another meeting of the Epistolarians.

My mood turned dark. I was depressed by Richard's weakness and spite, by my loneliness, by the black weather, by the claustrophobia of blackout-shuttered nights, by news of Axis advances in the Low Countries. I asked myself why I was in England. Because at heart I wanted to be an Englishman? Answers that had been plain a few weeks ago now seemed facile.

In mid-May, John Pendlebury was granted weekend leave from his army camp, and I was invited to supper. What a haven that small house was, overflowing with children and books, smelling of fresh bread and precious hoarded bacon! John, fresh from the train, looked magnificent in his cavalry uniform, crisp pinks and gleaming boots and shining brass buckles. His manner, always gruff but teasingly so, had taken on a martial edge. Nor did Hilda make apologies for him.

After supper he interviewed me rather fiercely on my academic progress. I told him that I was holding my own in mathematics, but that try as I might, I was unable to persuade myself that philosophy was not trivial.

"You are keeping secrets, Little Minos," he said accusingly.

"According to my sources, you are as famous among the dons as you were among the schoolteachers of Lasithi. The mathematicians speak of you in the same breath as that poor Indian, Ramanujan, who I'm told starved himself to death for love of numbers."

"My love of numbers is not so pure," I said, confused by this flattery.

"And then there is the physics, or whatever. A Professor Dirac—chap won the Nobel Prize, I'm told—said something about a paper of yours. Don't remember what. Remarkable only because the fellow rarely says anything at all."

"I didn't know that." I'd written a note on the theory of negative electrons for Dirac's seminar; the only response was a correction in the margin.

Pendlebury cocked his head at me. You would have had to know, as I did, that his left eye was glass to detect anything the least unusual about his penetrating stare. "Perhaps you think I am asking myself about the soundness of our investment in your education."

"You have every right to do so," I replied.

"In fact that's not what I'm after." He switched to Cretan-accented Greek, as if spies were lurking. "Because I trust you completely, I will tell you a secret. I'm going back to Crete."

"To prepare for an invasion," I said.

"I'm to be British vice-consul in Iraklion," he said, agreeing without saying yes.

"I've been thinking of going back to Crete myself."

"That's what I suspected, and that's why we are having this conversation. If you want to defend Ellas—and not only Ellas, but free men everywhere—you are far more valuable here."

"I don't know about Ellas. I want to defend Kriti. I know Lasithi better than anyone."

"There are others who know Lasithi almost as well, and I doubt that any of them would be of any use deciphering the enemy's codes or building new weapons against the enemy."

"Forgive me for saying so, *kyrie* Pendabri, but it sounds strange to hear you asking me to leave the defense of Crete to the English."

"The issue is larger than one island, Little Minos. This will be a world war, much more encompassing than the Great War. Every one of us must make use of his resources and talents."

"I understand your concern for the British Empire. But my talents are sheep and goat tending, cheese making, shooting, and the identification of broken pots. My shooting, at least, might be useful against Germans."

"See this?" Pendlebury took up the walking stick he had with him, not the rough old shepherd's stick he had carried in Crete, but a polished oaken staff with brass fittings. He seized its handle, gave it a twist, and with a flourish and a ring of steel he drew out a glittering blade. "A sword stick," he said, "wildly romantic, an affectation, according to my fellow officers. But I have been studying the German paratroopers. Never mind the Italians, there will be no taking of Crete without the Germans. Do you know that the German paratroopers cannot carry their weapons with them when they jump? Their arms and supplies must be dropped separately. Inside their coveralls they carry grenades and a Schmeisser machine pistol with a few rounds, useless at more than thirty yards. They cannot even defend themselves as they descend." He swung his sword, making it whistle, then jabbed it into the low ceiling. "A traditional weapon, but I think it will prove telling." He grinned wickedly and resheathed the sword inside the walking stick. "I'm not a fool, Manolis. Airplanes and tanks and submarines and radio communications have changed the nature of warfare. Equally ingenious devices will be devised in this war. You will help devise them. For our side."

"I'm a neutral," I said. "Your side does not consider me to be on their side."

"They will, my son, and very soon.".

I doubt he realized what he'd said. In Greek, everybody is "my child," but not "my son." By calling me his son, Pendlebury temporarily won my compliance. Despite my longing for Crete—which crystallized most vividly in my longing for Elpida and her teasing intelligence, her challenges, her fiery moods—I did not leave England for another year.

20

May 20, 1941, a Tuesday, began beautifully in the west of Crete. As the sun climbed above the morning hills, pearly coastal fog cleared to reveal a calm sea. Minutes later the smooth surface of the water was darkened by the shadows of Stukas and Messerschmitts in formation, flying from the north. Behind the fighters and bombers came swarms of Junker transports, many of them towing gliders. Their objective was a landing ground west of Hania, the closest to mainland Greece.

Seven months earlier, in October, the Italians had invaded Greece, but by December the Greeks had chased the unhappy fascists back across the border into Albania; Hitler cursed when he had to divert forces from his planned assault on Russia to bail out Mussolini. The Greek dictatorship reluctantly accepted help from Great Britain, but it was too little, too late. Greece surrendered in April, two weeks after the Germans attacked. The remnants of the Greek army and their British, Australian, and New Zealander allies fled to Crete.

A month went by before the Luftwaffe attacked Crete. That morning the defenders in Iraklion, eighty miles to the east, heard not a word of the airborne assault on Hania, a failure of communications for which there would never be an explanation—except that Tuesday had been a bad-luck day ever since the Tuesday in 1453 when Constantinople fell to the Turks.

"What marvelous timing, Androulakis! I'll want the story of how you got here just as soon as I have time to listen—you always were devious—but if you want to help us win, you have to swear to me right this minute that you won't let yourself get shot." Pendlebury was hunched over his desk in the British consulate, scribbling furiously.

"I cannot be killed by bullets," Manolis said without a hint of humor. He was dressed in a British army uniform with Greek insignia; he sported a trim mustache and a beret pulled down snugly on his head. A Marlin gun was slung over his shoulder.

"Oh, marvelous, a Cambridge moral philosopher who believes in magic." Pendlebury glanced up from his scribbling. Where his left eye would have been he wore a black patch. His glass eye sat beside him on the desktop, staring at Manolis independently. "Just because a shepherd boy with a birding gun couldn't hit you doesn't mean a German paratrooper with a tommy gun can't. Eh, Grigorakis?"

"You ask my advice, Pendabri?" A mustachioed gent in baggy trousers leaned against the wall, his arms crossed over his chest. "Use this one up quickly. See if he is as brave as he is stupid."

"Hear that, Androulakis?" Pendlebury still scribbled. "Here speaks a man with so many bullets in him they claim he is the devil incarnate."

Manolis feigned boredom, as he had learned to do at Cambridge. "I have heard of Captain Satan. Is it true, Captain, that you shot off your own finger because it failed you rolling dice? Surely that was an act of great . . . bravery."

Satan stood away from the wall, bringing his silver-inlaid carbine across his chest. His right hand gripped the small of the stock, and it was plain that his trigger finger had been severed at the first joint. "And I have heard that Manolis Androulakis was born without a father. Is a bastard mocking me?"

"No more discussion," Pendlebury said sharply, folding the paper and handing it to Manolis. "Take this to the Old Wolf at Knossos. Tell him that what we discussed has come to pass—except that we face Germans, not Italians. Then I want you to go to Krousonas, in the foothills of Ida. Can you find it?"

"Certainly. Why go there?"

"Because I order you to."

Manolis came stiffly to attention. *"SAH!"*

"Oh, give it a rest," Pendlebury said. "Somehow you talked yourself into the SOE against my express displeasure. But you're in my clutches now, child, and I'm appointing you my deputy liaison between the irregulars and the allied forces. That's a fancy name for a runner." Pendlebury stood up from his desk and snatched his sword stick. "If the Cretans possessed the ten thousand rifles I begged Wavell to give them, they wouldn't need allies."

"We have arms," said Captain Satan, hefting his carbine. "Everything we hid from the Royalists."

"Precisely weapons of that vintage, Grigorakis, and what few rounds of ammunition you have hoarded," Pendlebury said irritably, "which means that despite the bravery of warriors like you and your men, it will be a long fight." He turned to Manolis. "Knossos, then Krousonas. Wait for me there. We have important things to discuss."

Manolis snapped a salute. *"SAH!"*

Pendlebury returned it smartly, but when Manolis turned on his heel and marched out, Pendlebury could not suppress a grin.

At four o'clock in the afternoon, Stukas and Messerschmitts appeared over the city. The Messerschmitts strafed everything that moved on the quays. The Stukas had sirens under their wings to make them howl as they dived, and whistles on their bombs, the better to terrify those below. The bombs were aimed at the ships, not for the docks, which the Germans hoped to preserve.

A mile to the east the bombs were aimed for the defenses around the airstrip, not for the airstrip itself, but these hit only dirt; the defenses visible from the air were decoys, wooden guns manned by scarecrows. In the rocky hills, well-camouflaged British antiaircraft machine guns and Bofors guns held their fire, waiting for the German troop transports.

The Messerschmitts and Stukas emptied their magazines and bomb racks over Iraklion and, running low on fuel, retreated to Athens, to the dust storms and wreckage of the *Fliegerkorps's* crowded dirt airfields. For a long time, no transports appeared. Although the defenders of Iraklion could not know it, German plans had gone badly awry.

At last came the green German "Aunties," the trimotor Junker 52s, flocks of them full of paratroopers, low and slow and loud—a mere two hundred feet off the ground, fatally behind schedule and unprotected by air cover, the ripest imaginable targets. Only when they were close enough to be pinned in the gunsights did the British Bofors guns open fire.

Transports fell in flames—two of them, six of them, a dozen, fifteen Junkers—exploding in midair or going down trailing smoke.

Parachutists tumbled out of the crippled planes, their parachutes hanging up in the wide tail assemblies, or blossoming into flame as they opened, or never opening at all. Even at two hundred feet, those who survived the jump still had to endure five long seconds dangling in the air. White parachutes for the officers. Olive drab parachutes for the men. Much bigger and much slower than clay pigeons. Some died in the sky. Some came down into green fields and olive groves where soldiers jumped up to meet them with bayonets. Some hung up in the plane trees and eucalyptus trees, unable to escape their harnesses before they were shot.

Most of those who made it to the ground alive were separated from their weapons containers, which came down behind them trailing colored smoke. If they were lucky, the paratroopers were captured by British or Anzac regulars; the unlucky were hacked and beaten to death with scythes and flails by villagers who despised them for polluting the soil.

A very few landed safely, within reach of their weapons containers. They retrieved their weapons and huddled to defend themselves, waiting for the refueled and rearmed fighters and bombers to return, and for the next wave of transports.

"How will I find Uncle Manolakis, Sister? John Pendlebury gave me an important message for him."

"He went with the other men down to the airfield, to fight the Germans." Phylia Akoumianaki whispered so that her mother would not overhear. "The Polakis boy came running to tell them that they didn't need weapons, that they could take the German weapons that were falling from the sky. That's why Mother won't talk to you. She thinks you will encourage Father in his folly."

They were alone in the basement of the palace of Knossos, down a corridor and past the columns of the Queen's Megaron, where *kyria* Akoumianaki had made a campfire under the restored frescoes of leaping dolphins. When she heard bombs falling to the north, she had taken her youngest boy and her daughter into the ruins, trusting Sir Arthur's reinforced concrete more than their house in the village.

"Did they go east of the airfield or west?"

"They followed the old Minoan road."

"Now tell me, where's Elpida?"

Phylia avoided his gaze.

"Sister, you must tell me where to find her."

When she looked him in the eye, her expression was not friendly. "I'm sure she heard your voice."

"Just now?"

"We knew you were on Crete. You didn't come to visit."

"I'm in the army!" His face twisted in anguish. "Cairo to Hania four days ago—even the Germans got to Kastro before me."

"Tell her that when you see her," Phylia said coolly.

"If she'll let me see her."

"Stay here," Phylia suggested. "My father will return soon."

"I can't, I have orders." He seized Phylia's hand and looked into her eyes. "Even in England I never saw so many German airplanes in one day. If things go badly, move to Lasithi. To the house of Siganos, the schoolmaster in Tzermiado."

"Father says we must go to Katalagari, to Mother's family."

"To Katalagari, then."

"I told him I would not."

"Why not? It's a good idea."

"The Germans killed Micky." She turned her face aside. He could barely see her in the darkness. "I will kill Germans."

"Don't believe rumors," he said. "Micky could be on his way here right now."

After a moment she faced him again, her face dimly outlined by reflected firelight in the ruins. "Micky's dead. The Germans killed him in Epirus. I will kill Germans on Crete."

"First you must make sure your mother and your little brother are safe. And Elpida. Take them to Katalagari, as your father wishes. I will come as soon as I can."

She said nothing. In the shadows he could not read her expression.

He moved cautiously on the Minoan road that went to the ruined seaport of Amnisos—less a road than a footpath down the gullies and over the ridges. The night was moonless, but from the heights he caught glimpses of Iraklion away to his left, lit by ruddy grenade bursts and flashes of gunfire. German parachutists had landed on the coast road to the west of the town in the late afternoon; some of them must have gotten inside the walls.

Toward the airfield and the sea, all was darkness and silence. He saw the allied sentry silhouetted against the stars—the man's shallow helmet looked more like a cooking pot than a warrior's headgear, so he had to be a Brit or an Anzac. "God save the king," Manolis called out, crouching in the bushes.

The sentry squatted and waved his rifle. "Who's there?"

"I have dispatches from Captain Pendlebury, Special Operations Executive."

"Never heard of him. Who are you?"

"Androulakis, Greek army seconded to SOE."

"Stand up then. Hands over your head."

"I'll leave my weapon on the ground."

"Which I was about to recommend."

The sentry stepped into the path with his rifle leveled as Manolis stood. Manolis indicated the Marlin gun with a thrust of his chin, and the sentry bent to peer at it, then straightened. "Right. Well, I do believe you're a Greek, Leftenant. No fucking kraut would announce himself like the bleeding Second Coming."

Manolis silently agreed. No fucking kraut would have let the sentry live long enough to express an opinion.

Battalion headquarters was a dugout in the side of a gully. Officers of the Black Watch questioned Manolis for half an hour about his knowledge of German deployment around Iraklion; then they directed him farther down to a line of smoldering campfires under the banks of the dry stream.

He found his foster father crouched in the smoke among a dozen men and boys from the village of Knossos, a bedraggled but happy bunch sporting new Schmeissers and clips of German ammunition, boasting loudly of their exploits as they passed around a bottle of country wine.

"Uncle Manolakis?" Manolis called softly.

"Little Minos? Come here to me." Manolakis struggled to his feet and engulfed Manolis in his embrace. As always he wore mountain clothes, a black shirt pushed into baggy black breeches, a big curved knife and a Luger pistol shoved into his red sash, and a wide straw hat on his head. "You remember this rascal," he said to the others. A few of them apparently did, hailing him rowdily.

"You were safe in England?" one of the men demanded. "Why did you come back?"

Manolis fumbled for an answer. "All the people I—"

"To help us kill Germans," Manolakis interrupted, answering for him. "Isn't that so, child?"

Manolis hesitated before he said, "To kill Germans in England, you have to fly a fighter plane. In England the Luftwaffe come over every night with their bombs. As they came here today. Except there they come *every* night."

"And how many Germans have you killed since you came

back to Crete?" The questioner was surly, as if he sensed evasion.

"One," Manolis said. "He was lying in a ditch, tangled in his parachute. Those who tried to beat him to death hadn't finished the job. He begged me to do it for him."

"He begged you in Greek?"

"I had no trouble understanding his German."

The other men laughed, and the questioner muttered, "Too bad you didn't get there in time to steal his weapon."

"Uncle, I must speak with you," Manolis said.

He and Manolakis went a few steps down the gully, far enough to be out of earshot of the men carousing under the ledge, though still illuminated by their campfire.

"This is from Pendlebury." Manolis handed over the envelope.

Manolakis peered at it, then handed it back. "Your eyes are young. Read it to me."

" 'To Akoumianakis, twenty-one May. Greetings, Old Wolf. German paratroops have landed in force, west of Candia and east of the airfield. Vital to keep south road open for reinforcements debarking in the Messara. In Skalani you will find well-armed men who support our cause. Base your defense on the ridge above Makritihos. Go with God.' It is signed 'John.' "

"He wrote the twenty-first? That's tomorrow."

"He wrote in haste."

"How was he, Little Minos?"

"In high spirits. The Germans were attacking the Hania Gate. He and Captain Satan went to join the defense."

"I was wrong to leave Knossos," said Manolakis. "We must go back there at once."

"He will be glad to know that his message reached you."

"You're going into the city?"

Manolis nodded. To the west, the flashes and flares of sporadic fighting lit the walls of the town.

"When you find John, tell him that after all he is truly a man of Crete."

"Uncle, he will be proud to hear that from you."

*   *   *

Manolis made his way toward the town. Fifty yards past a British machine-gun emplacement he stumbled into a ditch full of bodies, swollen with corruption in the unseasonal heat. He lurched backward, and his heel squelched into softness; he heard a loud *"Aaaahhh."* He reeled in terror and tried to bring his gun to bear, but the groan bubbled away to nothing; it was a corpse's sigh.

He entered the darkened town through the harbor gate. Inside the Venetian walls and among the Turkish houses, his first challenge was from a Greek, who shouted at him from the shadows, "Freedom or death!"

"Freedom or death!" Manolis shouted back.

"Say who you are!"

"Androulakis from Lasithi. They say that there are beautiful weapons to be had here," Manolis responded, in an enthusiastic spate of rural Cretan, "that they fall from the sky, or else that all one has to do is pluck them from the Germans, who hang in the trees like ripe oranges."

The man laughed, a dry and cynical laugh. "Too late for easy pickings, my little *palikari.* Maybe you can get something off a German sniper, if you can kill him before he kills you."

It was almost midnight; sporadic gunfire came from the western part of town, toward the Hania Gate. Manolis loped through the narrow streets, keeping close to the walls. Twice bullets dug holes in the plaster close to his head; twice he threw himself into doorways and shouted, "Freedom or death!" and twice the answer came back, "Freedom or death!" in an accent no German could mimic, and he ran on.

The third time he shouted "Freedom or death!" a tight pattern of bullets struck the stone wall beside him at the level of his chest—one, two, three—spraying him with rock chips and smashing wood splinters out of the door behind him.

For a moment everything was quiet. Without streetlamps or lights in the windows, the rooftops were silhouetted against the stars. Manolis bent down as slowly as he could and groped about on the doorsill for a handful of the rock chips the sniper's bullets had cut out of the wall. He stood up and threw them hard, sideways, back the way he had come.

The sniper's bullets ripped the wall at chest height where the chips had clattered—one, two, three shots, no more. But his muzzle flash was bright, and by the time it blinked out Manolis had crossed to the other side of the street.

He climbed the stairs to the pitched tile roof of a deserted house and crossed to the next with a leap. The sniper was on the flat roof of the next building. Manolis lay sprawled on the sloping tiles, unmoving, waiting to learn if the noise he had made had exposed his position or panicked the sniper into flight.

The sniper waited a long time before he moved, not out of fear but from prudent caution, separating himself only by movement from the pale shadows cast by the stars.

Manolis shot him, once.

The man squealed in surprise, and when he realized what had happened to him squealed again, a sound more like despair than pain, but his panic had a perverse effect on Manolis, whose coolness—an actor's coolness; he'd been bluffing ever since he'd set foot on Crete in his new uniform; he'd never killed anyone, not even that pitiful half-dead paratrooper he'd found in the ditch whom he claimed to have killed—suddenly boiled away in a flash of bloodthirsty rage.

Manolis stood up and leaped across to the next roof, moving without caution, inflated with his image of himself as untouchable. Who was this man to think he could hide in the dark? To think he could kill in safety? He found the sniper pulling himself away from his abandoned Mauser, still squealing like a baby as if expecting a mother's pity, his bare, close-cropped head of blond hair white in the starlight, trailing a wide streak of blood that was black in the same starlight, and Manolis shot him again in the back of his head from two feet away, and he stopped squealing.

He staggered away from the body and sat down hard, desperate for breath, overwhelmed with physical hurt although he wasn't wounded, wasn't even bruised. He wasn't sorry for what he had done, no, though the sniper was an adolescent no older than he was, no, not sorry for killing a *xenos* who had tried to kill him, maybe had already killed his countrymen. So why did he ache as if his ribs would burst? Because this was war? Because killing seemed natural? Because it gave him a thrill?

At dawn Manolis retreated to the British consulate, carrying his Marlin gun and his newly acquired Mauser with its packet of ammunition clips. He was hoping to find Pendlebury, but a younger man was behind Pendlebury's desk, his head down, pawing through a file drawer.

When he raised it, the young man's irritated expression flickered into pleasure. "Manoli! Here at last!"

Manolis recoiled. "Richard!"

Richard stood up from behind the desk. "Pendlebury didn't tell you?"

"No he didn't."

"I thought . . . He went on at quite extraordinary length about you, when he found I knew you." Richard thrust out his hand. "It's very good to see you again."

Manolis hesitated, then put out his hand to shake Richard's. "Good to see you too," he said, businesslike, withdrawing his hand abruptly. "I have urgent news for John."

Richard clasped his hands behind his back. His uniform was spotless, his trousers creases knife-edged. "Quite sure you're all right?"

"Oh, quite." Manolis affected a laugh. "Busy night."

"Yes, it has been. As for Pendlebury, Corporal tells me he was here an hour ago—tells me he was fighting in the streets all night. Left again almost immediately. Wearing his glass eye, no doubt. It's gone from his desk."

"Where did he go?"

"Out the Hania Gate, says Corporal, in a car with one of those bandit friends of his."

"West?" Manolis rubbed his stubbled jaw. "The Germans are everywhere to the west."

"You're said to know him better than any of us, old chap."

"Where's Captain Satan?" Manolis demanded.

"To Krousonas. Left in the night."

"I'm off to Krousonas, then. Orders."

"Surely there's time for you to get some rest," Richard said.

"Couldn't sleep."

"Some breakfast then."

"Couldn't think of eating. Sorry."

"A drink if you prefer. Damn it, we ought to talk."

"Perhaps later."

The look between them, before Manolis turned and left, was freighted with resentment, but at the last moment Richard whispered, *"Andio, Manoli."*

Pendlebury was not in Krousonas. Satan was, but he claimed to have heard nothing from Pendlebury since Tuesday afternoon, when the two of them had been heavily engaged with German paratroopers in the streets of Kastro, near the harbor. Manolis waited in Krousonas a day and a half, until he could wait no longer. Then he went to join Manolakis at Knossos.

In the far west of Crete, things went badly. After a week of hard fighting, British and Anzac soldiers retreated over the White Mountains toward Sphakia-town on the south coast, pressed by German mountain troops and harassed by the Luftwaffe. Thousands of men in a narrow file many miles long lined up to board the Royal Navy's destroyers standing off the rocky shore. They could only be taken aboard a boatload at a time. Most waited as patiently as if queuing for a bus, although the last in line knew they would be left for the Germans.

To the east, Iraklion and its harbor and airfield held out, although German paratroops had occupied Knossos and the heights south of the city, and a German field hospital was installed in the Villa Ariadne. In the town, Allied commanders were advised that British ships would arrive on the night of May 28 to evacuate as many men as possible from the harbor. The British officers were instructed, for security reasons, not to inform the Greeks.

On the afternoon of the twenty-eighth, the Old Wolf, Manolakis Akoumianakis, led a party of Cretan irregulars up the steep Ailias Ridge opposite Knossos, toward an entrenched unit of German paratroops. At the same time a British platoon approached the Germans from the north, up the gentler seaward slope of the ridge.

For the past two days Manolis had worked to coordinate the attack; when the Old Wolf's men were within sight of the enemy position Manolis left them, running, to advise the British platoon leader that the Greeks were in position.

He climbed hard, dodging through a grove of young olives, when suddenly he heard the crackle of small arms and the staccato chatter of a light machine gun. A British corporal staggered backward, down through the trees. Manolis caught him and dragged him to shelter behind a slender tree trunk. Around them, other soldiers were taking cover. Bullet-clipped branches of gray-green olive leaves fell to the ground around them.

"Where are you hurt?" Manolis demanded.

"I ain't."

"Why aren't we advancing?"

"I don't see *you* advancing, mate," said the corporal. Facedown in the dry earth, he turned his face toward Manolis; his eyes were sunken with fatigue, he had a week's growth of beard, and he stank.

"Where's your officer?" Manolis demanded.

"Dead. Jerries got him soon as he stood up."

"Then you're in command, Corporal. Rally your men and follow me. The Greeks are attacking from the west."

"They got fucking machine guns up there!"

"One light machine gun. We've faced worse this week."

"Yeah, when we were in for it," the corporal snarled. "But who wants to be the last dead Britisher in this hole?"

"We've got to clear the highway. Do your duty, man."

The corporal rolled onto his back and brought his rifle to bear. "Get clear of me, wog, or I'll do for you myself."

Manolis knocked the rifle aside and grabbed the man by his collar, pulling his face close. "Open this road, or you and your mates have *nowhere* to retreat."

The corporal stared up at Manolis for a moment, then started giggling. "Always somebody 'asn't got the word, eh?" His gaunt, whiskered face looked like a much abused forty-year-old's, though he couldn't have been much more than twenty. "We're *already* retreating, you stupid shit. Stay alive and get back to town before midnight, that's *my* mission. Then the bleedin' Royal Navy takes me off."

After a moment the corporal's meaning penetrated. Manolis let him go to lie in his funk and ran back the way he had come.

The German fire was concentrated on the Greeks now, who were climbing a steep, wide slope that broke the crest of the ridge. Most of the Greeks were belly down among bright green stalks of wheat that had grown thigh high in the hot spring weather. It was their only cover; they had to rise to their knees to shoot back at the Germans.

"Where is Manolakis?" Manolis asked the first man he came to, a villager armed with a captured Mauser.

"Pinned, up there."

"Go back. Tell everyone you can find to retreat—slowly, carefully. We'll have to try another time."

"What about the English?"

Manolis hesitated an instant before he told the necessary lie. "The Germans are even stronger on the other side. Go, tell the others. I'll find Manolakis."

Manolis cradled his gun in his crossed arms and wormed his way through the young wheat, belly down, his nostrils filled with the rank smell of crushed vegetation. Lots of insects he had never seen before were squirming and hopping about under his nose. His progress was visible to the Germans; every few seconds bullets popped the air over his head and sprinkled him with clippings. He clung to the belief that no bullet would kill him—he had worked out a mathematical rationale for his blatant superstition, having to do with Riemannian manifolds and space-time coordinates—but he was not above caution.

He lifted his head out of the wheat just long enough to get his bearings. A few feet ahead of him, someone was moving. "Uncle Manolakis!" he cried. "Stay down! We must go back."

Either Manolakis didn't hear him or chose not to, for suddenly the old man stood up, a grenade in his hand.

With half his consciousness, Manolis noted his foster father's irrational courage and registered the image of his defiance—*they had killed Micky, his firstborn son, and to the devil with them*—Manolakis standing up in the young wheat, hurling a thunderbolt back against the sky, his wide-brimmed straw hat on his head.

What a target that made.

From their dug-in position the Germans concentrated their fire, catching Akoumianakis as he began his throw. He jerked backward; jets of gore expelled from his back propelled him forward again, onto his face. From reflex or habit he clutched at his straw hat, as if caught in a strong wind.

The live grenade fell behind him and bounced downhill toward Manolis, who, having overlooked the space-time mathematics of grenades, tried to bury his face in the earth. It went off three yards away. The shrapnel plowed his scalp and covered him with his own blood, bright red blood flecked with shreds of green wheat.

The Germans, terrified for their safety and moving fast through the wheat, counted Manolis among the dead. For a day and a half he lay unconscious.

As the sun was setting on the warm evening of May 29, Phylia Akoumianaki and Elpida Pateraki climbed the Ailias Ridge. Phylia came upon her father facedown in the dirt, his body scattered with earth, his hat clutched in his hand. She touched him; he was cold. With her bare hands, she scooped earth out of the wheat field and covered him over, defying the German decree that Greeks were not permitted to bury anyone who had taken up arms against them, on pain of death.

A little downslope Elpida came upon Manolis, crusted with blood and flies. She touched him; he whispered for water. His eyes were glued shut with coagulated blood.

In his dreams he was among the skeletons in the cave, sitting with them around a cold green fire, trading stories of betrayal as he tried to reassemble a shattered Minoan jar. Pendlebury touched his shoulder with a cold hand and gestured at the jar and then at his own face, a skull with one glass eye; he reached out to touch Manolis's eyes. . . .

In a panic, Manolis opened his eyes.

They were cleansed, unstuck. A woman's face was bent close to his, framed in black curls, her wide green eyes glistening with tears. Her hand rested on his brow.

"Elpida?" He blinked cautiously. "You're in Katalagari."

"I'm here with you, Manoli." Her long hair came down around him and her hot lips pressed against his.

She sat up again, pulling back. "No talk until you eat something," she said. "We have to make you strong. You are in danger here."

He moved his head and looked around. A wick burning in a dish of olive oil lit the walls of the Queen's Megaron with a dim and fitful light, like an offering to the dead. Painted dolphins leaped in the shadows.

"We're in the palace?"

"The only place we could hide you. The Germans are everywhere, but they don't come here at night. Can you eat?"

He sat up cautiously. "I could eat a donkey."

She'd brought artichokes and lamb stew, still warm from the hearth. After he'd eaten as much as he could—hardly a donkey's worth, for his stomach was shrunken with hunger—he leaned back and rested his head on the stone.

She gave him the news, most of it bad. Uncle Manolakis was dead. The Allied troops had vanished overnight, leaving by ship—all but those who were prisoners of the Germans or stragglers who'd escaped capture. The Germans had moved into Iraklion, and already they were shooting Greek hostages. They'd promised that for every one of their men killed since the collapse of the Allied defense, they would kill ten civilians.

"And for sheltering a fugitive?" he asked. She said nothing, but he knew. "I'll bring catastrophe upon Knossos if they find me here. I must leave now."

"I told you, the Germans don't come here at night."

"Why not?"

"Because most of the soldiers are farm boys with good sense. They're afraid to trip over people like us in the dark." In the guttering lamplight, she held up two German machine pistols, one in each hand. "And the educated ones, the officers, are superstitious. They think the palace of Knossos is—how do they call it?—'the cradle of Europa.' "

"You mean they're afraid of ghosts." Manolis tried to smile.

She laughed at that. "Sit up and eat more stew."

Perhaps it was the stew. By an hour before dawn Manolis felt strong enough to walk, a few steps at a time. Elpida threw a shepherd's cloak over his shoulders and led him out of the ruins, down to the reeds by the stream. Before the sun had risen they had crossed the road south of the guarded bridge and reached Knossos village unseen.

Elpida knocked once, then twice, and Phylia opened the door of the Akoumianakis house and pulled them inside.

Manolis spent the day dozing off in the heat of the upstairs room, while Elpida made a show of going about a village girl's work: washing, sweeping, shelling beans, and feeding the chickens. She and Phylia chatted with the neighbors and like them fell haughtily silent whenever a pair of German soldiers passed by in the narrow street.

As soon as it was dark, Elpida and Manolis said good-bye to Phylia and slipped out of the village. It took them most of the night to cross the fields and low ridges to the southeast of Knossos—Manolis was weak, and twice they had to dodge German patrols—but by dawn they were climbing the steep canyon of the Erganos stream, the back door into Lasithi. It was slow going; it would be days before Manolis could once more jump around the rocks like a *kri-kri*. When the stars dimmed in the ruddy sky, they found themselves many miles short of their destination, among peaks of bent and layered gray rock.

They took shelter in a shepherd's *mandra* and spread their cloaks on stone beds, huddling beside a brushwood fire to eat bread and cheese and oranges, tucking potatoes into the coals to roast for later. Their drink was cold water from a jug. Before he was finished eating, Manolis was asleep again.

For the second time he awoke to the sight of Elpida's face floating over him. The old rug over the door behind her kept out all but a few pencils of mote-spangled sunlight, crowning her with rays. He experienced such pleasure in the sight that he knew without question that he wanted this sight upon his every awakening for the rest of his life. "You look at me so fiercely," he whispered, touching her curling hair. "Like a goddess."

"I wonder what the great thinker is thinking."

He grinned wickedly. "I am thinking how desolate and miserable I would be if I had never met you."

She frowned and punched him hard in the arm. "Liar."

"And what are you thinking?"

She leaned away and released her piled-up hair from its pins. It fell over her shoulders. She inclined her head and pulled at the tangles. "Tell me about England. Tell me what you did there."

"England is dark and cold and wet and crowded with people and motorcars and bicycles. As for what I did there . . . I thought about you."

Her eyes glittered. "Don't be clever. You'll make me angry."

"All right, I confess that I spent more time thinking about mathematics and science. It was my job to learn. But I thought about you a great deal."

"With all those English girls about! They are said to be very free with their affections."

"I wouldn't know," he said archly. "I certainly had no time for them."

"Not even time to visit Mercy? Whom you so admire?" Her black hair lay loose and shiny on her shoulders and breast; she continued to comb it through her long fingers.

"Miss Money-Coutts lives in Oxford," he said reasonably. "I was in Cambridge."

"Sir Arthur lives near Oxford. You had time to visit *him.*"

"Yes, I had time for Sir Arthur." He paused. "How do you know all this? What do you know of Oxford and Cambridge?"

"You wrote letters to the Hutchinsons. The Squire showed them to Uncle Manolaki, and I . . ." She let her words dwindle.

"You're a spy!" He laughed.

"Why did you come back? Surely you were happy in England."

He grinned, knowing what she was fishing for. "That I have no family doesn't stop me from loving my homeland."

"Your homeland." She swung her arm as if to indicate the invisible mountains. "Oh yes, these are very lovable rocks."

"When I left I learned how lovable they are," he said seriously. "In England, no matter what I achieved, I was never anything but a foreigner. I persuaded my English schoolmasters to persuade the Greek government to give me a commission. The Greeks assigned me back to the English, and I soon began to realize how little we matter to the Brits—although we are, or were, their only ally in all of Europe."

"We matter to John."

He snorted. "You know where the British army put him first? In the cavalry. Fine terrain for cavalry charges, Crete."

"Still, they had the sense to send him here."

He fell silent. He reached out and carefully took her hands. "Have you heard anything about him?"

"Nothing. The day after the Germans came he left Iraklion by the Hania Gate."

"Yes, I heard that too." He drew a great breath and let it out slowly. He looked at her hands, not her eyes; he held them more tightly. "I was hoping you had heard something more."

"Have you heard that I love you?"

His surprise was so deep that he was sure she was teasing him. "When could I have heard that?"

"I suppose you couldn't have. We in the underground have very good security."

He laughed. "That must be why you never heard that I love you too."

"Is that why? All this time I thought it was a German trick."

He leaned toward her green eyes. "No joking: I love you, Elpida, and I want us to be married. John will be our *koumbaros,* if we can find him and make him stand still for a minute."

"This is a most irregular proposal," she said archly. "Our representatives haven't discussed your meager prospects, or my nonexistent dowry, or . . ."

So it was her turn to be funny. "Alas, you don't consent."

"Who will represent me? Who will represent you, if we can't find Pendabri? Given your famous affection for priests, who will crown us in marriage? A schoolmaster?"

He knotted his brows as if perplexed. "You're right, it's impossible. We can never be married. I apologize for asking."

Maybe she wasn't being funny after all, because she didn't go along with the gag. "We can be married without all that nonsense," she said. "We can be married now."

"You mean secretly?" She had confused him more profoundly than she'd intended.

She freed her hands and gripped his fingers, moving his hands to her breasts as she leaned into him. "I mean now."

He pulled her down beside him onto the stony bed and they lay kissing in a tangle of clothes, their hands moving urgently through folds of black cloth that had the scent of sweat and wild herbs and woodsmoke deep in them, unbuttoning buttons, unbuckling buckles, untying tapes, pushing at wrinkled masses of cloth. When he had opened all the buttons of her high-buttoned dress she sat up long enough to shrug it over her head and pull her white cotton undershirt after it. She wore nothing else except darned black stockings that ended below her knees; for the rest of her length, she was all white against the skirts of the black dress now beneath her.

But she was impatient with him, who had gotten no further than removing his shirt and loosening his trousers. "You are not allowed to be shy with me, husband," she whispered, and she stood up and pulled him to his feet and turned him around, wrapping her arms around him from behind, pushing her heavy breasts into his pale muscular back, her hard nipples like coins between them, and hooked her thumbs in his waistband and pushed his pants down around his bare feet. She would not let him turn around until she had tested the rigidity of his desire, softly mauled him with her long fingers, meanwhile biting the curls at the nape of his neck, growling and laughing into his fragrant skin—until he turned upon her, made impatient by her play, and they stumbled onto the stony bed.

* * *

Daylight was gone before they noticed. Reluctantly they dressed, each dressing the other as if they were playing with dolls, and both doing badly at it, not unintentionally.

They found the potatoes in the cold ashes of the fire, crusted black but warm and creamy inside. After their meager supper they shouldered their bags and pushed the rug over the door aside, watching and listening to the night.

"Wife," he said, and kissed her cheek.

"Husband," she said, and leaned into his arm. A moment later she let him go and went out of the hut, among the silvery peaks and the starry sky.

They made their way over the pass above Kaminaki and down into Lasithi, striking out across the flat fields, avoiding the villages that encircled the plain. Rich odors of cultivated earth thickened the air, and pale windmills, their sails hanging limp, gleamed like night flowers; the stars trembled like drops of liquid on the verge of falling out of the sky. Although the dusty lanes were at right angles to one another and their path was often crabwise, they made good time on their march; Manolis had recovered the spring in his step, and Elpida kept up with him easily, smiling to herself. They saw no one, and nothing disturbed them before they reached Georgios Siganos's house in Tzermiado.

Manolis ran to the door and knocked on it softly. The village dogs set up a racket. After a long time a muffled voice spoke from inside. "What do you want here in the middle of the night?"

"*Kyrie* Georgio! It's Manolis Androulakis."

The door opened and Georgios reached for Manolis. "Come in, my child. Quickly."

"This is my . . . I mean, this is . . ."

"Inside, both of you!" Georgios was fully dressed, wearing a white shirt and a dark wool suit. When he had closed and bolted the door behind them, he turned to Elpida. "Who did he say you were, child?"

"I'm Elpida Pateraki, *kyrie,* from Knossos," Elpida said, "and I think my dear Manolis was trying to explain that he and I are engaged to be married."

"What good news! Well, well! Come, come, sit by the fire. We must lift a glass of raki."

The coals were glowing on the hearth. Manolis and Elpida took chairs beside it, exchanging a questioning glance when Georgios addressed the shadows beyond the arch. "Pavlo, come out and meet our guests. A young genius just back from England. And his bride-to-be. We will make him tell us all about it."

A tall man leaned into the half-light. His full black beard was streaked with gray, and his baggy trousers and high boots and broad sash were those of a mountain man. He clutched the barrel of a Mauser in his left hand; the callused fingers of his right were wrapped around an unlit pipe.

Siganos said, "This is Pavlos Papalexakis, a brave fellow who has just now returned from Kastro."

"Your health, sir," Manolis said, with a bob of his head. "What is it like in the town?"

"It's wreckage, and it stinks." Papalexakis sat down heavily beside the hearth, leaning the Mauser against the wall. He picked up a burning stick and drew fire into his pipe. "The Germans put us to work digging graves, but there were too many corpses," he said between puffs. "The sewers are broken too. They bombed everything." Pavlos looked at Manolis warily. "What kind of uniform is that?"

"British. I'm Greek army attached to the British."

"Huh. There are no more British."

"This is Manolis Androulakis. He's a good man, Pavlo," Siganos said. "Pendabri himself sent him to study in England."

"Mm, Androulakis. Pendabri told me about him," said the guerrilla, sucking his pipe.

"And from him I heard many stirring tales of Papalexakis," said Manolis. "I wonder if you have any news of him."

"Siganos my friend, do you have any more of that excellent raki?" Papalexakis asked.

"Let me fill you a glass," said the schoolteacher.

Papalexakis thoughtfully rolled the glass in his grimy fingers before tossing it back. "They say Pendabri is dead. I talked to a woman who said she saw him die."

Elpida cried out, but quickly covered her mouth. Papalexakis stared at her balefully.

"John is dead?" Manolis had to force the words from his dry throat. "How did he die?"

Papalexakis raised his bushy eyebrows and looked at Siganos.

"Tell him what you know," said the schoolmaster. "This lad was like a son to him."

"This is what I heard. The day after the Germans came, Pendabri went out the Hania Gate. He was riding in a car that Georgios Drosoulakis was driving. They didn't get far. More parachuters were coming down, right there in Kaminia, so they had to get out and fight. They fought off the Germans, but Drosoulakis was killed and Pendabri was shot up. A chest wound. That was near where Drosoulakis lived, and later the Germans found Pendabri lying there and dragged him into Drosoulakis's house. This was an accident, the Germans didn't know whose house it was. And Drosoulakis's wife took care of him. A German doctor came and dressed his wounds. But then Drosoulakis's wife and her sister were taken off to the prison camp. And then other Germans came, the ones who wear black uniforms. And they dragged Pendabri outside and stood him against the wall. 'Where are the *andartes?*' they shouted, and he shouted, 'I will never tell you,' and they shouted, 'Tell us or die,' and he shouted, 'No, no, no,' and they shouted, 'Attention,' and then they shot him in the chest and the head, and they left his body there."

For a long moment everyone was silent, as if waiting for Papalexakis to continue. But he had no more to say.

"Tell me again. Who told you this?" Manolis asked quietly.

"I heard this from Kalliope Karatatsanou and Aristea Drosoulaki, the same day I escaped from that camp at Tsalikaki."

Again there was no sound but the creak and sputter of the coals, until Elpida spoke up. "For their sakes and ours, you must tell no one what you heard."

Papalexakis turned his bearded face toward her, as if replying to a woman who gave orders cost him an effort.

"That is only what I heard from those foolish women. What I know is this: Pendabri is alive in the mountains. With his glass eye he sees everything. He will make the Germans suffer." He pulled on his pipe. "You think I am not serious, woman?" When she did not answer, he said, "I am serious."

21

Manolis and Elpida were officially married on a hot Saturday afternoon in July, under giant kerm oaks in Yannitsi, a village of a few stone houses on the high Katharo Plain above Lasithi. Manolis wore his uniform; Elpida wore a borrowed dress of white cotton. The priest, a member of the underground, came up from Kritsa.

Pavlos Papalexakis stood in for the missing Pendlebury as *koumbaros,* waving marriage crowns of twisted vine shoots three times over the heads of the couple while the priest chanted the blessing. When the chants finally came to an end, the onlookers shouted gleefully and hurled fistfuls of almonds at the newlyweds. Lute and *lyra* made a sweet racket; everyone whirled in the dance. Guns went off as if there were no such creatures as Germans within a thousand miles.

In those days there was still food in the remote villages, and Yannitsi, in the shadow of Mount Lazaros, Dikti's third and easternmost peak, was one of the most remote. Lamb chops and stuffed sheep guts and boiled beans and peas graced the trestle tables under the oak branches, along with sweating jugs of wine. A round loaf of freshly baked sweet bread, brushed with sugar

water and garlanded with orange slices and tiny orchids, served
as a wedding cake.

But in the midst of speeches and toasts the wedding party fell
silent; boisterous voices suddenly trailed off as everyone turned
to stare at the strangers who were coming toward them across
the fields of ripe wheat. One was an old man some of them
knew from Ayios Konstandinos in Lasithi, but the other two
were strangers wearing ragged uniforms, who limped painfully
as they walked. The wedding guests reached for their guns.
Bolts slid and hammers clicked.

Manolis raised his hand. "Wait here. I'll speak to them."

He walked slowly toward the men and when he reached
them, bent his head to talk. Then he took their hands and
gripped their arms and turned to lead them to the banquet.
"Lower your weapons, friends, and welcome our guests. This
old man has brought us some English."

Before the war, when Pavlos Papalexakis was a small-time
smuggler operating a caïque out of Iraklion harbor, John
Pendlebury had occasionally engaged him in drinking contests
during which he dropped hints of British largesse to those who
were prepared to resist the fascists—rifles and boots and gold
for mountain men, and for captains who knew the coasts of the
islands not only gold but the opportunity to do a little trading
on the side.

But on unlucky Tuesday Papalexakis's boat was sunk in the
harbor, and he fell into German hands. Within days of his
escape, having decided that English rifles and boots would
have to substitute for the black market, he was back in the
mountains of his birth, organizing his relatives into a band of
andartes.

All over Crete the Germans did their best to help the formation of the resistance, by committing bestial atrocities against
noncombatants—thus expressing their disappointment that the
Cretans had not welcomed them as liberators.

Manolis was Papalexakis's second-in-command. They were
as different as vinegar and oil—Papalexakis could not read;
Manolis had never stolen anything worth mentioning—but they

blended well. Two days after the British stragglers arrived at Papalexakis's camp, a runner from the west brought a letter.

"Last week a British submarine surfaced at Preveli Monastery in Rethymno nome," Manolis read aloud. "An officer came ashore to organize the evacuation of the stragglers to Egypt."

"What's that to do with us?" Papalexakis sat at a plank table, busily spooning soup into the opening in his black beard. The late-afternoon sun shone through the heavy oak branches, dappling the stone walls with orange light.

"The next landing will be at Tsoutsouros two nights from tonight. We can put our Englishmen on that one."

"What's the hurry? Just now the Italians are practically offering to give away the weapons they don't know how to use."

Like ravens flocking to a kill, the Italians had landed in Sitia on the last day of the battle for Crete, and the Germans, eager to get on with the conquest of Russia, had given them the eastern part of the island.

"We can make fools of the Italians whenever we want, Pavlo, but we can never liberate Greece without the help of the British."

"Well, you are a great friend to the British. But if they can send submarines to rescue their foot soldiers, why can't they give us what we need to fight their battles for them?"

Manolis leaned forward, resting his hands on a low oak branch overhead. "Let me have one man. Old Siphis, if he agrees. We'll take the English to the submarine. I'll talk to the officer and make sure that we get our supplies."

"*Endaxi.*" Papalexakis stood up and turned away toward the house. "Bring back more English promises. While you're gone I'll see if the Italians have something real to offer."

"Good hunting," Manolis said.

"A shame you won't be with us," Papalexakis said sourly.

A village boy ducked into the house where Manolis and the English were packing their *sakoulis.* "*Kyrie* Manoli," he said excitedly, "more English are coming."

Manolis looked a hard question at the soldiers.

The sergeant shook his head vehemently, and the haggard private said, " 'Aven't seen any of ours for a month or more."

"All right, through the hole," Manolis said. "No noise."

There was a hole in the back wall of the house at floor level, through which the fugitives could squeeze under a pile of brush stacked against the outside. Manolis blocked it with loose stones and hauled a cedar chest in front of it.

He stepped outside and shaded his eyes against the low sun on the slopes of Lazaros. With his natural *teleskopia* he saw a group of men and a donkey approaching through the golden fields, raising an orange column of dust behind them.

"They came up the west side, from Lasithi," Elpida said. She sat beside the door, working at a loom upon which half a rug had taken shape, woven tight as canvas and red as blood, bordered by bright blue and yellow flowers. She, however, was dressed in black from her shawl to her long skirt, like all the village women; hardly a woman in Greece did not wear mourning. "Siphis went out to meet them. He's stirring up dust on purpose."

"He's a clever fellow."

Manolis strolled through the village, looking around with a critical eye. Old men and women sat in front of their houses, and a few children played in the dust or went about their chores. Yannitsi looked innocent, entirely unremarkable.

Minakis found Papalexakis and his men lurking in the rocks and prickly ilex trees above the village. "Germans," he said.

"Not Italians?" Papalexakis asked, disappointed.

"They wouldn't have the wit to disguise themselves as stragglers. You and the others must leave now, while I get the English away from here."

"Only three? We'll slaughter them."

"And the Germans will come back and slaughter every male they can find and blow up every house in the village."

"We'll stay here until you get the English out," Papalexakis grumbled. "Take your wife. She's as good as Siphis or any man."

Minakis took the big man by his shoulders. "Don't wait for us, Pavlo. Your job is to rob Italians. Go do it."

* * *

Old Siphis, a practiced deceiver, hid the amateurish Gestapo pretenders in Papalexakis's own house and offered to introduce them to the local resistance, and when they expressed delight he immediately went off to report these "English" stragglers to the nearest Italian outpost in Lasithi.

As soon as it was dark Manolis and Elpida pulled the real English out of their hole. Elpida wore a shepherd's cape over wool trousers; like her husband she had a Schmeisser slung across her back along with her *sakouli*. They set out over the pass for the south coast, under a sky clotted with stars.

Their progress was slow. The shadows under the pines were so thick that the air itself felt dense, and despite rest and food the English soldiers were still weak. They did not reach Christos until the Libyan Sea was already a plain of purple emerging from the gloom.

The schoolmaster and his wife greeted them as warmly as they had greeted Manolis and Pendlebury five years earlier, putting the English in the storeroom under the house and giving Manolis and Elpida their own bed. They slept like innocents in the shuttered room.

In midafternoon they awoke together. He buried his face in her fragrant hair and she ran her fingers along the stubble of his jaw. "Do you think we can go back to Yannitsi?" she asked.

"Siphis knows how to handle those Germans. Who knows, the village may get a reputation for being friendly to the occupation."

"That's too easy." She snuggled closer.

"We may have to stay away until the fascists lose interest. Before I met Pendlebury I lived most of my life alone in these mountains, afraid to go home to my own village. There are people all around who will do what they can to help us."

"We'll need their help."

He raised himself on an elbow to look at her. "Why?"

"You and me and John. Or Sophia."

"John? Sophia?" He stared at her a long time without getting the message.

Finally she smirked. "John for Pendabri. Sophia for your

mother. If you like those names. I don't know who's coming
first, but one of them is on the way."

Comprehension dawned. "Elpida! Wife! I love you!"

"*Sshh,* don't shout."

He engulfed her, holding her close, then holding her suddenly away again as if afraid to smother her.

She laughed out loud. "That old prude Papalexakis made us
get married just in time."

"How can you joke about it?"

"How can you not?"

He jumped off the bed and began pacing, pausing long
enough to pull on his boots. "You must stay here," he said.
"Christos is a good, safe place. The schoolmaster will take
care—"

"First let's get the English aboard their submarine."

They argued urgently, but after a long time Manolis conceded that her condition wasn't delicate and that the English,
not to mention Manolis himself, would be safer with her
help.

"I want this war to be over," he said passionately. "I want us
to have a place to live, and work for our hands and our minds,
and a safe place for our children to grow up. And . . ."

Her graceful hands tugged at his sides, begging comfort. "All
I want is you, Little Minos."

When it was dark, they took their leave of the schoolmaster.
The English were bone weary and their feet were swollen and
bleeding, but they kept up without complaint, spurred by the
hope of rescue. Before daybreak the little band was asleep on
hard ground, sheltered only by a rocky overhang, hardly moving all day except to take turns standing watch.

As the sun went down beyond the volcanic landscape they
set off down a steep westerly ravine, toward the rendezvous.
Waves seethed against the shingle, a rhythmic, perpetual slide
of wet gravel that masked other sounds. By two o'clock in the
morning they had reached the beach below Tsoutsouros.

Through the thick sea mist they could see only the diffuse
silvery glow of the young moon that had risen behind them.

Manolis signaled a halt, and they crouched in the reeds. "There are other *andartes* here, bringing English to be picked up," he whispered to Elpida.

"How do we find them without getting shot?"

"The runner gave me a code phrase."

"That's reassuring," she muttered.

They went ahead cautiously. A dozen steps farther down the beach they heard gravelly footsteps, and the slick slide of bullets entering chambers. Manolis stretched out his left arm, his hand palm down, and Elpida and the English flattened themselves on the wet shingle.

"Good evening to you," Manolis called softly. "Any fresh *mizithra?*"

"Fresh as in May," a voice replied. "Come forward, where we can see you."

"I'd rather see you first, Captain Satan."

There was laughter in the mist, and the voice replied, "Together then, Little Minos."

Manolis stood up, and immediately Satan loomed out of the ·fog in front of him; their guns were leveled at each other. They grinned, two sets of teeth bright in the mist, acknowledging that neither had fooled the other. Then they aimed their weapons skyward and embraced.

They were a long time catching up, trading a thousand and two questions and lies, and Satan made an appropriate fuss over Elpida. He had good news: her cousin Micky Akoumianakis had survived and was living in Knossos, working for the underground.

Satan's men had two dozen stragglers hidden in the darkness, but there was little chance of signaling the submarine until the fog lifted. "So we sit here on the beach until daybreak flashing our torches, and pray to Saint Nicholas they can get their man ashore."

As he spoke, there was a splash offshore, audible between the gravelly beat of the waves. A few seconds later a rubber boat grounded on the shingle not ten feet away. A man crouched in its bows whispered loudly, speaking Greek with a strong British accent, "Any fresh *mizithra?*"

His answer was a chorus out of the fog. "FRESH AS IN MAY!"

A half-dozen *andartes* ran barefoot into the surf to help the Britisher, a small, neat lieutenant wearing battle dress that had been cleaned and pressed, who looked as if he would have been more at home in a yachting party. The Greeks lifted him out of the boat and put him down high and dry on the shingle, along with his kit, before helping the first group of stragglers aboard.

"Yank that line sharply now," the lieutenant called when the boat was full, "and you'll get a free ride to Egypt." The soldier in the boat did so, and the line stretched taut. Out in the fog, persons unseen began hauling the boat in.

Three more times the *andartes* pulled the boat back by the rope they had payed out behind it, running into the surf to bring it safely through the low breakers. In half an hour all the refugees were safely aboard the submarine, which sank into the depths of the Libyan Sea, never having been visible from shore.

"Grigorakis, good to see you again," the lieutenant said heartily, extending his hand, which Satan gave a firm yank. "Now those chaps are safely off, I look forward to meeting your men."

At the moment Satan's men were imps in the mist, collecting the boots and weapons that the departing British, with fervent thanks to their rescuers, had dropped behind them on the shingle, and busily packing the booty alongside the lieutenant's gear on a pair of donkeys.

"First meet these," said Satan. "Papalexakis on Dikti sent this one. Minosakis. Or do you know him already?"

"Yeia sou, Richard," Manolis said calmly.

"You were dead!" exclaimed the astonished lieutenant. "I mean, we thought . . . Oh, Manoli, what a . . . How glad I am to see you!"

"Satan didn't tell me it was you."

"He didn't know. I was lucky to get this mission."

Manolis turned to Elpida. "Darling, this is Richard Wingate, Lieutenant, SOE. Richard, my wife, Elpida."

She towered over him on the foggy beach and thrust out her hand to shake his like a man; Richard smiled as graciously as if they were meeting in a London drawing room. "Charmed, *kyria* Androulaki. My friend is surely lucky to have found you."

She eyed him curiously. "I am lucky too."

Satan, who had been paying close attention to the exchange, laughed heartily. "These two are the brains behind Papalexakis's troop of amateur clowns."

"Good, glad to hear it," Richard said heartily. "SOE want to put some men and resources into his region."

"You will be lucky indeed," Satan sneered, "if he uses what you give him to fight the enemy."

"Come with us now," Richard told Manolis. "I'll make arrangements by radio with Cairo." He turned to Satan. "Captain, hadn't we ought to put some distance between us and this beach?" There was already a hint of light in the east, much diffused by the thinning mist.

"Waiting on you, my little *palikari*." They fell in behind Satan and his second-in-command, a gap-toothed ruffian named Siphakas. The others followed, tugging the overburdened donkeys.

"What did Satan call you?" Richard whispered. "Minakis? Something like that?"

"Minosakis, Little Minos. A nickname John gave me."

"Have you heard anything of Pendlebury, then?"

"There's said to be an English captain on Psiloritis," Manolis replied, "leading a band of *andartes*. A tall man with a glass eye."

"That must be the story they tell on Dikti," Satan put in; he was a shameless eavesdropper. "On Psiloritis we tell the same story, except the one-eyed captain is in the White Mountains."

"He's everywhere," Elpida said. "The Germans are terrified."

Richard understood them: Pendlebury was dead. "Sometimes people do come back, as if from the dead," he said cheerfully. "Androulakis here. Case in point."

Manolis said nothing, but Elpida crossed herself.

The sun was well up in the clear sky by the time they reached their bivouac, a shallow cave in the dry mountains of the south coast. Satan's headquarters were more than twenty miles away across the long, low Messara Plain, and German troops were stationed in strength along the highway. The *andartes* pulled the packs off the donkeys and led the animals inside the cave, then lay down on the cold earth at the cave mouth and curled up in their cloaks. A few dragged on cigarettes and talked in whispers. Before long even these were fast asleep.

Outside the cave, Manolis and Elpida spread their cloaks on drifts of little prickly leaves beneath a stand of holly oaks, in shade fretted like a net—bright, but better for sleeping than the clotted darkness of the cave. They were drifting into unconsciousness when Richard appeared and squatted beside them.

He took a thin cigar from his jacket pocket and lit it with a cylindrical brass lighter. "Too excited to sleep," he confessed. "First time behind enemy lines."

"You'll get used to it," Manolis mumbled. Beside him Elpida yawned mightily.

"Well, I won't keep you. I just wondered . . ."

"What?"

"Why Cairo thinks you're dead."

Manolis squinted at the high sun and sat up. Elpida sat up too, sensing his unease. "Glad you're here. You can set them straight."

"Planning to tell them, then, were you?" When Manolis said nothing, Richard shrugged. "I mean, could be awkward. Now you're married."

"SOE left me, Richard. I didn't leave them."

Richard sighed. "The British army's a lot of things, but not often reasonable. Can't speak for the Greeks, of course."

"What are you saying?" Elpida demanded, catching more from Richard's manner than from his abbreviated English phrases.

"Your husband's gained valuable experience fighting behind German lines, *kyria* Androulaki," Richard explained. "There are a lot of places SOE might find a use for him besides Crete—the Balkans, Palestine, North Africa. . . ."

"Forget him," she said. "You never saw him."

"I understand your sentiment, but I can't pretend he doesn't exist. For one thing, he's my liaison with Papalexakis."

"Call him what you called him before: *Minakis*"—a name that meant nothing in Greek. "You never saw this Androulakis."

Richard drew on his cigarillo and studied Manolis. "You?"

"We'll talk later." Manolis glanced sidelong at Elpida.

"Right, then." Richard stood up and brushed the dust from his trousers. "Dreadfully sorry to have disturbed you," he said to Elpida, avoiding her gaze.

As he climbed away uphill, Elpida seized Manolis and pulled him close. "He is not your friend."

"He is. He'll do what he can for us."

"When he calls on his radio, I'll be standing over him," Elpida whispered fervently. "The British won't take you away. I'll kill him first."

Manolis held her close and hugged her, searching helplessly for words that were not only comforting but true. He found none.

There was an eruption of dry leaves beside them, a sudden crackle of rifle fire from the ridge across the ravine. They flattened themselves in the prickly oak leaves; then, grabbing their weapons, they half ran, half crawled uphill toward the mouth of the cave.

Richard ducked out of the cave, his Marlin gun in his hand. "These Greeks are half asleep. You and me."

Manolis nodded. "Inside," he told Elpida, and to Richard, "We'll go upslope, pick them off if they try to—"

"No. Down there," Richard yelled. "We can't hit anything at this range."

"Neither can they," Manolis yelled back, too late. Richard was already sliding toward the bottom of the ravine, bullets popping in the air and digging up the dirt around him, a one-man frontal attack. Manolis muttered curses only his grandmother would have understood and plunged after him. Now it was a two-man frontal attack.

By the time they reached the dry streambed, Satan's guerrillas were returning fire from the shelter of the cave. Among them were marksmen who had a chance of hitting someone, while Manolis and Richard were mere targets, taking what shelter they could behind the basalt blocks that cluttered the watercourse. Richard leaned against a boulder and checked the chamber of his Marlin gun. "Let me get a little farther up this gully. If they try to come across, we'll have them pinned."

"They're green boys, Richard. Stay here."

But Richard was in no mood to take advice. "Make them keep their heads down," he ordered, and hurled himself into the open.

Manolis threw himself against the underside of the boulder and fired at the hurrying shapes on the slope above him, squeezing off shots as fast as he could aim. One German soldier sat down abruptly, and others dived for shelter. He saw Richard stumble and fall—

—then crawl a few feet forward on all fours and get up again, sprinting to shelter under the eroded stream bank. Crouching, he waved back at Manolis, a smile lighting his face, his dark hair gleaming in the sunlight, looking as natty as ever. Manolis cursed and gave him the five fingers of his open hand, then returned his attention to the Germans.

High above him a German officer was screaming at his men, threatening to shoot them himself if they did not press the attack. A machine gun opened fire, shooting over the heads of the frightened soldiers as they stumbled reluctantly downslope toward the streambed, the shortest route to the cave.

Meanwhile Satan's guerrillas had left the cave and were climbing the ridge behind it, gaining the high ground even as the Germans were leaving it. Within moments the first Germans would reach the gully between Manolis and Elpida.

Manolis was astonished to see that they really were children, inexperienced and frightened. What fantasies of Aryan triumph and revenge had brought them here to be slaughtered? He waited until the first of them tried to jump the gully to the slope opposite; he shot the boy in the spine as he struggled for balance. Two more Germans jumped the gully. Richard got one, who flopped down and lay screaming, and Manolis shot the other in the back of the head; he dropped without a sound.

They were children, but there were a lot of them. As if by instinct Manolis clicked his weapon to full automatic a second before he heard a slide of rock behind him, turning just as a

German sergeant crashed down the slope. Manolis fired a burst, three bullets at close range. The sergeant lurched toward him and fell dead—no boy but a bold, unlucky man. Manolis snatched up his weapon and ammunition clips.

Too many Germans were getting across the gully. The boulder and the stream bank that a moment ago had shielded Manolis and Richard were now at their backs. There was nowhere to hide; the machine gun upslope kept up a raking fire. Manolis saw Richard dive for cover in the dry watercourse. It was an awkward place from which to aim.

Manolis wormed his way backward, keeping his belly to the rock. Up the hill there was the sharp bang of a grenade, and the machine gun fell silent. He kicked the dead German sergeant aside and peered out. Satan's *andartes* had seized the ridge.

But opposite, the Germans had almost reached the cave.

Suddenly there was a sustained burst of fire from the cave mouth; three Germans fell among the sparse oaks, and the others groveled on dry slopes which gave them no shelter.

Manolis had the sensation of leaving his body, of taking in everything at a glance—and when he stood upright and raised his hand in a commanding gesture, it was as if time stopped, as if his silent command was instantly communicated to everyone on the field. The lethal popping of gunfire ceased. There was not a breath of air or a whisper of shifting dirt.

A loose pebble clattered down the slope.

The German soldiers raised their hands above their heads and stood up cautiously; the *andartes* stood up against the sky and shouted and leaped and slid down the slopes of the ravine on all sides, herding the Germans toward the dry watercourse.

Already Manolis was limping uphill toward the cave, his leg muscles cramped from crouching behind the rocks. He found Elpida lying in the cave entrance, watching him, her gun still aimed downslope. He sat down beside her. "I'm sorry I left you," he said. He put his left hand on hers and with his right lifted away the Schmeisser; it was so hot he almost dropped it.

"Is it over?" she asked hoarsely.

"For now." He glanced across the ravine. Down below, Satan and his second-in-command, Siphakas, were in a shouting match with the German officer, a young lieutenant who clutched his right hand to his bloodied side while he gestured and swung at them with his left, screaming in German. Richard was making his way uphill, shouting at them to let him translate.

Too late. Siphakas snatched up the German lieutenant's pistol where he had dropped it and shot him in the face; his body pitched forward, out of Satan's grip, and landed facedown in the dirt a dozen yards uphill from Richard. Now Richard began screaming at the Greeks.

"Elpida, I need your help," Manolis urged.

"I'm sorry," she whispered.

He bent to her, suddenly afraid. She was curled into the shade of the cave mouth as if seeking protection. Gently he sought to turn her so that he could look at her face. Her skin was pallid; her lips were blue. She turned her green eyes on him, but he could not tell what they saw.

"My love, where are you hurt?"

She sighed and rolled away, opening to him. Her chest was a mass of blood-soaked clothes through which the dark blood bubbled and oozed like water from a slow spring.

"All-Holy Mother," he whispered.

"You do love me, Manolis?"

He made himself look away from her wound to her chalky face. "With all my heart. I have never loved anyone but you."

Her blue lips were thin as she smiled. "Not even Mercy?"

"Oh, don't tease me now." He tried to smile too; the tears spilling from the tip of his nose were pretty funny, after all.

"Remember me to her."

"Don't say that."

"Don't pretend," she said, groping for his hand. She held it over the wound beneath her collarbone. Her blood welled over his fingers.

"I will remember you to the end of the world."

"Let me kiss you," she whispered.

He held her for a long time, holding his mouth against hers lightly, for her breath was shallow. Finally it ceased. The life and breath drained out of her, and he knew that she was gone, and that John and Sophia were forever gone with her.

* * *

Maybe seconds, maybe minutes passed. Manolis folded his wife's hands across her chest and stood up unsteadily, bouncing his head off the low cave roof so hard that his scalp bled. He didn't notice the blood or the pain. He stumbled down to the ravine, to where the *andartes* surrounded the German prisoners.

"What are you doing?" Manolis demanded of Satan, looking at the Germans.

They stood barefoot in the gravel; a few feet away their boots were piled beside their weapons. Their white faces and close-cropped scalps were smeared with dust and blood, but through the dirt their stiff new uniforms gleamed.

"Don't concern yourself." Satan turned away and raised his voice. *"Now!* Let no one escape."

"Wait, *wait!"* Manolis lurched toward the muzzles of the raised guns, waving his bloody hands. Siphakas grabbed him from behind and threw him sideways. Richard leaped at Siphakas, cursing savagely, but another man seized Richard by the throat, threw him to the ground, and sat on his chest.

The remaining *andartes* took haphazard aim and began firing. There were twelve remaining Germans. Some knelt and bowed their heads as if receiving Communion; some ran a few steps down the dry streambed or tried to climb the slopes before they were shot too.

Satan's men left the bodies unburied and moved down the gully as far as they dared, wondering when the German patrol would be missed. As soon as it was dark they set out across the Messara, crossed fields of pungent onions, forded the shallow river and ran across the car road, and at last pushed up into the foothills of Psiloritis. One of the donkeys was more heavily laden than before with extra weapons and ammunition; the other's added burden was a corpse.

They came to a stony gorge where the water spilled noisily from above and made their way cautiously up the treacherous cliffside path. When at last the sky reddened with dawn, they had cleared the gorge but were still far short of their goal; they were exhausted, every one of them, and the danger of moving in daylight was extreme. They huddled under tall pines as the sun rose over the peaks. Manolis lay down on his cloak between the roots of a massive pine and sank into despairing sleep.

He swam up through blackness, pulled on a taut line, trying to understand the voice whispering in his ear: *". . . next submarine would take them off as prisoners, but he couldn't afford to take prisoners, couldn't leave them to tell tales, and never mind how many innocents the Germans slaughtered . . ."*

He awoke to find Richard squatting beside him, rocking back and forth, staring into the sun that filtered through the pine branches as he drew on a thin cigarillo. "Not talking Geneva conventions here, y'know. Talking plain human decency . . ."

For a long time Manolis said nothing while Richard, perhaps not really caring to be understood, talked to himself.

Finally he sat up and interrupted him. "Do you think I would have treated those Germans any differently than Satan did?"

Richard glanced sidelong, still rocking. "You tried to stop him." The shadowed sunlight moved over his tired features. He hadn't shaved in more than a day. On a Greek, his whiskers would have made him seem a regular fellow. On an Englishman who cared about appearances they looked shifty.

"I wasn't trying to stop him," Manolis replied. "I wanted to know which of them shot Elpida."

Richard paused in his rocking and rubbed his whiskery jaw. "I see."

"I don't think you do. We had to kill them, and leave no doubt that it was done by the resistance and not the nearest villagers," Manolis said. "The whole thing's a bloody shambles. I'm not apologizing. Why are you apologizing to me?"

Richard studied the burning stub of his cigarillo. "Do you know that SOE take the pair of us for Communists?"

"What do I care what they think? I'm not anything."

Richard laughed bitterly. "Who would believe that a Greek has no politics? SOE already know about our careers at school, that we were Epistolarians. . . ."

"Why are you *apologizing* to me, Richard? Because when you tried to get yourself killed you involved me in your stupid heroics? Because you thought it would be grand for us to be killed together, fighting for liberty in the cradle of liberty? Little Lord Byron and his Greek friend?"

Richard flinched at the ferocity of Manolis's sarcasm, opening his mouth as if to protest but saying nothing.

"Go away, leave me alone," Manolis said, "long enough to bury my wife."

The burial was at dusk, quick and unceremonious. Under pines that caught the rusty afterglow of sunset, Elpida's body was laid in a shallow grave. The *andartes* filed past, sifting bits of soil from their fingers and mumbling prayers over the mound of earth.

Satan paused to say his condolences to Manolis, who had not moved from the graveside; the donkeys were already loaded, and the men were anxious to start.

"What is the name of this place?" Manolis asked. A stony peak was visible through the trees. At its apex a chapel smoldered like a coal against the fading sky.

"That peak is Ambelakia, my child."

When all the Cretans were gone up the mountainside into the gathering shadows and only Manolis was left beside the grave, Richard approached him. "I'm terribly sorry for your loss, *kyrie* Minaki. I want to say . . . Well, please don't worry about me shooting my mouth to Cairo. I never saw you here. Crete is your home. This is where you belong."

Manolis turned red eyes upon him, studying him with fierce concentration. "Before Elpida, it was John who made it my home. I came back for them both. When John died, I still had a home in her. Without her, what do I care about Crete?"

"Oh my dear friend"—Richard hesitated and reached out a tentative hand—"what can I do?"

"Stop moping. You didn't kill her."

"I can't bear to have you think I put her in harm's way."

"Well, I'm a realist." Manolis leaned over the mound of fresh earth as if he intended never to leave the place.

Richard said, "We can talk when we get to Satan's camp. About how you want to spend the rest of the war."

"I'll tell you now," Manolis said. "I want to spend the war where I can end it faster than one child at a time. Which is not on Crete."

"Right, then." Richard cleared his throat; having found time to shave, he was once again the model of upper-class diffidence. "I'll do what I can to see you get back to England."

22

The elements of my character, like the impure bronze of a statue, had been poured together and left to cool. I stopped forming, growing, the day I buried Elpida. On that day I became who I am in every essential. Time did not stop, but the rest is weathering.

They were the last scribbled sentences of Minakis's manuscript. Anne-Marie let it drop on the table. Her eyes stung with tears, and she wiped at them impatiently. She should be frustrated, even afraid—there was not a word about the cave or the objects in it—but against her own interests she was coming to care as much about the man she was trying to deceive as about his treasure.

Still she needed to find it. She wondered what would happen if she simply explained her predicament—if she asked him?

The old house was cool inside, but outside the courtyard was bright in the afternoon sun. The air was suddenly heavy with spice. Minakis's silhouette appeared in the open door, filling the rectangle of light.

"I picked these on the mountainside." He came into the room and handed her a prickly bouquet.

"Thymos. Rigani." She inhaled. "I read that in ancient times sailors could smell the herbs before they could see the island."

"Yes, and not so long ago. But not any longer." He nodded toward the manuscript. "You finished the screed?"

"A few minutes ago." She laid the herbs on the table and stood. Hesitantly she stepped forward, then on impulse wrapped her arms around him and leaned her head on his chest. "She is in your heart as if she died yesterday."

He said nothing. He put his hands on her shoulders and held her for a moment, then gently stepped away. "I have errands to do. Surely you need sleep?"

"No. Let me come with you."

As they walked toward the village square they were avidly inspected by women in black, seated with heads together in the gateways of their courtyards, whispering. Anne-Marie pretended not to see them, though they pressed for her attention.

"You ended the manuscript by saying nothing had changed since your wife died. I can't believe that."

"How did I become a scientist, you mean? Where did the yacht come from? The details you need for your magazine story?"

"They would be worth knowing," she said coolly.

He nodded as if this were the right answer. "There's something on the mountain you ought to see. Do you have enough energy to climb there with me?"

Her heart lifted. "Yes," she said. If what he wanted to show her was a cave, she had enough energy to climb Everest.

"We'll have a stroll before supper. I'll tell you the rest."

They crossed the square and entered Louloudakis's place, past old men gaping in curiosity. Inside, the middle-aged proprietor was boiling coffee over a propane-fired gas ring.

"Good day, Haralambos. How are you today?" Minakis said cheerily.

Louloudakis looked up from the foaming *briki*. "Very well, *kyrie* Minakis, and you?"

"Well, thank you. And your wife? And your sons?"

"All very well."

"May they live long. This is my guest, *i kyria* Brand. A magazine photographer."

Anne-Marie offered her hand. When Louloudakis took it she saw the speculation in his eye—"A pleasure to meet you, *kyria*"—his gaze flickering over her as if to ask, Where are your cameras?

Minakis touched the man's arm in a friendly way to reclaim his attention. "I spoke to your boy Dimitri this morning about hiring a pack animal."

"He went down to Kaminaki to get her. He'll be here soon."

As the men talked, Anne-Marie looked around. She was standing next to a freezer case full of Belgian ice-cream novelties and German butter. Steel propane bottles lined the floor. There was a telephone on the wall beside the door. The shelves were stacked with Dutch lightbulbs, French canned goods, Italian dried pasta, and English socks and underwear. Her eye was caught by a shelf of audiocassettes: Sting and U2 had joined Maria Pharantouri on the Ayia Kyriaki hit parade.

She tried to imagine the place as young Manolis Androulakis had known it, with an oil lantern on a shelf instead of an electric bulb overhead, with sacks of grain where propane bottles now stood. Only the back wall seemed a remnant of that time: two stuffed pine martens and the head of a *kri-kri* ram with immense curving horns were mounted above a couple of shotguns on pegs. The ram's head was very old; the endangered Cretan ibex hadn't been seen in Lasithi nome for a hundred years.

She wondered why Manolis did not seem as ancient as the ram. No one else in the village had escaped time—

". . . as soon as he arrives," Minakis was saying to Louloudakis, who nodded agreement. "You may depend upon him."

—certainly not the man he was talking to, the son of his boyhood enemy, who was already middle-aged. Minakis, seen in a certain light, looked younger. If he was a statue, half a century of weathering had not spoiled his finish.

Anne-Marie changed into jeans and fetched her camera bag from the house. In the courtyard, Minakis pulled a tarpaulin from a pair of small, heavy bundles packaged in blue plastic.

"What are those?" she asked.

"Laboratory equipment."

She looked at him quizzically. "Where's the laboratory?"

"Let me surprise you."

A boy arrived at the gate, leading a sad-eyed donkey with a packsaddle. Minakis introduced them: "Dimitri, this is Anne-Marie Brand. Anne-Marie, this is Dimitris. And"—he indicated the donkey—"this is Irini."

"Dimitris Louloudakis?" Anne-Marie asked the boy.

"Malista, kyria," said the youngster. He wore a tattered sweater-vest over a dirty white shirt tucked into stained black trousers; his shoes were scuffed brogans.

"This is indeed Dimitris Louloudakis," Minakis said, "whose father is Haralambos Louloudakis, whose grandfather is Dimitris Louloudakis, whose great-grandfather was Haralambos Louloudakis, whose great-great-grandfather was Dimitris Louloudakis . . ."

"Endaxi, I get it. I'm very happy to meet you, Dimitris."

While Minakis and Dimitris loaded the donkey carefully, insuring that the heavy packages could not slip, Anne-Marie circled and clicked away, occasionally reaching into her camera bag to change lenses.

Minakis indicated the bag. "Irini can carry that."

"I'm used to lugging it."

"Feel free to change your mind."

They followed the bank of the arroyo toward the saddle at the head of the dry falls. Anne-Marie noted the rubberized cables on the ground paralleling their route, turning west where they turned west, taking a path that pitched up the slope of shattered rock to the northwest of Dikti's long crest.

The donkey's dainty, iron-shod hooves repeatedly slipped

and struck sparks from the rock with metallic rings like hammer blows. Anne-Marie scrambled to get far enough ahead to photograph the little caravan against the background of the plain; she had to scramble again to catch up after she had waited for them to pass.

The world quickly opened below them, a bowl of golden mountains filled with green trees, a tiny village perched at its edge, the whole under a sky deepening to twilight, brushed with feathery vermilion clouds. The altitude and the steepness of the path were daunting. She stopped taking pictures and fell in beside Minakis, taking lungfuls of air. "Now tell me the rest," she said.

He didn't slacken his pace; when at last he spoke he sounded as relaxed as he had sounded yesterday morning, sitting at a café on Mykonos. "As for the war, you may have heard stirring tales of kidnapped German generals and the like. Those were English adventures, worse than useless to the Greeks. As for me, I had no reason to stay on Crete, but neither did I have a means of leaving.

"Any prospect I had of becoming a boffin in war research had died with John—and with Sir Arthur, who died shortly after he learned of John's fate; he was a few months past ninety. After a few more months, Richard returned from a trip to Cairo with news of yet another death."

"My father is dead," Richard told Minakis, as they crouched beside a smoky fire in a dripping cave high on Mount Lazaros. A half dozen *andartes* lay curled in the shadows; a British sergeant in filthy garb lay on his stomach at the cave entrance, fiddling with a wireless.

"I'm sorry," Minakis said after a long silence, though he felt nothing.

"I should be sorry too, I suppose." Richard fancied that he was disguised as a shepherd, but he wore his wool cloak regally. "A hunting accident, they say. Not likely. They called him a traitor behind his back. He could never abide disapproval." He reached beneath his cloak, brought out a packet of cigarettes, and offered one to Minakis. "Cigars a bit of a luxury, these days." Minakis thrust out his chin, and Richard handed the pack around. He smiled apologetically. "Thing is, the family business is obscenely successful—all these uniforms, you know. And I'm the heir. Rather an embarrassment."

Minakis watched his friend with unblinking eyes, saying nothing, for there was nothing to say to comfort a man whose grief over the loss of his father was already many years old.

The *andartes* lit their cigarettes from smoldering branches; the cigarette pack came back almost empty. Richard lit his own with his brass lighter. "Some good in this. Lots of Father's old pals on high are friendly to his survivors." He reached beneath his cloak again and brought out a pair of letters in brown envelopes. "These for you."

Minakis took them and read them quickly. One was from SOE relinquishing him to the command of the Greek army. The other bore the heading of the Greek general staff temporarily housed in British Cairo, ordering him to complete his degree at Cambridge University, whereupon he was to report to the Radar Research Establishment as scientific liaison from the Greek government in exile.

Richard said casually, "I understand there's a scholarship at King's—it says that, does it?—and army pay, of course."

"Does it?" Minakis asked dryly.

"These days, when Churchill says 'jump,' the Greek government asks 'how high?' " Richard replied airily. "If Suggs here can raise them on the wireless, the *Hedgehog* will take you off tomorrow night. Already a week into Michaelmas, you know." He was talking fast to divert his friend's brooding sense of honor, knowing it was one thing for a boy to accept help from his *sadalos,* quite another for a grown man to accept a lavish favor from a colleague. A foreign colleague at that. "Not sure Malvern'll make the best use of your talents, but the places that could really use you are not places anybody can . . ."

Minakis held up his hand; Richard faltered in midsentence. "I'll go to England, Richard. You can have Crete."

When the commanding hand came down, Richard nodded vigorously. "Right then. After the war I'll let you stand me to a drink."

"You must stay alive to collect it." Minakis's tone was neutral; he meant no more than he said.

Cambridge was colder and darker and offered even fewer distractions than before the war. By June 1943, Minakis had done the maths tripos with honors, and for the next two years he worked on radar—not theory, a fait accompli, but practical problems of mass-producing lightweight sets for aircraft. He learned the techniques of generating high-power microwaves. He learned the properties of silicon detectors. He read Cavafy and Seferis and T. S. Eliot:

> There will be time, there will be time.
> To prepare a face to meet the faces that you meet;
> There will be time to murder and create,
> And time for all the works and days of hands
> That lift and drop a question on your plate. . . .

Minakis was happy for his colleagues when the war ended but felt little on his own account or that of the country he had left; the Greek government was a British prop that could not feed its people, the Communists and the monarchists were at one another's throats like savage dogs, and civil war was inevitable.

Better to return to grim Cambridge, where, having indicated that he would apply for British citizenship as soon as he had met residency requirements, he was offered a fellowship in applied mathematics (Cambridge-speak for theoretical physics) and a research post at the Cavendish to go with it.

His solder-splattered wooden bench-top was cluttered with electronic valves and copper switches and bulky resistors and capacitors; its centerpiece was a tiny crystalline slab mounted in a vise, connected by fine wires to a greenly fluttering oscilloscope. Minakis tweaked the oscilloscope—a piece of equipment that had survived the Blitz, if barely—and studied the racing curves on the screen. As he bent to his slide rule there was a knock on the laboratory door—

—and simultaneously a terrific bang on the bench, a flare of pink light, a tinkling glissando of valve fragments.

Minakis swatted at the flames with his bare hands. He turned to find Richard Wingate standing in the doorway.

"Oh my," said Richard. "I hope I didn't do that."

"Hello, Richard." Minakis's mustache twitched, but he didn't smile. "I see you took my advice."

"Oh yes—I'm alive. You owe me a drink, I believe."

They studied each other solemnly, separated by dense smoke and the stench of burned insulation. Slowly Minakis bent toward his friend, stepped forward, and took him firmly by the hand.

They caught up over lunch at the Eagle Pub. After four years behind enemy lines in the Aegean and France, Richard had returned to take up his doctorate, leaving the family business in the hands of the functionaries who had run it during the war.

"Not that I haven't shocked the old dears by insisting on a number of reforms. The board think me radical, but I daresay they have no idea how fast society is shifting. Just look around—most of the undergraduates here are as old as we are, and not at all the sort of person one encountered before the war." Richard sipped daintily at his sherry. "And you? What are you up to in that cubbyhole Bragg has put you in?"

"I'm looking at surface effects in semiconductors."

"Is that work for a theorist? You know what Pauli said about solid-state physics—this after he personally *invented* the field—'One shouldn't wallow in dirt.' "

"Wallowing in dirt is my nature," Minakis said.

Richard reddened. "I didn't mean to suggest . . ."

"I'm quite serious. Potsherds were my first love. Silicon is a substitute. Interesting in its own way."

Richard raised his glass. "To silicon."

For several weeks neither Minakis nor Richard made an effort to contact the other—Minakis from bad habit, because he avoided social contact and buried himself in research, sleeping on a cot in the laboratory and spending his weekends climbing mountains or bicycling to exhaustion.

One day Richard decided to drop by the Cavendish again. Minakis was using a helium cryostat when Richard knocked on his door. At that moment a fluid line ruptured. Liquid helium spurted out, and the air filled with dense white vapor.

Richard poked his head in. "I say, I hope I didn't . . ." Amid sounds of shattering glass, Minakis leaped to block his entry.

"Don't touch anything, you could freeze your fingers."

Richard waited in the hall for half an hour while Minakis and a porter cleared the mess away. When Minakis came out Richard insisted on paying for the damages, and Minakis accepted his offer with a curt nod.

"Last time we talked you mentioned Pauli," Minakis said. "Have you heard of the Pauli effect?"

"Well, he did just win the Nobel Prize. . . ."

"I don't mean the exclusion principle. I mean that whenever Pauli enters a laboratory, something breaks. But he always escapes unscathed." With a firm hand on his shoulder Minakis guided Richard toward the main entrance. "We'll simply have to meet somewhere besides my laboratory from now on."

"Dinner in my rooms?" Richard suggested meekly. "Actually, I came by to ask you about electrons in nonmetals."

"It will be good to talk physics with you," Minakis said, thinking it would be a relief to talk any subject with Richard without first having to clean up after him.

They talked physics often, but they never talked of the past.

Richard's respect for his friend's work grew, even as that work was anticipated by others better funded. Minakis was well on the way to creating a solid-state amplifier when Bell Laboratories announced its patents on a similar device, which it called a transistor. Minakis turned to semiconductors made of intermetallic compounds, but the giant Siemens combine in Germany was the first to achieve practical production methods.

Richard suffered setbacks of his own. He decided that his doctoral work was a mere footnote to the theory of quantum electrodynamics worked out in the United States and Japan.

He left to spend a summer on the Continent, and when he returned to London he asked Minakis to join him for dinner at his club.

"I haven't any talent for the scientific life," Richard told Minakis, when they had finished their roast beef and potatoes and the waiter had removed their plates. "I was born to be a businessman; I admit it. Unlike my effect on laboratories, looms don't break down when I walk onto the mill floor."

The two men, glowing with health in the mirror-reflected light of chandeliers and sconces and polished paneling, were older than their years in every way but their looks—Richard, sleek and sunburned, barely thirty-two years old, was impeccable in fine-woven tweeds; Minakis was a smooth-browed twenty-nine, with long black lashes and black eyes and a glossy black mustache, wearing the same suit that had served him since the end of the war.

"What became of your Communism?" Minakis asked with a smile.

"You're an ex-Greek, I'm an ex-Communist. My employees don't complain as much as most."

"I'll miss our talks," Minakis said mildly. He sat back as the waiter returned with a bottle of Five-Star Metaxa and two snifters.

Richard nodded for the waiter to pour the brandy. He lit a thin cigar, puffed a stream of smoke and studied the burning ash, then eyed Minakis, who was watching him steadily. "Cloth is a bore, Minakis. I've decided to branch out."

"Into?"

"I'm thinking of buying an instrument factory in Switzerland. Add a research arm to the place. Change the name, change the direction. Miniaturized solid-state electronics. Digital computation machinery. The coming thing."

"I'm sure you'll do well."

"Manolis, give me your attention." Richard's eyes narrowed, and he spoke with barely suppressed heat. "How do you *like* struggling to teach undergraduates the fundamentals of quantum theory for what, the fifth year now? How do you *like* making bits and pieces of gear out of glass valves because Bragg can't spare you the money to buy the sort of solid-state instruments you invented? It's been ten years since John died. Since your wife died. Aren't you tired of wearing that bloody hair shirt?"

Minakis found himself fascinated by Richard's display of temper: perhaps the man wasn't condemned to eternal politeness and guilt after all. "Am I tired of my life?" Minakis set his brandy snifter on the table and rotated it thoughtfully. "I am indeed. What do you suggest I do about it?"

"Be my business partner. The brainy half of Androulakis and Wingate, inventors and entrepreneurs. Make us impossibly rich."

Minakis tilted his head to one side, his eyes hard as glass. When he smiled his teeth gleamed in the warm light. "Why not?"

23

"Microelectronics made our fortune, as Richard predicted. You'll have to ask him how he did it. I only ran the lab."

"Is that what renewed your interest in life?" Anne-Marie asked, her breath coming hard, something she was getting used to in Minakis's rarefied air. "Money?"

"After Andwin was established, I could pursue my own projects."

"Which were?"

"What I'm taking you to see is a kind of prototype."

"Oh." Her disappointment was plain—she could stop searching the rocky slopes for a cave entrance. "Tell me when we get close enough to spot this laboratory of yours."

"It was never out of sight," Minakis said. "It's right up there." He pointed.

A tiny chapel built of fieldstone perched high on top of the conical tor. A cross of welded scrap iron at the end of the chapel's barrel vault was silhouetted against the lurid sunset.

"What are you doing up there, calling God?"

Minakis laughed, loud enough to make the donkey shy. "Don't tell the metropolitan. After a very substantial donation to the church, I secured permission to use this place on the promise that my work had not the least religious significance."

They reached the lofty chapel, surrounded by purple sky, the air colder than the stone underfoot; the night's first stars glittered like quartz. To the southeast, Dikti formed a gray wall across the horizon; far to the west the snowfields of Psiloritis were pale in the afterglow of sunset.

The chapel door was locked, but an old iron key rested on top of the lintel, in the first place anyone would look for it; the door was locked only against the wind. Inside, under a vault of bare stone, oil lamps flickered on a wooden stand in front of a bleached paper icon of the Metamorphosis. Someone had been here not long ago, saying prayers.

The chapel was too poor and remote a place to merit an iconostasis; where one might have stood there was a sturdy construction of steel struts mounted on leveling jacks, supporting a platform covered with a heavy plastic sheet. The platform was at the level of a slit window in the center of the apse, which neatly framed the snowy mass of Psiloritis. A computer terminal, also shrouded in plastic, sat on a table against the wall.

"Well, it's a picturesque place for a physics experiment." Anne-Marie reached into her bag and pulled out a flash unit that she snapped to the Canon. She turned to find Dimitris hovering in the doorway, displaying his dazzling grin.

"Polaroid?" he asked.

She thrust out her chin. "Be patient, child."

Minakis had pulled the milky plastic covering off the platform, revealing a perforated steel bench. Answering Anne-Marie's questioning look, he said, "Essentially it's an interferometer." He named the components: "Primary laser and guide-beam laser, mirrors, rotating prisms, solenoid shutters, sighting scope . . ."

"Just look at me a second . . . that's good." Peering at him through the viewfinder, she bounced the flash from the vaulted ceiling, bathing the whitewashed interior in light, three times in quick succession.

"Forty-five kilometers west of us, this side of Psiloritis, is the peak of Ambelakia," Minakis said, "almost as high as the one we're standing on. Two years ago, with the cooperation of the local shepherds there, I installed a compound mirror, a mirror that can reflect a laser beam straight back where it came from—here, that is."

"To do what?" she asked, framing him in her viewfinder against the high slit window. Her flash washed him in white light.

"I and my former colleagues have used the interferometer to test Cramer's transactional interpretation."

"Which is? If you told me already, remind me."

"I discussed it with Peter. Cramer's interpretation removes uncertainty from quantum events—gets rid of the collapse of the wave function, resolves apparent dualities like the wave-versus-particle nature of a quantum event, and emphatically gets rid of the observer required by the Copenhagen interpretation." He smiled. "So one doesn't have to imagine Schrödinger's cat half dead and half alive before one looks in the box."

"You mean the cat's dead or it's alive. Really."

"And the moon exists, whether we look at it or not."

"Kind of takes all the fun out of quantum mechanics."

"Not at all." He was bending over the machinery, sighting along the light paths. He groped in a tool chest and found a can of compressed air and used it to flick dust from the surfaces of the mirrors. "It's true that the transactional interpretation is only an *interpretation,* a different way of looking at the same events; it uses the same mathematics as standard QM and makes the same predictions. But Cramer assumes that information travels backward in time."

"Time travel?"

"Not material bodies, only information. By his interpretation, cause and effect work backward as well as forward, everywhere and always—cause and effect are an agreement, a 'handshake,' between something that happens now and something that happens then."

Minakis had made whatever adjustments he wanted to make

and turned, focusing his attention on her. She snapped three more frames, up close, full face. He said, "The core of Cramer's idea is that the signal moving backward in time, from effect to cause, quite naturally selects from among all the possibilities that are moving forward in time the only one with real results."

"And you've tested it."

"Yes."

"With this machine?"

"Yes. What we've built here is a fancy version of the two-slit experiment—QM's oldest paradox."

Like Schrödinger's cat, the two-slit experiment had been familiar to Anne-Marie even before she met Peter, for it was beloved of literary theorists who had only the vaguest sense of its physical meaning. "If both slits are open, light's a wave, but if only one slit's open, light is particles," she said, putting it baldly.

"*Endaxi.*" Minakis shrugged. "You can do it with a single photon. It interferes with itself if it goes through both slits; if only one slit is open, it makes a discrete hit. But how does it *know*, before it gets to the barrier, whether it will encounter two slits or one? How does it *know* whether to behave like a particle or a wave?"

"You think, because of this signal moving backward in time."

He nodded. She was quick, perhaps a little too quick; she wasn't listening so much as keeping him talking, a photographer's trick. "At the moment the photon is emitted, a signal from the future tells it the outcome. The catch is, the signal moving backward in time covers exactly the same interval as the signal moving forward in time."

"So it could never be detected," she murmured, her fist pressed against her lips as she held the camera to her eye and rapidly shot more frames.

"Which is why it *normally* goes undetected," Minakis said, gently correcting her. He patted the optical bench. "What we've done is to shrink time along one leg of the transaction—shrink it in the forward direction, so to speak. Warp time like a bow."

"I get it. . . . I think." She let her camera fall to her chest. "By speeding up time along one leg of the path, you spoil the transaction."

"*Malista*. The result comes back before the photon goes anywhere. 'One slit is closed,' says the future signal—or in this case, 'One beam path is closed'—so the photon expects to behave like a particle. Meanwhile the experimenter fools it and opens the other slit, the other beam path, too. But the outcome has already been signaled, and the result is a particlelike splotch, not the wavy interference one would expect of superposed paths. Impossible! Or if the photon thinks both paths are open, the experimenter closes one, and in this case a single path produces wavelike interference. Impossible again!"

"That's what you've done with this setup?"

"I'll show you. This laser is the photon source. The beam splitter sends part of the beam to Ambelakia."

He invited her to peer through the aiming telescope, and she bent to the eyepiece. Centered in the crosshairs was an array of corner reflectors cemented to the roof of a chapel, reflecting only the evening sky.

"Half the beam goes forty kilometers and comes back. The other half follows a parallel path of the same length—because it is reflected numerous times by these spinning prisms. Then the beams are recombined, as in an ordinary Michelson interferometer. According to the Copenhagen interpretation, each photon is taking two superposed paths, both possible, neither definite, like Schrödinger's alive-dead cat, until somebody observes the result."

Minakis paused and grinned at Anne-Marie as if he were about to reveal a secret. "We're interested in which path the photon *really* took." He tapped a key on the computer keyboard and a heavy disk rotated, snapping an instrument into position on the tabletop. "You see, we can arrange the path so that each time the distant beam comes back to the tabletop it goes through this black box."

The "black" box was in fact a gray box of painted steel a foot long, with thickly filtered, lenslike openings aligned between two mirrors on the steel bench. "A photon spends *no* time in here. I mean that literally—it gets through this box faster than light."

Sticking with what made literal sense to her, Anne-Marie said, "So you're splitting a photon and messing with half of it. You can mess with what information it gets from the future—what it knows about what effect it is supposed to cause."

"Nicely put," he said dryly. Perhaps she had been listening.

"Where's the crunch?"

"Ah, the crunch. It's here, where the two light paths recombine."

In train behind the black box was a larger steel box, as wide and tall as a ream of business stationery, fitted with an optical tube in its center and hinged to the bench along its edge. Minakis folded it back, revealing a flat metal plate as big as a sheet of paper, coated with a dull sheen. "It's a CCD, a charge-coupled device that sends information about photon hits to the computer." With a long finger he tapped the thin plate. From it, flat strips of optical fiber ran to the computer against the wall. "When photons arrive here, the computer counts the hits and constructs either an interference pattern or a discrete splotch—according to whether two beams are open or only one. But if the black box is in the second beam line, the photons are getting information of outcomes before there have been any outcomes. So the computer shows us whether information from the future has changed the photon's past."

"Do I get to watch this miracle?" Anne-Marie asked quietly.

"You call it a miracle?" Minakis replaced the hood over the CCD plate and snapped it into place. "Perhaps it is a miracle—that the world is real."

The rotating prisms spun with an ear-needling whistle. Minakis and Anne-Marie peered at the computer screen.

"Without the black box, here's what one beam looks like," Minakis said. The computer screen showed a glowing white splotch in the middle of an otherwise dark screen, brightest in the middle, fading toward the edges, like a burned-out picture tube.

"And here's both beams." He tapped the keyboard. Under the

scream of the prisms Anne-Marie could hear the soft click of a
solenoid shutter snapping out of the beam path. The computer
screen instantly flipped to a pattern of concentric circles, bright
lines alternating with black lines, the crests and troughs of
interfering waves of light.

"Now we put in the black box." Minakis tapped the keyboard. The turntable whirred, sliding the black box into place,
momentarily interrupting the beam. The interference fringes
vanished and the plain white splotch reappeared.

Anne-Marie leaned forward to peer over Minakis's shoulder.
"How do I know that's just because you blocked the second
path with the black box?"

"You're a skeptic. Excellent." He tapped a series of commands
on the keyboard, the alphanumerics appearing in a stripe down
the side of the screen. "I'm instructing the shutters to leave both
paths open until a packet of photons has reached the beam splitter, but to close the first beam before they can be recombined.
This will happen very rapidly and repeatedly, in order to build up
an image. In the interim, both beams will be blocked."

Minakis pressed Enter. The screen went dim, but within a
second a perfectly circular interference pattern had assembled:
the photons traveling on a single path to Ambelakia and back
were behaving as if they had traveled along two paths.

If Anne-Marie were to believe what she saw, the simple display on the screen was evidence that Minakis could trick the
future—even recover the past, a few milliseconds of it.

"Of course, this could all be in the computer itself, just a program I'm running to fool you," Minakis said happily.

Anne-Marie's smile was a grimace. "I doubt I'm worth the
effort."

"I have to go home now," Dimitris announced loudly. All this
time he had been standing beside the door, listening to their
conversation in English. Evidently he had abandoned the
attempt to understand. "My father will want me at the taverna."

"Thanks for your help, Dimitri." Minakis turned from the
screen. "You and I will talk later." He groped in his jacket and
handed the boy a brown envelope. "If I were you, I wouldn't let
your father have all of this. You did the work."

Dimitris grinned. "There are lots of good hiding places on the way back to the village, *kyrie*."

Minakis and Anne-Marie went outside and watched as Dimitris led the donkey down the stony track. Relieved of her burdens, Irini stepped lightly.

Anne-Marie sat on the rocky ground, settling her back against the chapel wall, to watch the moon rise over Dikti, while Minakis went inside to turn off the switches and rewrap the interferometer in its plastic shroud. When he came back out, he dropped easily to the ground beside her, as flexibly as a teenager. For a few moments they savored the spectacle of moonrise over the bare cliffs.

"I observe that the moon is rising," Anne-Marie said soberly.

Minakis threw back his head and laughed, and he was still wiping tears from his eyes when she turned to him, a sly grin on her face.

But her grin soon faded, and his chuckles died. "What next?" she asked. "Why haven't you published what you've done? Why hasn't the world heard all about it? Especially my husband."

"My former colleagues have published, although my name is not on their papers. Anyone who wants to spend the time and money can replicate our experiment." His smile was sour. "Meanwhile reports of superluminal photons go into the hopper of unbelievable results, along with naked quarks and the like."

"Why isn't your name on those papers?"

"I didn't want it there. I don't publish fragments. What I've showed you is not what I set out to do."

"All this hinting! Just tell me."

He acknowledged her temper with a wry smile. "Call it a telescope into the past. Or think of it as bait for your husband. If Peter has studied what's in that envelope I gave you, he will know that what he wants to prove can be proved."

"He wants to prove the world is real. It's all he talks about these days."

"Then he must accept that the past is shaped by the future as much as the future is shaped by the past."

"That sounds as if you think the future *causes* the past." She bowed her head and rubbed her temples.

"You saw it tonight. Does it disturb you?"

"Yes," she said emphatically. "It's like saying that every bad thing that happens to us, we cause ourselves by what we do later."

"Every good thing too, by that reasoning."

"Isn't the past hard enough to live down without worrying that we're making it happen all over again?"

"If we're speaking in metaphors, that would be a good way to describe memory."

"Memory isn't cause," she said unhappily.

"Cause and effect are illusions. We do not say, when we travel from Paris to Athens, that Paris causes Athens. These places exist in a fixed spatial relation; only the order of our experiences differs. Time is a dimension like the dimensions of space. Just because we experience time as a one-way street doesn't mean it *is* a one-way street."

"And if someone puts a bomb on the plane, would you call that cause and effect?"

"Some events are inextricably entangled."

"What you showed me tonight was patterns on a computer screen. Do they mean we can go back and change the past?"

"*Oshi*." Minakis thrust out his chin. "Even if we could go back—not in person, of course—it wouldn't change anything. When you go from Athens to Paris, Paris is Paris."

"Assuming your plane gets there." Anne-Marie pushed herself away from the wall, suddenly restless.

The level space at the top of the peak was hardly wider than the chapel itself. She circled the building, surrounded by a sweep of stone and sky and starlit sea, and when she rounded the last corner, Minakis was on his feet, waiting for her.

"I didn't tell Peter where to find you," she said defiantly. "I didn't want him here."

"Perhaps he will find me anyway."

"Do you know what scares me? What if he has to choose between me and that machine inside, and he chooses the machine?"

"What kind of choice would *you* face?"

"No choice; I made it before I married him. My son."

"You can have them both," Minakis said.

"What do you mean?" she demanded.

"I brought you here on purpose. I think you know that."

"Yes."

"I know what you want."

"Yes," she said. "What do I have to do to get it?"

Cold air swept down the slopes; the wind sifted through the thorny plants that clung to the crevices among the rocks, a sound like falling water, like the breeze in a pine forest.

"We'd better start down," Minakis said. "It's getting cold."

24

They sat beside an oak fire. He had given her food and wine and the answers to all her questions but one, and now he questioned her.

"Does Peter know about Alain?"

She shook her head. "I've never told anyone the whole truth."

"Are you willing to tell me?"

"Will it change anything?"

"I don't know." His worry beads wound themselves around the fingers of his left hand, clicking softly.

For the past two days she had shared Minakis's losses and hopes so deeply that she had come to feel a great affection for him. Now he had retreated again, playing god. Since there was no more to gain by hiding, she stroked her throat with an open hand, coaxing herself to speak, and made her face into a mask.

"Papa was always on tour when I was little. We moved a lot because Mama was anxious to stay as close as possible—Milan one year; New York the next for what seemed forever, probably six months while he was doing the States; Vienna—it must have been expensive moving us around, and she made up for it by installing us in the cheapest places. Alain and I shared a bedroom and sometimes a bed.

"I was as curious as he was, the first times we explored. He was sweet, not insistent, not . . . pokey. I got bored before he did, but I didn't think much about it.

"When I was eleven we learned that Papa was having ' 'affairs,' although we didn't know what affairs were exactly. We couldn't ask Mama, it upset her too much—their fights were how we heard the word in the first place, how we knew it had something to do with other women. Which was as much as I wanted to know. But Alain was thirteen, he had sex on the brain.

"That year was the first time he rolled on top of me, pushed my knees apart, pulled up my nightgown. Nothing happened except he made a sticky mess on my belly, but the next time he tried it I slapped him as hard as I could and started screaming. When Mama came running in, I said I'd had a bad dream.

"Alain didn't bother me again, as long as she was around, although when we were alone there were times he pawed at me like a zombie, with no control of himself, apologizing all the time—'I'm sorry, I'm sorry'—but coming at me anyway.

"When I was fifteen we moved back to Paris. One night Papa came home late from a performance, drunk—he was drunk a lot that year; I suppose his career was starting to slip—and demanding money for a taxi at the top of his voice, which Mama refused to give him. He hit her. We'd never seen him do that.

"Alain went crazy. He attacked Papa with his fists. He was sobbing so hard he could hardly see, but he couldn't stop himself. Papa was shocked—he wouldn't use his hands to defend himself, all he could do was run, and Alain ran outside after him and threw a handful of coins on the sidewalk and yelled at him not to come back.

"Next day the police came and told us Papa was dead. Later we found out he'd been with a man's wife, and the man found them and shot him. Both of them.

"I don't remember much about that day except that the apartment was full of people all day long and Mama was in hysterics and somebody, a doctor I suppose, made her take sleeping medicine. When everybody finally left she was snoring like a freight train. Alain came at me and begged me to help him forget what had happened—what *he'd* done to Papa, he said. . . ." Anne-Marie broke off, the words sticking in her dry throat.

Minakis said, "You don't have to . . ."

"Yes I do," she whispered. "And you have to listen." She reached for her glass and sipped the last of the wine, then held on to the empty glass, squeezing it in her fingers. "He kept at me. He had his hand clamped over my mouth so I couldn't scream, and I almost passed out. When it was all over he started crying again, all of a sudden desperate for forgiveness. I forgave him. It was the only way I could get him off me." She relaxed her grip on the empty glass and set it on the table.

"From then on I slept on the couch. I told Mama why, and even though Alain denied it, and she tried to make excuses for him—even though she knew it was true and it horrified her— it wasn't in her to spend money on a bigger place for us to live.

"I started classes at the Sorbonne, officially living at home but spending as little time there as I could. I had some girlfriends. I told them lurid tales about imaginary lovers; they told me about contraception. There were boys I wanted to know, but whenever I daydreamed about them needy Alain would loom up in my thoughts, blotting out everyone else. There were nights when I stood on a bridge staring at the Seine, wondering how long it would take to drown.

"Meanwhile Alain got a job with an antiquary in the rue Dauphine. He had no formal education beyond the lycée, but he'd always haunted museums and galleries—he was a quick study and a social charmer. When he was twenty-one he got his trust fund—Mama had made Papa set up trusts for both of us— and he left Paris to work for the gallery's Zurich branch.

"When I came into my own inheritance I didn't tell Mama where I was going; I told only my bank. I spent the next year working my way across North Africa. I was a party girl, an arrogant, manipulative bitch, someone I wouldn't want to know"—she smiled crookedly at Minakis—"until I landed in jail in Algiers for smuggling hash. They let me go, but I can't go back. I'm persona non grata.

"I wasn't celibate, but the idea of marriage turned my stomach. In Egypt I had a German boyfriend who was a stringer for Reuters. I picked up photography from him, and pretty soon I was selling snaps of my jet-set acquaintances to magazines like *Stern* and *Paris Match*.

"I got to Crete on a seagoing hotel owned by a Saudi arms dealer and came ashore half blind with migraine from a permanent hangover. By the time my hands stopped shaking and I could focus a camera again, they'd sailed without me.

"So I stayed. I still had hangovers two or three nights a week, but I was getting used to them, and besides, I promised myself I'd become a better person soon. I was scouting a fashion shoot for some German magazine at the archaeological museum in Ayios Nikolaos when I saw Alain. It was the first time I'd laid eyes on him in half a decade. . . ."

"I really am on vacation, my dear, believe it or not."

"Here's to your vacation." Anne-Marie held up her glass and glanced it off Alain's. "Are you having any fun?" she asked, sipping the cold, astringent white wine.

"I am, actually. I'm quite the amateur scholar these days. Not a great reader, not compared to you, but I've taken an interest in old books. As objects, you know. I'm an antiquarian at heart, incapable of ignoring any nearby museum. The one here is small but choice." They were sitting at a table on the terrace of the class-A Minos Beach, west of town; Alain's bungalow-by-the-sea was a few steps away. "And you're a photographer. I've seen your work in the magazines. Very, mm, what shall I say? Engaged? *Strong.* Social commentary with a sense of style. I applaud that. I'm proud of you."

"Kiss my ass," she said without humor. "Snapshots of drunken socialites. Their groupies and gigolos and whores. Not-quite-dirty pictures."

"You earn your living. I earn mine."

"A good one, it seems. Congratulations."

"Which makes us grown-ups. Not like before."

"You don't look as happy as you claim to be," she said.

"I have no reason to be unhappy." His smile was thin; he avoided her eyes.

"Maybe it doesn't work that way. Maybe what we need is a reason to be happy."

"And how are we doing in our search?" he asked quietly, looking up.

She resented her brother for being such an attractive man. She wished she could censor her odious comparisons of him with the rich creeps who took up too many of her days and nights. She felt a moment of panic. They were not through their first drink—had they already run out of safe topics?

"Alain! We've been looking for you!"

Alain recoiled at the sound of loud American voices across the terrace; he winced and grinned and waved in one fluid suite. "We're stuck," he whispered to Anne-Marie, "but not for long. Don't lose hope." He pushed his chair back and stood as two men approached from the bar, carrying their drinks. "Anne-Marie, allow me to introduce my friends Howie Thomas, Charlie Phelps. . . . Gentlemen, my sister."

Both men were in their late twenties and both wearing Bermuda shorts and Hawaiian shirts, their bare feet stuck into boat shoes, but while Howie was short and rotund, with peeling freckled skin and thinning orange hair, Charlie was as tall and slim as Alain, his otherwise unremarkable features made exotic by a tan almost as deep as Anne-Marie's.

"Happy to meet you, Anne-Marie." Charlie managed a bow, then turned to Alain. "You didn't mention you had a sister."

"If she really *is* his sister," Howie muttered, with a pop-eyed leer he evidently meant as a compliment. "My God, Alain, where have you been hiding this gorgeous woman?"

"This is actually the first time we've seen each other in years," Alain said. "We were just catching up."

"Why don't you both sit down and tell me where Alain's been hiding *you* two?" Anne-Marie had assumed a glassy vivaciousness. "He *claimed* he was alone."

"One drink," said Charlie, his eyes fastened upon her. "We

don't want to break up a family reunion." He and Howie
dragged chairs to the table while Alain signaled a waiter, who
hurried to take their orders. "As for us," Charlie continued,
"your brother's been on board for a week, ever since we ran
into him on Rhodes. A bunch of us from San Diego are doing
the islands on a charter." He glanced sidelong at Alain. "Sorry
if I'm blowing your cover, but you did call us over."

Alain shrugged, but Charlie was watching Anne-Marie.
"Have you ever done that? A yacht charter? It's a wonderful
way to experience Greece."

"It must be wonderful," Anne-Marie replied, lifting her glass
and gulping the wine. On how many yachts had she been a pas-
senger? She'd come to think of island-hopping as a good way
to avoid experiencing anything.

"Alain has been a terrific guide. To the ruins, you know? And
what's in the museums? We couldn't have hired . . . well, that's
a stupid thing to say. He's a friend."

"You're very kind," Alain whispered.

"What do you do when you aren't experiencing Greece,
Charlie?" Anne-Marie asked brightly.

Howie smirked and bounced in his chair. "He makes money."

"Oh? You must tell me how you do that."

Again Howie answered for him. "Real estate, venture capital,
oil. Hollywood even. How many people do you know who make
money investing in movies? Meet Charlie Phelps. Hardly thinks
about it, he's so rich to begin with. Maybe that's his secret."

"You've got a big mouth and a weird sense of social
chitchat," Charlie said.

"Oo, ow. Hit me again, Chuck." Howie rolled his eyes and
sucked at his cocktail.

"Probably we ought to get on over to Tracy's," Charlie said.
"We've organized a buffet in Tracy's bungalow," he explained
to Alain. "You two must join us, after you've done your catching up."

Alain assumed an expression of deep regret, but before he
could frame his excuses, Anne-Marie said, "We'd be just
delighted."

* * *

By the time they got to the party, Alain had grown sullen. He pushed through the crowd to the makeshift bar in the kitchen, leaving Anne-Marie in the bungalow's overflowing suite, which was crammed with young American and German and French tourists and a Japanese couple in stylish white linen and the crew of the charter boat. Charlie forced his way through the press in her direction, reaching her just ahead of the nearest hot-eyed Greek sailor.

Half an hour later she still hadn't been able to shake Charlie and his determination to make investment banking seem romantic. She'd sought safety in numbers, but this was too much, really oppressive.

Almost every time she turned in Alain's direction he was staring at her, and then suddenly he was leaving. She pushed herself away from Charlie—actually pushed him away, her palm on his chest—pleading a need to use the toilet; once across the room she slipped through the open doors to the little terrace overlooking the beach.

She ran across the lawn and down to the sand. It was pale in the starlight. The sea was a silent, light-sucking void, barely visible or audible where it splashed feebly on the shore. She pulled her espadrilles off her bare feet and let the lukewarm waves lap her toes as she walked toward the lights of the town, which seemed to recede as she approached. Something about the night's nonevents, just like all the nonevents of her nonlife so far, had tipped her into a slide. She wasn't even drunk yet, and blackness was descending.

A torrent of recorded bouzouki music from tinny speakers announced a beachfront taverna; it had a trellis with little white lights twined among the grapevines. She paused and looked back toward the hotel and saw Charlie Phelps trudging toward her through the sand.

What followed would forever remain hazy in her mind. She could have run—escaped outright—but she didn't. Why not? She could have escaped another way, by playing the nitwit, the airhead, the rah-rah girl, stroking his ego and soon enough his dick; she could have stood one more one-night stand and in the morning gotten rid of him. Why not? What she did instead was sit in the taverna and talk to him. And long before the crescent moon had risen over the lifeless sea, she'd agreed to marry him.

To marry him. A man she did not know and, if he'd been described to her before she'd met him, a man she would have avoided. Instead, in response to his passionate arguments, his recitation of his vita and prospects, his conviction that in her he had found his destined mate, she put him off with a cruel promise and sealed it with a practiced kiss and left him there grinning stupidly as the moon rose, having made him swear not to follow her as she walked back up the beach. She planned to vanish before sunrise.

As she trudged along the beach past the hotel, Alain came out of the darkness and seized her arm. "We must talk," he said reasonably, even as she struggled against his bruising grip. "There are things we must have done with."

They did not have done with them. Instead there was a new and more horrible beginning.

"It comes back when I'm dreaming or when I'm daydreaming of other things. Suddenly I'm on that beach again. The moonlight, the struggle. The way he beat me. The rape."

"What courage you have. What a stupid and insensitive game I've been playing." The last flames fluttered among the coals. Minakis's worry beads, silent for long minutes, began to click again. "Please accept my apology. Please know that I'll give you whatever you need to satisfy Alain."

Anne-Marie nodded wary thanks. "To satisfy Alain I need to see that treasure of yours for myself, take my own pictures."

"It's a hard climb, an all-day trip. Let's talk about it in the morning."

"You agree?"

"I'll give you what you want, Anne-Marie." He pocketed his beads and stood up. He took a candle from the mantelpiece and lit it with a match, then turned to look at her. "I wonder why you haven't told Peter what you've told me. He seems to have great affection for your children."

"Yes. We were in love before I even knew I was pregnant with Jennifer. A happy ending, it seemed." Hot tears flooded her eyes. "As illusory as all happy endings. The morning after Alain raped me, even Charlie seemed like a savior."

"Did you ever think of telling Peter the truth about Carlos? Or Charlie the truth? Before now?"

Anne-Marie pushed away from the table and stood up unsteadily. "I thought about it, when I knew I was suffocating again, when I was ready to do anything to get some air. But I'd lied so persuasively before—I even managed to get myself run over, that night after Alain left me alone, so I could explain the bruises." She shivered. "Only by a motor scooter. Still . . . Charlie's the kind who needs proof."

"But Peter. Surely you can tell Peter everything. He can only admire you for your determination to recover your son."

"We'll see." Her smile turned into a yawn. "At least he's not a Greek."

"This Greek will tell you that a grandmother like Katerina was worth much more than an absent father. A *sadalos* like John Pendlebury was worth more to me than an absent father."

"Yet you were eager to know your father."

"In those days I dreamed he was an English soldier." Minakis gave her the candle; her blue eyes were liquid in the light of its flame. "Imagine my disappointment if he had turned out to have been an American investment banker—or a Swiss anti-quary, for that matter."

"Don't you still think about him?"

"What does it matter, after all these years?" He opened his palms, signing helplessness. "Go lie down on the bed, before you fall asleep standing up. We'll talk tomorrow."

25

The Sea of Crete rolled in a strong northwest wind. Peter watched the seething blue water come up fast beneath his oval window before land appeared abruptly beneath the wings, dry white and bright yellow; then tires squalled and the Airbus settled heavily to the runway.

Outside the terminal, Peter found a dented gray Mercedes taxicab and showed the driver the address of the foundation.

"No problem!" the man said heartily.

"How far is it?" Peter asked.

"Get in," said the driver.

"I mean, should I find a hotel first? Or can that wait?"

"No problem," said the driver.

"No problem for me? Or for you?"

"Get in," the driver said impatiently.

Peter got in.

The foundation was south of town on the road to Knossos, housed in a concrete heap that looked more like a bunker than an office building. The taxi fare was modest. So what if the driver had no English? No problem. Peter tipped him better than he would a New York cabbie and got out, dragging his suitcase and his laptop behind him.

"Peter, good to see you again." Markos Detorakis grabbed Peter's hand and punched his shoulder. "And how is Kathleen?"

"Fine, I hear. You know she's remarried?"

Detorakis was a mathematician Peter had known at Berkeley—not his colleague so much as his ex-wife's colleague—and a hulk, as tall as Peter but substantially wider, with a luxurious growth of hair on his face that made him look like a slovenly monk. "And you too. I hear you're a newlywed. How's your wife? Keeping her happy?"

"I try," Peter said.

"Good. Good for you." Detorakis led him down waxed-concrete corridors to a small office with a view of the parking lot. Beyond the parked cars were green vineyards and chalky hillsides.

"Nice," Peter said politely.

"I like it well enough." Detorakis shuffled the papers on his desktop, selected a couple of pages, and held them out. "Here's what I could find by your guy, what's in English."

"Thanks for doing the search."

"I should thank you. This guy Minakis is big. Wish I'd known about him before now."

Peter glanced through the photocopied pages, articles from *Nature* and *Reviews of Modern Physics* and *Scientific American*—old-fashioned typeface, words and diagrams so close-set as to make a jeweler squint, having to do with Schrödinger's cat and Wigner's friend and the arrow of time. Einstein-Podolsky-Rosen. Wheeler and Feynman and Cramer.

"This stuff is over ten years old," Peter said, looking up. "No wonder I couldn't find it on the net."

"Notice the hardware."

"I wouldn't call it hardware." The diagrams in the old papers were precursors of the device in the sketches Minakis had left for him. "Thought experiments, maybe."

"Then maybe you know we have a pretty good laser-optics lab here, one of the best in Europe. Within the past six months the director has signed off on femtosecond lasers, other stuff I couldn't describe, all of it charged to an account that doesn't show up on anybody's budget. Want to guess who?"

"Minakis." Peter slid the papers back onto the desk. "How did you learn about it?"

"Asked. It's no secret, even if Minakis shies from publicity. Director says it's his private project, fully endowed by Andwin-Zurich. FORTH have no liability. Any unspent funds remain with us."

"What's his address? Don't tell me Athens."

Detorakis winced. "A yacht: *La Parisienne,* home port Piraeus. Anyway, you can see why the foundation is happy to help him—happy enough to lend him a government account number and address. Even helpful with the metropolitan."

"What's the metropolitan?"

"He's the head of the Orthodox Church here. It seems Minakis has been permitted to use certain chapels for scientific purposes."

"Where are they?" Peter asked.

"Yes, that might answer your question." Detorakis settled his bulk into his armchair and began stroking his beard. "You have two sites to choose from, unfortunately: a mountain called Ambelakia and a peak near Dikti, thirty miles apart and neither of them easy to get to."

"Which would you choose?"

"I never heard of this guy until you called." Detorakis gave him a gnomish look. "Flip a coin."

Peter fished a fifty-drachma piece out of his pocket. He flipped it and called, "Heads Ambelakia, tails Dikti," and slapped it on his wrist. "Ambelakia it is."

"Not today," said Detorakis, "and not in those clothes. Let's get you a hotel, get you some hiking gear, rent you a car. You've got a trip ahead of you."

Anne-Marie rose through layers of dream imagery, hovering over mountain precipices, floating through sunlit clouds, finally awakening beneath cotton sheets and embroidered wool. The whitewashed ceiling above her was hazy-bright with reflected late-morning light. Until the last shreds of her dream had dissolved, she didn't know where she was.

She was alone in Minakis's bed, in Minakis's house in the mountains of Crete. Last night she had talked to him as she had never talked to anyone. The thought of what she had told him made her shiver. She kicked off the sheets and put her bare feet on the cold flagstone floor and pulled on a thin Japanese robe. She went to the curtained arch that divided the bedroom from the rest of the house and peered out.

The outer room was empty, full of shadows. On the table in front of the cold hearth, a piece of paper was bright in the diffuse light. She picked it up and read it.

"I have gone up to the chapel. Join me if you wish. If not, I look forward to seeing you this evening."

She pictured him at work, fiddling with this and fiddling with that, as fussy about his gear as she was about hers when she was calibrating a new lens. Better to leave him in peace for a few hours. She wished she hadn't slept so long, but she'd desperately needed the rest. And he had promised to give her what she wanted.

She got oranges and honey from the wall niche and fresh yogurt from the new refrigerator. After she ate, she dressed and took her cameras and went exploring.

She passed a young woman in black sweeping her courtyard and three men discussing how to reassemble a motor scooter that lay in pieces at their feet. They all stopped and stared as she passed, exclaiming, *"Kalimera, kyria,"* eager to talk, but she smiled and mumbled and kept on walking. Once upon a time she had made a career of photographing more-or-less real people, and these were certainly real people, but nevertheless she felt she had already met them on postcards. Ayia Kyriaki no longer looked quite like the village of Minakis's tale, a village seen from a child's point of view, but instead like a grubby miniature of that place. The town square was deserted except for a couple of Nordic tourists on Louloudakis's terrace. Avoiding them, she went into the church.

The church was empty inside, dark except for the dusty light that sifted through the slit windows at each end. Oil lamps

flickered in front of icons with patinaed tin *tamata* pinned to
their frames. The desiccated wood of the iconostasis could have
been a hundred years old.

Older still were the peeling murals—but only a couple of
centuries old at most, crudely drawn and painted, no great
Byzantine treasures. Yet an air of faded vitality clung to them.
On the rear wall was an implacable Christ in majesty, surrounded by angels and demons, caught in the act of dividing the
saved from the damned, the sheep from the goats. On one side
of the vault Michael with his flaming sword barred the gates of
Eden, and on the other side flocks of saints and holy men
eavesdropped on Gabriel's message to the Virgin Mary. Mold
and dampness had attacked the teeming scenes; patches of
paint had fallen away, leaving blooms of lime on the stone.

Anne-Marie stepped closer to the mural of the Virgin. Here
Maria and her mother, Anna, the saints after whom she herself
had been named, were seated on thrones to receive the
archangel, whose wings were those of an eagle. The damage
this mural had suffered was not just from mildew or moisture.
Mary's eyes had been scraped out, down to the bare rock.

To Anne-Marie, more comfortable photographing living
faces and bodies in motion, recording the damaged paintings
was a technical challenge; to make them vivid was a greater
challenge. She took her time, setting her flash unit on the floor,
on a chair, anywhere that would give texture to the light without obscuring details. She worked for an hour, forgetting the
time.

Outside the church, the sunlight momentarily blinded her. She
went through the deserted schoolyard to the back of the church,
to the walled burial ground. The graves were raised boxes of
stone or concrete filled with gravel, most with inscribed
plaques at their heads, some with cases built of marble and
panes of glass containing a photograph of the deceased, a polychrome of the name saint, an oil lamp. A few had offerings:
flowers, a bottle of oil or raki, a slab of honeycomb, a cigar that
hadn't been smoked much. Inside some of the cracked glass
cases, wasps and spiders were at work.

She expended half a roll of film on the graves before she came to one with a cracked limestone plaque upon which was inscribed KATERINA K. ANDROULAKI, 1886–1935. Another name had been inscribed below it but had been crudely chiseled away until only the dates remained: 1908–1922. The missing name was Sophia's. This grave had no case of marble and glass, no photographs, no pictures of saints, no burning lamp, no offerings, only a few wildflowers lying on the gravel, already wilted and drying to weeds. Who but Minakis would have left them?

Anne-Marie shot the rest of the roll, then reloaded, but the sun was too high for romantic photos in a graveyard.

Louloudakis's place was busier now, and young Dimitris was serving and taking orders from French and German tourists who had arrived by car. The local old men were planted at their accustomed iron tables, staring at Anne-Marie as she crossed the square. She gave them and Dimitris a cheerful *kalimera sas* as she passed among them and entered the store.

Haralambos Louloudakis was busy over the propane stove, brewing coffee in a copper *briki*. "*Kalimera, kyria,*" he called happily. "How can I help you?"

"You can let me take your photograph," she replied, holding up her camera.

"You want to photograph *me?*"

"Why not?"

"You are here to photograph the philosopher."

"True, but I have to place him in his surroundings. Where does he buy his lightbulbs? Who sells him coffee?" She smiled and raised her camera to her eye.

"I understand." He stood there beaming as she clicked and flashed away, until the boiling *briki* overflowed behind him.

At that moment Dimitris stuck his head in the door. "Quickly, Father! What's taking so long?"

"Enough of that insolence," Louloudakis shouted at him, and to Anne-Marie, said, "Excuse me, excuse me, please." He poured the coffee into tiny cups and set them on a tin tray with glasses and a carafe of water, which he handed to Dimitris to carry outside, then followed the boy onto the terrace to soothe any ruffled feelings.

Like any seasoned lens-slinger, Anne-Marie shot first and asked questions later, spending six frames on the moth-eaten *kri-kri* and the martens and the shotguns mounted on the wall. Then she lowered her camera and tried to see the objects not as they appeared through her viewfinder but for what they were: the remains of rare animals; a massive rusty shotgun that could have dated from 1866; a beautiful slender birding gun, its barrel chased with silver.

"Tell me the story of that beautiful gun," she demanded, when Louloudakis came back inside.

"You think it is beautiful?" His smile faded.

"Who wouldn't?" she asked, surprised by his change of tone.

"You are a woman."

"I'm a photographer."

He grunted. A photographer, was she? Every tourist had a camera. "My father is outside, finishing his midday meal," he said, moving impatiently to his stove. "Get him to tell you the story of that gun."

The elder Dimitris Louloudakis sported baggy black trousers below and a bristling white beard above. He was only a few years older than Minakis, but to Anne-Marie he looked like a holdover from a different century. It was his eyes, she decided, milky from staring into mountain light, and his skin, wrinkled into worn parchment. Hard to picture this old man as the teenage bully who had tried to kill young Manolis.

He fastened upon her eagerly, pressing her with questions that she had learned to answer automatically—husband, children, home, job, where she had learned Greek—while he prevailed upon her to accept a glass of his son's raki. But when it arrived accompanied only by a plate of chopped cucumber, he shouted abuse at his son through the open door, and young Dimitris came running out with plates of olives and cheese and a dish of marinated bulbs and a basket of bread.

Satisfied that he had cowed her with his hospitality, old

Dimitris deigned to answer her question. "The gun belonged to a Turkish spy," he said. "In those days there were many Turks."

The two other old men at the table, a priest and a shepherd, wagged their heads in agreement.

"Turks? Or Greek Muslims?" Anne-Marie raised her camera to frame Dimitris's picturesque face.

He irritably lifted a hand. "You cannot make photographs."

She lowered the camera to her lap. "I'm sorry. I should have asked." Still he looked at her silently, suspiciously. Ostentatiously she twisted the lens off her camera, capped its ends, and put it in her bag. "You were telling me about Turks."

Mollified, he settled into the iron chair. "I was a boy then. There were many Turks as well as Mussulmans about. I knew this one was a spy, because my father told me he was." He looked to the others, and they nodded. "He came up to photograph the passes. Lasithi is a natural fortress, everyone knows that. That's why the conquerors always tried to keep us out of the mountains."

"This Turk was a photographer like me?" Anne-Marie asked.

They all had a good laugh at that. "He was a *real* photographer," Dimitris told her. "His camera was *this* big." He held his hands a couple of feet apart.

"What happened to him?"

Dimitris eyed his companions, who seemed to be thinking heavily, their lips pursed and their brows bunched. The priest reached for a chunk of bread and stuffed it into his mouth. Anne-Marie had noticed him when she first arrived in the village, an ancient graybeard, hunched and sly; she realized he must be Kriaris, son of Papa Kriaris, and Manolis's long-ago guardian. And the shepherd? One of the Michalis boys, perhaps?

"You must have heard what happened to him," she prompted. "A spy, a photographer. People must have talked about him a lot."

Dimitris shrugged. "We were children."

"He fell," mumbled the priest, his mouth full of bread. "He fell off a cliff. It was icy."

"No one found him for days. They said ravens had been at

him," said the shepherd, crossing himself vigorously. "And dogs."

"They even carried off his shoes, those animals," said the sullen priest. Unexpectedly he laughed, spilling bread crumbs into his beard.

"And his gun?" Anne-Marie asked. "How did that come into your father's possession, *kyrie* Louloudakis?"

Dimitris did not answer. The priest grinned slyly at the shepherd and said, "Perhaps a dog brought it to him."

Anne-Marie kept her attention on Dimitris. "Is that how your father got the gun, *kyrie*? A dog brought it to him?"

A fleeting expression crossed his face, bitter and bright and sly, a look she could not have described but fervently wished she could have photographed. "I don't know how it came to him," he said, a smirk twisting his mustache, "but in any case, it is impossible not to steal beautiful weapons."

At that everyone laughed, for it was an old saying and certainly true, and its truth covered many lies.

Anne-Marie laughed with them, enjoying their wit. "And cameras," she cried happily. "Who would not steal a beautiful camera? Who got the Turkish spy's camera?"

The old men's laughter died in confusion. They traded glances, sharing the quick, bitter thing she had seen in Dimitris's expression, before they turned sullen, weary faces back upon her.

She thanked them for their hospitality and went back inside Louloudakis's place. "I need to call a taxi," she said, giving him a large banknote; he had the only telephone in town. "And buy those men a round of drinks. Tell them it's on you."

Louloudakis made the call for her; after negotiations that would have sounded fierce to someone less fluent than she, he assured her that a taxi would call for her at Minakis's gate in forty minutes.

She packed a change of clothes into her camera bag and left a note on Minakis's table: "I look forward to another dinner with you—not tonight, but tomorrow night. Until then, with much affection . . ."

* * *

When it came to the written word, Anne-Marie was experienced at getting what she wanted, which had as much to do with getting access to documents as what was in them. By midafternoon she'd talked her way past a phalanx of clerks and policemen in the headquarters of the Hellenic Police in downtown Iraklion with a tall tale about doing a magazine story on the Dikti Mountains.

Rows of steel shelves held faded logbooks and bundles of papers covered with dust. She untied ribbons and lifted fragile official forms printed in uneven type on cheap paper, the blank spaces filled in by many different hands, elegant-looking by the handwriting standards of the 1990s but hard to read, and the ink itself vanishingly pale with age. Her hopes rose and sank again. Many records had been destroyed in the war; there must have been more losses after the war, when files from all over the island were moved to Iraklion, the new administrative center of Crete. Much of 1922 was missing; what remained were scorched folders almost too fragile to handle.

At first Anne-Marie could find nothing from Lasithi nome, but this proved to be an accident of organization; when she untied the last bundle, the piece of paper she was looking for was near the bottom, still where it had been placed on the last day of January 1922.

Summary of investigation regarding the accidental death of Konstandinos Didaskalos, male, 26 years old, of Athens.

Report of gendarme Sergeant N. Bounialis, Tzermiado, 15 January 1922, as follows: "On the evening of 12 January 1922, M. Michalis and S. Ariakis, herdsmen residing in the village of Ayia Kyriaki in the Limnakaros Plain, discovered a body at the foot of the scarp of Mount Dikti approximately one mile east of the village. On the morning of 13 January these men, accompanied by H. Louloudakis, reported the discovery to this office. . . .

"I was able to observe that the body was that of a young man with brown hair, wearing a blue serge suit and white shirt. His shoes and other outer clothing he may have been wearing, such as an overcoat, were missing. Although the flesh was well preserved by the cold, the soft parts of the face, hands, and feet had been eaten by animals. A thorough investigation of the site at the base of the cliff and of the top of the cliff two hundred meters above uncovered no additional evidence. The clifftop was slippery with ice and extremely dangerous. The man was known to be an admirer of wild scenery. It is possible that he approached the cliff too closely and lost his balance. . . .

". . . through these and other interviews it became evident that this was the same young man who had arrived in Ayia Kyriaki on approximately 18 December, bringing with him a pack mule. He stayed in the household of M. Michalis, to whom he identified himself as K. Didaskalos of Athens. He was known as a photographer, having previously visited the region to make scenic pictures. On this visit, however, he seemed interested in making portraits of the inhabitants, including various unwed young girls. He also made photographs of the frescoes in the chapel. . . ."

As she struggled to read the puristic Greek, Anne-Marie felt the skin of her brow tighten. The report was written in the passive, conditional voice of bureaucracies everywhere—It became evident. It is possible—with a marked lack of enthusiasm for further investigation. To this end, Sergeant Bounialis had done more than merely distance himself. The dead man had "seemed interested in making portraits of . . . various unwed young girls," he had written, and his meaning was plain enough: accident or not, the dead man deserved what he got.

What happened to the man's mule, Sergeant? To his camera? Having mentioned these valuable properties, Bounialis's report made no further reference to them. She read on.

Supplemental report of gendarme Lieutenant S. Sarakatsanis, Lasithi nome, as follows: "Subsequent inquiries to Athens revealed that one K. Didaskalos, a law student residing with his aunt N. Didaskalou in Athens,

had been reported missing after failing to return from
Crete on 15 January as expected. An amateur photographer, Didaskalos had been touring the island to make
scenic pictures. On 21 January, *i kyria* N. Didaskalou
arrived in Neapolis, accompanied by her cousin, *ton
kyrio* S. K. Didaskalo, also of Athens, and identified the
body of her nephew. *I kyria* Didaskalou was permitted to
take the body with her for burial. . . ."

Anne-Marie closed the file. Though she had not been permitted to take notes in the archive, she would have no trouble
remembering the contents. Outside police headquarters she ran
to catch a taxi to the airport.

She reached Athens after sunset. An hour after the airplane
touched ground she checked into a tourist hotel in the Plaka;
she ate *mezethes* in a tourist place on Tripodon Street and went
straight back to her room, yanking the curtains closed against
the cliffs of the Acropolis, ablaze with artificial light.

Morning on Crete came softly, the salt sea breeze mingling
with the scent of oranges in the courtyard of Peter's hotel. After
breakfast he drove his banged-up little rental Fiat out of
Iraklion; at the first hill he wondered if he would have done better to hire a taxi. But an hour later when he arrived at the lonely
monastery of Saint Nicholas, thirty miles southwest of the city
and a mile from the nearest village, at the foot of a spectacular
gorge down which spring torrents poured from the pine-
forested heights, he was glad he had his own transportation.

His tourist map indicated that Ambelakia was over 4,500 feet
high and that the climb was mostly vertical. Peter stood at the
trail head listening to the cascading water, trying to persuade
himself that Minakis would not have chosen such an isolated
spot for scientific work—yet if the coin had fallen the other
way, he would have had as steep a climb on the slopes of Mount
Dikti. He was glad Detorakis had made him buy boots and
khaki trousers.

He locked the car and set out upon the uneven path that clung
to the wall of the gorge, forcing himself to stretch his long legs.

An hour passed before the pine forest gave way to a meadow covered with meager new grass; flocks of sheep and goats were busily stripping it bare. Ambelakia loomed seventeen hundred feet higher still—all stones, no more falling water—and for the first time he could see the stub of a chapel on its peak.

He stumbled over ankle-breaking eroded limestone, climbing toward the peak. At last he pushed through the unlocked door into the empty chapel. Three oil lamps burned with pale yellow flames under the stone vault; the only furniture was the decrepit wooden stand supporting the lamps. There was no sign Minakis had ever been near the place.

He went outside and settled himself against the sunny wall of the chapel, stretching his aching legs. His feet were tender in the stiff new boots; he tugged them off and pulled off his wool socks and wriggled his toes in the cool air. No blisters yet, only bright pink patches, but he'd be raw by the time he got back down. Was this the way to search for reality, climbing mountains crowned with empty chapels?

Reality was that the woman he loved had walked away without a word. Last night Markos Detorakis had taken Peter to dinner at a fish taverna; he was full of questions about Anne-Marie, and at first Peter had been delighted to tell him about her, her beauty, her talent, her quick intelligence rooted in the world of things—so different from his own weakness for abstractions—and the way his heart had jumped when he'd laid eyes on her the first time, after his divorce from Kathleen had convinced him that he'd never fall in love again. But Detorakis kept pressing him for details, and somewhere between the cuttlefish and the red mullet things got awkward. Peter could hardly admit that she was off doing some kind of in-depth interview with the same guy he was looking for and didn't know how to find.

Maybe she wasn't with Minakis at all; maybe that was just smoke. When he thought about it, this freelance magazine assignment had sounded fishy from the start. Not Anne-Marie's style, leaving Jenny with her mother, even if it was less than four days now. And what did her brother have to do with it? She'd barely mentioned his name until the phone calls to

Geneva started last fall—then got prickly and evasive when he'd asked about the charges. Not that he'd cared; he was just curious.

Frustrated, he stood up, the stones cold under his bare feet. He would go straight back to the hotel and call Madame Brand in Paris and ask her the humiliating questions he'd avoided before. Face it, he'd wanted to believe Anne-Marie was with Minakis because it gave him an excuse to track down Minakis's intriguing experiment. But it wasn't worth the price of not knowing. . . .

A jolt of fiery pain shot up Peter's right leg. He hopped back as if he'd stepped on a live coal, holding fast to his ankle; a bee's stinger, a thread of entrails attached, was lodged under his little toe. He brushed the stinger away and stood on his heel, arching his head backward, gasping.

In a crack in the wall under the roof of the chapel bees came and went, buzzing in multipart harmony. A few feet away from their nest, on the east end of the vault, sat a glass corner reflector as sturdy as the corner reflector the astronauts had left on the moon, cemented to the wall and aimed toward Dikti.

For a moment Peter ignored his throbbing foot. Far to the east, the Dikti Mountains were hazy gray under the high sun. He ran his fingers through his hair, as if trying to massage some sense into his head. Ambelakia. Dikti. The two places Detorakis had named were in line of sight of each other, something he could have seen from the map if he'd thought to look. And Minakis's interferometer had a long leg. . . .

One more day, then. Tomorrow—if he could get his bee-stung foot back into his boot—he would climb a different mountain.

In Athens the morning smelled of Aleppo pines and diesel exhaust. From her hotel in the Plaka, Anne-Marie walked to the cemetery, up the hill beyond the vast ruined temple of Olympian Zeus, a short walk made tortuous and long by rush-hour traffic. Once she was inside the cemetery gate the traffic sounds fell away and the air seemed cleaner. Doves wobbled along the yellow sand paths, calling sadly; a priest chanted a memorial service somewhere up the hillside. Among black cypresses and pines that shivered in the fitful breeze, pale marble glowed, greenly phosphorescent. There were funeral stelae in the manner of classical Greece and florid modern allegorical statues of grief and eternal life. There were miniature Orthodox churches, miniature ancient temples, and miniature neoclassical mansions. The graves were family homes, housing the dead and tended by the living. Women in black swept leaves from in front of the mausoleums, washed down the marble pavement with hoses, set fresh flowers in bronze urns, lit the oil lamps, and set smoking sticks of incense in front of the ceramic plaques that were likenesses of the dead.

Everywhere the faces of the dead looked back at Anne-Marie, photographs turned to stone: gray-haired old men and old women and young men in uniform, as one would expect, but so many children too, and so many young women, full of hope, innocently beautiful, fashionable in the fringed satins of the 1920s or the angled suits of the 1940s. In these decades the death dates clustered, rising to a crescendo by the end of the 1920s—here lay the victims of the Catastrophe—rising again in the 1940s, when the Germans and Italians ruled, but peaking only after they had left, after civil war and famine had killed tens of thousands.

It was a sprawling plot of ground, crowded with trees and graves, and she searched a long time before she came upon a stained and untended slab of marble with a cracked glass case at its head, empty except for a picture in a tin frame that was bleached to whiteness. The gravestone was inscribed KON/NOS M. DIDASKALOS, 1896–1922. The vanished picture in the frame had no doubt been of Saint Constantine, but there was no ceramic portrait of the dead man. Unlike most of the others in the cemetery, Konstandinos Didaskalos lay alone in his plot, sharing it with no relatives.

"He was an orphan, never married, raised by his maiden aunt, my grandfather's cousin. My grandfather bought the plot for her—well you must know that, that's how you found me—but

she was buried with her own family in Thessaloniki, so there
has been nobody else to put there."

Anne-Marie said nothing but only leaned forward with an
encouraging look toward the speaker, an attractive middle-aged
woman with stiff yellow-blond hair arranged in a coiffed helmet, who twisted her round face now comically, now tragically
as she told her tale.

"I do feel badly about neglecting his grave. After all, he is
my . . . my . . . Let me see, he was my grandfather's cousin's
nephew, so . . . oh, dear." Seeing Anne-Marie smile, the woman
understood that she had permission to laugh at herself. "Well, I
promise to do better."

They sat sipping tea from a china service on a silver tray laid
upon a carved Chinese table, in a penthouse in the fashionable
Kolonaki district of Athens. Anne-Marie, seated on the bro-
caded sofa, had a view through open French doors to an iron
balcony facing Mount Likavitos; *i kyria* Kargioti sat close by in
an armchair sumptuously upholstered in satin. Everything in
the room—the furniture, the heavy drapes, the gold-framed
prints of Mont Saint Michel and Versailles and the Eiffel Tower
on the wall—spoke of a yearning for France. Guessing this,
Anne-Marie asked, *"Parlez-vous français, madame?"* and
when the answer was a happy *"Mai oui, madame,"* Anne-Marie
continued the conversation in French, to the delight of her host-
ess.

Soon they were drinking Napoleon brandy with their tea, and
Anne-Marie was telling stories of the exciting magazine-
publishing scene in Paris, and shortly Madame Kargioti—she
insisted that Anne-Marie call her Nitsa—was rooting in her
closets for a photo album. Her grandfather having died in the
famine of 1945, his cousin having died twenty years earlier of
malaria, no one had looked at the album in years. She had
almost forgotten she had it.

With a triumphant cry Nitsa found the dusty book. She
placed it on Anne-Marie's lap, then collapsed in her chair and
poured herself another brandy. Anne-Marie lifted the cover.
The album was filled with Kodak snaps, Brownies having been
to the 1920s as video camcorders were to the 1990s. Anne-

Marie leafed through pages of prints mounted in black paper corners: families at the beach, families on ferryboats, families posed in front of ruins.

"Who are these people?" she asked.

Nitsa shrugged happily. "I don't know. Oh, that one—that's Aunt Niki. And there's my grandfather, I think."

Anne-Marie kept looking. Midway through the book she came upon a photograph of a young man wearing a shirt and tie and a dark suit, standing against a backdrop of sky. He could have been standing on the edge of the Acropolis, or on Areopagos or Pnyx or Likavitos, or not in Athens at all; there was no clue to his whereabouts except bare rock beneath his feet and storm clouds behind him. "Is this Didaskalos?"

Nitsa leaned over Anne-Marie's shoulder to peer at the photograph. "Yes, that's him, I think."

"Who took the picture?"

"I don't know. Aunt Niki?"

"She took a good picture. Where did he get the gun?"

"I don't know that either. Maybe my grandfather's graduation present to him? When he completed law school?"

Anne-Marie hesitated. "I don't know how to ask you this. . . ."

Nitsa giggled. "Just ask me."

"Can I take this picture? I promise I will send it back to you within the week."

Nitsa leaned back, rolling her glass of brandy between her fingers. "I would like to have it back. But I confess it really doesn't mean that much to me." She didn't need to repeat her earlier confession, that she had not even tended the man's grave. "Maybe if you take it, it will acquire some meaning."

Anne-Marie carefully lifted the photograph from its mounting and held it close and studied it—the handsome young man in his suit and tie, standing against the stormy sky, holding the silver-chased gun that now hung on the back wall of Haralambos Louloudakis's store.

26

He was your father. I'm sure of it. There are ways you can prove it." As always when they were climbing, Anne-Marie hurried to keep up, for Minakis's stride seemed to lengthen as the pitch steepened.

"One could ask to exhume the body, I suppose; one could test the DNA."

She could not see his expression, but she could hear his distaste. "He must have written letters to his aunt, sent pictures. I'm sure *kyria* Kargioti would be happy to find them."

Minakis stopped when they reached the saddle above the village, where the crest of Dikti lifted away to the east, and the chapel's isolated peak rose to the west. "Forgive me, I should be grateful for the work you've done. Before Pendlebury found me, I wanted desperately to know who my father was. Afterward it no longer mattered; when I lost Pendlebury, I lost the only father I ever knew."

"So I wasted my time. *Merde.*" The heat and his lack of interest provoked her; perspiring fiercely, she loosened a button of her cotton shirt and hitched up her jeans as if preparing for battle. "Why did you come back here, then? You could have set your stuff up lots of places, a lot more convenient places."

His response was cheerful. "Revenge perhaps?"

"Revenge?" she said sourly. "Have you ever told Louloudakis who you are?—I mean that old monster who was the kid who tried to shoot you with your own father's gun? Have you ever told the priest's son, who was supposed to look out for you, who inherited everything that was yours? Who probably sold your grandmother's house back to you?"

"Why warn them? I'm planning to slit their throats in their sleep," he whispered, full of menace.

"How can you make a joke of it?"

He shrugged. "I do thank you for what you have done. For one thing, you have given me the name of the man who persuaded my disreputable grandfather to leave Limnakaros."

"You could have found out for yourself. Perhaps you already have. Perhaps this is all a charade."

"You're wrong." He leaned toward her, resting a hand on her shoulder. "As far as I knew, that gun was always the property of the Louloudakis clan. If Katerina knew it was the photographer's—not likely—she didn't think it mattered enough to mention."

Anne-Marje turned away, shrugging off his touch. "Doesn't it make a difference that they murdered him for it?"

"Oh Anne-Marie," he said quietly, "if my grandmother didn't know that, how can you know it? Nothing but ragged coincidence suggests that that man was my father. Nothing at all connects me to his relatives—relatives so distant they do not even tend his grave."

"You don't want it to be him, do you?" she said, red-faced and sweating. "Maybe you wish your father was a god, like some old hero's. That would make you half a god yourself."

His expression was cool and opaque. "I promised to take you to the cave. We have a long way to go."

It was the worst climb she had ever undertaken. Nothing technical about it—just seven hundred vertical feet of loose gravel

and greasy clay lying at the angle of repose. Every step was a
landslide, like climbing an endless escalator running backward,
except that an escalator doesn't suck at your shoes.

She stopped for breath often. Minakis paused, watching
without sympathy until she was ready to go on, not offering to
help with her cameras: this was her trip. When she resumed
climbing he went along beside her easily, almost dawdling, no
doubt thinking of other things as she struggled toward the high
ridge where the clouds boiled, flashing into existence out of the
clear, rising air.

When they reached the crest she bent over, gasping for
breath. They were immersed in blowing mist; she heard the liquid sound of the wind sifting through the shattered rocks and
the ground-hugging thorns, which crawled with orange lady-
bird beetles lifted here on the wind from the fields below. She
tried to imagine Sophia and Katerina and little Manolis climbing this murderous slope again and again, sometimes daily, as
if they were climbing apartment stairs.

When she straightened and stepped off along the path she
was still heady with fatigue, but at least they were no longer
going uphill. The path divided, and she knew without asking
that their route was the faint trace to the left. Before long a
tumbled heap of stones emerged from the mist, the ruins of a
shepherd's hut: in front of it the edge of a cliff with wet fog
blowing over it into nothing, and beyond it, coming clearer
with every step, a low scarp of limestone where a trickle of
water seeped from a dark crevice edged with ferns and
lichen.

Minakis paused at the entrance. "This will be dangerous and
messy. Now you've seen the place—do you really need to go in?"

"I told you why."

"Stay close and do exactly as I say."

Inside the narrow mouth of the cave she saw a coil of knotted rope, stiff and new, secured around a sturdy outcrop of
stone.

"How many times have you been in here?" Anne-Marie
asked.

"Once during the war, to see if Pendlebury missed anything

in '38. All I found was sherds. Since I came back to the village, I've been here twice. I went deeper than before."

"And found more than sherds."

His answer was a grunt. He tested the rope against its mooring, then tossed the coil into the depths. She looked at the narrow passage through which they must go, past a block of limestone covered with dripping moss; it was a black hole that soaked up her flashlight beam. The flesh rose on her forearms.

"They're still in there, aren't they?" she said.

"They won't bother us." He was stone-faced, as if her question were a breach of etiquette. He went first into the darkness, showing her how to lean back on the rope and plant her feet against the slope. She followed him cautiously down the muddy slide. With her flashlight hooked over her waistband, she could see nothing but a diminishing patch of pale skylight above her; the only thing she could hear, besides her own breathing, was the trickle of water. But the breath of the cave was dry; the lower she went the warmer it seemed. She was inside the earth now, out of the sky's cold turbulence.

"Stop a moment. Aim your torch down here," Minakis called.

Her pale beam found him resting his back against a massive block of stone that loomed out of the darkness. The rope had fallen away over a ledge, disappearing from view. "It's steeper and muddier from here on. Keep a tight grip." He swung over the side and soon was out of sight.

She let herself down until her feet touched the block. She shifted her grip and lowered herself cautiously down what was now an almost vertical drop; her flashlight, at waist level, lit only a circle of slippery green moss in front of her. The sound of running water was louder.

Then Minakis had her by the waist and the arm, steadying her as she let go of the rope. Her feet were on flat ground. "This way," he said. "Stay behind me. Don't get off the path."

She flicked her flashlight beam over the ground around her: she saw no jewels or weapons sparkling among the crumbling human remains, only moldy ribs and pale round skulls. She was in a boneyard, ranker than anything she had imagined from

Minakis's tale. Sixty years had passed since he had found these people; it was now almost 130 years since they'd died. All that time the spring had poured from above.

She took her camera from its bag and filled the cave three times with blinding light. Minakis waited patiently until she was done and then led her on a winding path across the floor, among the scattered bones, to the far wall. Lit from this angle the wall seemed blank and smooth, but when they had felt their way along it for several yards a vertical black shadow suddenly opened under Minakis's light. He aimed the beam into a narrow crevice.

"We go up in here. We'll have to crawl part of the way."

Minakis moved as confidently as if he could see in the dark, bending over, squeezing sideways through tight spots, dropping to his hands and knees when the floor rose—while behind him her flashlight beam made puzzling shadows and highlights of the roof and walls of the low passage—until the passage opened out into the darkness of a larger chamber.

"Just shine your torch on the ceiling; that will be light enough for the moment."

She pointed the flashlight beam upward. The roof was hung with slender stalactites and veils of stone.

A match flared beside her with almost painful brightness. Minakis crouched to light the wick of an oil lamp, then another and another, three lamps clustered on the floor of the cave.

"Save your batteries now," he said. "Wait here. I'll be back in a moment."

He left one of the lanterns where it sat and carried the other two with him as he walked deeper into the cavern. Among the groves of stalagmites the floor was sandy, not muddy like the chamber they had left behind. When Minakis passed behind a column, masked from her view, amber light flickered over the formations and walls of the cave; when he re-emerged he was momentarily blinding to her eyes, a creature of fire. For a moment it was as if he were walking across a bridge of air. Then she realized she was seeing the cave's intricate ceiling reflected in a still pool of water, as if in a perfect mirror. Minakis bent to place one lantern on a low pedestal of travertine. He walked a few steps and put the other on a ledge.

Her breath caught in her chest. Gold glistened between the lanterns and reflected from the still pool: two *labryses,* double axes of incised gold leaf, were set upright in sockets on a low sill of clay. They framed a pair of shattered goddesses, large shards that once had been deft sketches in orange clay, bell-skirted, bare-breasted, and dove-crowned. At their feet and beside them on the sill was a heap of pottery, scattered jars and cups and inscribed plaques and little clay figures of worshipers, male and female, the females skirted like the goddesses, with arms raised, the men loin-strapped, their backs arched at attention, their right fists clenched against their brows in the salute of adoration. This was the treasure she had been sent to find, far richer than anything Alain could have imagined.

Anne-Marie reminded herself to breathe. She lifted her camera and flooded the cavern with light half a dozen times; the utter stillness was punctuated by the camera's click and the levered advance of film. She blinked and peered into the lamplit darkness. There was no sign of Minakis in the inky shadows.

"Manolis, where are you?"

A shadow moved in the labyrinth of shadows cast by the three lanterns, and he stepped into the light. There was something odd about his pace as he came toward her, something measured and solemn. In front of him, in his right hand, he held an object she could not quite make out, except that it gave off flashes of reflected light.

"I want you to have this," he said.

She looked first at his enraptured face, then at the thing he held. "What is it?"

"Middle Minoan workmanship, made at the height of their glory. Tell me what you think of it." He sounded reasonable, as if he were asking her advice.

She started to reach out but hesitated. He grasped her reluctant hand and turned it, laying the object in her palm. Her dark hair fell past her ears as she bent to study it in the wavering lamplight.

It was a pendant less than two inches across. Two *kri-kri* were depicted in thin beaten gold, kneeling with their heads bent together, their thick necks and muscular shoulders neatly embossed in the metal, their legs folded beneath them. The altar on which they knelt was decorated with a running spiral of tiny beads of gold, and from it dangled gold disks rimmed with beads and fine wire circles of gold. Between their enormous, backward-curving horns the two *kri-kri* supported a larger beaded disk, attached to a loop through which passed a twisted strand of wool.

"I apologize for the wool string. I pulled it out of my *sak-ouli*," Minakis said. "It should be a golden chain."

"Who knows about this?"

"Three others know it exists, but only you and I know where it is. Didn't your brother show you the picture?"

She said nothing, only raised her gaze to study him.

"Yes," he confessed, "everything here is stolen, in the sense that I haven't reported it. After I bought my grandmother's house in the village—from Kriaris, as you surmised—I decided to do a thorough job of following up Pendlebury's original suggestion that the cave was a sanctuary. In 1938 he found only sherds, but his mind was on many other things. When I came here during the war, I was a sleepwalker—I was as taken with the notion of joining the guardians out there as with buried treasure." He indicated the shrine across the pool. "This is how I found it. I only cleared away some dust and rubble. On my second visit I took the pictures. There's more here, a lot of it at the bottom of the pool, all undisturbed. The chamber must have been sealed off in 1866, or else the people outside would have gotten in. So no one's been in here for thirty-seven centuries. Only me. And you."

He took the pendant from her hand, where she still held it as if mesmerized. Opening the loop of yarn in his fingers, he held it toward her. "Wear it for me."

In his dark eyes she saw what she could not have imagined seeing in him when they first met, the final melting of a cold, controlling man. His passionate entreaty bordered on worship. It excited an answering heat in her.

If only she could help him discover what he longed for in the inmost chambers of his heart. . . .

On impulse she bowed her head and felt him slip the loop of wool over her hair; she let him arrange her hair on her shoulders; she felt the warmth of his hands against her neck, and the weight of the warm gold between her breasts.

She straightened, and Minakis stepped away from her. "You are truly Diktynna," he whispered.

"What are you saying, Manolis?" But she had heard him plainly enough; he had called her by the name of the goddess for whom the mountain was named.

" 'For there is no place here/ That does not see you . . . ,' " he said in his full voice, smiling now. "Indeed, you have changed my life. I hoped the god would do that for me, but I never found the god."

Her heart raced. "Manolis, whatever you think I am, I'm not." She was suddenly afraid that he would come at her with the desperation with which other men came, projecting their want and need upon her, taking what they pretended to give.

"It doesn't matter what I think," he said. "Take the pendant. Offer it to your brother if he agrees to tell the truth."

She said nothing. What he suggested was not only a crime but a betrayal of what he claimed to hold dear.

His coal-bright eyes were fixed upon her. "You know I lured you here—because I thought I could give you what you wanted, a way to have your son. And because I thought I could make you love this island. So that you would not object when Peter wanted to work with me."

"You were so sure he would want to work with you?"

"I was sure of too many things. I've been sleepwalking for half a century." Minakis took a step toward her. "Give this to your brother, Alain. An artifact, that's all it is. You can hold it in your hands; he can hold it in his. Any child is worth more."

She groaned and covered her eyes. When he reached out to steady her she leaned toward him, letting him envelop her in his arms, relaxing her weight into his encircling arms. She tried to suppress the sobs that racked her.

She stopped shaking but still hid her head in his chest. "I'm sorry I told all those lies."

"I made you lie. I lied first," he said. "But no matter, we always know when the other is lying. I even lied on the way here, and you knew it."

"About your father."

He nodded. "I loved John Pendlebury, but I never stopped wondering about my real father."

She brushed the tears off her nose and cheeks. He fumbled in his jacket and fished out a cotton handkerchief. She laughed when she saw it—not a Kleenex, a cotton handkerchief; after all, he was an old-fashioned gentleman—but she took it and dabbed at her eyes. "This was the place your father came to meet your mother. You must know that."

He shook his head. "Whenever my thoughts start in that direction I become restless, I let anything at all distract me. Maybe I do want to believe he was a god."

"They never found his camera. It must still be here."

For half an hour they searched different sections of the chamber; Minakis was bolder than Anne-Marie in wriggling into narrow passages that led nowhere, but she was luckier.

"Manoli! Come here."

He hurried to her, carrying a lantern. Beyond the pool and the shrine, at the back of the chamber, behind a veil of limestone, he followed her through a winding passage into a raised chamber with a sandy floor and a ceiling of delicate crystals that caught the lantern light and shot it back in a thousand warm glints. On the floor lay a telescoped wooden tripod with brass fittings, still bright, and beside it a metal tray of the sort used to hold magnesium powder to make flash pictures.

And two leather cases. Anne-Marie knelt in the sand and opened one of them, lifting out a view camera of pebbled black leather and chrome fittings, bright as new, its lens a well of polished glass.

The other case was the same size. She lifted it, hefting its weight, and shook it. "These must be the plates. It ought to be safe to open this—the negatives ought to be in sleeves—but I don't want to take any chances." Anne-Marie looked at Minakis. "Your mother's picture is on one of these," she said with conviction.

"After seventy years?" He put the lantern down and sat on the sand beside her, folding his legs easily beneath him.

"It's cool in here," she said, "the temperature is the same summer and winter, and it's been dark. Why not? I can borrow a darkroom in Iraklion—maybe at the newspaper—or make a darkroom in your house. I'll develop them." She saw his troubled expression and leaned toward him, encouraging him. "You can see your mother's face."

"I've always been able to see her, in my imagination." He shook his head irritably. "Are we obliged to know everything we *can* know?"

"It's meant as a gift."

"If I accept, will you take the pendant?"

Her gaze darted back to him and she lifted the pendant from her breast. The golden ibexes gleamed in the flickering light. "I'll take it, then," she said, "and I'll make my bargain with Alain. And I'll tell Peter why." She leaned toward him and pressed her lips against his. When she leaned away her lips were full and moist, and her skin was bright; her pale eyes glistened in the lantern light. In the shadows of the open collar of her shirt, the golden ibexes rested between the curve of her breasts. She let the tips of her fingers brush his cheek.

He bowed his head, then raised it to watch her face. "I have come to adore you, Anne-Marie—from a distance of years that cannot be bridged, except in this: before I knew you existed, I knew Peter was like me, that in some sense Peter *was* me. My hubris was to want to control him, to watch myself in him. You came instead, to remind me who I am."

Peter's rented Fiat was chugging on three of its four cylinders as he pulled into the square of Ayia Kyriaki. He circled the cistern and let the car die in front of the church. Wearily he climbed out and, limping on his bee-stung foot, went past the old men who sat staring on the porch of the *kafenion*.

Inside he found a middle-aged man at a wooden counter, slicing a block of dripping white feta into cubes.

"Excuse me, do you speak English?" Peter asked.

The man thrust out his chin and wiped his sweating face with a towel; "Dimitri! *Ela!*" he shouted, and went back to his work.

A curly-haired teenager ran into the store. *"Nai?"*

"Milaei anglika," the man said, jerking his head toward Peter.

"You are English, sir?" the boy asked.

"American. Perhaps you can help me. I'm looking for Professor Minakis. Do you know him?"

The boy shrugged.

"All right. I'm looking for a chapel on a peak near here."

"There are many peaks near here, *kyrie*."

"Where someone has been carrying machinery?"

The boy studied him. "What is your name?"

"Peter Slater. What's yours?"

"I am Dimitris."

Peter put out his right hand. The boy grasped it gently in his own tough, deeply soiled hand.

"How do you know *ton kyrio* Minaki?" Dimitris asked.

"I met him a few days ago. He asked me to visit."

"Do you know the photographer?"

"A woman with dark hair? Light blue eyes?"

Dimitris nodded.

"She is my wife."

"Ah, your woman. Come outside, I'll show you the path to the chapel."

The weather-bleached wooden door of the chapel was locked, but Peter felt along the lintel and discovered an iron key. Before the door was half open he saw that he had found the place.

Cautiously he rolled back the plastic shroud and studied the steel test bed and the instruments mounted on it, which corresponded to the sketches on the papers he carried folded in his shirt pocket. He peeked through the eyepiece of the telescope: the corner reflector on the roof of the chapel on Ambelakia filled the circular field. A black dot drifted across the bright backdrop: a bee.

He bent down and craned his neck, sighting along the light paths, from laser source to beam splitter to prisms and back. Here was the "black box" wave guide; here, behind where the beams recombined, he folded back a metal cover to reveal—

—a thin steel frame, holding an irregular shape between

glass sheets. Peter frowned. It was not what he had expected to find.

He fumbled in his shirt pocket and brought out the sketches, crumpled and sweat-stained by now and scribbled over with his own notes. He smoothed them on the bench beside the computer monitor. On one of them the unit under the hood was clearly labeled as a very large CCD, a charge-coupled device—far larger, in fact, than was needed to compare pinpoint beams of photons.

Peter bent closer to inspect the object in the glass frame. It appeared to be a fragment of pottery painted black and red on pale gray, deft spiky lines that could have been thorn branches. Flakes of paint were missing, but despite the blemishes it gleamed as if it had been applied yesterday—as if it had just emerged fresh from the kiln.

Peter stood back and looked around the chapel, puzzled. He had found Minakis's laboratory, but where was Minakis? Where was Anne-Marie?

Her flashlight beam played over rotten skeletons half sunken in muck, the skulls glowing brighter than before, luminous growths like magical mushrooms. In the darkness she lost her bearings and felt herself sway on her feet.

"Are you all right?" Minakis demanded, invisible.

"Yes, I'm . . . I'll be right there." She trod carefully among the skeletons and joined him beside the falling water.

He had the knotted rope in his right hand. "Here, let me." He took the leather case of plates from her hand. "Loosen your belt and tie it behind you."

"Okay." She settled her camera bag between her shoulders. He gave the plate case back to her and she looped it through her belt, letting it bounce against her rear. "All set."

"I'll give you a boost."

Minakis's hands made a stirrup under her foot. The knots in the rope were hard and slippery smooth in her grip; she pulled, one hand after the other, grateful for Minakis's hands relieving her of part of her weight—and then she was on her own, too high for his help, and it was only her knees against the wet rock as she reached higher up the rope, again and again, desperate to keep her grip on a rope as stiff and slick as a steel cable. She only had to get herself to the ledge, another ten or fifteen feet . . . after that it would surely be easier.

She groped for the lip of the shelf and rolled sideways against the leaning boulder. Beyond the edge, the cave's opening was visible above, a palely glowing delta in the darkness. "I'm on the ledge," she called down to Minakis.

"All right, I'm coming up."

She felt the rope stiffen again and felt it twitch from side to side as he swiftly climbed toward her. He pulled himself over the ledge. In the diffuse daylight from above, she could just discern his expression. "I'm really getting too old for this." He sighed melodramatically, and when she laughed, he growled, "You think that's funny?"

"I know twenty-year-olds older than you," she said.

"Oh dear. Are they wiser too?"

She thrust out her chin, a curt Greek no.

"Good. Maybe there's some compensation." In the half-light his teeth gleamed. "Go on. I'll be right behind you."

She hauled herself up the gentler slope on her knees, long past caring about mud; her jeans were thick with it. Within a minute she was squeezing through the crevice at the top of the slide, blinded by the white daylight at the cave mouth. At that moment, half through the narrow passage and unable to see clearly, she thought she heard something on the threshold of sound, an exhalation of the earth almost like a groan. . . .

She scrambled into the light, dragging the case of plates through the aperture. Kneeling, she loosened her belt buckle and freed the case and pushed her head back through the crevice to call to Minakis. "I'm safe. . . . I mean I'm up."

"All right, I'm coming," he called back.

She could see nothing of him; her vision swam with motes that came from inside her dazzled eyes. "Hurry!" In the diffuse light of the cave entrance, everything seemed too sharply focused; every particle of stone and flake of lichen insisted upon its own presence. The rope tautened and jerked and a few seconds later Minakis was pushing his broad shoulders through the opening in the rock, looking up and smiling at her, his black eyes bright in his mud-streaked face—

—and at that moment the ground moved under her knees with a grinding sound, like an animal's deep-throated bellow.

"Manolis, give me your hand." She said it with urgent calm; they might have been boarding a boat.

Still smiling, still cheerful, he reached out his hand to her. She took it just as the mountain heaved itself sideways, massively. Anne-Marie was thrown to her side; chunks of rock fell from the ceiling, bouncing into her, but she kept her grip on Minakis's hand. The moss-slickened boulder that towered beside the crevice leaned and fell, crushing Minakis below the shoulders. Anne-Marie cried out in terror, but he only sighed; the look on his face was one of astonishment more than pain.

More rubble fell, a cascade of gravel, and the air was thick with dust. Anne-Marie saw the end of the climbing rope whip past and vanish through a crack in the rocks beside Minakis like a snake making for cover. "I'll bring help," she blurted. "I'll bring help. Oh God. Oh please . . ."

He squeezed her hand harder and a wordless groan escaped his lips. He lay beneath the stone, so powdered over with rock dust that he seemed made of stone himself, a half-carved statue with wet black gems for eyes.

"Oh please don't give up. I'll bring help soon." She had to tug her hand from his rigid grip.

Peter had gone a few steps down the path from the chapel when the ground moved under his feet. He stumbled and tripped over his own sore foot and sat down. Rocks bounced and skittered past, clattering down the mountain. He waited until he thought the tremor was past, but as he was getting back to his feet there was a sharper jolt; the whole mountain moved sideways, and he sat down harder.

He sat still, his thoughts knocked askew; something seemed to have let go inside him, as if the unsteady earth had robbed him of confidence. He was suddenly afraid for Anne-Marie, for her children; he was afraid for himself, afraid for their life together. He was startled to find tears welling up hotly.

He brushed his palms on his dusty trousers and wiped the back of his hand across his eyes. Still seeping tears, he stood and began, unsteadily, to walk. He could not relate his sudden grief, his sense of loss, to anything but frustration.

He had reached the saddle where the paths forked when he saw someone moving high on the side of Dikti, half running, half falling down the slope of loose stones that spilled from the crest. Recognition went through him like an electric charge. He ran toward Anne-Marie, but that effort lasted only a few yards; the incline soon had him sobbing for breath. He stretched his protesting muscles, climbing as fast as he could.

She came tumbling down the mountain, bringing herself up short a dozen feet away as he struggled toward her, peering at him as if frightened. He saw her wide eyes, the dried mud smeared all over her clothes and face and hands. "Are you hurt?" he cried.

Her dizziness passed. She knew him and stumbled toward him and fell into his arms, slack and exhausted, her weight almost bringing him down with her. "We have to get help."

"Who's hurt?"

"Minakis. It crushed him."

She burst into violent sobs but just as suddenly stopped herself short. "I'll go down to the village, there's a telephone." She shivered with the effort to maintain control. "I don't have the strength to climb back up there now. You go up, stay with him until help comes."

"Anne-Marie, listen. You're hurt too. I'll go with you."

"No!" she said fiercely. "You can't leave him alone."

"But I don't know where . . ."

"Climb straight up. As you start down there's a path to the left. Half a mile, less, you'll see a collapsed shepherd's hut. There's a cave behind it. We were climbing out. Then the earthquake . . . He's just inside. Go before it's too late."

"But *you* might be injured. We ought to—"

She shook her head sharply. "Go on, I'll come later."

He left her to climb the mountain, to wander in the blowing mist, shivering in shirtsleeves, sure he had lost his way.

After almost an hour he walked past the tumbled stones of the collapsed hut without recognizing it; at the last moment he stumbled back from the cliff edge. Turning beside the dry watering trough, seeking any landmark, he saw the dark mouth of the cave.

Inside, Minakis lay still beneath the boulder that pinned him. His eyes were closed, but Peter saw the barest movement of air in his throat. Somewhere Peter had read that wounded people— or was it people with concussions?—should not sleep.

"Minakis, it's Peter Slater. Can you hear me?"

He took the man's hand where it lay in the rubble and rubbed it between his own. Minakis's gritty eyelids parted.

"Can you hear me? Help is coming." Peter hoped that was true. "Can you talk?"

Minakis said nothing. Anne-Marie's camera bag lay on the ground, near a leather case. In the dirt next to it was a flashlight. Peter picked it up and played the beam over the collapsed roof. When he saw how massive the block was that weighed upon Minakis, a cold current of fear went through him.

He groped in the camera bag and found a wide-angle lens; he pulled the deep plastic cap off the back of it and used it as a cup to catch the water that dribbled haphazardly down the fallen boulders. When he had a cupful he held it to Minakis's lips, first wiping away the dust with moistened fingertips. Minakis opened his eyes. Awkwardly Peter poured the water into his mouth, a few drops at a time.

He said, "Peter," barely audibly.

"Right here."

"Tell you . . ."

"What?" Peter bent closer, but he could not hear words in the breathy whisper.

He kicked at loose stones and cleared a space to stretch out flat on his stomach, his ear close to Minakis's lips. "What did you say?"

"Fi . . ." Minakis swallowed. "File."

"File. A computer file?"

"In the chapel."

Peter wasn't sure what Minakis said next—it sounded like "jar," and then a weak humming sound, "mmm," repeated, "mmm," dwindling as Minakis's breath leaked away. He closed his eyes.

There was nothing for Peter to do but wait.

A dozen shapes appeared in the mist, led by Anne-Marie and the boy Dimitris, who ran ahead of the others to the cave. He knelt beside Minakis. "Kyrie, o kyrie, poli ponai?"

Peter was astonished to see a tiny smile on Minakis's lips. "Nai, ligo," he whispered.

Anne-Marie pushed into the narrow entrance beside them. "People are coming from the fire department in Neapolis," she said as Peter backed away. He said nothing; he wondered if the rescuers had thought to bring rock drills, and maybe a big sky-hook.

Faces crowded the cave mouth, peering in, mustachioed men from the village and a couple of young German tourists, all staring at Peter as if he could tell them what to do. A villager said something in Greek; Peter raised his palms helplessly. One of the Germans said, "He asks if the man is alive."

"Yes, but he can't be moved. He's badly hurt."

The German translated, and the villagers began a heated discussion. The German said, "Let me have a look at him, I'm trained in—"

Whatever he was about to say, he was cut short by a wave-like lift and subsidence of the earth and a grinding, continuing bass rumble. The crowd at the cave entrance shouted and retreated. Dimitris staggered back, frightened, and Anne-Marie knelt to grab Minakis's hand.

"No!" she cried, as if she could command the shaking earth. Rocks shifted in the aftershock; again the air filled with choking clouds of dust.

Minakis groaned in anguish, his wide eyes staring at nothing. His hand squeezed Anne-Marie's fiercely and just as suddenly let go. He fell away from her, into the cavern.

Peter caught her by the waistband of her jeans and dragged her back as an awful crescendo of rock signaled the collapse of the ceiling of the chamber beneath them; the sound went on for endless seconds.

27

The editor said they were too busy with the earthquake," Anne-Marie said to Peter, translating the meeting they had just left, "that even if there was anything on our old plates they weren't news."

They hurried down the hall of the *Kritika Nea* newspaper offices behind a gangly fellow with long legs, long black lashes, long black hair, a sparse mustache, and a spectacular Adam's apple.

"Did you tell him where they came from?"

"I didn't even tell him where *we* came from. It's better if we keep Minakis's name out of it." Before they'd left Ayia Kyriaki she'd washed the mud off her face and changed into a clean blouse and skirt and sandals. Under her tan she was pale with fatigue.

"Who's our friend?" Peter asked.

"His name's Iliakis, he's their photographer. He told the editor he'd printed everything for the next edition and he had to throw the soup out anyway, so why not see what we had. . . ."

Iliakis led them into a room hardly bigger than a closet, closed the door behind them, and flipped a switch; a dim red bulb came on overhead. In an instant the three of them were standing closer than old friends.

Anne-Marie set the leather case on the bench-top, and Iliakis lifted the lid and carefully extracted the first of the plates. To Anne-Marie he said something with a question mark, pointing toward one of the cameras on the shelf. "Den xero," she answered with a shrug. He returned his attention to the plate, carefully extracting the sheet of film from its holder and submerging it in a plastic tray, talking as he worked.

"What's he saying?" Peter asked.

"He's a camera nut, a collector. He says these plates are German made, fine grained, celluloid backed, intended for use in cameras like that one, a Voightlander-Alpin view camera"—the array of old cameras was barely visible in the dim light, packed among the bottles and packages of chemicals on the shelf above the sink—"very classy back in the twenties."

She bent and peered at the rectangle of film lying in its chemical bath. Peter peered over her shoulder, trying to see what was happening.

"Den enai kala?" Anne-Marie asked Iliakis.

The photographer sighed. "Ti krima."

"Tell me what's going on," Peter whispered urgently.

Anne-Marie wiped her hand across her damp brow. "Nothing's going on," she said tiredly. "There's nothing on that plate."

"It was never exposed?"

"No, it's fully exposed."

"What does . . . ?"

"Too much light. Like somebody held it up to the sun."

There were a dozen plates in the box, and an hour later Iliakis had developed the lot. His voice was full of sympathy as he poured the spent chemicals out of his trays, down the drain.

Peter followed Anne-Marie out of the *Kritika Nea* offices, past staffers who gave them amused looks. When they reached the crowded street he asked her, "What do we do now?"

"I don't know. Give up, I guess."

Peter put his hand gently on her shoulder. "Look at me, just for a second." She looked resolutely past him instead, onto the busy street, but finally she turned, her eyes brimming, and leaned her head on his chest. In a few moments his shirt was soaked through with her tears.

"You never told me what you expected to find on these photos. You haven't told me why you followed Minakis to Crete— or why you made me track you down. I don't know whether I figure in your plans anymore at all."

"Oh yes, you do, Peter," she whispered, "and I want to tell you everything. But don't make me tell you standing on this street corner."

"Then we'll go back to the village. I want to visit that chapel one more time."

Ayia Kyriaki was quiet and dark after sunset, with no sign of unusual activity; the rescue team had gone back to Neapolis, announcing they would not attempt to recover Minakis's body while there was still danger of aftershocks.

Peter parked the Fiat in the narrow street beside Minakis's front gate. They had expected to talk their way past a police guard; no one was in evidence, but the house was undisturbed.

"Things have changed since Minakis grew up here," said Anne-Marie. "They would have looted the place by now."

"Someone on his yacht will know whom to notify about his personal things," Peter said. "Tomorrow I'll call FORTH about his experiment."

Anne-Marie made a fire in the hearth. She found oranges and hard cheese and bread on the shelf; they should have been ravenous, but neither had much of an appetite. There was a bottle of white Bordeaux in the shiny refrigerator; she poured two glasses and sipped from hers before sitting down across the table from Peter. Cradling the glass, she leaned back in her chair and stared into the fire. He waited quietly.

"This all started when I was a little girl," she said. "There's a lot I never told you about my family. About Alain . . ."

Peter listened with all his senses, hearing what she said but also hearing the sad melody of her voice and seeing the morose beauty of her face in the firelight, the weariness in the drape of her body on the chair. Her aroma was a strange bouquet of wine and spicy perspiration and wild herbs and sharp photochemicals—or was that acrid scent the odor of limestone?

What she told him saddened him and made him feel angry and weak, but though it was news, it came as no real surprise. There had always been a brittle insincerity about her attitude toward her brother. As for Charlie, her unwillingness to concede that he had any rights to her children had always baffled him.

As she came to the part of her story that dealt with her appearance on Mykonos, her voice faltered. Alain had called her to Geneva to make a deal, she said—he would sign an affidavit and provide a blood sample proving that Carlos was his son, not Charlie's. But his cooperation had a price.

"I agreed to find out where Minakis kept his Minoan artifacts. You probably know the magazine story was a lie."

"Do you know where they are?"

"Oh yes. Buried under tons of rock, on top of a mountain, with no road to the place. And Minakis buried with them." She put a worried hand to her temple.

In the silence that followed, Peter tried to cut through the hundred questions that jostled in his head. He said simply, "I love you, Anne-Marie, and I love your children. I'll do anything I can for you."

"Tell more lies for me?" She wasn't teasing.

"If I have to."

Tears welled in her pale blue eyes. "If only . . . oh, Peter, if only I had trusted you from the beginning, instead of trying to do it all alone. You do love me, don't you?"

"From the first night." He smiled. "When you told me I couldn't play the piano as well as your father."

"I didn't say that, exactly." She reached a hand across the table, taking his fingers in hers.

He got up and went to her and held her as she stood—embraced her, kissed her, squeezed her tight. "Is there a bed in this house?"

"Why? Are you sleepy?"

"Too much awake."

"Me too."

He bent and lifted her off the floor, carrying her easily into the darkness under the arch.

Later, he brushed the dark hair gently from the bruise over her temple. Her eyes were bright in the darkness, watching him. "I will get Carlos back, you know."

"You'll share him with me?"

"Oh Peter . . . With all my heart." She tugged at his hand.

He kissed her forehead. He sat up in the bed and kicked at the sheets. He should have been pleasantly sleepy by now, but he was full of nervous energy. "You never told me what all that was, about the plates."

She sat up beside him, as restless as he was; the night air was electric. "Because I promised him I'd find out what was on them. No, that's not true, I made him agree to *let* me find out. Minakis's father was the photographer. I think Minakis was conceived there, where I found the plates. His mother was only fourteen." She turned to Peter, her pale eyes reflecting the new moon. "I think the men in this village murdered Minakis's father. Maybe his mother destroyed the plates accidentally—maybe she held them up to see what was on them, after he was gone. . . ."

"You got to know Minakis well."

"Well enough. He brought you and me both to this place. At first it was all because of you. He wanted us to move here; he wanted you to work with him; more than anything, he wanted you to understand what he was doing. But he showed me the cave because he wanted to give me back my life."

"I wish I could have talked to him one more time."

"My fault for keeping him to myself." Her gaze flickered away. "I thought there would be lots of time later for you two to go off and talk physics."

"Time is what I wanted to talk to him about. But all he said to me was something about a file." He lay back, his head on his hands, looking at the shadowed ceiling. "Did he show you how his experiment worked?"

"I was too busy taking pictures to pay close attention. He talked about transactions between the past and the future, said they got rid of paradoxes in quantum theory." She snuggled down beside him. Her fingers crept across his belly. "Which made me wonder why theorists cling to their long-standing paradoxes. But that I didn't ask."

Peter laughed. "We cherish our paradoxes. Every year thousands of graduate students learn to suppress reason and find in quantum mechanics the true faith." His hand caught hers and gently trapped her fingers. "We're all like German Lutherans, the ones who believe in consubstantiation. Come to think of it, a lot of the early quantum theorists were born Lutherans."

"What difference does that make?" Abruptly she sat up and swung her legs off the bed.

"Communion. The Eucharist, the Mass. Most Protestants believe that the bread and wine are just symbols. Catholics like you . . ."

"I *was* a Catholic." She went naked to where their clothes were piled in a heap on a chair. She found something among her clothes and picked it up.

He watched her, propping his head in his hand. "So you were taught to believe in *tran*substantiation—that even if the bread and wine retain breadlike qualities and vinous qualities, they turn into the actual body and blood of Christ. That may be magic, but it's not a paradox. To Lutherans, the consecrated bread *is* bread, and at the same time it *is* the body of Christ. The wine *is* wine, and at the same time it *is* the blood of Christ. Bread, body—wine, blood. Waves, two paths—particles, one path. Superposition."

"Quantum mechanics as Communion?" Her voice betrayed a wan smile. "Minakis promised the metropolitan his work had no religious significance."

"I won't tell the metropolitan if you won't."

She turned to him, her naked body long and smooth, pale and deeply shadowed in the moonlight. "Are you religious, husband?"

"Only in unguarded moments. You, wife?"

"Oh yes. My religion is very old." She came toward him, her dark hair moving on her shoulders. Between her full breasts a golden pendant gleamed.

*   *   *

As the sun rose behind them the morning mist brightened and grew iridescent with a wavering rainbow. They climbed in muffled silence, a hard climb over slick rock. Near the top of the peak the blue sky appeared through curls of vapor; the stone chapel caught the early light.

Inside the chapel, a shaft of sunlight streaming through the eastern window illuminated their vaporous breath. Peter took the cover off the computer. He carefully pulled the plastic sheeting off the test bed and lifted back the hood where the beams recombined.

He indicated the fragment of pottery in its glass mount. "Did he say anything about this thing? What it was for?"

"That wasn't there when I was here. But I didn't see him for two days—he was up here by himself." She looked closer. "It reminds me of something he talked about. It's like the potsherds he found in that cave when he was a little boy. But those would be over thirty-five hundred years old. This looks new."

"Could it be a piece of a jar?"

"I suppose."

"He said 'file.' He said 'jar'—at least I think that's what he said. Let's see what's in the computer." Peter switched on the computer and pushed the mouse across its pad, clicking on icons. A file directory appeared on the screen. "Greek, what else? Can you help me with this?"

She watched as he scrolled. "I can read the words . . . but it's Greek to me too. What's a four-momentum propagator?"

"Never mind, we're looking for a file named 'jar.' "

"*To doheio,* okay. Wait, slow down. E.M., M.M., L.M.— those are archaeological periods. There's a list of objects under each heading—cups, figures—there's a jar, Middle Minoan I."

Peter clicked on the file name. The screen went blank, then slowly began to paint a picture in high resolution, line by line. A net of irregular polygons stretched over a rounded surface, most of them sketchily filled in; missing pieces were indicated in thin white lines. The whole picture was of a widemouthed pot with two handles.

A click of the mouse made the figure rotate.

"Isn't that the broken piece, the one in the mount?" Peter

said excitedly, indicating one of the polygons with the cursor. "Except here it really does look thirty-five hundred years old!"

A strip of icons had appeared across the top of the screen; Peter clicked the little picture of a flashlight. Polygons brightened and came into sharper focus, one after another, until the whole pot shone like new, a sturdy but shapely vessel decorated with thorn branches as sprightly as a *zenga* ink painting.

All but for a single section. Yes. The final piece waiting to be restored by the computer animation *was* the one still resting in the mount on the bench.

Which excited their curiosity.

They rummaged in the computer files. Other objects were pictured in other files, some restored, some still represented as unretouched assemblies of ancient sherds.

In shallow drawers beneath the computer bench, Peter and Anne-Marie found the sherds themselves, material objects they could hold and feel. Some were dim with age. Some were bright as new.

Peter pulled the crumpled and stained sketches from his shirt pocket, the papers Minakis had left him on Mykonos. "See what he wrote here? 'More is implied by light-speed tunneling than the confirmation of Cramer's hypothesis—including the possibility that some physical processes may be reversible.' I couldn't make sense of that before. Now I think he meant he had found a way to reverse the chemical aging of these surfaces."

"Yes," she said. "He wanted to build a telescope into the past."

For three hours they searched the computer files, she translating, he sometimes querying her reading, sometimes moving impatiently to another file, sometimes drifting away for minutes at a time in rapt thought.

He came out of one such trance with a start. "Those plates you found in the cave—where are they?"

"I left them in the car. Oh . . ." Anne-Marie frowned. "They're worthless. There's no picture information left on them."

"If someone just took an unexposed plate out of its sleeve and waved a torch at it, exposed it all at once, there's nothing we can do. But if the photographer made a good exposure to begin with and got an image on the plate, and sometime later the plate was exposed a second time, we may have a chance."

"How? Either way all the grains have been exposed. That's why the negatives are plain black."

"There's no physical or chemical difference among them, but there is a *time* difference. I think we can make the grains that were exposed later revert first."

"You are going to try to *un*develop an exposed negative?"

"Well, let's see," Peter said. "Let's just see."

Peter plucked out the glass-framed sherd and adjusted the bracket to fit the Voightlander's film holder, bending its thin metal springs. Then he lowered the hood over the mounted negative, turned, and tapped instructions on the computer keyboard.

Glass prisms accelerated to a near-supersonic whistle. Starlike points of laser light gleamed on their surfaces—surfaces spinning so rapidly they seemed like motionless, multifaceted columns of glass. Although the laser beams were invisible in the sunlight, their incident stars were reflected on the surfaces of mirrors and lenses along all the paths of the interferometer.

"This is a different setup from the one you saw—something he didn't tell me about either. *This* is his telescope into the past."

Peter backed away from the mechanism until he was standing beside Anne-Marie in the rear of the chapel—any flaws in those rotating chunks of glass could cause them to explode. "When a photon in the time-reversed beam hits the objective—in Minakis's case a scrap of pottery, in our case the overexposed negative—it gets information about the molecule it encounters. The waveguide barrier advances the information a few trillionths of a second backward in time. Then the information goes to the computer, but more importantly it resets the chemical reactions in the object itself."

"What are you saying?" Anne-Marie shook her head. "What are you talking about?"

"Sorry. Just this: we're causing the past to remanifest itself a few trillionths of a second at a time. Within those few trillionths of a second another wave arrives and sets the chemical-reaction clock back that much more. And another wave, and another after that, and each one ratchets the clock back, instant by instant. And that's the way we undevelop the picture."

The spinning prisms sang, the solenoids clicked, the scanner murmured. They stood watching the monitor screen. The screen was black—plain black, meaning there was no information to be had.

"If there's a picture on that negative, it was taken seventy years ago," she said quietly. "I don't think I want to wait that long."

"For most of those seventy years that plate was in the pitch dark," Peter replied. "Photochemically, nothing happened. We're skipping the time nothing happened. When nothing happens, going back in time should take no time at all."

As he spoke, the black on the screen softened almost imperceptibly to a mottled gray, in which shapes like distant clouds suggested themselves.

"I forgot to reverse the polarity," Peter said suddenly. He leaned over the keyboard, tapping commands, clicking the mouse, peering at the screen, and tapping and clicking again. "Damn it, I don't know how to do this."

"I can read a negative, Peter." Anne-Marie gazed at the screen in near reverie.

"I can't," he said, still trying. "I want to see it too."

Meanwhile the image grew clearer every moment, emerging from the bright chaos on the screen. An arch like a halo appeared above a pale luminous oval with stark little ovals set into it: they were eyes, with gray irises like gemstones and white lashes under thick white brows, and a mouth whose curved white lips were delicately closed—a human face framed in hair that glowed unearthly white.

Anne-Marie could see the crisp resolution of the image and its fine gradation of tones, growing crisper and finer with each passing moment, but despite her claim that she could read negatives, she could not read the subtleties of expression on this young woman's face—until Peter found the right keys, and the image reversed with a tingle of electricity. Everything bright was now dark; everything dark was now bright.

"My God!" he whispered.

Anne-Marie said nothing but only stared at the portrait on the screen. The woman was very young indeed, although she had a serenity of purpose that seemed older than her years. Her wide pale eyes under dark brows looked deep into the eyes of the watchers, and her mouth enclosed a secret in its gentle smile, and her cascading dark tresses curled about her cheeks and glistened in the artificial light. Her shoulders were bare under loosened hair; behind her, soft chiaroscuro suggested the interior of a cave. On her slight bosom rested a gold pendant depicting two kneeling *kri-kri*.

None of these details had caused Peter's exclamation. "Is that really . . . ?"

"That's Sophia, Minakis's mother," Anne-Marie said. "She was only fourteen."

"But you see the resemblance. Surely you see it."

Anne-Marie reluctantly nodded. Time adds the marks of experience to a face, but it does not change that face beyond recognition. The picture on the monitor screen was an exact likeness of Anne-Marie herself, at the age of fourteen.

Peter hastily struck keys in hopes of storing the image in computer memory. Then they could only watch as the image clouded over and brightened to white while Minakis's busy time probe, looking ever farther backward, erased it from the negative that had first captured it almost seventy years ago.

Within a few seconds the camera negative was as fresh and blank as it had been when it was new, never exposed.

Anne-Marie said, "I didn't think of that."

Peter raised a brow. "Didn't think of what?"

"I wasn't surprised that it can bring back the past. But it hadn't occurred to me that it can erase the evidence."

28

The only things not covered with dust in Alain Brand's cramped and windowless office were the telephone on his desktop, on which he had just taken a call from his sister, and the audio equipment on the shelf behind him, playing a version of Schubert's *Winterreise* recently remastered to compact disc, on which the piano accompaniment was provided by the late Eric Brand. Alain owned every edition of his father's recordings, but only in moments of stress bordering on panic did he listen to them. After Anne-Marie's call he'd brushed aside his ledgers and his correspondence and pressed the CD into its tray, and now he sat enveloped in a chill landscape of sound.

She'd done as he'd asked; she'd found Minakis's collection of Minoan artifacts; she was already in Geneva; she was on her way over to give him the details. Not a word of apology for being four days late in calling—and every minute of that time Alain expecting a visit from Karl. He didn't have the courage to tell her the deal was off, that he'd completely lost his nerve, that not hearing from Karl was almost as frightening as facing him across the desk—that he was afraid to walk home alone at night. He'd assured Anne-Marie that he looked forward to her visit. Then hung up gently. Then swore.

Fifteen minutes passed before the intercom buzzed. "Monsieur? Vôtre soeur est ici."

He flung open the door and swept into the shop through aisles of books, all smiles, his lips already pursing for a kiss. "Anne-Ma*rie!*"

She raised her camera and aimed it at him, snapping a frame as he stumbled to a halt.

"Put that away!" He wiped the lank hair off his forehead with a motion that turned him away, his hand half hiding his face.

"Oh my. You said you admired my photography, Alain," she said cheerily, and dropped the camera into her bag. "Where shall we talk? Here? Or somewhere darker?"

"In my office." Alain glanced nervously at his clerk, not last week's tall, haughty brunette but her successor, a tall, haughty blonde with plucked eyebrows and bright red lipstick, who stared back at him in wide-eyed puzzlement. "We are not to be disturbed," he told her, too loudly.

He led Anne-Marie into the office and closed the door behind them, squeezing behind his desk. She stood a moment, listening to the music. *"Winter Journey?* Excellent choice. Pure self-pity."

Alain twisted in his chair and savagely hit the power button, killing the sound.

She sat opposite him and withdrew a map from her bag, leaning forward to spread it across his desk—a German topographical map of Crete, four feet long, with tattered edges.

"Do we really need that?" Alain asked, barely glancing at it.

"You'll need it. Did you suppose Minakis kept the artifacts in his house? They're in a cave on a mountain. No roads for miles. A strenuous climb."

He looked where she was pointing, at the elevation lines that bunched and meandered, indicating rough country. "And just how is anyone supposed to pay a discreet visit to a cave on a mountaintop on Crete without every goatherd in the neighborhood watching every step?"

"It's a challenge," she agreed cheerily, "but consider the

rewards." She took a handful of color prints from her bag and spread them over the map. "You will recognize these. Three Middle Minoan painted cups . . . a carved alabaster vase . . . a Late Minoan *labrys*. The pieces you showed me."

He looked at the pictures. They were the same objects as in his Polaroids, but in sharper focus, better lit. Her work.

"And these, that you didn't show me." She fanned more prints. "A necklace of gold and faience beads. Two clay statuettes of the goddess. Bronze and ivory votive figurines. More painted pottery. Another gold *labrys*."

Alain fished in the detritus on the shelf behind him and found a magnifying glass. He took up the prints and peered at them one by one. They displayed an unprecedented treasure, far richer, because far rarer, than any unexcavated tomb in Tuscany or Sardinia, the sort of plunder with which he was familiar.

She let him look at them in silence until she was sure she had his attention. "And nobody knows where, except you and me."

"You forget Minakis."

"He's dead. Didn't you read about the earthquake?"

Alain gaped. "He's *dead?*" Perhaps there had been news about an earthquake in Greece; it hadn't made an impression on him. "You're the only one who knows about this cave?"

She nodded. "I've done what I promised. And you promised, in writing, to give me your affidavit."

His fear came racing back. How could he know if she was telling the truth? "I'm afraid that . . . Anne-Marie, I . . . Anyway, no court in the world will uphold an illegal agreement."

She looked at him without expression, so coldly and openly that his heart shriveled. Clearly she had expected nothing better. "I want my boy back, Alain. If you won't honor our agreement, I'll make you a different proposal."

"What do you mean?"

She pushed another color print across the desktop. "You told me not to steal. I ignored your advice."

His chest tightened involuntarily. "You stole this?" he whispered. It was the one piece whose picture Karl had given him that he had never shown her, the one piece against which his greed had no defense.

"It's in a safe-deposit box in a vault at the Berthelier Bank, ten blocks from here. Come see it for yourself."

His smile was desperate, as brittle as dry clay. "How can I possibly refuse?"

The bank guard stood by while Anne-Marie removed the steel drawer from the vault. She carried it to the private carrel where Alain waited, outside the vault's round steel doors—which were mostly for show, but inside a cage of quite practical steel bars. She set it on the table, inserted the key, and lifted the lid. Alain bent to look inside.

"The animals are *kri-kri*, wild goats," she said. "According to Minakis it's a little younger than the bee pendant from Malia."

"May I?" He was surprised at his own hoarse whisper.

"Please."

He lifted the *kri-kri* pendant into the cool neon light. Up close, the workmanship was more exquisite than even Anne-Marie's photograph had suggested, the animals swelling with naturalistic vigor. "Extraordinary," he murmured. So extraordinary that it posed a dilemma of the sort he had never faced before, for he knew as soon as he saw it that he was willing to steal it from his own client, even at the risk of his life.

He laid the treasure back in the strongbox. "What you want is an affidavit?" As if he didn't know what she wanted.

"Stating that you believe you are the father of my child."

"I don't see a problem with that."

"And a blood sample to back it up."

He would have promised her anything. "All right. But how do I know you won't take my confession straight to those German scandal rags you work for?"

"I'll put the box back and we'll go upstairs. After you cosign for your own key we'll discuss terms."

The high-ceilinged, marble-columned lobby of the Banque Berthelier had been built in a more genteel era; its present owners had cluttered the echoing space with cheap cubicles where computer screens glowed and telephones burbled. The harassed young woman behind the desk made it clear she had better

things to do than rent safe-deposit boxes, especially since the
rent on this one had already been collected this morning by one
of her colleagues. She glanced over Alain's identification and
compared his signature to the one on the card he'd signed,
authorizing him, along with Anne-Marie Brand, to have access
to the box. It took her only a few seconds to tap the pertinent
information into her terminal. She returned his documents and
placed the card in an interoffice folder. "Here's your key, Mr.
Brand," she said.

As Alain reached for it Anne-Marie deftly took it from the
woman's hand. "I'll hold on to that for now," she said. "We
have to hurry, Alain; we have an appointment at the clinic."

The clinic was a pay-as-you-go commercial health clinic on the
rue du Rhône, three blocks away. The receptionist showed
Alain and Anne-Marie to an examination room where a bored
nurse in a starched white uniform asked Alain to remove his
jacket—just take one arm out of it, that was fine—and roll up
his shirtsleeve. Did he prefer the left arm? That was fine too.
All he had to do now was rest his arm on the table and make a
fist.

He barely felt a prick as the big needle went into the vein
below his elbow and the fat syringe filled with dark blood. The
nurse pulled out the needle and slapped an alcohol-soaked pad
on his arm and told him to squeeze.

As she left the room a ruddy crew-cut fellow with a silk suit
draped over his considerable bulk came in through the same
door. He didn't pause to introduce himself. "At Ms. Brand's
request I've drafted a document for your signature, Mr.
Brand"—not a doctor, then, a lawyer—"in your words, first
person, so let me know if there's anything you object to saying.
I've got my laptop right here and we can fix it up on the spot."

Alain read the printout. It rehearsed events he had tried long
and hard to forget: "As a boy I often pressed myself upon my
younger sister with erotic purpose, and upon occasion sexually
assaulted her."

The events at Ayios Nikolaos were recounted in more
graphic detail: "I struck her repeatedly about the face until she

stopped struggling. I forcibly removed her undergarments. Although she still resisted, I penetrated her. While still inside her, I ejaculated. . . ."

"Christ!" Alain felt trapped, his jacket half off, his shirt-sleeve unraveled, his arm clenched to close his leaking vein.

"Everything all right, Mr. Brand?"

Alain ignored the lawyer. "What's to keep this pornographic fantasy from getting into the hands of the press?" he demanded of his sister, but she stood watching him with wordless contempt.

"As you see here, on the next page," the lawyer put in cheerfully, "there is an agreement of confidentiality already signed by Ms. Brand to the effect that this document may only be shown to Mr. Phelps—or used in judicial proceedings."

"Oh, oh! Very nice, very nice! You promise to be good," Alain said to Anne-Marie. "What am I supposed to do when you cheat?"

"I'm very sure everybody involved would prefer to keep the matter quiet," said the lawyer.

"*You*, not him," Alain shouted at her. "Talk to me. Is that your idea of a guarantee?"

Wordlessly Anne-Marie held up the safe-deposit box key.

Alain glared at the key and then at her. He snatched the pen the lawyer offered him and almost violently scrawled his signature across the bottom of the papers.

"We appreciate your cooperation, sir," said the lawyer.

"I can leave now?"

The lawyer glanced at Anne-Marie. She still held out the key, unsmiling. Alain snatched it from her hand and left the room.

He walked fast, pushing his way through midday crowds along the rue du Rhône toward the bank. He shouldered through the old-fashioned bronze-and-glass doors and marched to the nearest unoccupied teller. "I want to get into this safe-deposit box." He laid his key flat on the marble counter and gave the young woman the number.

"Certainly, sir. I'll need some identification. And your signature on this card . . ."

A minute later the bank guard stood by while Alain removed the drawer from the vault. He took it to a carrel, laid it on the table, inserted the key, and lifted the lid.

The box was empty.

Peter yawned and yawned again, shaking himself like a dog to stay awake, pacing the quays of Lac Leman, waiting and watching to see his wife and her brother leave the Banque Berthelier—waiting until the coast was clear.

They had flown into Geneva late last night, and the first thing this morning she had dragged him to the bank where they'd rented the safe-deposit box, paid for it, signed for it—she signing with his last name, Anne-Marie Slater—and then they'd left to find a photo shop with one-hour processing, and finally gone to breakfast, which somewhat restored *his* spirits, although she was so adrenaline-rushed it would have been hard to notice the difference in her, and afterward she was off to make other arrangements—while he was off jewelry shopping.

All of it happening so fast that Peter wondered, now that he had time to think, how she could have planned it so thoroughly. The only business she had not thought through was what to do with the pendant after Peter recovered it. An artifact divorced from its context, no matter how valuable, was a mere curiosity. Collectors and the museums that dealt with them did more to corrupt the past than to preserve it, were in fact a plague upon the past.

Surely Minakis would have recorded somewhere the circumstances of his exploration of the shrine; if the *kri-kri* pendant could not be returned to the cave, its proper place was with his records. Peter and Anne-Marie would have to find Minakis's executor, and meanwhile Peter would have to take the pendant back to Crete. This was their vacation.

It was after noon when Anne-Marie and Alain came out of the bank on their way to the clinic on the quai du Mont Blanc. Peter watched them cross the bridge over the Rhône. Then he hurried to the bank, presented his identification to the clerk, signed his name, went to the vault, and removed its contents. What could be easier?

But what was Alain Brand going to do when he found that he'd signed for a box in the name of Anne-Marie Brand that contained nothing? Would he realize that he'd inspected the contents of a neighboring box, one in the name of Anne-Marie Slater?

Maybe she intended him to know; Peter hadn't asked her. He was satisfied to embrace the passionate and loving and loyal side of her; the furies in her he would prefer to honor at a distance.

He walked quickly to the railroad station on place Cornavin and took the next train to the airport. It was a short ride. Soon Anne-Marie would be in the terminal, on her way to Paris by way of Air France, but there was no risk they would encounter one another; his flight was to Athens. Last night she had smuggled the *kri-kri* pendant out of Athens, assuring him that she was an expert "mule." By comparison he was worse than an amateur mule, but his burden was easy; all he had to do was smuggle a Greek treasure back into Greece, one nobody was looking for because nobody knew it existed. It rested in cotton in a cardboard box with a Cartier label and a sales slip listing its value as 750 Swiss francs, tax included.

He had already passed through the security gate when a man with a blond ponytail came swiftly toward him in the crowded corridor. "Professor Slater, my name is Rudi Karl. There's someone you should meet."

"Do I know you? How do you know me?" Peter felt himself blush to the roots of his hair. He must be radiating guilt.

"Please don't worry, Professor. We have no intention of telling anyone about the pendant." The man's bright blue eyes were icily compelling. "If you'll come with me . . ."

The neat little man rose from his easy chair in the VIP lounge and dismissed Rudi with a nod.

"I'm Richard Wingate, Professor Slater. Please sit down, I'll only keep you a minute. I was a longtime friend and business partner of Manolis Minakis. I'm also the executor of his estate. I wanted to give you this in person." He handed Peter a large brown envelope.

Peter sat, feeling tired and distinctly rumpled by comparison to the tailored older man sitting opposite who smelled so freshly of cologne. He looked at the envelope warily. "What is it?"

"His will. Subject to probate of course, so please regard it as confidential. He hoped you would be willing to work with him and, if necessary, take over his work. Unfortunately the need has arisen sooner than he expected."

Peter twisted in the heavily upholstered chair as if trying to distance himself from the envelope without dropping it. It was a message from the grave. "I hardly knew the man."

"A year ago Manolis decided to—if I may put it bluntly—recruit you. He was a very confident man who liked to keep his affairs current. Although the owner under Greek law is the Foundation for Research and Technology, Hellas, you are to have the use of his house in Ayia Kyriaki and the equipment he has set up near there. I believe you have acquaintances at FORTH?"

Peter nodded, speechless.

"Of course you are under no obligation," Wingate said. "Whatever you decide, you will have my complete cooperation. I hope you will come to regard me as a friend."

Peter straightened in his chair. "Do you know what he was doing with that experiment? Do you understand the implications?"

Wingate smiled thinly. "I believe I do. It will change the world, would you agree?"

Peter said, "Mm." A joke, perhaps, but not that funny.

"Would you like a sandwich, a drink? Your plane doesn't leave for an hour."

Peter looked at his watch. "All right, a drink if you'll join me. Scotch, neat."

Wingate signaled an attendant. When he turned back, Peter was watching him.

"You understand I'll need confirmation."

"All sorts of legal correspondence will follow. Meanwhile, guard the *kri-kri* pendant. An awkward business, that, but I'm afraid Manolis didn't understand your wife's predicament when he wrote his will. Well, she wasn't your wife then. Nevertheless, Rudi tells me she handled the matter deftly."

"My wife is a remarkable woman," said Peter. "More remarkable even than she appears. What remains to be done can only be done by her, if it can be done at all."

Their drinks arrived. Peter raised his glass to Wingate. "Do you believe in reincarnation?" he asked. "The eternal return? The seamless continuity of past and future? The implicate order?"

"I confess I have been unable to take these matters seriously." Wingate raised his own glass. "To your health."

Behind them a silvery jetliner screamed into the sky against the backdrop of distant Mont Blanc.

"Nor have I. But I intend to look a little deeper. I assume you'll be going to Crete to see to Minakis's affairs."

Wingate nodded. "Perhaps I'll see you there."

Peter said, "One of these days you must let me show you a photograph of Minakis's mother."

A week later, on their way home from Athens to Paris to Honolulu, Peter and Anne-Marie and Jennifer stopped for a day in San Diego.

Charlie Phelps's office had thick oriental carpets on the floor and a glass wall overlooking San Diego harbor in the distance, thirty stories below. Charlie, looking efficient and relaxed, with a golfer's tan, stood up from behind his desk as his secretary ushered his visitors in. "Anne-Marie, it's very good to see you. And Peter, good to meet you at last."

"Charlie. Same here."

They shook hands, a quick firm shake. Charlie turned to Anne-Marie. "Dad called to report, soon as you dropped off Jenny. Says he can't believe how much she's grown. Certainly made his day," he said affably. "Thanks for saving me a trip to Hawaii."

"Yes, your dad looks good," Anne-Marie said quietly.

"Let's sit." Charlie waved them to the library corner, furnished with a leather sofa and chairs and a low round table. "Coffee, tea, mineral water? Anything? No?" There was a moment's leaning back and fidgeting, a straightening of seams, a clearing of throats. Charlie kept his eyes on Anne-Marie, working at seeming unhurried.

"Thanks for seeing us like this," she said hoarsely. Her voice was threatening to desert her.

"I only wish it could have been sooner. There's something you wanted to tell me about Carlos?"

"How is he?" she asked.

"Happy and healthy, except for two scabby knees. Fiercest soccer forward I know, for a six-year-old." He paused. "Can't wait to visit his mother next month. Wants to know if you'll teach him to surf. I said I hoped so. Wasn't sure."

Anne-Marie smiled tightly, avoiding Charlie's eye. Peter said, "We'll see what we can do."

The silence stretched, and no one chose to end it until Anne-Marie turned her gaze back onto Charlie, her smile gone. "I had to see you. To give you some bad news. Something I should have told you a long time ago."

He tilted his head. "Shoot."

She leaned forward, nervously circling her wrist with her fingers. "Do you remember the morning after we met on Crete, how I was cut up, had all those bruises? I told you I'd been hit by a scooter, that I'd fallen down in the road?"

"Oh yes."

"It wasn't true. I mean, it was true, except that it wasn't an accident. I made sure that boy hit me—I threw myself in front of him—to cover up what really happened. I was raped and beaten that night. I didn't want you to know."

Charlie looked concerned, ready to do what he could to help. "I'm very sorry to hear that."

"Charlie, listen to me. Carlos isn't your son. You're not his real father."

His friendliness faded. "Anne-Marie, whatever you have in mind, I intend to abide by the court's decision. I urge you to do the same."

"I was pregnant when we were married. That's why I married you—because I was pregnant. Even though I didn't want to be, even though I was a bad Catholic, I couldn't do anything about it because abortion was murder. I believed that. And there you were."

"You had already agreed to marry me, when this hadn't happened yet," he said sharply.

Anne-Marie tossed her head and pushed her hair out of her eyes. "I said yes that night to get rid of you. I was going to run away. You weren't ever going to see me again. But then, after the rape, you were . . . insurance, I guess."

"You tell me this now." Charlie stared at her in disgust. "Is this some kind of sick revenge? Because if you think it makes any difference in the way I feel about Carlos . . ."

"Charlie, please. You have to hear the truth."

"The truth is, Carlos *is* my son. From the minute he was born I've loved him. He is *my* son, and nothing you can say, *nothing* you say can change that." He stood up. "In fact I think you've said more than enough already."

Peter said, "It's important that you hear her out."

"I don't believe I asked for your advice."

"Please, I'm not saying this to hurt you." Anne-Marie looked up at him. "I'm sorry I lied to you. No more lies now, I promise."

"There's more? What next? You're going to tell me who the guy was? Like it makes any difference?"

Anne-Marie looked at Peter, then back at Charlie. "No, it doesn't make any difference. I came to say I'm sorry, Charlie. Not just for the lies. For hating you when you were doing the best you could for me and Carlos . . ."

Charlie paced in circles, shaking his head. "Wait, wait. You kick me in the gut, and then you *apologize?*"

Her voice gathered strength. "I'm sorry I couldn't let you love me, Charlie. I couldn't forgive myself. All that hatred rubbed off on you. It made me blind. And I was wrong, wrong."

"Why *are* you here? What do you want?"

"I want you to know. A little while ago I met a man who made me realize it doesn't much matter who a person's real parents are. But it took time for the lesson to sink in."

Anne-Marie stood up unsteadily. Peter, caught off guard, stood quickly and put a hand on her arm.

"I don't want anything, Charlie," she said, "except your help in giving Carlos and Jenny the best life we can give them. All three of us. That's all I wanted to say. We'll go now. But I hope we can talk later."

"Imagine my surprise," Peter said as they waited at the curb for their taxi. "Any second I was expecting Alain's affidavit to come out of your purse."

"Thanks for reminding me." She pulled a thick envelope from her purse, walked to the nearest sidewalk trash bin, and tossed it in. When she came back she looked at him almost shyly. "I hope you're not disappointed. After all I put you through."

"Far from it. You have a big heart. Bigger than I knew."

She laid cool fingertips on the back of his hand. "It was you Minakis was talking about when he said that about parents, not himself. And when I thought about you and the way you love Jenny—and Carlos, knowing everything you know—it finally clicked. Poor Charlie, all those years. I was such a harpy. He never did do anything really wrong."

"He bored you."

She gave him a wry look. "That's true."

"Tell me, is an investment banker inherently more boring than a theoretical physicist?"

"You wish."

29

Dimitris had finished lashing the plastic-wrapped computer monitor to the top of Irini's packsaddle when Peter leaned out of the chapel door. "Why don't you go on down? I'll catch up."

"Nai, kyrie." Dimitris slapped the donkey on the rump, raising a cloud of dust; the careful beast stepped off daintily over the stones.

Peter went back inside the chapel. The bare floor and stone vault gave no hint that anything as strange as an optics experiment had ever occupied the serene space. Where the steel test bed had stood there was only a crudely painted icon of the Metamorphosis resting on a wooden stand. Peter took a match from the box on the stand, struck it, and held it to a wick floating in a dish of oil.

He watched as the transparent yellow flame took hold. Then he smothered the match in the sand tray in front of the icon. He emptied his pockets of coins, leaving them in the sand. Outside, he locked the door against the gusting wind and put the iron key back on the lintel, where the next person who needed to worship could find it.

* * *

Approaching the village from above, Peter inhaled the early-summer landscape, the sweet blossoms on the feathery green branches of the almond trees dappling the plain. Below he saw Dimitris and the donkey nearing the courtyard of Minakis's house. Suddenly the gate was flung open and a dark-haired little boy raced out, calling to Dimitris in a high, clear voice. Dimitris halted, and Irini the donkey did likewise. The boy ran up and took the halter Dimitris offered him and tugged hard; the donkey understood what was required and followed the little boy down the street.

Anne-Marie came out of the courtyard and watched the caravan pass on its way to the village square but made no effort to follow. Jennifer ran out of the gate and clutched at her mother's skirt, pointing excitedly toward the retreating donkey. Anne-Marie scooped her up in her arms and turned and looked up the hill, in Peter's direction.

He waved and hurried to meet them.

They were sitting down to lunch at the table Anne-Marie had spread in the sunny courtyard when Carlos came back through the gate, leading Dimitris by the hand. "Eat with us, Dimitri," Anne-Marie said to him in Greek. "You've done too much work this morning to go hungry."

"Thank you, *kyria,* but I have no appetite."

"All right, but take some of these stuffed peppers with you." She scooped a pair of them from a serving dish into a shallow bowl. "Peter made them himself, last night."

"If you wish, *kyria.*" Dimitris peered into the bowl as if this were not a recommendation, but he took the bowl, sketched a wave, and was gone.

"Takis isn't hungry because he wants to play with his new computer," Carlos informed them, leaning across the table for the stuffed grape leaves.

"Aussi, je voeux le poivron ça," Jennifer announced, clambering onto her chair to reach for one of the oil-drenched peppers in the dish.

"Doucement, Jenny, attende un moment." Peter deflected her

grasp and emptied the spicy rice filling of the pepper onto her plate. When he set the plate before her, she beamed with satisfaction.

"Merci, Dada."

Peter was Dada to both children now, a name that made him feel ten years older and too whiskery. But since Charlie Phelps was Daddy to Carlos, and Anne-Marie wouldn't have them addressing Peter by his first name, and Father was a stern antique, Dada he was.

"Dada, why can't you understand Greek?" Carlos asked. "You understand lots of other languages."

"I learned the others when I was still a boy, like you." To the extent that he had learned them at all. "It's hard to learn new languages when you're a grown-up. So learn all the languages you can right now. As for me, give me time."

"Okay," said Carlos, unconcerned, as he bit off half a slippery dolma.

Then Peter experienced a moment of . . . not bliss, exactly, but of happy comprehension. A Zen moment. He knew the feeling well enough not to cling to it, having experienced it only once before, in connection with a mathematical insight—not with children (as much as these two were his own, his chosen children, he could never pretend to own them), not with a woman (not even Anne-Marie, his chosen and rechosen mate), not with the food on the table or the sun in the sky or the cliffs of Dikti looming above the rooftops.

This evanescent instant of enlightenment had only to do with love and how love expands, infinitely . . . or for a moment, so it seemed.

In the village square, beside their rented car, Peter swung Jennifer round and round in the air, she dizzily shrieking, "More! More!" while Anne-Marie went into the churchyard to lay a wreath on a gravestone, and Carlos, out of curiosity, tagged along with her.

Three names, three sets of dates were deeply carved in new dark granite: KATERINA K. ANDROULAKI, 1886–1935; SOPHIA A. DIDASKALOU, 1908–1922; MANOLIS A. D.

MINAKIS, 1922–1997. Anne-Marie's wreath of chrysanthe-
mums, bought the day before in Iraklion, was big enough to
cover them all.

"Who are they?" Carlos demanded, tugging at her hand.

"One was a friend of mine," she said.

"And Dada's?"

"His too." More than his friend, his *sadalos,* his sponsor,
although she was not at all certain he would have approved of
Peter's decision to move their work to Switzerland.

Her son, bored with graves, tugged urgently on her sleeve.
"Are we ready to leave yet?" he demanded. Anne-Marie got a
grip under his bottom and lifted him to her flank, and they left
the graveyard.

Catching sight of them, Peter wearily set Jennifer on her feet.
She was still calling, "More! More!"

Anne-Marie brushed strands of dark hair from her perspiring
forehead and jerked open the passenger-side door of the rented
Mercedes. "Inside, kids. Dada's taking us home."

They tumbled in and settled themselves. The car circled the
cistern and bumped over the cobblestones, heading downhill
through the almond groves. Through the back window the children waved and made faces at the old men in front of Louloudakis's place. The old men stared back unsmiling.

Afterword

John Pendlebury and his family and colleagues are historical figures I have treated fictionally here. Dilys Powell's *The Villa Ariadne* gives a good account of the Knossos community, British and Greek, yet much of Pendlebury's remarkable story remains to be told.

In several trips to Crete I attempted to retrace the ancient routes Pendlebury describes in *The Archaeology of Crete*, but I've made slight necessary adjustments to Pendlebury's itinerary and the geography of the Dikti Mountains—there is no village of Ayia Kyriaki in the Limnakaros Plain—and it's important to stress that none of the nonhistorical characters in this book, good or bad, is based on a real person.

I'm indebted to Dr. Catherine de Grazia Vanderpool, U.S. director of the American School of Classical Studies at Athens, for substantially assisting my research in Greece, and to Margaret Cogzell, librarian at the British School at Athens, who provided me with photos of Pendlebury and his companions, plus contemporary maps and other documents, and who helped me determine that it was his left eye which was glass. Among other *xenoi* who helped, I owe much to Rosemary

Barron, Willy Coulson, Steve Frisch, Sue Haas, Stephana McClaran, Karen Preuss, Mona Helen Preuss-Guillemot, and Kent Weeks.

Among natives of Crete, Christophoros Veneris and his brother Georgios were endlessly helpful and generous, as were the Kargiotakis and Siganos families of Tzermiado. I'm especially indebted to Sophia Lenataki-Gallagher, once of Sitia, now of San Francisco, who instructed me in Cretan usage and pronunciation and tried valiantly to teach me Greek—but was finally forced to correct my numerous errors, including social blunders, by reading the manuscript herself. *Efharisto poli, Sophia!*

Cramer's transactional interpretation of quantum mechanics is not fiction—a simplified account of it can be found in John Gribbin's *Schrödinger's Kittens*—but although John Cramer was good enough to comment on the manuscript of *Secret Passages,* he is not responsible for my far-fetched use of his work.

For encouragement and good criticism I am thankful to Ursula Le Guin, Vonda McIntyre, Virginia Beane Rutter, Steven Yafa, Lynn Yarris, and my long-suffering agent, Jean Naggar; to Allen Dressler, Molly Giles, Kate Pelly, Michael Russell, and Debra Turner, who were meticulous in telling me just how to write and rewrite the book on a monthly basis; and to Charles Brown and David Hartwell, who crucially helped me focus a story that had become a years-long labor of love.

TOR
BOOKS The Best in Science Fiction

MOTHER OF STORMS • John Barnes
From one of the hottest new names in SF: a shattering epic of global catastrophe, virtual reality, and human courage, in the manner of *Lucifer's Hammer*, *Neuromancer*, and *The Forge of God*.

THE GOLDEN QUEEN • Dave Wolverton
"A neatly plotted novel that combines swashbuckling action with hi-tech SF....This is an enjoyable story. Recommended." —*Starlog*

TROUBLE AND HER FRIENDS • Melissa Scott
Lambda Award-winning cyberpunk SF adventure that the *Philadelphia Inquirer* called "provocative, well-written and thoroughly entertaining."

THE GATHERING FLAME • Debra Doyle and James D. Macdonald
The Domina of Entibor obeys no law save her own.

BEGGARS RIDE • Nancy Kress
The Triumphant Conclusion to the Award-Winning Beggars Trilogy
"Read them and marvel at how SF can be hard and still have a heart." —*Locus*

THE VOICES OF HEAVEN • Frederik Pohl
"A solid and engaging read from one of the genre's surest hands."—*Kirkus Reviews*

MOVING MARS • Greg Bear
The Nebula Award-winning novel of war between Earth and its colonists on Mars.

BILLION DOLLAR BOY • Christopher Sheffield
A luxury intergalactic cruiser goes awry, stranding a spoiled teen on a mining colony twenty-seven light-years from home.

TOR
BOOKS The Best in Science Fiction

LIEGE-KILLER • Christopher Hinz

"*Liege-Killer* is a genuine page-turner, beautifully written and exciting from start to finish....Don't miss it."—*Locus*

HARVEST OF STARS • Poul Anderson

"A true masterpiece. An important work—not just of science fiction but of contemporary literature. Visionary and beautifully written, elegaic and transcendent, *Harvest of Stars* is the brightest star in Poul Anderson's constellation."
—Keith Ferrell, editor, *Omni*

FIREDANCE • Steven Barnes

SF adventure in 21st century California—by the co-author of *Beowulf's Children*.

ASH OCK • Christopher Hinz

"A well-handled science fiction thriller."—*Kirkus Reviews*

CALDÉ OF THE LONG SUN • Gene Wolfe

The third volume in the critically-acclaimed Book of the Long Sun. "Dazzling."—*The New York Times*

OF TANGIBLE GHOSTS • L.E. Modesitt, Jr.

Ingenious alternate universe SF from the author of the *Recluce* fantasy series.

THE SHATTERED SPHERE • Roger MacBride Allen

The second book of the Hunted Earth continues the thrilling story that began in *The Ring of Charon*, a daringly original hard science fiction novel.

THE PRICE OF THE STARS • Debra Doyle and James D. Macdonald

Book One of the Mageworlds—the breakneck SF epic of the most brawling family in the human galaxy!